The Illuminator

Brenda Rickman Vantrease

St. Martin's Griffin

New York

www.stmartins.com

Design by Kathryn Parise

Library of Congress Cataloging-in-Publication Data

Vantrease, Brenda Rickman.
    The illuminator / Brenda Rickman Vantrease.
       p. cm.
    ISBN 0-312-33191-6 (hc)
    ISBN 0-312-33192-4 (pbk)
    EAN 978-0-312-33192-4
      1. Bible—Translating—Great Britain—Fiction. 2. Illumination of books and manuscripts—Fiction. 3. Inheritance and succession—Fiction. 4. Scribes—Fiction. 5. Widows—Fiction. 6. Great Britain—History—14th century—Fiction. I. Title.

PS3622.A675 I45 2005
813'.6—dc22
                                              2004030095

10 9 8 7 6 5 4

For Barney and Arlene

THE ILLUMINATOR

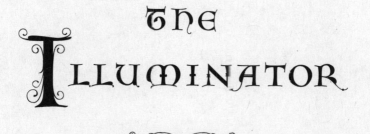

PROLOGUE

OXFORD, ENGLAND
1379

John Wycliffe put down his pen and rubbed tired eyes. The candle burned low, spitting tendrils of smoke. It would burn only minutes longer, and it was the last. Only the middle of the month, and he'd exhausted his allotment. As master of Balliol College, Oxford University, he was afforded what would be adequate for most clerics—for most, who worked by day and slept by night. But Wycliffe scarcely slept during the nighttime hours. Purpose drove him from his bed early and kept him from it late.

The orange glow from the charcoal brazier did little to dispel the twilight thickening in the corners of his Spartan chambers. The candle sputtered and guttered out. The girl would be here soon. He could send her to the chandler, paying out of his own purse. He would not call attention to his work by begging more from the bursar or borrowing from colleagues.

At least the chargirl's delay gave him a much-needed respite. The muscles in his hand ached from holding the quills. His head hurt from squinting in the dim light, and his body was stiff from hours bent over his desk. Even his spirit was fatigued. As always, when he grew tired, he began to question his mission. Could it be pride, intellectual arrogance, and not God, that called him to such a gargantuan task? Or had he simply been pushed down this treacherous path by the machinations of the duke of Lancaster, John of Gaunt? The duke was on his way to gaining a kingdom and had no wish to share its wealth with a greedy Church. But it was no sin, Wycliffe reasoned, to accept the patronage of such a man, not when together they could break the tyranny of the priests and bishops and archbishops. John of Gaunt, the duke of Lancaster, would do it to serve himself. But John Wycliffe would do it to save the soul of England.

King Edward's death had been a blessing, in spite of the political struggle now going on between the boy king's uncles. Too much lasciviousness had swirled around Edward; the taint of sin corrupted his court. He had consorted openly with his mistress. It was rumored Alice Perrers was a great beauty, but Wycliffe thought her the devil's tool. What black arts had the scheming baggage practiced to gain the soul of a king? At least with Edward's death, Alice Perrers was gone from the cesspool that had been his court. John of Gaunt was now regent. And John of Gaunt was on his side.

For now.

Wycliffe pushed his chair away from the desk. He faced the window that looked out over Oxford. From below, he heard revelers, students with too much ale already in their bellies and now in pursuit of more, though where they got the money for an endless supply was a mystery to him. He guessed they drank the cheapest, the last pouring, though it would take more of that than a fat man's belly could hold to produce such an excess of exuberance. For a moment, he almost envied them their innocence, their wanton joy, their singular lack of purpose.

The girl should be here soon. She was already an hour late. He judged this by the deep indigo reflected in the window—a glazed window to honor his station. He could have translated two whole pages from the Vulgate in that time—two more pages to add to the packet going to East Anglia on the morrow. He was pleased with the work the illuminator had done for him. Not too ornate, yet beautiful, worthy of the text. How he loathed the profane antics of beast and bird and fool inserted for amusement in the marginalia, the ostentatious colors, the lavishness that the Paris Guild produced. This illuminator worked cheaper than the Paris masters, too. And the duke said he could be trusted to be discreet.

Voices drifted up from below, laughter, a snatch of song, then receded. Surely the girl would not be much longer. He must finish more of the translation tonight. He was halfway through the Book of John. Shadows flickered around the room. His eyelids drooped.

Jesus had faced down the temple priests. Wycliffe could face down a pope. Or two.

The coals shifted in the brazier, whispered to him. *Souls perish while you dawdle.*

He dozed before the glowing embers.

※ ※

Joan knew that she was late as she rushed up the stairs to Master Wycliffe's chamber. She hoped that he was so busily engaged with his writing that he would not notice, but she had seen no candle glow from his window. Sometimes, he hardly noticed she was there as she collected his soiled linen, swept his floor, emptied his chamber pot. Wouldn't it just be her luck that today he would be in one of his rare moods, asking about her family, how they spent their Sundays, if any of them could read?

It wasn't that she resented his curiosity—in spite of his abrupt manner, he had kind eyes, and when he called her "child" he reminded her of her father who had died last year—but today, she didn't want to talk to him. She was sure to cry and besides, he would not approve she thought, as she fingered the relic hanging from a ribbon attached to a hemp string. It girdled her waist like a rosary.

She smoothed her unbound hair beneath its shabby linen cap, took a deep breath, and knocked lightly on the oaken door. When she heard no response, she rapped again, louder, cleared her throat. "Master Wycliffe, it's me, Joan. I've come to clean your lodgings."

She tried the handle on the door, and finding it unbarred, opened it just a crack.

"Master Wycliffe?"

From the interior gloom, gruffly: "Come in, child. You are late. We waste time."

"I'm so sorry, Master Wycliffe. But it's my mother, you see. She's very ill. And there's only me to see to the little ones."

She scurried about the room while he watched, lighting the rush lights, their flames flickering as she opened the window and slung out the contents of his chamber pot. She collected his soiled linen into a bundle, conscious of his eyes on her. She never disturbed the papers on his desk. She had learned that the hard way.

"Shall I replace the candle, sir?"

"Umph. I've naught to replace it with. I've been waiting for you. So you could fetch more."

"I'm sorry. I'll go right away."

She hoped he would not report her tardiness. Who knew when her mother would be well enough to return to her own work as a charwoman. He turned his chair away from the window to face her, held up his hand in a halting gesture. "Your mother is ill, you say?"

"Her fever is very high." She blinked back tears, then blurted out her confession. "I've been to Saint Anne's to beg the priest to pray for her.

His mouth pressed into a tight line above the gray hairs of his beard. "The priest's prayers are no better than yours. Perhaps not as good. Yours may well come from a purer heart."

He stood up, towering over her, austere in his plain robe and tight woolen cap that scarcely covered the gray hair flowing over his shoulders and mingling with his beard.

"What's that you have hanging on your belt?" he asked.

"My belt, sir?"

"Beneath your arm. Something that you call attention to in trying to conceal."

"This, sir?" She held up the item in question. She felt her face flame. Why did his piercing gaze cause her to doubt what had seemed so right less than an hour ago?

" 'Tis a holy relic," she said, dropping her head. "The finger bone of Saint Anne. I'm to hold it when I say the Paternoster. The priest gave it to me."

"I see. And what did you give him?"

"A sixpence, Master Wycliffe."

"A sixpence," he sighed, shaking his head, and then repeated, "a sixpence, out of your wages." He held out his hand. "May I see this *holy* relic?"

She fumbled with the ribbon attached to her girdle, then handed him ribbon and relic. He examined it, rubbing it between his thumb and forefinger.

"It is soft for bone," he said.

"The priest said that's because of Saint Anne's gentleness."

Wycliffe weighed it in his hand, the scarlet ribbon dripping like blood between his fingers. "It is pig's cartilage. It will do naught for your ailing mother."

"Cartilage?" The unfamiliar word twisted in her mouth.

"Gristle. The stuff of a pig's ear, or tail, or snout."

Gristle? The priest had given her a pig's ear to aid her prayers? He'd said he was giving it to her cheap, out of Christian charity. Said it would usually cost much more. Pig's gristle for her mother? She couldn't stop the tears then, the tears that had been building up inside her all day. Now what was she to do?

He handed her his clean, ironed kerchief, a kerchief that she recognized from last week's laundry. "Listen to me, child. You don't need a saint's relic. You don't need a priest. *You* can pray for your mother. *You* can confess your sins directly to God. *You* can pray for your mother in our Lord's name. Our Father in Heaven will hear you, if your heart is pure. And then, *then after you have prayed,* go to an apothecary and buy your mother a physick to heal her fever."

"I have no money for a physick," she said between sniffs.

"I will redeem the relic from you."

While she mopped at her eyes with his now soggy kerchief, he went over to the table to retrieve his purse, reached into it and extracted a shilling.

"Here. If there's aught left after you buy the physick, use it to buy a chicken to make a broth for your mother."

"Master Wycliffe, how can I thank——"

"You don't have to thank me, child. Your church at least owes you that much—not to steal from you. I'm only returning what is yours." He unfastened the object from its cord and patted her hand. "I'll keep the *relic*. You take the ribbon." He smiled, softening his austere features. "It will be pretty in your hair."

In her relief, she wanted to hug him, but his dignity forbade it. Instead she dropped him a deep curtsy.

"Hurry before the apothecary in King's Lane shuts her door for the night. Be off with you. I will say a prayer for your mother. And it will cost you nothing."

It wasn't until the chambermaid was gone that Wycliffe remembered the candles. He would have to go himself. But the night was still young. He could do several pages before fatigue overtook him and he started to make mistakes. The nap had revived his body, and the circumstance that had just transpired had plumped up his resolve. He carefully locked the door behind him—who knew what prying eyes might be abroad—and hurried down the narrow stairs and out the door in pursuit of light.

ONE

NORWICH, EAST ANGLIA
1379, JUNE

One. Two. Three. How many bells? Half-Tom the dwarf huffed his way to Norwich market, squinting at the sun overhead and counting. Twelve peals called the monks to sext. He pictured them in his mind's eye—walking in black-robed silence to midday prayers, arms tucked in opposing sleeves, two abreast, one long line, writhing soundlessly through the cloister walk, like the eels that parted the marshy waters of the fens where he lived. He would not trade his own green sanctuary of willow and reed for all their cold and splendid stone.

The road was dusty and the sun hot on his back. He quickened his pace. If he didn't look smart, Thursday market would break up ere he got there. Thor's Day—that's what Half-Tom called it. He liked the old names celebrated in the stories he'd heard as a boy. Days when the Danes struggled with good King Alfred for the rule of Anglia. Bloody tales, some, but filled with brave men. Heroes—all. Bold, strong.

And tall.

Half-Tom had never met a real hero. The monks said they lived only in the old bards' songs. They were certainly not abroad in Edward III's England. Was Edward still the king? He would ask in the market.

More bells now. Their clappers raucous, strident, like children clamoring for attention, they answered the cathedral's mother bells. Behind the city walls there were churches everywhere, built by wool merchants with cash from Flanders. Bribes to God or monuments to pride? Half-Tom sometimes thought that if the North Folk shire had as many holy souls as it had churches, he'd see more of heaven and less of hell. Though he knew one holy soul—only one—and that no hero, but a woman. He'd planned to visit her today; now there'd be scant time.

He'd left the marshy fens at daybreak, his willow baskets on his back, and run the usual gauntlet of pilgrims, thieves, and beggars on the hard-rutted road from Saint Edmund to Norwich. His stubby legs had pumped hard to make the weekly market by midday. They cramped in protest. His shoulders ached from balancing the bulky pack, and his wits were weary from sparring with runaway villeins and laborers who indulged in a bit of dwarf-baiting to break the boredom of their own journeys. Sport for them. Danger for him. He'd already bartered two eels and a long-necked stoppered eel basket to rogues bent on using him for a football.

The unwieldy pack on his shoulders bumped with every step, chafing the skin beneath his jerkin. Sweat stung his eyes. He didn't see the sow and suckling pig that blocked his path until the beast grunted a warning. As he careened sideways to avoid this last hurdle between him and the town gates, his pack shifted, snapping its leather strap, and crashed to the ground. Its contents spilled higgledy-piggledy into the muck.

"Blast the bishop and his swine to bloody hell," he cursed.

The hog snorted and shook her snout at him, baring her incisors. A broad frown split the dwarf's round face as he kicked at the empty air, stopping just short of the pig's hind flank.

Half-Tom was angry. But he was no fool.

The sow heaved herself over, crushing a large round basket. The dwarf swore again at the sound of splintering willow. A week's labor shattered under the pig's belly. A whole week, gathering and stripping the willow wands, weaving them lightly, deftly, in spite of his clumsy hands, into the graceful long-necked baskets that would trap the eels or be traded for a bit of cloth or a sack of flour, and if the day was prosperous, a pint of ale. Vain hope, that. He'd be lucky to salvage enough to buy a half portion of flour.

He flung a string of spittle at the offending beast.

Bloody sow—it was the bishop's hog, aright; he could tell by the notch on the ear—making a stinking hole right here on the main road leading into the third-largest city in all of England. Wallowing in her own offal, living off the leavings of the nobility and gorging herself on food that might have fed a yeoman's starving brood for a month. Her floppy ears, lined in pale gray, mocked him—a bishop's dingy miter.

Half-Tom's stomach rumbled his frustration. The bit of bread and dripping he'd eaten in the pre-dawn was long since gone. He thought of the stiletto blade in his boot and eyed the suckling pig. So what if it was Church property. There was some what thought Holy Church had too much property. There was some what said a man could say his own prayers, didn't need a priest. Heresy, others called it. But Half-Tom reckoned one thing was true—he could say his own blessing over roast pork as good as any taller man, be he Benedictine or Franciscan.

Anyway, didn't the bishop owe him for the ruined baskets?

He wiped sweat from his forehead with the ragged sleeve of his doublet and glanced around. The road lay empty—even the beggars had abandoned the roadside for the town market—except for one lone rider approaching from the south. A mere speck on the horizon. Too far away to notice, if he did the deed quickly. A convenient clump of bushes screened him from view of anyone coming and going outside the gate. There was a peasant's hut behind him, but no sign of life, except for a child—hardly more than a babe, too young to give witness—playing with a chicken in the doorway.

Still, to steal the bishop's pig . . . It'd be like poaching the king's deer. At the very least a stint in the stocks—a punishment especially painful for a dwarf who drew more than the usual number of tormentors. Maybe even a hanging offense if caught red-handed.

He pulled his scraggly chin hairs. The speck on the horizon was taking the shape of a horse and rider.

Swearing loudly, he kicked the air again, but this time his wooden clog connected with the flank of the sow and not gently, though with not enough force to satisfy his temper. The hog lumbered to her feet. Half-Tom, preoccupied with inventorying his damaged goods, ignored her.

He ignored, also, the child that wobbled on unsteady legs across the hut's threshold and out to the edge of the road. Usually, he enjoyed the children who were drawn to him by his child size—not the older, pimply-faced youths who tormented him, but the little ones. He'd even been known to plunder his shrunken purse for a penny to buy a sugarplum or two. But just now, he was too distracted by his anger, and by his temptation, to pay much attention to this blond cherub who watched him with large, round eyes.

The suckling pig—probably the runt of the litter, for Half-Tom saw no others—got to its feet and, squealing indignantly at the interruption of his feeding, followed the sow. Half-Tom looked up in time to see the child reach out a chubby hand toward the piglet. She grabbed at its tempting curlicue of a tail, and holding it in her fist, she pulled. The piglet's squeal became a screech. The child laughed and pulled harder.

"Let go the pig's tail!" Half-Tom yelled, dropping a basket. "Don't—"

But the squealing pig had already gained the sow's attention. She was making for the grinning child as resolutely as a thousand-pound mother could waddle. Her warning grunts punctuated the piglet's squeals. Still, the child did not release her hold, but at the sight of the angry animal, the little girl's laughter changed to a whimper. Frozen, she held on stubbornly to the pig's tail.

The sow charged.

The child's cries mingled with the grunts of the hog as the sow knocked her prey to the ground and began to maul it. Her piglet safe—or maybe forgotten at the prospect of the unexpected and oh-so-tender feast—the sow, snorting and slobbering, began to chew on the child's leg.

Half-Tom leaped onto the back of the hog, but he might as well have been a fly on the flank of a horse. The child's cries spiraled into ragged screams. A gaping gash on her leg oozed blood and bits of chewed flesh.

His knife blade flashed in the morning sunlight, and the sow's warm blood spurted onto his face, blinding him. The sickly, sweet smell of it thickened in his nostrils. He wiped his bloody face on his sleeve and slashed again.

And again.

And yet again.

More blood now, not spurting, just pouring, like dark ale from a spigot, until the bishop's hog lay silent, her body twitching, her stained snout pinning the child's leg. A bit of chewed flesh showed between her bared incisors.

The little girl's cries stopped abruptly. Half-Tom lifted her in his short arms. She was not moving, not breathing. Blood trickled from the ragged wound on her leg and her foot hung awkwardly.

He had not been quick enough.

And he had killed the bishop's swine for nothing.

He looked over his shoulder. The lone rider was closer now; he could hear the pounding of the hoofbeats. Or was that his own heartbeat?

The child's body stiffened and jerked in his arms. A death tremor? Her breath seemed stuck in her throat, like a trapped butterfly struggling to get out. Her throat quivered ever so slightly. His stomach answered with a quiver of its own. He rocked her back and forth in his arms. A fluttering movement of her chest, then a gasp, and she began to cry, a small weak sound that wrung the blood right out of his heart.

"It's all right, little one. Hush, now. Old Half-Tom'll keep ye safe. Hush now," he crooned, rocking back and forth, back and forth, then muttered to himself, "He may swing for it, but he'll keep ye safe."

It seemed like hours, but the whole fracas took less than a minute. Half-Tom suddenly became aware that he and the child and the dead hog at his feet were not alone in the world. From the doorway of the hut a woman ran toward them, her arms reaching out, her skirts flying behind her like great gray birds. When she saw her child she began to cry, keening, unintelligible sounds. They writhed in the air like the eels crawling from their ruined baskets.

⸺❧⸺

Enjoying the main road after his two-day journey from Thetford through dense forest and brackish swamp, Finn was, at first, unaware of the struggle between the dwarf, the sow, and the child. Indeed, from a distance, the horseman mistook the dwarf for a child in a tantrum. Green fields, grazing sheep, the warm sun on his back, the thought of a pork pie and a mug of ale before he continued the twelve miles on north of Norwich to Bacton Wood and Broomholm Abbey: all conspired to lull him into a sense of false peace.

Then he saw the woman come screaming from the cottage.

Finn dug his heels into the sides of his tired horse sufficiently to spur his borrowed nag to a gallop. He reined in only long enough to assess the wounded child, the distraught mother, the dead animal. He didn't dismount but shouted at the woman, who held the mangled, silent child in her arms.

"Does she breathe?"

The mother merely stood, looking at her baby dumbly with wide, staring eyes.

"Is the baby breathing?" he shouted again.

The woman did not answer but held the child up to him like one offering a sacrifice to a god. The small form was very still. Finn took the child and cradled her against him, being careful to support the foot. The pig's snout had snapped the bone just above the ankle. The flesh was badly mutilated, but the bleeding had stopped. He thought he detected the tiniest heartbeat.

The dwarf stepped forward. "The babe may yet be saved, milord, she has not turned blue. But you must hurry. There's a holy woman I know who lives by Carrow Priory in the Church of Saint Julian. She will care for the child and pray whatever miracle can be formed. The anchoress at Saint Julian's. Anybody can tell you. Ask for Julian."

"There's no time to find the way," Finn said.

And before the little man could finish protesting that he did not wish to enter the city—Finn could well guess why: he'd noted, too, the notched ear on the carcass of the sow, the dwarf's clothing and dagger smeared with pig's blood—he scooped the dwarf onto his horse and headed toward the town gates.

"We'll come back for you later, as soon as the babe's safe," Finn shouted over his shoulder to the woman, who stood gazing after them as though she'd been turned to stone.

They galloped through the gates of the city, almost colliding with a cart of hogsheads at the first crossing. The dwarf pointed with his right hand. Finn spurred his horse in that direction. His arm ached with holding the child cushioned against the shocks from the pounding hoofbeats. He glanced down only briefly. She was as still as a doll. He prayed there was still a quiver of life in her.

"King's Street and Rouen Road," the dwarf shouted in his ear. The dwarf was holding on for dear life, making Finn's small-arms belt cut into his side.

Finn reined in his horse in front of a small church built of flint. He was about to head for the heavy wooden doors when the dwarf grunted and pointed to a tiny hut attached to the sidewall of the church, hardly more than a lean-to. Finn recognized immediately the cell-like appurtenance of a hermit, attached to but not contained within the church. In two leaps, he crossed the patch of herb garden and was at the outside portal, which stood open to the mid-summer noontime.

From within, a woman's voice called in the singsong voice of an oft-repeated litany, "If you're wishing to visit with the anchoress, you should go around and enter through the anteroom at the other end. Tap at her window, and if she is not at prayer, she'll craw back the curtain."

Finn ducked his head, still holding the child securely in the cradle of his arm, which had gone numb, and entered the small bare room. He was about to protest to the short, wide-hipped woman bent over the fire pit in the center of the floor that he had no time for holy protocol when she turned around. She had a frown on her face and the scolding words obviously already on her tongue. Her gaze halted on the child in his arms

"Bring her here," she said, indicating a window with a wide casement that opened into the next chamber. She hastily removed a milk pitcher and used trencher. Finn guessed immediately that he was in the maid's room of the two-room dwelling and this large window was the table where the maid passed the holy woman her food. There was also a heavy wooden door separating the two rooms. It was bolted from the maid's side.

"Mother Julian, you have—"

The face of a woman in wimple and veil appeared at the window and, without waiting for introduction or explanation for the interruption of her solitude, reached through the window to receive the child.

"Alice, quickly. Bring me water and clean rags. And pound some Saracen's root into a mash."

Finn watched through the window. The anchoress laid the pale, unmoving child on a cot, which, along with a slant-topped wooden writing table and stool, constituted the room's only furnishings. Mother Julian, as the dwarf had called her, appeared a slight woman of about thirty or so years, but it was hard to tell as she was swathed in unbleached linen from head to toe, her veil and wimple revealing only her face. She had two bright, deeply set eyes in a face that might have been called gaunt except for its peaceful countenance. Her voice was low and musical, like wind playing through pipes. Softly chanting a lullaby cadence, she soothed the child, who stirred, whimpering from time to time, as in a dream.

Finn had not had time to question the dwarf's suggestion, although he had little faith in holy hermits or their prayers, no more than he had in holy relics or the pardoners and priests who pandered for the Church. But he had even less faith in the pretentious doctors of medicine from the university, few of whom would soil an academic gown for the sake of a bleeding peasant child. As Julian's fingers worked over the wound swiftly and efficiently, gently washing it with the juice and then making a plaster of the mashed comfrey to set the bone, he blessed his choice.

The dwarf, unable to watch because the window was set too high, paced back and forth, his short legs churning in silent rhythm, his eyes darting nervously through the outside portal.

"Will the babe live, Mother Julian?" Half-Tom shouted so that his voice could carry through the window.

Julian left the sleeping child and came over to the window, looked down. "I cannot say, Half-Tom. She is in God's hands. Only God knows what is best for this little one. The bone will set, but if the animal that attacked her was diseased . . . we must trust His will in this. As in all matters."

Finn was enchanted by her smile. It was wide, all-encompassing, like sunlight breaking through a cloud. "The two of you come around to my supplicant's window. You are making my maid extremely anxious lest my reputation be compromised. We will be better able to talk, and Half-Tom, you will be better able to see the child."

Finn went back out into the churchyard and re-entered the little anteroom built at the other end of Mother Julian's anchorhold, which allowed her visitors to be out of the elements as they conversed through her window. This window was narrower than the maid's window, but wide enough so they could talk, though it afforded a much lesser view of the anchorite's "tomb." The curtain had been pulled back as wide as it would go. Half-Tom sat on the visitor's stool; Finn stood beside him, bending slightly so that the anchoress could see both of them as she tended the child.

"It was the bishop's swine," the dwarf said.

"A crime for which the animal has paid, thanks to the bravery of my companion," Finn said. "If the child lives, it is Half-Tom we must thank. And you, sister. But it seems that the two of you are well acquainted."

The child stirred. The anchoress brushed her forehead with a kiss, stroked her hair and again chanted softly the half-lullaby, half-prayer. When her patient was once again quiet, she answered softly, "I am no *sister*. Just Julian, a humble hermit seeking God. Half-Tom visits me on market days and brings me a gift from the waters. On such occasions Alice and I eat well."

The dwarf flushed crimson. "I have no gift today, mistress," he muttered. "The bishop's cursed pig—"

"Dear friend, you brought me a wonderful gift. You brought me this child to tend, another with which I can share His love. I am grateful to you, to both of you, Master—"

"No *master*. Just Finn."

"Finn," she repeated. "You have a gentle heart but the manner of a soldier. You have fought in the French wars?"

He was taken aback by her perception and her frank manner. "Not since 1360. Not since the Treaty of Bretigny. I have been a man of peace these nineteen years."

He did not add: Since the birth of my daughter, since the death of her mother.

"You will not join the bishop's cause then, you will not take up arms for the Holy Father in Rome against the usurper at Avignon?"

"I will not fight for the bishop or either of his popes."

"Not even for a holy cause, in a holy war?"

"There is no such thing as a holy war."

He thought he read approval in the bright flash of her eyes, the lift of her brow.

"Except in the minds of men," she said.

She covered the sleeping child with a blanket, then wiped her hands clean of the ointment she had spread on the wound.

"Can you fetch the mother of this child, Finn? There is no substitute for a mother's healing touch. It most closely resembles, of all earthly feelings, the love our Lord has for us."

"Of course, anchoress. I promised the mother I would be back for her. I'll fetch her straightaway."

"Half-Tom will stay with me until Alice fetches him clean clothes. We will pray for the child, and its mother. And for you."

"Aye, mistress." Half-Tom looked at the dried blood on his palms. "And I'll be praying, too, that the bishop doesn't find out who killed his pig."

Finn would have laughed at the dwarf's wry tone if he had not known the seriousness of Half-Tom's situation. He would be completely at the bishop's mercy—a quality for which Henry Despenser was not widely praised. A dwarf from the fens, who grubbed his living from earth and water, against one of the most powerful men in England. Despenser would swat him like a fly, perhaps even take his life as payment for the pig's.

The anchoress looked up at the window. "Do not be afraid, Tom. Our Lord is a much greater judge than the bishop and He sees into the heart."

"I just hope He's paying attention is all," Half-Tom muttered under his breath.

Finn placed his hand on Half-Tom's shoulder. "Friend, would you be offended if I called upon the bishop and claimed for myself the honor of saving the child? I have some connections with the abbot at Broomholm. That would surely add weight to a reasoned argument."

Finn didn't know whether to read discomfort or relief in the dwarf's face. A mixture of both, probably. But after a brief hesitation, his fear won out over his pride.

"I'll be in your debt," he said. He didn't look as if the prospect made him altogether happy. "For the rest of my life or yours, whichever ends first."

The anchoress thanked Finn with her eyes.

⁓⁓

With Alice's help, Finn discarded his bloody tunic and sponged the stains from his shirt. He did not want to distress the mother with the sight of the bloodstains.

She was still standing by the roadside waiting. She looked as though she had not moved.

"Your child lives. I'll take you to her." He held out his hand.

She did not answer but climbed dumbly onto the horse, behind him.

"Put your arms around my waist," he said.

As they rode, he could smell the fear on her, pungent and biting, mingling with the smell of rancid fat and smoke from her cottage cook fire. He thought about what the anchoress had said, about the power of a mother's love. His own daughter had never known that. But he loved her. Hadn't he provided for her every need? Sometimes, they had to hire an extra cart just to carry her satins and laces. But the anchoress had implied that a mother's love was greater in some mysterious way than a father's. Under other circumstances he might have hotly disputed that with her. Rose's protection and comfort guided his every decision. No father could be more devoted. It was a vow he'd made on Rebekka's deathbed. And he'd kept it.

He urged his horse faster. The day was fleeting, and he'd not yet found suitable lodgings. Rose, housed at Thetford with the nuns, was unhappy about the separation. He'd promised to find a place for them today, but now there would be no time.

Had he been too rash in offering to take the blame for the dwarf? True, he was well connected and his reputation commanded respect, but he had secrets of his own, secrets that would not endear him in certain society. And then there was the matter of the papers. He should, at least, dispatch those before he called on Henry Despenser. It would delay his meeting with the abbot at Broomholm and mean another night in an inn, but it couldn't be helped. If the illuminated texts were found in his possession, it would prejudice the bishop against him, make him ill-disposed to consider the slaughter of the pig as the only reasonable action. It might even cost Finn the abbot's patronage.

The hedge lining the field to his right painted a short shadow. After he delivered the mother to her child, there would be time to find a messenger to carry the papers to Oxford. He wouldn't send for his daughter until he had settled this affair with the bishop. It could be a tricky business.

Behind him, he thought he heard the child's mother start to cry.

TWO

Will then a man shrink from acts of licentiousness and fraud, if he believes that soon after, but with the aid of a little money bestowed on friars, an active absolution from the crime he has committed may be obtained?
—JOHN WYCLIFFE, 1380

Lady Kathryn of Blackingham Manor pressed the heel of her palm hard against the bridge of her nose as she paced the flagstones of the great hall. Damn that sniveling priest! And damn the bishop he pandered for! How dare he come here again, for the fourth time in as many months, peddling his indulgences.

The pressure under her left cheekbone was excruciating, but it was no use sending to Norwich for a doctor. He would hardly stir his learned bones in this heat to tend the monthly migraine of a woman no longer in the bloom of youth. He would send the barber surgeon to bleed her. Bleed her! As if she had not bled enough this week. Already she had stained two of her best linen smocks and her green silk kirtle.

And now there was *this*.

The hawthorne hedge had barely sprouted its tight white buds when the bishop's legate came the first time, demanding money to buy masses for the soul of Sir Roderick, who had "g ven his life so valiantly in the service of his king." Surely the widow would want to ensure an easy passage for her husband's soul. The *widow* had given him three gold florins, not because she gave a farthing for the state of Roderick's soul—he could roast on the devil's spit for all she cared—but there were appearances to maintain. For the sake of her sons.

When this priest—he'd introduced himself as Father Ignatius—learned that her own father confessor had died at Christmastide, he'd chided her for neglecting her soul and the souls of those entrusted to Blackingham. He'd offered to send a replacement. She thanked him warily. His manner did not foster trust, and since she could il afford the upkeep of another gluttonous priest, she'd put him off with vague assurances that the void would soon be filled.

A few weeks later, on May Day. Father Ignatius came skulking back. "To bless the festivities," he said. Again he inquired about the status of her priestless household, and again she put him off, this time by claiming a close relationship with the abbot at Broomholm.

"It's a short ride to Broomholm. and the abbot is glad to hear my confession. There's also the new Saint Michael's Church in Aylsham. And we are frequently visited by friars—black friars, gray friars, brown friars—who, in exchange for a joint of meat and a quart of ale, will see to the souls of the vilest sinners among my crofters and weavers."

If he heard the sarcasm in her voice, he ignored it—only wrinkled his heavy furred eyebrows into a single black line—but he warned again of the perils to the unshriven soul. Then, to her relief, he appeared to let the matter drop. But the day of his departure, as he feasted at her board, the priest commented that he had lately become much distressed upon hearing that her dear departed husband might have forged, before his death, an alliance with John of Gaunt, who was a patron of the heretic John Wycliffe. Although any such alliance was probably innocent, unscrupulous persons could make even the innocent appear guilty. Would the widow like to buy another round of prayers? For appearance's sake?

Lady Kathryn knew full well that her gold florins—for which the sly priest thanked her "in the name of the Virgin Mother"—went to finance the ambition of Henry Despenser, bishop of Norwich, in his campaign for the Italian pope. Better soldiers for Urban VI, she supposed, than jewels and women for the French pope at Avignon. And besides, what choice did she have but to pay? Her estate was ripe for plucking by Church or crown, should the slightest hint of treason—or heresy—be breathed.

Not that she thought her late husband capable of treason. Roderick had not the fortitude for it. If indeed he died in a skirmish with the French, as she was told, he must have been struck in the back. But he had a fox's instinct for sniffing out his own interest. And he was very capable of the kind of petty, inept intrigue that could get her and her two sons put off their lands despite her dower rights. In pledging his allegiance to the more ambitious of the young king's uncles, Roderick had played a dangerous game. John of Gaunt was regent now, but for how long? The duke was making enemies within the Church, powerful enemies—enemies that would be no match for a widow alone.

By the saints, how her head ached. Her left temple throbbed, and she felt the bit of capon she'd eaten at nuncheon threaten to return, bringing the boiled turnips with it. Squinting against the afternoon sun, she thought longingly of her cool, dark bedchamber. But not yet. First, she must see the steward to receive his quarterly accounting of the wool receipts and the rents. He was already late with the collections by a fortnight, and she would not feel easy until she felt the weight of the coin in her hand. She knew at the first indication of a womanly weakness or lapse in vigilance, he would strip her clean as a beggar's bone.

Her supply of gold florins already plundered, she had been forced to satisfy the priest's third extortion with her ruby brooch. He had shown up on the Feast Day of Mary Magdalene and suggested that, if she paid for prayers for King Edward's soul, the loyalty of her household could not be questioned, even by those who might wish her ill.

And now—today. Today, the greedy priest had taken her mother's pearls. Smiling greasily, Father Ignatius had slid them into his cassock. They are only pearls—she'd steeled herself against the loss—only pearls. A creamy strand of gleaming stones, the necklace that her dying father had pressed into her hands in a rare display of affection. *I gave them to your mother on our wedding day. Wear them always near your heart,* he'd said. And she had, putting them on every morning like some good-luck charm, some angel's token of her mother's guardianship. They had become as much a part of who she was as the chatelaine's keys that nestled between the folds of her skirt. But they are only stones, she reminded herself. Not brick and mortar. Not lands.

Not deeds. And she had no daughter whose hands she could press them into saying, *Wear them next to your heart. They belonged to your mother and her mother before.*

"I have nothing left to pay for prayers, Father Ignatius," she had said, her voice husky with unshed tears. "I trust our souls and our persons are now divinely protected. You have no further cause to trouble yourself on our account."

He had inclined his head in what she hoped was silent acquiescence, but as she ushered him to the courtyard where he mounted his horse, he spoke to her in the unctuous voice she loathed.

"Lady Kathryn, in a household such as yours," he said, looking down at her from his horse, "with a breath of scandal hanging over it, you would do well to wear your *natural* piety like a garment. A *resident* priest is a requirement of a truly devout household. I'm sure your friend, the abbot of Broomholm"—the sly smile, the veiled gaze beneath the scraggly black line of brow—"would agree. Would he not?"

So. He had found her out. He knew she had no friends at the abbey.

That was when she first felt the familiar, squeezing pressure around her left eyeball. He would try to plant some spy so that he could keep a tighter grip upon her purse, or, worse yet, insert himself into her household on a permanent basis.

He didn't wait for her reply, but pulling on his horse's reins, said over his shoulder, "Think about what I've said. We'll talk about it when I return, next month."

Next month! By the saints and by the Virgin, too.

There must be some way to rid herself for good of that extortionist priest.

❧

When the steward finally waited upon her an hour later in the great hall, Lady Kathryn's left temple throbbed. She could not concentrate.

"If my lady is indisposed, I'll just leave the bag with the rent receipts. She need not bother herself with the details of the reckoning. Sir Roderick often—when he was busy—"

She picked up the bag and weighed it in her hand.

"Sir Roderick was more trusting than I, Simpson," she said evenly. "You would do well to remember that."

"I meant no offense to your ladyship. My only desire is to serve you well." The words were right, but not the tone. There was an insolence about the man that made her uneasy—the slump of his large shoulders, the sullen eyes with their hooded, lazy lids.

"Leave the ledgers with me and attend me tomorrow at this same time," she said as she unconsciously rubbed her temples.

"As you wish." He placed the sheaf of pages bound with string on the sideboard and backed out of her presence.

At last. Now she could seek the sanctuary of her bedroom. If she could make it that far without retching.

✼

Dusk was thickening in her room when she awoke, several hours later, to the sound of a door creaking on its iron hinge.

"Alfred?" she asked, keeping her voice low lest she wake the sleeping beast inside her head. It was an effort just to form the word.

"No, Mother, it's me. Colin. I came to see if I could get you anything. I thought maybe some food would help. I brought you a cup of broth."

He held it to her lips, gently. The smell made her stomach lurch. She pushed it away. "Maybe later. Just let me lie here a bit longer, then have the lamps lit in the solar. I'll come down by and by. Have you eaten? Is your brother home?"

"No, Mother. I've not seen Alfred since prime. Are we to have vespers in the chapel? Shall I go and find him?"

"Father Ignatius is gone." The taste of bile was on her lips, or maybe the bitterness was just the priest's name in her mouth.

Her elder son, elder by only two hours, was probably at the tavern and would come home drunk and stagger to his bed—his father had taught him at a tender age. But at least, she reasoned, the boy had been obedient, had abstained while the priest was in the house.

Her younger son stirred, reminding her of his presence.

She patted his hand. "No, Colin. We are spared the tyranny of praying the hours for a little while."

In the dim light she could make out the pretty shape of his head, his pale hair falling in a shimmering curtain over one eye.

"It wasn't so bad, Mother. To have the priest, I mean. I think the ritual beautiful in its way. The words fell on the ear almost like music."

Lady Kathryn sighed, and the beast sleeping inside her head stirred, sending shooting pains into her temple. So unlike his twin. It was just as well Colin would not inherit. He had not the heart for it. She wondered, not for the first time, how Roderick had begot such a gentle creature.

"I've learned a new song. Shall I sing it for you? Would it soothe you?"

"No." She tried to answer without moving her head. It felt as though it were stuffed with soggy wool. The linen sheet beneath her was warm and moist. She would have to change her smock, find more linen rags for padding. "Just send Glynis to me, and close the door. Gently," she whispered.

She didn't hear him leave.

❧

When Lady Kathryn entered the solar two hours later, Colin was at supper. And he was not alone. Her pulse quickened when she saw the back of the Benedictine habit.

"Mother, you're better. I was telling Brother Joseph about your headaches."

"Brother Joseph?" The question rode out on a relieved sigh.

Colin got up from his stool. "Do you want the rest of my supper? It'll make you feel better."

He pushed the half-eaten fowl toward her. Queasiness threatened. She shook her head. "I see that you have divided your supper once already." She pointed to the bird that had been neatly halved, then turned to look more closely at the unexpected visitor, who had risen when she walked into the room. She held out her hand. "I am Lady Kathryn, mistress of Blackingham. I trust you have found my son worthy company." She hoped he mistook the relief in her voice for hospitality. "If you're passing through, it would be our pleasure to provide you shelter for the evening. Have you a horse that needs grooming?"

"Your son has already seen to it; and since the evening grows late, I'm grateful for your kind hospitality. However, Lady Kathryn, I am not just passing through. I have come on a mission. I have brought you a message from Father Abbot of Broomholm Abbey. He has a request to make of you."

"A request? From the abbot of Broomholm?"

Had the priest stirred a hornet's nest with his inquiry? Blackingham could not satisfy the greed of an abbeyful of monks.

"How can a poor widow serve the abbot of so esteemed a company of Benedictines?"

"My lady, you look quite pale. Please, sit."

He indicated the bench upon which he had been sitting. She sank down on it and he sat beside her.

"Please, don't be distressed, Lady Kathryn. We heard through Father Ignatius that you desire friendship with our abbey. What Father Abbot and Prior John suggest will cost you little but will offer you a chance to serve our abbot in a profound way and ensure you and your household the friendship of our brotherhood."

The friendship of the brotherhood? But it was unlikely she would be granted *gratis* that which she had falsely claimed.

"Please, Brother, tell me how my humble household may serve his lordship."

The Benedictine cleared his throat. "It is a simple matter, Lady Kathryn. Blackingham Hall has ever been known for its hospitality. With the death of Sir Roderick, I'm sure this tradition will continue. Therefore, our abbot and our prior feel that this request would not place too heavy a burden on your ladyship."

He paused for breath.

"And what request might that be?" she asked, impatient for him to get beyond his rehearsed speech. "I hope I may not seem as slow to grant your request as you are to voice it."

The monk looked momentarily disconcerted. He cleared his throat and began his recital again. "As you know, my lady, we at Broomholm are blessed with many holy treasures, including a relic of the true cross on which our Lord suffered. However, we have few books of note. Father Abbot thinks that so esteemed an abbey should have at least one manuscript worthy of its glory, one to rival *The Book of Kells* or the *Lindisfarne Gospels*. We have a scriptorium and several monks who toil daily in copying the Holy Scriptures."

She nodded impatiently.

"Although our brothers do a passing job as copyists and scribes, we have no illuminator of reputation to enhance our texts. It has come to our attention that a very gifted artisan would be willing to serve as illuminator for the

Gospel of Saint John, except that he is unwilling to attach himself to our abbey. It seems he has a young daughter of marriageable age"—here he laughed to ease the awkward moment—"well, your ladyship can see how lodgings in a company of monks would be unacceptable."

"Can the daughter not lodge with the nuns at Norwich or at Saint Faith Priory?"

The monk shook his head. "It seems the illuminator dotes upon her and will only undertake employment with us if we can provide suitable lodgings."

"Ah, so your prior and your abbot think to attach the young woman to my household?"

He hesitated just a moment before answering. "Not only the daughter, my lady, but the father as well."

"The father? But—"

"He will do his work here, with your permission, so that he can be close to his daughter. Along with food, lodging, and the use of a horse, he will require but a small place with good light . . ." The monk must have sensed that she was about to plead the poverty of her newly widowed state, because he held up his hand to forestall her protests. "Along with his sincere appreciation, Father Abbot is willing to pay for their board and all expenses incurred. He would not wish to impose on a poor widow."

If only her head were clearer. Could this be the answer to the troublesome priest? If she did the abbey a favor, then she could in truth plead friendship with the abbot of Broomholm. Colin was eagerly querying the priest about the proposed lodgers. He would be pleased to have an artist in the house. And Alfred would be pleased to have the girl, no doubt. That could be a problem, especially if the chit had a pretty face. But the friendship of the abbot *and* extra income . . .

There was Roderick's room. It had good lighting. And it was far enough removed from her own not to cause gossip among the servants or endanger her privacy. She and Roderick had been able to avoid each other for weeks at a time.

Her son interrupted her thoughts, his blue eyes bright with interest. "Mother, what say you to this idea?"

She could tell from the excited pitch in his voice that he found the plan appealing. He must get lonely. She was always so busy and his connection with his brother seemed to have ended when they exited her womb.

[25]

"What say you, Colin?"

"I think it a fine and noble idea," he said, smiling broadly.

"Well, then, I suppose we might give it a trial."

She was rewarded by the look of pleasure on his face. "Brother Joseph, you may tell your Prior John and your Father Abbot that I and my household are pleased to be of service. We will prepare to welcome your illuminator and his daughter."

THREE

Christ and His Apostles taught the people in the language best known to them . . .
The laity ought to understand the faith . . . believers should have the Scripture in a language which they fully understand.

—JOHN WYCLIFFE

Lady Kathryn spent the next two days supervising the cleaning of Roderick's chambers. His best clothing she put away for Alfred to grow into. Colin was much too fine-boned. The elegant brocades and velvet finery would hang heavy on his slender frame.

It was a burdensome chore in the summer heat and fraught with emotional peril, so she was relieved to be at the bottom of the chest when she came upon a folded piece of parchment, half-hidden beneath a moth-eaten tunic, among the residue of aromatic herbs. A love letter from one of Roderick's many conquests? He shouldn't have bothered to hide it. She was long past caring. The more paramours he had, the less he claimed from her the onerous marriage debt. But upon examination, the document proved to be no billet-doux but some kind of religious tract headed in scrawling script, *On the Pastoral Office*. It was not illuminated but hurriedly transcribed and signed simply at the bottom, "John Wycliffe, Oxford." She recognized that name. That was the man the bishop's legate called a heretic.

She might have burned the damning paper immediately, except the way it was written caught her notice. Not the subject or even the style, but the language, if language it could be called. It appeared to be the midland Anglo-Saxon dialect spoken among the peasants and the lower classes, hardly a tongue appropriate for a scholar's document. Norman French, the language of her father, was the language of books and court documents. Religious documents were written in the Latin Vulgate. Few of the people who spoke this doggerel could read. And they would never be able to afford the cost of books, not even hastily copied parchments such as these.

Out of curiosity she began to decipher the unfamiliar spellings and found the content even more shocking than the language. No wonder the priest had called Wycliffe a heretic. This document charged that the Church was filled with apostasy, even in its highest offices, and called for the withholding of funds from immoral and negligent clergy. Dangerous language, even for an Oxford master with a patron at court.

It was not that she disputed the truth of such a position—the bishop of Norwich, Henry Despenser, had certainly shown more interest in raising money to set an army against the French antipope, Clement VII, than in saving souls. It was rumored that the bishop even ordered the withholding of the sacraments pending a contribution to his cause. She thought bitterly of her ruby brooch and her mother's pearls. But verity aside, this was a dangerous document to have in one's possession. Proof of heresy. The priest's sly smile slid into her mind.

She'd heard talk before. She knew that Wycliffe had followers not only within the lower classes but among some nobles as well—the presence of this tract among Roderick's possessions was proof—but for different reasons. It wasn't moral outrage that wooed John of Gaunt, the duke of Lancaster, and his conniving courtiers to Wycliffe's call for reformation. As regent to the young King Richard, the duke would be jealous of the pope's authority over civil matters, would want such authority for the crown. Power and wealth: the Church embraced these twin whores. And the crown lusted for them. John of Gaunt saw Wycliffe and his following as a means of plundering the Church's bulging treasury. But that wasn't her concern. Her concern was more personal. The duke of Lancaster had allied himself with

Wycliffe and Roderick had tied himself to the duke, leaving her and her sons on a ship floundering in the shallows, drifting toward a rocky shore.

She set a torch to the parchment and watched it curl and blacken in the cold grate. Roderick had been a fool to embroil himself in royal intrigue. Who knew which way the political winds would blow? Best to keep her own council in matters of religion and politics—a beast with two heads. If only her husband had been wise enough to do the same.

As she closed the lid on the heavy clothing chest, she took comfort in remembering the two gold sovereigns the abbot had given her as surety for her new lodger. More than the Holy Scriptures was being enriched by the illuminator's art. This new alliance would give her much-needed revenue and make good her claim of powerful friends.

Anything to keep that hateful money-grubbing priest at bay.

∗ ∗

By late afternoon, the room was cleared of her late husband's belongings. Kathryn surveyed the space with a calculating eye. The great four-poster with its velvet hangings might give the humble colorist illusions of grandeur. But all in all, it was a room well suited for his purpose—well lighted with that singular light born in the North Sea, sometimes golden, riding in the sun's chariot, and sometimes silver, spilling watery luminance over everything it touched. The pellucid light even penetrated into the adjacent sitting room, where she had placed a daybed for the daughter.

She closed the chest and looked up as Glynis entered the room, bobbing her perfunctory curtsy.

"Did you send for me, milady?"

"I need you to help me move the writing desk under the window. The illuminator will need the light. And did you change the ticking in the mattress?"

"Yes, milady. Just like you said. I put fresh goose-down in milord's mattress and Agnes is stitching a new straw mattress for the daybed."

"Good." But Lady Kathryn was rethinking the straw mattress. Suppose the girl was spoiled and put on airs? She leaned her tall frame against the edge of the oversize desk and strained, nodding curtly at Glynis to do the same.

Again the half-curtsy. "Beggin' milady's pardon, but shouldn't we get some help to move this?" the girl asked in her thick North Country brogue.

"I'll fetch Master Alfred. It would be naught to the likes of him. He has his father's manly build," she said eagerly.

The ghost of yesterday's pain stirred in Kathryn's head as she watched the girl skip away a little too merrily, obviously more on her mind than her mistress's poor back. Glynis was a good worker. Kathryn would hate to let her go because of a swollen belly. God knew she'd lost enough maids to Roderick's whoring. Alfred was only fifteen, but already she'd heard gossip about him and the tavern wench at the Black Swan. She hoped his experience did not go beyond the sighs and gropings of green youth. But he already wore a thin little stain of a mustache, and if he had inherited his father's whoring nature, there might be little she could do about it except to teach him discretion. Harmless flirtation with tavern maids was one thing, but she would not have him fouling their nest with his lechery.

They returned quickly. The maid, with flushed cheeks and simpering manner, followed Alfred into the room.

"Glynis said that my lady mother had need of a lusty lad with a sturdy back. So here I am. I'm your man." One rust-colored curl escaped the leather thong that bound it and bobbed against his cheek.

"More boy than man, I would say. Though for want of any other, you'll do. Put your sturdy back to shoving that desk beneath the window."

If the boy wondered at the curtness of her response, he made no mention of it, but good-naturedly set himself to the task.

" 'Tis easy enough," he said, pretending less strain than the heavy oak furniture would cause a man full-grown. She wondered what else he'd done to impress the plump little chambermaid.

Giving the desk one last, red-faced push so that the mullion window was exactly centered above it, he asked, "Why did you want the desk beneath the window? And I see you've cleared Father's belongings." He blew a breath at the offending curl to clear it from his blue eyes—the only feature he shared with his brother.

"You may leave us, Glynis," Lady Kathryn said. "I'll put fresh linen on the bed." She waited until she heard the girl's footsteps fade away.

"We are to have a lodger, Alfred." She picked up the sheet Glynis had brought and turned to the bed, talking to her son over her shoulder. "I would have told you about it sooner, but you have seen fit to deprive yourself of your mother's company for the last two nights."

"Colin said you had a headache, and I didn't wish to disturb you." He rapped his knuckles against the oak table.

Too much restless energy, she thought. He reminded her of a simmering pot working up a head of steam. She whipped the sheet in the air. It settled with a snap onto the bed. "Well, in any case, I doubt you were in any condition to wait upon your mother, whose pain would have only been enhanced by the sight of her oldest son so far in his cups he could barely walk, and at such a green age—a boy scarcely weaned, who cannot hold his beer."

Good. She had at least succeeded in bringing a deeper blush to his naturally ruddy cheeks.

"I see Colin was ready enough to tattle—"

"Your brother, sir, told me little enough. Agnes told me how she had to clean up the puke from your linen. I will not have my son made the butt of jokes among serving wenches and villeins. And while we're on the subject, you make too free with my maid. I've seen the calf-eyed looks that pass between you."

The boy at least had the grace to look embarrassed, though he did not hang his head in shame. But neither did he flare back at her as a young Roderick would have done—though whether his temper was checked by discretion or affection, she couldn't say.

"I fear I've been too lax with you. From now on, you will be home by vespers."

"Vespers," he whined, his eyes sparking like flint on stone. He shook his head, loosening another shaggy curl. "I hate that priest. Is he—?"

"No, Alfred. Father Ignatius is not moving in. And if he were, I would hardly give him your father's quarters. We are to have lodgers."

"Lodgers! By God's wounds, Mother, surely we are not so poor that we must rent out my father's—"

"Don't take that tone with me, Alfred. And you may indulge your temper and swear like a rogue while in the company of villeins but you will not do so in the presence of your mother."

This time, he did hang his head. But in shame or merely to hide an insolent expression? Whichever, she resolved to soften her manner. A wise mother did not provoke her son to wrath.

"I have hit upon a plan to rid us of the priest whose company you find so confining," she said. "Though a few prayers would not hurt any of us.

However, I don't see why we should be forced to pay for them. I don't recall that our Lord charged for his services."

"Who is our lodger, then, and how will he keep the priest away?"

"*They*, not *he*. There will be two of them. A man and his daughter. The abbot at Broomholm has asked us to lodge them as a favor to the abbey, and what's more, he's willing to pay. Between the king's purveyances and the rising cost of prayers, you'll have nothing left to inherit if the bleeding isn't stopped."

"But, I still don't understand. How will—"

"Don't be such a dullard. If we befriend the abbot, he will befriend us. The lodger is an illuminator of some renown who is coming to illustrate a Gospel for the abbey. He could not stay with the brothers there because of his daughter."

Alfred's face lit up like sunshine breaking through a cloud. "How old is the daughter?"

The light from the north-facing window poured over the boy as he hoisted himself up onto the desk and sat facing her, swinging his legs, curiosity chasing away any resentment at his mother's tongue-lashing. No wonder the girls flitted after him like swallowtails to bluebells. It lightened her own heart just to look at his merry eyes and toothy grin, but she would not let it show.

"It can make no difference to you. You will have nothing to do with the illuminator's daughter. Do you understand me, Alfred?"

He held up both hands in a gesture designed to halt the rising pitch of her voice.

"Just curious, that's all. She's probably ugly as a crow, anyway." He laughed as he slid off his perch. The light behind him backlit his unruly mane of copper hair, making it into a fiery halo. He scowled petulantly. "Does that mean we have to go back to praying the hours, since we have a spy from the abbey?"

"I don't think so." She absently fingered the jet beads of the rosary at her belt. "A small demonstration of our religious devotion is probably all that's required. You can manage a daily visit to the chapel, can't you? That should be enough. After all, the man's an artist, not a monk."

"And nobody at Blackingham has need of a monk, right, Mother?"

Ignoring her son's impudence, Lady Kathryn turned her back on him and strode from the room.

The illuminator and his daughter came on Friday. At midday on every other Friday, Lady Kathryn met with Simpson in the great hall on matters of the estate. She rarely looked forward to these meetings, and today was no exception. But she had two important matters to discuss with the overseer, and she hoped to cover both before the arrival of her lodgers.

The first concerned a plea from one of her crofters. The woman, one of the weavers, had come to her, distraught and weeping. Simpson had taken her youngest daughter as a house servant. As steward, he was within his rights to do so, since both mother and child were serfs. The mother was not one of the free women who worked for rent and a pittance wage, so Lady Kathryn was her only recourse. Kathryn had promised the woman she would see that her daughter was returned. And so she would. The steward's action was intolerable. Not only was the welfare of the child at stake, but the mother, as one of Blackingham's best weavers, would pass the ski l on to her daughter. Kathryn would have prevented it without the mother's tears had she known. She confronted Simpson before he'd completed his simpering greeting.

"A six-year-old child is not old enough to go into service. You will return her to her mother and find someone more suitable to empty your chamber pots and scour your boots."

Simpson clutched his cap in his hands, kneading the velvet roll that banded it. She found his plumage and his overpowering perfume offensive. If he dressed up, as she suspected he did, for these Friday reckonings to impress her, it had the opposite effect.

"Milady, the girl is big for her age. And Sir Roderick was much opposed to coddling. He said it made for poor workers."

"I should have thought you'd learned by now, Simpson, that I do not care what Sir Roderick said, cared about, or would have wanted. Your argument is not served by quoting him to me. As you are of yeoman status and are paid a generous wage, you should hire a groom out of your wages to attend you. Blackingham serfs are for service to Blackingham Hall and its lands. You will return the child to her mother. And you will not replace her with another."

She watched with a mixture of satisfaction and apprehension his obvious struggle to curb his temper. It rankled that she needed this odious man, but she had none with whom to replace him.

"I do not mean to be unreasonable in this matter," she continued. "If you wish to choose one of the crofters' wives, and if she is agreeable to working for you, then I will pay her a small wage as an addendum to your salary. That is the best I can do. I will expect to see the child returned within the hour." She leveled her gaze at him and lowered her voice, enunciating each word carefully, lest he misconstrue her peace offering as weakness. "In the same condition as when she left her mother's hearth."

"As you wish, milady." He lowered his head sufficiently so that she could not see his eyes and, giving a token bow, backed away.

"We aren't finished. There's one more thing. There is a shortfall in last quarter's accounting of the wool receipts."

He stopped dead in his tracks and looked at her. She watched surprise, then resentment, register in his face. He closed his eyes briefly in a pose of remembering.

"Perhaps milady has forgotten the foot rot in the spring. We lost several sheep."

"Foot rot?" She scanned the ledger that she'd brought with her from last quarter's accounting. "I see no expense in the accounting for tar."

The steward shifted on his feet. "The shepherd did not report in time for us to buy the tar to treat the feet of the afflicted beasts I—"

"You are the steward. It was your responsibility, not John's. Anyway, you should have had enough tar on hand to treat a minor infestation. How many sheep did we lose?"

Simpson shifted his hulking frame and his left hand twitched. "Eight ... . ten head."

Kathryn stiffened her spine. "Which is it, Simpson? Eight or ten?"

The steward clenched and unclenched his left hand several times, then mumbled, "Ten."

250 pounds of wool lost! 250 pounds she'd been counting on.

She looked down, pretending to be occupied with binding the fasteners on the account book, but continued to watch him from beneath lowered eyelids.

"Well, at least you harvested some of the wool from the dead sheep."

A sly look chased surprise across his features before he answered. "Unfortunately not, milady. We weighted the carcasses and threw them in the marsh. To keep the rest of the herd from being contaminated."

She raised her head and met his gaze levelly. "How very judicious of you. Who knows how contaminated the pelts would have been from the foot disease."

It was fortunate for the steward that at just that moment the sound of horses' hooves interrupted his interrogation. But the look Lady Kathryn shot in his direction, as she went into the courtyard to greet the arrivals, was clearly meant to say the matter was merely postponed.

The visitors were just coming to a stop in the courtyard. Kathryn squinted into the sunlight. She recognized only Brother Joseph from the abbey. A young girl of about sixteen rode on the back of a donkey being led by a tall man with an angular face. For a moment it was as though an apparition, a holy vision of the Virgin riding into Bethlehem, had graced her courtyard. But clearly this girl carried no child. Even the chaste cut of her dark blue kirtle revealed her slender form. Her dress was simple but of excellent cut and cloth. Kathryn's own weavers produced none so finely woven. The girl's only ornament was an exquisitely worked brooch of intertwining knotwork with a tiny pearl-encrusted cross at its center, which she stroked nervously with thin, pale fingers. The pendant hung from a crimson cord around her neck. A matching cord circled a gossamer veil covering hair black and shiny as a raven's neck. She had an exotic look: large almond eyes in an oval-shaped face, features so perfect they seemed to be chiseled in marble, and skin more olive than cream. Not the plain lump of a maid Kathryn had been hoping for. And she carried herself with a dignity that, like her dress, was far above her station.

That must be the father walking beside her, leading the donkey, watching its every step with sea-green eyes. He was tall, not brawny, sinewy in build. He leaned in toward the daughter protectively. He was clean-shaven and hatless, and Kathryn noticed his gray hair was thinning slightly at the crown. His tunic was knee-length, a light pale linen of good weave and spotless, its only adornment the small dagger hanging from a leather belt that girdled his waist loosely. Father and daughter could have been a tableau from a Christmas mystery play staged by the Mercer's Guild.

As he helped his daughter to dismount, Kathryn stepped forward to greet them. He smelled of Saracen's soap and some unfamiliar, subtle scent, linseed oil, perhaps. The hand that reached for his daughter's was narrow in the palm, with long, graceful fingers, and though the nails were carefully manicured, a hint of ocher-colored pigment clung to the cuticle of his right forefinger. He looked fastidious. She hoped he was not going to be a demanding guest.

Brother Joseph spoke first. "I've brought your guests," he said, taking her hand. "But I fear that we——"

A cadre of mounted men clattered into the courtyard in a cloud of summer dust, drowning out his words. Surely it did not take so many men—one of whom she recognized as the sheriff—to escort one man and his daughter to their lodgings.

"Sir Guy," she said, acknowledging the newcomer, "it has been too long."

He had been a frequent visitor when Roderick was alive. With their falcons, they'd hunted together for sport in the meadows around Aylsham, and sometimes, with their bows, for wild game in Bacton Wood. He had not darkened her door since her husband's death. She was not happy to see him now.

He leaned down from his horse and raised her hand to his lips. "Indeed, it has, Lady Kathryn. I offer apologies for my neglect, and now I fear I must confess that this visit is an official one."

She quickly surveyed the three mounted men behind him, looking for a familiar face as she scanned the courtyard in search of her sons. Had Alfred's temper involved him in some escapade that would embarrass her, or worse yet, prove costly?

"Official?" She forced a smile.

The sheriff pointed to a horse being led into the courtyard. At first glance it appeared to be riderless, but closer scrutiny showed what looked like a human form wrapped in a blanket and slung across the horse's back. A summer breeze lifted the edge of the blanket, and Kathryn wrinkled her nose in distaste. Whatever, or whoever, was wrapped inside was very ripe. The horse stamped its feet and whinnied as if wanting to be rid of its noisome burden.

The sheriff motioned to the man who held the horse. "Back him away. That's not a fit smell for a lady. She doesn't have to stand that close to identify the body."

Identify the body! Lady Kathryn felt the ground swirl beneath her. Again, she scanned the courtyard, urgently this time. *Alfred! Where was Alfred?* And she hadn't seen Colin since that morning. *What if it were Colin!* She moved toward the body on the horse, holding one hand against her chest to calm her heart.

Sir Guy must have seen the fear in her eyes; he put out a restraining hand. "I've frighted you for naught, Lady Kathryn. 'Tis not young Colin or Alfred. 'Tis only a priest."

She thought she would faint with relief. The tall stranger standing beside Brother Joseph stepped forward and placed his arm around her to keep her from falling. She leaned for the briefest moment against the illuminator, grateful for the strength of his arm. The feeling passed, and she disengaged, stepping away. He also backed away, a mere half-step, but enough to place an appropriate distance between them.

"Thank you," she said. "A mother's foolishness makes me weak."

The illuminator nodded and gave her a half-smile. "A mother's love is never foolish, my lady." His voice sounded like the sifting of river gravel worn smooth by the current. "And my experience has not found it to be weak."

Sir Guy's horse stamped and snorted. The sheriff jerked the reins sharply.

Having regained strength enough to speak, she addressed him. "A priest, you say, Sir Guy? What has your priest to do with Blackingham?"

He dismounted before answering, and Lady Kathryn motioned for a groomsman. A small knot of servants had gathered around the stable to see what was happening. One of them scuttled forward to hold the sheriff's horse.

Sir Guy nodded toward the body. "I think he's the bishop's legate. And if he is, there'll be hell to pay. Henry Despenser has set up a great hue and cry looking for him. Says he dispatched him to Blackingham to attend your ladyship several days ago. He was expected back at Norwich by compline on Monday." He strode back to the horse that carried the body. "We found him in the marsh that borders your lands, his head bashed in."

He drew back the blanket to reveal the muddied cloth of a Benedictine habit. As he dragged the lifeless monk upright in the saddle for her to see, she recognized, through the bloated features and the dried blood, the black-furred eyebrows. Father Ignatius. She turned her face away in revulsion, a natural-enough response that bought her time. Her mind was spinning now, whirling, leaving her light-headed, forcing her to lean once again on the stranger's strong arm. What should she say? Admit the priest had been there? Expose her sons to questioning? Bring her fragile status under scrutiny? Had she mentioned to anyone in her household how threatened she felt, how angry she was at the priest's extortions? Had they guessed? Where was Alfred on that night? Alfred with his father's fiery temper, his reckless impulses. Had the priest provoked him beyond reason? She breathed deeply, then stood upright once again under her own power.

"I knew him to be the bishop's legate, but I've not seen him in many weeks," she said. Her voice was scarcely above a whisper, but her gaze never wavered. "He must have met with his untimely death on his way to Blackingham."

FOUR

here had simply been no other course but to invite Sir Guy to stay for dinner. She had hoped he would plead the necessity to return the priest's body to Norwich, but he had merely dispatched his men, telling them he would follow.

Now, as Lady Kathryn sat at table, she listened with half her mind to the small talk going on around her. The other half skittered between the lie she had told and her duties as a hostess. She used those duties to push the implications of that lie aside. Best to deal with them in the calmer light of solitude. And truly, entertaining Sir Guy at the last moment had been challenge enough to keep her preoccupied.

Fortunately, she had instructed her cook, Agnes, to prepare a more elaborate meal than usual for her new lodgers and Brother Joseph. She had not planned to dine in the great hall, thinking that her lodgers could be led to settle for a tray in their new quarters—best to set that precedent—while she ate alone with her two sons and Brother Joseph in the solar. But Sir Guy's presence demanded more, so she had hastily summoned the groomsmen and had the trestles brought in and the board dressed with a silk cloth. Agnes had complained—it was a month until harvest and the larder was depleted—but with characteristic loyalty and cleverness had stretched the simpler fare into something more in line with Kathryn's unexpected guest's expectations of hospitality. All this had left her little time to reflect upon the circumstance that had brought him to her door. Now, however, the subject she'd been avoiding surfaced again.

"Whoever the culprit is, the killing of a priest will weigh leaden against his soul," Sir Guy said as he cut a piece of the larded boar's head the carver offered. "No respect for holy men. You can blame that on the heretical teaching of the Lollards."

"Lollards?" Lady Kathryn asked, to keep the conversation going. Not that she cared. She was only half listening, her mind preoccupied with the bloated corpse of Father Ignatius. There was an image she'd like to forget. Fearsome enough in life. More terrible in death.

"A bunch of ragtag self-styled *priests*, followers of Wycliffe, who go around mumbling heresy. He's playing a dangerous game. Oxford has already forced him out."

Suddenly alert and thinking of the damning text she'd found in Roderick's trunk, Kathryn said, "Thanks to the Virgin, no such poison has found its way to Blackingham," but she wondered how much Sir Guy knew of her late husband's alliances.

She motioned to the carver, who placed a double serving of sturgeon on the trencher that Sir Guy, as guest of honor, shared with his hostess. She had scavenged from her impoverished cellar a small leathern bottle of wine, which the butler poured into the silver cup they also shared and from which she took only tiny, pretend sips lest the bottle be emptied before Sir Guy drank his fill. The butler poured ale in pewter mugs for the others who sat at table with them. Colin and Brother Joseph sat next to Sir Guy on Kathryn's right. The illuminator, Alfred, and the illuminator's daughter sat to her left.

Brother Joseph, obviously inflamed by the very name of Wycliffe, leaned his tonsured head in front of Colin so that he could address Sir Guy. "They say the heretic Wycliffe even dares question the Miracle of the Mass. Calls the transubstantiation of the Host a *superstition!*" His voice cracked with outrage on the last word. "The University will force him out, and what's more, it's rumored among the brotherhood that since the king is dead and unable to come to his support, the archbishop is about to bring him up again on charges of heresy." He stabbed at the air with his knife as though it were Wycliffe's heart. "He'll hang, if he's not careful. Though I'd rather see him burn."

The heretofore gentle-mannered monk smiled smugly, as though he would take delight in torching the fire himself. Lady Kathryn could almost see the flames reflected in the little black pupils of his eyes. She felt her throat close as she chewed unsuccessfully on a bit of pheasant pie. Her father had taken her to a burning once, as a girl, and she'd never forgotten the terror in the eyes of the woman who'd been charged with witchcraft. As the bailiff lit the faggots and the smoke billowed up, Kathryn had cried and hid her face in her father's sleeve. But that had not shut out the stench of the charring flesh.

Tiny beads of perspiration popped out around her hairline. She dabbed at them with her silk handkerchief. The long twilight had not dispelled the July heat. Moisture formed in between her breasts, and the linen of her shift clung to her skin, sticky and damp. Odors from the kitchen fires, smoke from dripping fat and roasting meat drifted in through the open windows of the great hall, mingling with the sweat of Sir Guy, whose day in the saddle lingered in his clothing. Was it her imagination, or did his scent also carry a hint of the dead priest's putrefaction?

She should have offered her guest at least a change of linen, but she had been too absorbed with stretching the small repast. If the sheriff stayed the night, and he probably would—even a man of Sir Guy's prowess with arms would be hesitant to ride the twelve miles back to Norwich through wood and marshland during the black of night—she would have to drag out Roderick's smallclothes.

Suddenly, she became aware of silence around her, an awkward, intrusive silence.

"What did you say, sir?" The sheriff, his posture taut, leaned across her, gazing intently at the illuminator.

"Not *sir*. Just Finn. My name is Finn. I am an artisan, not a member of your noble estate."

There was an archness in his tone just short of sarcasm. His voice had the same smooth-gravel quality that she remembered from earlier in the day, when he had kept her from falling, only now the edge was honed.

"I said, 'He'll never burn.' Wycliffe will never burn. And he'll not hang. He has too many friends in high places."

"He'd better beware lest he be perceived as having too many friends in *low* places." The sheriff laughed as he split the back of a partridge with his knife before spearing it and raising it to his mouth.

"Ah, I take your meaning," Finn said slowly and without raising his voice. "But high and low may not necessarily make strange bedfellows. I suspect, if you listen closely, you may hear the devil laugh at many a papal edict."

Brother Joseph gasped.

Kathryn had to stop this line of talk before it got out of hand. As she clapped her hands for the carver to reappear, she looked askance at this new-comer. She hoped he was not going to bring more controversy at a time when she was trying so desperately to cleanse her household from any stain of unorthodoxy.

"Please, kind sirs, no more talk of burnings. It is not comely conversation at table. You should not misconstrue the words of my guest, Sir Guy. He's not the humble artisan he proclaims himself to be. He, too, has friends in high places. He's an illuminator of great renown here on business for the abbot. Perhaps he only seeks to draw you out for the sake of conversation. Here, try some of the smoked herring with murrey sauce."

She motioned for the butler to squeeze a few more drops from the leathern bottle as the carver ladled a generous portion of the fish swimming in its red mulberry sauce onto Sir Guy's side of the trencher. She placed her hand over her own side to decline, shaking her head. "Give my portion to Brother Joseph, I find the heat has destroyed my appetite."

Smiling, Brother Joseph eyed the generous portion before him, his shock at the illuminator's heretical words forgotten in anticipation. "My lady's loss is my gain," he said. "I'll see it does not go to waste."

As if anything were ever wasted at Blackingham, she thought. The servers with hungry mouths at home would see to that, as he well knew. Still, it was amusing to watch the monk's exceeding pleasure. His little round belly testified that he did not consider gluttony the deadliest sin.

"By the by, milady, I've brought you something from our apothecary for your headaches," he said between mouthfuls, "ground peony root with oil of roses." He reached inside the deep pockets of his habit and produced a small blue phial.

"How kind, Brother Joseph. Please give my thanks to your apothecary as well."

And she meant it. Hard to believe this gentle man who took such care to assuage her pain was the same firebrand who a few moments ago had anticipated the burning of a fellow human being with the same enthusiasm with which he now attacked his food. And all in the name of God. Well, no matter. She was glad for the medicine. She would have need of it, if this dinner did not end soon. Thankfully, the talk had settled to more mundane things. Colin talked in Brother Joseph's ear of the guild pageants he'd seen at Eastertide in Norwich. Sir Guy interrogated the illuminator about the nature of his commission.

But no sooner was one fire put out than here was another. Alfred had moved closer to the illuminator's daughter and leaned forward to whisper something in her ear. The light from the tallow candles on the wall behind him sparked fire in his red hair. Lady Kathryn heard his familiar, merry laugh and saw the girl's olive skin turn pink like the blush on a peach.

The illuminator had introduced her simply as his daughter, Rose—not Margaret, or Anna or Elizabeth. Just Rose. Like the flower. A strange name for a Christian child, she had thought at the time. It was after the priest's body had been removed, after her sons had wandered in, summoned by the commotion in the courtyard. As soon as she saw the look in Alfred's blue eyes and recognized it for what it was, she decided what her course of action should be. Now, she was more sure of her decision than ever.

Finn inclined his head and spoke low in his daughter's ear, scolding, Kathryn deduced, from the fleeting frown that turned down the corners of Rose's mouth before she lowered her gaze. Her fingers fidgeted with the pendant at her throat, fingering it like a talisman. Kathryn would attend the girl tonight, but she could not play nursemaid forever. Tomorrow she would have to tell Alfred of her decision.

～✦～

Finn also found himself distracted as he sat at table in the great hall. He had noted the irritation in the voice of his hostess, who sat at his right, and so resolved to make no more political statements. He did not want Brother Joseph carrying tales back to the abbot at Broomholm that the abbey had a heretic in its employ. He had already called undue attention to himself by confronting the bishop of Norwich and confessing to killing his sow. He had tried to be deferential to the impudent stripling of a bishop—even offered to pay for the pig and her suckling—but deference didn't come easily to Finn, and he feared he'd botched it. But by taking the blame on himself, he had saved the dwarf from the stocks or worse.

He hoped the abbot would forget any indiscretion on the part of his new employee when he saw the carpet pages for the manuscript. They would be glorious. On the journey to Aylsham from Broomholm, Finn had had plenty of time to think about the end-papers, the pages that would precede the beginning of Saint John's Gospel. The background would be the rich red of the mulberry sauce soaking into the bread of his trencher and smothering the partridge on which he chewed.

"I hope you find the sauce pleasing, Master . . . Finn."

"I find much to please me here, madam." Was it his imagination, or did her face redden? He hastily added. "You are fortunate in your cook. The bird is well-seasoned."

She smiled at him—a real smile, not the strained grimace he'd seen heretofore.

"Agnes has been with me since I was a child. She was my nursemaid. She is very loyal."

Finn saluted her with his knife. speared another bite. Agnes, he thought. A name worth remembering. It was always good to make friends with the cook. Nor did he want to incur disfavor with Lady Kathryn. If she prized loyalty, he must say nothing else to make her wary of his own, but he sincerely hoped hers was not one of those pious households where he would be constantly required to invent excuses for his absence from a numbing ritual of daily prayers. And he really did not want Rose to be influenced by an excess of religious fervor. He'd seen the dark underbelly of that kind of piety. Balance in all things was best, and especially in religion. That's what he wanted for his daughter—devotion to the Virgin, yes, but balanced by intelligent reasoning. His life had been ruled by the sign of the cross—hadn't he dedicated his art to it, even carried it before him into battle? But he had been born under another sign: Libra, the sign of the scales—reason in one, piety in the other.

It would help if he knew why Lady Kathryn had agreed to board him and his daughter. He suspected more than loyalty to the Church; the abbot was probably making it worth her while. Hers was a prosperous household, if the silver cups and horn spoons tipped with silver carvings were an indication, but the table she kept, if respectable, could not be said to be extravagant, and he'd noticed the careful manner in which she directed the pouring of the wine. He and Rose would be served simpler fare in future. She was probably hard-pressed to stretch her income to meet taxes and tithes.

He couldn't help but notice that the widow had other pressures as well. The hawk-nosed sheriff on her right, with whom she shared cup and trencher, brushed her sleeve too often and would have buried his long nose in her cleavage had she not pulled back from him. Some might call her beautiful, but Finn's taste ran to dark-haired, buxom girls with friendlier ways. This woman was too tall, and carried herself too proud, and despite the pleasing bulges above the neckline of her square-cut bodice, she could not be called buxom. Her hair was certainly her most remarkable feature. She couldn't be more than forty, but her hair was gray—almost white—with one black strand above the left temple that threaded like a velvet ribbon through the intricate knot bound in a blue snood at the nape of a slender neck. He wondered what she would look like naked in the moonlight, the whole great mass of hair loosed and flowing over her breasts like melting silver. He was surprised how quickly this lecherous thought had inserted itself—he had not thought the woman that attractive.

"A toast to Lady Blackingham." Sir Guy raised his glass. "To the beauty of our hostess and the bounty of her table."

Fawning bastard, Finn thought. Was the sheriff toasting her thighs or her pasturelands? But he raised his glass so as not to appear ungracious. One insulted a sheriff at one's peril.

The room was warm, and he was vaguely aware of an odor of musk on his right. He noticed how the flimsy fabric of Lady Kathryn's kerchief clung to her breasts. He felt a tightening in his loins and was glad he didn't have to stand to drink the toast. He'd been celibate too many months. Celibate, not because he'd been on pilgrimage or fasting, no such nonsense—he'd leave that to the monks—but celibate out of convenience and squeamishness. Traveling with his daughter made dalliance difficult. The doxies who offered themselves smelled of the hovels they lived in, and their bodies were infested with lice. Even in the brothels run by the bishops, there was still the danger of catching the pox.

Finn became aware that his companions had fallen silent and were looking at him expectantly. The rotund little monk was leaning across the table, shouting in his direction.

"Do you not agree, Master Illuminator?"

"I'm sorry, I didn't—"

"Brother Joseph, please. Have another sweet?" Lady Kathryn beckoned to the server. "Agnes made the custard tarts especially for tonight."

The monk held his spoon at ready and his eyes lit up in anticipation, his inquisition forgotten.

Whatever the question, it was obvious to Finn that his hostess had not trusted his answer. She was cunning. He remembered her reaction when the sheriff brought the priest's body, the too-straight way she'd denied seeing the priest. What involvement could be there? Whatever it was, it was none of his affair. He had his daughter to think of. The murder of a priest was a dangerous thing to know about.

Alarm bells in Finn's head pulled him back from his reverie. A different voice this time, coming from his left, hushed, intimate, "I could show you the best place for drawing—a little inlet overlooking the sea."

He recognized the tone of the jackanapes beside him, whose red head was bent much too near his daughter's. Their lips were almost touching.

Finn spoke loudly enough to pull Alfred away from his amorous pursuit. "Inlet by the sea, you say. Rose and I will be glad to see it, won't we, Rose?"

Alfred hummed and hawed after the manner of a thief caught with his hand in the herring barrel. His daughter blushed, anger at her father sparking in her beautiful eyes. A harmless flirtation, perhaps; still, the boy needed warning that he was being watched.

The meal dragged on interminably. What a relief when his hostess rose. Now he could excuse himself and retire to the pleasant quarters she had provided. He said a polite good night to the others, saluted Lady Kathryn once again for her hospitality, and pulled his daughter from the clutches of her ardent admirer. But before he could make good his retreat, a servant approached him and handed him a scrap of sealed parchment. "This message came for you, sir. I was instructed to give it into your hand."

The seal was not familiar, but the holy cross embossed upon it gave some clue to its origin. Probably some afterthought instructions from his patron.

"Did the messenger wait for an answer?"

The sheriff had stopped talking and was taking a noticeable interest in this exchange. This rankled him, just as Sir Guy's earlier probe into the nature of his commission had rankled.

"No, sir," the page said. "The messenger said to tell you something else, though. He said to tell you 'Half-Tom pays his debts.'"

The dwarf. But why would he bring a message from the abbey in Broomholm? The abbey was in Bacton Wood, several miles east of Aylsham, and that through forest. And Blackingham was miles out of his way—at least twelve miles north of Norwich. Half-Tom was from the edge of the fens, west of Norwich. The question could be cleared up easily enough by opening the dispatch, and he had started to do just that when the sheriff stood up and, crossing behind him, peered over his shoulder. Nosy bastard. Instead of breaking the seal, Finn tapped Rose on the sleeve with the folded parchment, then gently shoved Alfred aside and took his daughter's arm.

"Come, daughter. It's time to retire to our quarters. Let Lady Kathryn take leave of her guests in privacy." He nodded at the Benedictine. "Good night, Brother Joseph. You may assure Father Abbot when you return to him on the morrow that his illuminator is hard at work. I wish you good journey. You also, Sir Guy." The *sir* did not trip easily from his tongue.

"But you haven't opened your message," the sheriff said.

"It might be from a lady," Finn replied, "and therefore better enjoyed in the privacy of my chamber." He pushed back from the table.

For the second time that evening, Lady Kathryn loosened the tension by inserting herself into his conversation. "In that case, Finn, we will bid you good night and speed you to your pleasure." She took a rushlight from a sconce, but when Alfred reached to take it from her, she frowned at him and summoned her other son, whom Finn had hardly noticed. Handing him the rushlight, Lady Kathryn said, "Colin will light your way. The stairs are dark and unfamiliar. You would not want Rose to stumble."

With a measure of relief, Finn turned his back on the whole lot of them. As they mounted the stairs, he thought about the hurt child for the first time since his arrival at the manor. How easily she had slipped from his memory. How had she fared? Of course. Half-Tom. The seal of the holy cross. The message was from the anchoress. When they reached their room, he grabbed the candle beside his bed and tore open the seal

The child had lived only three days.

⧓

"You sent for me, Mother?" Alfred wiped the sleep from his eyes, trying to keep reproach from his voice. He stumbled in the pale light of pre-dawn that scarcely penetrated Lady Kathryn's bedchamber. The torches flickered in their sconces, wicks burnt low.

She didn't answer him right away, but paced back and forth, her leather-bottomed slippers making little shuffling noises in the stillness of early morning.

The bedcovers of his mother's bed had already been replaced, or maybe, Alfred concluded after noticing the bluish circles that ringed her eyes, maybe the bed had never been slept in. Was it one of her headaches? He forgot his own annoyance at being summoned from his dreams and watched her anxiously as she paced back and forth. She was still wearing the clothes she had worn the night before. Sweat stains ringed the silk of her tunic beneath the armpits. She had removed her headdress, and her silver hair fell in a tangled, unkempt mass below her waist. Her face looked haggard in the gray light.

"Mother, are you all right?"

She halted in her pacing and glanced at him as if startled by his appearance in her bedchamber.

"Alfred, you're up early. Is something wrong?"

"My lady mother sent for me," he said, unable to mask the irritation in his voice. He had only just gotten to bed. His head felt foggy and his tongue thick. He'd gone out with some lads from the village to a cockfight. But best not tell her that.

"I didn't mean for Agnes to awaken you so early," she said.

"Well, the old cow did, and seemed to delight in it, too." He waited for his mother's chiding, but it didn't come. Instead she just stood there looking at him, as though she didn't know what to say. Unusual for his mother to be at a loss for words, she who wielded words like a rapier.

"Are you unwell, Mother?" he asked, feeling suddenly like a child again, panic rising inside him. What if they lost her suddenly, too, like their father? Alfred had loved his father, but it was Lady Kathryn to whom he and Colin looked for support and whose wrath they feared whenever they strayed. Roderick had often been away for months at a time, fighting the French or playing courtier to the king.

She shook her head, sat down on the bed, and patted the space beside her, inviting him. "I'm all right. Come. Sit beside me. I need to talk to you about a matter of great importance."

Now, this was a change. She was usually either autocratic or indulgent with him: sometimes stern disciplinarian, occasionally doting mother; but this tone sounded different, almost as though she were seeking his advice. True, he would be sixteen in another year, the age of majority under Danelaw, but he knew that he would never really rule Blackingham as long as his mother was well. She had brought Blackingham with her to her marriage, and retaining her dower rights had been in the terms of her nuptial contract. Nobody could wrest it from her but the king himself.

He sat down on the coverlet beside her, and she turned to face him, raising one leg up onto the bed and leaning against the bedpost for support. She reached up and smoothed his hair. Suddenly he was a child again, and she was trying to explain to him that putting the little green snake in his brother's bed had been a cruel joke—not funny at all. But she'd not seen Colin's little baby mouth screwed into a tight little O while he danced around on one foot, screaming, "A snake, a snake." Alfred wanted to laugh now just remembering. He hadn't a clue what he'd done this time—or had she found out about the cockfight after all?

"Alfred, you know these are not easy times. The king's death left a great hole, and his sons are seeking to fill that hole and gain power for themselves. Lancaster and Gloucester will probably not allow their dead brother's eleven-year-old-son to assume the throne without a struggle. And then, of course, there are the French wars and one too many popes to carry on our backs."

"What has that to do with me?" he asked. She would hardly summon him to discuss the politics of court and Church with him.

She smiled at him and shook her head in a gesture of exasperation. He knew that look. It always made him feel like a simpleton.

"It has everything to do with you, Alfred. With Blackingham. If we appear to cast our lot with the wrong faction, and that side loses in the struggle for the throne, then we—you—could lose everything." She touched him gently on the chin with long, tapered fingers. Her eyes caressed him. "Including that beautiful red head of yours."

"But Father and the duke of Lancaster were friends."

"Exactly. Your father made a foolish alliance with John of Gaunt. What if the duke falls prey to his own machinations? It wouldn't be the first time. What if young Richard grows tired of both his uncles' conniving and comes under another's influence—say the archbishop? John of Gaunt is not popular with the bishops because he defends the cleric Wycliffe and his teachings against the power of the Church. They stir up the rabble against the pope. If the bishops turn against John of Gaunt, the lord of Blackingham could go down with the duke, charged with treason, his lands forfeit. That would be you. Do you understand that, Alfred?"

"I think so." Maybe Colin was the lucky one after all, he thought, suddenly feeling the weight of his birthright. "What do we do?" he asked soberly.

"We feign ignorance of your father's alliances, proclaim ourselves neutral whenever possible. We make ourselves invisible."

"Invisible?"

"We walk a narrow road. We maintain the appearance of loyalty in a very quiet way. We express no unsolicited opinions, and when asked where our allegiance lies, we weigh our words like gold." She licked her forefinger and held it up for him to see. "And we are always alert for the winds of change."

"You mean don't brag about our friends."

"I mean neither 'brag about our friends' nor appear to threaten our enemies."

"And keep our mouths shut in the presence of important people," he said, nodding. "Not like the illuminator."

"Exactly." Her wide mouth turned down, making her face even more haggard. "He should never have been so outspoken in front of the sheriff and Brother Joseph. It could hurt him and, by association, us."

"Will you tell him?"

She looked thoughtful. "I think not. Somehow I don't think a man like Finn would keep silent for the sake of judiciousness."

"You mean he's brave," Alfred said.

"I mean, he has no lands to confiscate, no sons to place in danger. He's a gifted artisan not tied to any guild, and because of his gift, he enjoys the protection of the Church."

"He has a daughter."

"Yes, he has a daughter." She looked away. "But I didn't drag you out of your bed to talk about Finn and his daughter."

"I know. You wanted to warn me to watch my mouth."

She nodded. "That and to ask you to begin to assume your responsibility as lord of the manor."

Here it comes, he thought, the lecture about responsibility, too much drinking, too much carousing. He remembered how angry she'd been at him. He shouldn't have been so familiar with Glynis in front of her. She must have heard him sneaking in during the wee hours after all.

"But I'm not old enough to be lord of the manor. Remember. You told me so."

"You're old enough to begin to learn how to protect your lands and your family." She held up her hand to stop his interruption. "I'm not talking about bearing arms. I know your father taught you how to wield a sword and use a dagger. And where did that knowledge get him? No, I'm talking about protection of another kind."

She got up and began to pace the floor again.

"I have reason to believe that Simpson is stealing from us, from you. And in any event, he has valuable knowledge about the tenants, the sheep, the preparing and selling of the wool: knowledge that you need."

"If you think he's stealing, why don't you just sack him?"

"Because between the plague and the French wars, precious few men are left. Laborers are hard enough to find: common yeomen, shepherds and weavers—harder still those who can read and cipher." She turned to look at him. Her gaze was level, direct. "So I'm asking you to go and stay with Simpson. You can keep an eye on him and learn from him at the same time."

"You mean like an apprentice! Me? The future Lord Blackingham, heir of Sir Roderick, apprenticed to an overseer?" He heard his own voice rise in a childish whine but couldn't help it. "Why can't Colin go?"

"Because Colin's not the heir to Blackingham Manor. You are. Besides, it wouldn't be apprenticed, exactly, Alfred. Simpson will still be servant and you master. He will respect that. He's too greedy not to. He'll probably even try to ingratiate himself with you. He knows I have no love of him. And you'll learn from him—he may be a thief, but he knows wool—but more importantly, you'll watch him, protect yourself and us from his thievery."

"For how long?"

"As long as it takes you to catch him." She shrugged. "Michaelmas, maybe."

Alfred, after his first flare of indignation, began to weigh the merit of her argument. So, he was to be a spy. The idea of such an adventure was not without its appeal. He could lead old Simpson a merry dance. And he had to admit it might be nice to be away from his mother's watchful eye. Sometimes her apron strings tugged painfully. He'd thought about asking to go as squire, maybe to the sheriff, Sir Guy de Fontaigne. His father had spoken about it before he died. But this might be better. Close and not too close.

"Needless to say," she added, "you'll be excused from prayers. I don't know how much show of piety will be required of us with our new abbey connection. I expect we'll see more of Brother Joseph. And there may be couriers between Blackingham and the abbey's scriptorium. We must keep up appearances. But Simpson's presence is only required at chapel on Holy Days. Of course, if you stay here, as future lord of the manor, you would be expected to be more in attendance than you have been in the past."

Well, that settled it!

"When would I have to leave?" he asked.

"Tomorrow. Simpson always brings the accounts on Fridays. Yesterday we were interrupted. I will send for him tomorrow. You will, of course, be present, and he will be made to understand your new status. Now that I think of it, he should give this accounting to you. I will stand in the background to answer any questions you might have later. But Simpson will see you're in charge. You can even tell him that it's your decision to observe his goings-on for a while—so that you can learn the wool trade—you don't want to put him on his guard."

This new adult status was scary but had a certain excitement too. Stay here and take orders from his mother or go with Simpson and be able to give the orders? What's more, he could do with a little male companionship. He missed his father.

"I'll do it, Mother," he said, nodding soberly—as if the decision had been his to make. "Don't you worry, I'll catch the bugger for you."

"Good." Lady Kathryn smiled. "I knew I could count on you." She exhaled deeply and the lines in her face relaxed. "Now, go along and tell Agnes that you want your breakfast."

She gave him a kiss on the cheek. Her lips felt soft, and her hair smelled of lavender. At least this time he had made her happy. And it hadn't been all that hard to do. Playing lord of the manor to surly Simpson might even be fun. And then he thought of Rose and sighed with regret. He'd completely forgotten about the illuminator's pretty daughter. What a time to have to leave. Maybe he could get away from Simpson once in a while to check on progress in the improvised scriptorium.

⋅※⋅

Lady Kathryn sank with relief onto the bed. From outside, she could hear the first clanging from the courtyard. Smoke from the struggling kitchen fires scented the early-morning air. Blackingham was shrugging off its slumber: the grooms, the maids, even the hounds sleeping in the stable, all were stirring to life with the first graying light. And she had not slept at all. She had passed the night considering the best way to get Alfred's cooperation, but her careful planning had paid off. She could have ordered him to obey, but he was happy this way. It was all a game to him.

Alfred and his games. How she'd loved watching him as a boy, a stick strapped to his side for a sword, dragging his makeshift shield behind him, devising battle strategy—he himself always the hero among his imaginary battle mates—punctuating gallant speeches about honor and courage with violent shakes of his red curls. She could still hear his shouts of "Forward, lads. Cut the blackguards down." And in frustration he would shake his sword-stick at Colin, who had wandered off to examine the colors of a butterfly. She allowed herself the briefest fancy that she was back there with her young sons—watching them play, loving them, stroking their heads, singing them to sleep, binding their scrapes and bruises, doing the things that mothers do. How much she'd taken those simple pleasures for granted.

Playing spy to Simpson would be just another game to Alfred, but it would keep him away from Rose. And he could profit from Simpson's learning, and the overseer did, indeed, need to be overseen. Alfred was bright. If Simpson was stealing, Alfred would discern it, and together they could put a stop to it. Still, she would miss having her merry-hearted son underfoot. He could always make her laugh. And if Simpson was not the best influence, what harm could he do to Alfred's character that Roderick had not already done by example?

The lark outside her window started to sing—impudent fellow, to herald a dawn come too early. She would have hurled her shoe at him were it not ill luck to harm a lark. And Kathryn needed no more ill luck.

So much to remember, so much vigilance required. Sometimes, she felt like a dried leaf buffeted about by the wind in winter. No direction. No control. If she could only rest a little while, then she would have the strength to see that Finn and Rose were settled in their new quarters.

Just before she closed her eyes and drifted off to sleep, she remembered there was one thing she had forgotten. She had not questioned Alfred about his whereabouts on the night of the priest's murder.

FIVE

*On your altar let it be enough for you to have a repre-
sentation of our Saviour hanging on the Cross: that
will bring before your mind his Passion for you to imi-
tate, his outspread arms will invite you to embrace
him, his naked breast will feed you with the milk of
sweetness to console you.*
—AILRED OF RIEVAULX,
RULE FOR THE LIFE OF A RECLUSE (1160)

 he anchoress lay prostrate before her altar, before the image of
her suffering Christ, and offered up her own anguish. Her contemplation was
broken, her prayers intruded upon by the terror her mind could not quench.
She remembered (as though it had been days and not years) the bishop's face
as he chanted the mass of the dead, the sound as he shot the bolt on the massive door, sealing her in the symbolic tomb. The sound of the clanging of the
lock and the scraping of the great oak door along the floor still rang in her
ears even as she lay before her altar in a well of silence. She lay in darkness,
too. And she lay in the cold sweat of her fear.

It was the highest calling of all that had summoned her, the call to live in
solitude, to close herself off from the world, from family, from friends—not
even allowed the comfort of monastic community—so that she might become

an empty vessel to receive Him. The woman she had been was dead as far as the world was concerned, giving up even her name for the name of the church, the Church of Saint Julian, in whose eaves her hut sheltered. A mere appurtenance, it was built outside the church walls as a symbol of the hermit's solitary status. She had willingly answered the call to this life, denying herself both ecclesiastical and worldly community, agreeing to live fully dependent on the charity of others for her sustenance, to abide in communion with her Lord, her solitude interrupted only by the occasional visitor who came seeking solace or prayer. And that had been enough.

Until tonight.

But tonight was as the first night, when her heart hammered in her chest like the heart of a caged bird. She felt again the rising panic, wanted to scream and beat with her fists at the great wood barrier that barred her from the world.

How long had she lain here in this heavy darkness, mouthing prayers that could not bridge the faithlessness of her broken communion?

Was that a lark? The cathedral bells tolled matins. It was not yet morning.

Her limbs were stiff, her flesh bruised by the clammy stone, sweating in the August heat. To live a life of contemplation, to shut out the swirling vortex, the *danse macabre,* to close her ears to the cries of mourning, to the never-ending dirges—the reaper walked abroad, gleaning souls like ripe grain—to listen instead for the Still, Small Voice: that was the way she'd chosen when she pledged herself to God.

And she had been content until the illuminator brought the broken child to her.

She'd cradled the wounded child in her arms and crooned a lullaby. But by the time the illuminator returned with the mother, the "anchoress" had receded into the shadows, and in her place was a woman filled with regret, a woman painfully aware of all she'd left behind.

Her menses had ceased with her enclosure in the anchorhold.

"Her name is Mary," the mother had said, as they bathed the skin of the burning child. Her voice broke on the last word, her face grotesque with pain, frozen like the tragedy masks the mummers wore for their mystery plays. "I named her for Our Lady. So She would protect her."

But the Virgin had not protected the namesake child. Nor had the Christ to whom Julian prayed. Did the mother know how much Julian envied her that little girl? Even a dead child lived in memory. First came envy and then doubt. Then, what other sins might creep through the crack in her faith?

The stone tasted of mold and death beneath her lips. *"Domini, invictus,"* she pleaded. But Mercy had departed for a season. Her body was rigid from lying so long on the cold stone floor. Could she will its locked joints to move, if she tried? I will die here, she thought. I will die, and they will find my bones before the altar, the flesh falling away like rotten fruit falling away from its seed. The fingers of her left hand, palm pressed flat against the floor, began to twitch convulsively.

I never even knew the mother's name, she thought.

Julian had tried to speak words of comfort. But the words had fallen like pebbles in the silence, hard and brittle as grief. How to speak of mercy when none is offered?

For three nights after they buried the child, Julian had dreamed the devil was choking her. She had awakened, struggling for breath, to the cries from beyond her servant's shuttered window, cries of the mother calling out in her sleep for her dead child. Julian tried with all her will to still the yearnings the child had wakened in her. She'd made her choice—blasphemy to gainsay it now.

"Pastor Christus est . . ." Her lips could no longer form the words. *Forgive my frail flesh, Lord. I thank you for this unanswered longing. I offer my suffering to you as sacrifice.*

But she could not stop the hot tears that puddled beneath her face. Did she weep for the suffering of her Saviour, for baby Mary, for the grieving mother? Or did she weep for her own empty womb?

In the garden outside, the first call of the lark presaged the dawn. Inside the church, rats scuttled about, seeking some lost crumb of host. How fragile was this thing called faith.

"Lord, if it be your will, take away the longing. And if it is not your will that I should be free of all womanly desire, then turn this yearning into a better understanding of your perfect love."

In answer, the first breaking of pearly light gathered and flowed, like fickle grace, beneath the door of her cell. Julian heard Alice's early-morning preparation on the other side of her door: the crunching twigs of a fire being laid beneath the cook-pot, the whoosh of the shutters opening on the small window through which Julian received her food. She rose from her position, surprised that she could will her reluctant limbs to obedience.

"Has the night passed?" she asked as Alice placed a clean stack of linen on the ledge.

"Aye, and the mother has gone," Alice said. "Her cot was empty when I got here. She's probably returned to her husband."

"That is good. Now she can begin to restore her spirit."

To Julian's relief, Alice made no comment about the seeming injustice, though her mouth twitched with wanting to. 'Have you been at prayer all night?" she asked as Julian removed a clean veil and wimple from the stack on the ledge.

"The Holy Spirit gives balm to wounded souls."

"Well, the body needs a bit of comfort now and then, too." She bustled like a wren lining a nest. "Here, take this egg to break your fast."

As Julian took a bite of the boiled egg, then returned it to its cup, she noticed the newly sharpened quills peeking out from the basket Alice was placing in the window.

"I see you brought more pens. I shall eat later. After my work is done."

The servant's mouth pinched tighter, but she swallowed her protest. "I brought an extra poppy-seed cake for the dwarf " she said. "He may be half a man, but he hath the appetite of a giant."

"And the spirit of a giant. But you may take the cake to the alms gate or give it to the birds. Tom won't be back. He's returned to his eel traps. He took a message to the man who brought the child to us. I thought that he would want to know."

Alice poured water from the church well into a basin and, shoving the half-eaten egg aside, placed it in the window. "Now, that one is a strange duck to be certain. He's doing monk's work, drawing for the abbey, but he's no monk. He has a daughter."

Alice laid out soap and towels and fresh herbs in the weekly ritual. Julian insisted on this frequent bathing over Alice's objection that " 'tweren't healthy." Julian undressed as Alice gossiped.

"I wouldn't have took him for a family man. He had the stubborn look of a Welshman, but he spoke Norman French as well as you. And that don't fit 'cause I never knowed a Welshman without a brogue. I'd bet my maidenhead, if I still had it, he's a vagabond Celt. More pagan than Christian. And working for the Church. They should stick to hiring God-fearing Saxons."

Julian turned her back to the window and removed her shift. The little cell, which was usually cold, had become uncomfortably warm with August heat. The water felt good against her bruised skin. Was this weekly bath a fleshly indulgence that she should deny herself? Or could she think of it as a kind of baptism? She half listened to the older woman's chatter, inhaled the soothing fragrance of the lavender-scented water. Another indulgence? But God made the lavender sweet—a gift from a loving father.

"God-fearing Saxons, that's what I say."

Julian had long been aware that, like others of her class, Alice harbored many prejudices in an otherwise good heart. No use trying to argue with her.

Alice rattled on. "He was uncommonly clean, though. Did you notice his hands? Smooth like a woman's. And the fingernails. Except for the little ridges of paint, they were clean as a chicken bone gnawed by a beggar." She gave a sly look from under lowered lashes. "But there was nothing womanly about him."

A pause. A sigh. Julian knew what was coming.

"But I don't suppose ye notice such."

"I've taken a vow of chastity, Alice. Not blindness. But more important, he seems to have an honest soul."

Alice harrumphed, "Not too honest to lie to the bishop about who killed the pig. I know 'twere the dwarf. He told me so. Said he was fearful of the stocks. Last man who stole the bishop's property had his nose slit fer it."

Julian, finding no holy reason to draw out her bathing and wishing her soul could be so easily cleansed, slipped a clean shift over her head. It smelled of lye, sharp and acrid. It stung her nose.

"'Twere a noble lie, though," Alice said grudgingly. "The bishop being more tolerant of an employee of Broomholm Abbey than to an eel-catcher from the fens. And a good thing it happened last week instead of this."

"A *noble* lie, Alice? I'll have to meditate on that. As for the timing, what difference could it make?"

"Ye haven't heard then. I thought maybe the dwarf might have told ye."

"Told me what?"

"The bishop's legate was returned to him in a sack. With his head bashed in."

"What—?"

"'Tweren't no accident, neither. And Henry Despenser says he'll see the murderer hanged, his head on a pole, and his entrails burnt."

"But what could that have to do with the illuminator?"

"Well, he were a stranger, that's all. And everybody knows the Welsh are a wild lot. Anyway, the bishop flew into a great temper when he heard the news. Said whoever struck the blow, he'd lay the blame to John Wycliffe for working up the people against Holy Church. Said if Oxford wouldn't shut Wycliffe up, he'd go to the French pope."

Julian handed her dirty clothing back through the window. Alice reached for it, her string of talk unbroken. "Though I don't know where that would get him, since everybody knows he's robbing rich and poor to finance the Italian pope's claim. Two popes. One in France. Another in Rome. Holy Mother of God. Isn't one enough? How is a God-fearing person to know which is right? Probably neither." And then she mumbled, "Mayhap I'll just declare myself pope, and then we could have three. And one a woman."

Alice must have seen from Julian's expression that she'd gone too far.

"Well, I'll just go tend the herb garden and leave ye to yer writing." She opened her chamber door into the morning sunlight. Through her window Julian could see the light from the open door paint the gray image of a tree branch on the wall. A shadow leaf fluttered in a remembered breeze. She could smell the green morning. She longed to feel the sun on her face. Second-hand light filtered through her interior window onto her writing table. That was her portion. And she would be satisfied with it.

Alice's voice drifted in. She must be just beside the door, talking to herself as she pulled weeds among the thyme and fennel. A muttered curse, then "two popes. 'Tis an evil world. The anti-Christ is abroad."

Julian turned to her manuscript and began to write:

OF CHRIST'S SUFFICIENCY

I knew well that there was strength enough for me (and indeed for all living creatures that shall be saved) against all the fiends of hell, and against all ghostly enemies.

At first, Blackingham's cook felt much abused that there would be two more mouths to feed from the gaping kitchen hearth she tended. As she flattened down the red embers under the white-hot ash to make a level cooking base and swung the heavy pot into place, Agnes grumbled to her husband, John, that her poor old back would not hold out much longer.

"Then where would milady be?" she asked.

"Like as not between the same rock and hard place she is right now."

She knew she shouldn't complain to John. It only made him more resentful, and that was not what she wanted at all. He'd begged her to leave years ago, after the plague swept the country in 1354, killing many of the able-bodied laborers.

" 'Tis our chance to break with the land," he'd said. "I've heard they be paying wages in Suffolk. A man can hire himself out to whatever job he wants. Leave when he wants. No questions asked. After a year in Colchester, we'd be free. Blackingham would have no hold on us."

"The king's law forbids it. We'd be outlaws for a whole year. I'll not wear the wolf's head even for ye, John; I'll not be hunted in the forest like a wild thing. Lady Kathryn's been good to us. Ye bide yer time right and Sir Roderick might make ye overseer someday."

John had been a good stout man in those days, and smart. He could do anything, and did. Single-handedly, he'd built the flocks to where they produced enough wool to keep every hand they could find busy with the fleeces; shearing and rolling, grading and packing. He'd been a proud man then, but things had not turned out the way Agnes had planned. Her John had not been rewarded for his loyalty and hard work. Instead, Sir Roderick had hired that surly bailiff, Simpson, who lost no time putting John back in his place, lording it over him, never calling him by name, just "Shepherd."

"Shepherd" John had remained, and he'd lost all joy in his labors. He still supervised the shearing and the pulling of the fleeces and much else besides—work that rightfully should have been done by Simpson. This very day Agnes had had to leave the kitchen and go to the wool room to help, because they were shorthanded. It was already late in the season and time for the haying, and John was with the mowers, laborers hired by Simpson who would be paid a wage. She and Glynis had rolled the washed fleeces skin side up and laid them out on the clean-swept floor of the wool house—she and Glynis and young Master Alfred, who'd stopped and offered to help.

These days, John came home at sunset too tired even to eat and sought his comfort in a flagon of ale. But Agnes didn't begrudge him, even though it hurt to see her once gentle John loutish and bitter. She had betrayed him for her mistress. Had it not been for her loyalty to Lady Kathryn, her John would be a free man today, working for the dignity of a wage, instead of as a lackey to the likes of Simpson. It hardly seemed fair that she should complain now about her lot, so she determined to say no more about the extra work.

But extra work or not, it didn't take the illuminator long to charm his way into her good graces. After two weeks, she had to admit that Finn's pleasant demeanor and undemanding ways offset the burden of the added chores. She even looked forward to the mid-afternoon break that had become his habit. She had learned to like his wit. He wasn't Norman French like her mistress, or even Danish like Sir Roderick, but Welsh impudence was more to be tolerated than Saxon brutishness. And she admired a man of learning.

"Might you have a glass of ale or even a sip of perry for a poor scrivener, Agnes?" he'd said that first afternoon when he came into her kitchen. He loomed large in the doorway, shutting out the light.

She looked up from the meat she was grinding to a paste, not happy with the interruption, and grunted as she poured him a tankard of pear wine.

To her surprise he settled on the high stool next to her, and resting his elbows and his cup on the chopping block where she worked, began to talk. "You're making mortrewes, I'll wager. My grandmother used to make that. She was a fine cook. Your food reminds me of hers." He motioned toward the mixture of bread crumbs and meat that she was kneading to a flattened ball. "Do you roll it in ginger and sugar? And saffron? I remember hers was the color of saffron."

Agnes frowned, begrudging her answer. "Sugar's too costly. Most times I use honey. The secret to good mortrewes is in the texture. It has to be boiled to the right stiffness. But don't ye need to be getting back to yer own work, and leave me to mine?"

"I left young Colin and Rose mixing colors. He asked if he could be my apprentice, said since his brother was heir and he didn't want to be dependent, he'd like to have a trade. I told him I wasn't a guild master, so I couldn't take an apprentice, but that he could watch and learn. Rose can be a hard little taskmaster. She'll teach him."

Agnes pummeled the concoction. "And Master Colin's a quick learner. You can trust yer daughter'll be safe with him. Now, if 'twere the other one, Alfred, ye might shouldn't leave them alone, if ye get my meaning."

"Colin is harmless. The abbey will probably claim him one day, and Rose enjoys his company." Frowning, he rapped his knuckles on the tabletop and looked off into the middle distance. "I worry that she's lonely. Lately, I've noticed a restlessness about her. She was such a sweet, contented child. Colin plays his lute, and they sing. They talk about music and colors, faraway places. Sometimes their chatter distracts me so, I have to shoo them out just to work in peace. But thanks for the warning. I'll be vigilant lest young Alfred finds the time from the tasks his mother has set him to steal what isn't his."

He took a long drink from the cup. "Excellent perry, Agnes. Do you ferment the juice in barrels?"

"Oaken," she said.

"Ah, that's what gives it this delicious, woodsy undertaste."

Agnes had smiled in spite of herself.

After that day, she found herself looking forward to the illuminator's visits. She always had his mug of perry—even though they were near to the bottom of the barrel and this year's pear harvest a month away—and sometimes a sweet cake, besides. She enjoyed chatting with him and allowed him to pump her for information. But always within limits. Peasant though she might be, she had lived long enough to be aware of the perfidy of the times in which she lived, and knew a wagging tongue could bring down great and low alike.

They were sitting at the chopping block, Finn coddling his tankard of perry as Agnes plucked a brace of geese for roasting on the turnspit. Cool winds from the North Sea chased the July heat that had collected in the room. Peat smoke from the perpetual fire on the stone hearth mixed with the smell of pottage in the great iron pot that Agnes kept continually simmering with beef bones, barley, and leeks. She always had a bowl of broth and an oatcake to offer a hungry villein or beggar, whoever came to her door.

"Blackingham is a fair-sized manor, and I've heard that Sir Roderick had friends at court, was even a friend of the duke of Lancaster," he said.

"Aye. I suppose you could say that. John of Gaunt visited here once. He and Sir Roderick went hunting with that hawk-nosed sheriff. A big headache fer me was that, I can tell ye. Nothing would do for the duke but a roast peacock. I nearly wore myself into my grave a baking and a roasting and then putting them fancy feathers back on that bird, all trifling like."

"And Lady Kathryn? Is she loyal to the duke now that her husband is dead?" Finn asked.

Agnes shrugged, realizing that she was wading in dangerous waters, but she was enjoying Finn's company and knew as long as she answered his questions, he would linger. She answered carefully.

"Lady Kathryn is loyal to her sons. And to Blackingham. She fears the dukes and their struggle for control over the young king."

"Lancaster seems to have won that struggle. They say he's in complete control of young King Richard. I met John of Gaunt once. Rather liked him—though I didn't have to cook a peacock for him." He grinned that sideways grin that Agnes found disarming. "But he's cunning, I'll give him that, the way he's using the preacher, John Wycliffe, to drive a wedge between Church and king. Rich and poor alike are tired of the Church's taxes."

"Aye. Greedy Lancaster's in control, all right. Time being. 'Tis him we have to thank for that wretched poll tax. Mark my words, Illuminator, poor folk will not stomach this tax. You can only push so far, even a peasant has his breaking point. Ye'd be ill advised to hitch yer wagon too soon. Young Richard's other uncle"—she groped for the name—"Gloucester, should not be discounted. Tides change. Wise men don't get washed out to sea."

"Good advice, Agnes. I'll try to remember it." He picked through the strongest quills among the feathers, testing their strength against the tips of his long fingers. "Is Lady Kathryn loyal to the pope, then? Come to think of it, I notice a conspicuous lack of prayers in her daily rituals—not that I'm complaining, you understand. I just assumed Lady Kathryn's sympathies lay with reform."

Agnes pointed at the illuminator with a pin feather she had just plucked from the denuded fowl.

"Milady is devout, Illuminator. Don't ye go carrying tales to the abbot. Her devotions are private, and she's paid enough to the bishop to pray even that rogue of a husband of hers out of purgatory. Ye remember the dead priest, the one the sheriff found in the woods? Well, he used to be hanging around here regular-like, tormenting milady with veiled threats, always asking for money. He 'bout bled her dry."

She thought she saw a flicker of surprise cross the illuminator's face and felt a moment's pang that she might have said too much. She reached for a cleaver and brought the blade down sharply on the neck bones of the bird, first one, then the other.

Finn scooped them onto the flat blade of his knife and added them to the simmering broth on the hearth. "And what about you, Agnes? What do you think about John Wycliffe and his idea that Holy Church has no right to tax what belongs to the king?"

"Me? You're asking me what I think!"

"You're a wise woman. You must have an opinion."

"Aye. And if I do, I'll be keeping it to myself. How do I know you're not a spy for the bishop? Yer doing monk's work. The proper place fer it would be the abbey. It could just be an excuse to spy. Ye might be a viper in our very bosom."

She'd said it half in jest. But still, what did she really know about this stranger who had shown up the same day the bishop's legate was found murdered? Maybe she'd already said too much.

"If I were a mind to spy, it would not be for that green bird Henry Despenser. Youth and unseemly ambition can be a dangerous combination."

Agnes approved of that opinion. She'd seen the bishop last year, when she went to Norwich with John to deliver the fleeces to the wool buyers from Flanders. Bishop Despenser had been supervising repairs on the Yare River bridge. The huge wool cart with its load of fleeces had been detained for an hour while he harangued the stone workers. She had resented his arrogance and the way he flaunted his ermine robes.

Finn drained the last sip of his wine and rose to leave.

"Since you've reminded me of my work, Agnes, I'd best get back to it. Rose will come looking for her father any minute now."

☙

But Rose didn't come looking for her father. She was much too happily engaged.

"I'll teach you how to play the lute," Colin had promised her the week before as they cleaned her father's brushes.

"That would be wonderful. I could surprise my father. He likes me to learn new things." She straightened Finn's manuscripts out of habit. Her father held neatness next to godliness.

"Well, if you want to surprise him, we shouldn't do it here." Colin's voice has music in it even when he isn't singing, she thought. Sometimes she had to remind herself to concentrate on his words. "Do you think you could get away long enough?" he asked.

She pondered the question, fingering the pearl-encrusted cross at her throat. She liked touching the intricate filigreed work, the smooth pearls—it was her very favorite ornament. Touching it helped her think. "Father quits painting every afternoon when the light shifts. He goes into the garden to sketch the next day's work before the daylight fails. Or, if it's too rainy or cold to sit in the garden, he goes for a walk. I'll just tell him I'm going to work on my embroidery with Lady Kathryn."

A frown wrinkled Colin's high, smooth brow. "Rose, I wouldn't want to deceive him. I much admire your father." He straightened an ink pot, touched the stack of manuscript pages, traced the outline of the gilded cross in the center of the mulberry carpet pages—the endpapers that were overlaid with an intricate knotwork of black and amber. "What if he found out?"

"Then we'd tell him the truth, you silly goose, and all would be forgiven." She loved the way his shining cap of pale hair hung just above his jaw line, like a smooth silken curtain. "He wouldn't blame you. He'd be thrilled. You know how my father loves your lute. Haven't you noticed how much better he works when you play?"

His frown vanished. "I think I know a place where we could meet and nobody would see or hear us. The wool house. Nobody ever goes there except at shearing time, and then just to pack the fleeces."

⁓

The afternoon sun was warm, the air fat and lazy like the dog that lay beside the path, when Rose opened the door on the eighth day and slipped inside. Every day for a week, in the late afternoon, Rose had met Colin in the wool room. She sat on the clean-swept floorboards made smooth with years of lanolin from the fleeces, with her legs folded under her. Sometimes, Colin sat behind her with his arms around her, his fingers guiding hers on the strings. Sometimes, he sat across from her, instructing her with painstaking care how to pluck the strings. And during these lessons she learned more than how to hold the lute. This youth, with his gentle manner and silken blond hair, stirred feelings in her that she had not known before. His breath on her neck, the touch of his hand pressing hers made her heart race. Sometimes she grew so light-headed she couldn't think.

The first thing she noticed today was the heavy, pungent odor of wool, not the usual lingering scent of lanolin that had soaked into the floor but a much stronger, more immediate, smell. She saw that the bare floor was littered with freshly clipped fleeces at about the same time she heard the voices. She was so taken aback that someone else was in their secret place that she instinctively shrank into the shadows for fear of being seen. At first she thought she must have imagined it; the room appeared to be empty except for the fleeces. Then she heard it again: voices, groans and giggles. They were coming from behind the large wool sack strung up on the rafters, waiting to be filled. She listened, her nervous fingers caressing the cross pendant for reassurance, feet pegged to the floor by the whispered words.

"Let go now, Master Alfred, milady will be furious with me. With you too, most like, if she finds out what we've been doing." A squeal and a giggle and then: "I should have known ye weren't helping Cook and me roll the fleeces just to be nice."

Rose felt her face flame. Sheltered though her young life had been, she had an inkling of the occupation wherein they were engaged. She recognized Glynis's high, strident voice at the same time she saw four feet sticking out behind the wool sack. There was a scuffle among the tangled limbs and some muffled words, but Rose didn't wait to listen to more. She bolted for the door and scurried behind the back of the shed. She was leaning against the rough boards, trying to collect her thoughts, wondering if she had been seen, when Colin found her.

"Rose, what are you doing out here?"

"I . . . there was somebody inside. I didn't want them to see me."

She looked over his shoulder, not seeing the black-nosed sheep grazing in the meadow beyond, not hearing the drone of bees in the border hedge hard by, seeing only Colin's hands plucking the strands of his lute, hearing only the sound of her heart beating in her ears.

"It was probably just John laying out the wool. But he won't tell. Come on, it doesn't matter. We can find a corner for our lesson."

"All right," Rose said, but she lingered behind, following Colin, wanting to be sure the room was clear, and all the while thinking about what use the other couple had put the same space to. She felt the warmth creeping up her neck. What if Colin could read her mind?

The room seemed different with the fleeces in it, alive somehow. Even the sound of the music was different. The notes didn't echo in the emptiness but had a softer, more muted sound. It was calming. Colin strummed and sang a few lines.

> *I live in love-longing*
> *For the seemliest of all things*
> *Who may me blisse brang,*
> *And I to her am bound.*

The words were hauntingly, wistfully played, evoking in Rose a longing of her own, though a longing for what, she wasn't sure. It was a strange, new sensation.

"Oh, Colin, that is so beautiful. Can you teach it to me?"

Without saying anything, Colin handed her the lute, then bent over her to show her how to place her fingers to make the notes.

"You smell good, Rose, like summer," he said over her shoulder.

She was glad she had washed her hair in lavender water. She could feel his closeness in a way she'd not ever felt close to another human being—not even her father, who stood so stiff when she hugged him he might have been made of wood, not flesh. He used to cuddle her when she was little. She remembered the roughness of his beard on her child's cheek. But he'd not done that in a very long time. She wondered if Colin would shrink away if she touched him. She sat as still as a fawn, lest she break the spell.

"*I live in love-longing*. Sing it with me and I'll move your fingers," he said.

Her fingers were trembling so, she could hardly press the strings.

"*And I to her am bound.*" He sang it softly into her hair, like a lullaby.

She could feel his breath. She thought of the tangle of legs she'd seen behind the wool sack. She knew what they were doing. She'd seen animals coupling once and asked her father in disgust if that's what people did. He'd answered curtly, "Pretty much," and she'd resigned herself to a perpetual state of virginal ignorance.

But with Colin it might be different. Glynis certainly hadn't seemed to mind.

Colin put down the lute and touched her face. If she sat very still, he might kiss her. What would his lips taste like? They looked like ripe cherries. She had an almost irresistible urge to nip his full lower lip with her teeth.

She closed her eyes and Colin kissed her. A shy, gentle brushing of lips at first and then more urgent, a gentle probing with his tongue, and Rose's childish resolution melted like snow in spring rain. After the kiss he continued to hold her, burying his face in her hair, singing to her, "Rose, my Rose, to which I am bound," and the love song sounded like a promise.

⚜

They lay in each other's arms until the daylight faded into gloom, tentative, exploring, both embarrassed by this newness, when she heard a soft rustling, almost a whisper. She sat bolt upright.

"What's that?"

"I didn't hear anything." He nuzzled her neck with his lips.

"Listen, there it is again."

A gentle heaving, like the stirring of leaves in a light breeze, disturbed the quiet of the wool room.

"Don't be afraid. It's nothing. Just the cooling of the wool. See how a mist is forming over the fleeces. They're warm and alive. The wool is only breathing in the cooling night air."

And true enough, as Rose looked more closely, she could see a white mist hovering over the fleeces, could hear the fibers expanding, whispering to each other. It was a nice sound, but there was sadness in it, too, like the ghosts of old lovers sighing for remembered embraces.

"It's late, Colin. My father may be worried. We should go." But her hair had come unbound and was trapped underneath his shoulder. She made no move to disentangle herself.

"Just one more kiss. Please, Rose. You are so beautiful. I love you. I've wanted to tell you. But I was afraid you'd laugh at me. You're the first, you know. I'm not like my brother."

"I would never laugh at you, Colin." And then some new disturbing thought poked its head like a serpent into her paradise. "Colin, do you think what we've done is wrong? Do you think we will be punished?"

"I love you better than anybody, Rose. Better than anything." He traced the outline of her lips with his finger, reverently, just as he'd earlier traced the cross on her father's manuscript. Then he sat up, and propping himself on one elbow, looked down at her. He looked serious, even a little alarmed. "How can it be a sin, Rose? You will be my lady. I will pledge my heart to you like in the song of Tristan and Isolde. I will love you forever. I even love you better than the music."

"Then you love me truly," she said, laughing.

And as she lay in his arms there amid the hovering mists on the wool room floor, she thought her love for him was as joyful and pure as the white wool fleeces that sighed their approval.

SIX

Lady Kathryn surveyed her new lodger's quarters with approval. An ordered work space bespoke an ordered mind, and there was certainly order here: small pots of color, lined up like sentinels across the back of the desk; brushes and pens, clean and neatly organized by size; stacks of vellum, carefully and lightly lined to guide the artist's hand—these, she knew, her youngest son had helped to prepare. She approved of this too. She liked to see her sons happy.

It was Colin she'd come looking for, and she was surprised to find the chamber empty. She'd supposed the illuminator might be drawing in the garden's fading light but thought to find Colin, for no particular reason, except that she missed the company of her children. She saw little of Alfred since he spent his days with Simpson, and lately even Colin had been stingy with his company. He'd always come to her chamber in the late afternoon. He would sing to her or tell her about some new adventure—a swan's nest he'd found hidden in the reeds or some new poem he'd discovered among the few volumes Roderick had acquired more for prestige than love of verse. Sometimes, they would say vespers together in the chapel—he would murmur the prayers and she would kneel silently beside him, in communion more with her son than with God.

Colin must be with the illuminator in the garden, she thought. No matter. She would not begrudge him this relationship, would endure the loss of his companionship willingly if learning a vocation would save him from a monk's cowl. Too many mothers sacrificed sons to king or Church. She would not be counted in that number. It was good that he could learn from the master artisan. But she must warn him to be careful in his conversation. Not to give away too much. What did they really know about this illuminator? On the surface, he appeared to be who he said he was. Agnes certainly liked him. She even provided him with special little treats, which Lady Kathryn did not begrudge because, after all, the abbot was paying her well for his keep. But then, the cook was a simple soul, easily pleased by a charming manner. Charming manners could cloak a dead heart and a cunning mind. Her husband had been charming. In the beginning. Before he gained control of her lands.

The chamber was cool after the heat of the day. A last ray of northern light lay on the desk, picking out the brilliant colors on the half-finished page of illuminated text. *In Principio erat verbum.* "In the beginning was the Word." The vertical shaft of the initial letter was colored a deep sea-green and exquisitely lined with filigreed knotwork in red and gold. The dropped *I* sheltered the rest of the text, forming a delicate shrine to Saint John and sprouting green leaves and vines that twined and trailed in an elaborate border so finely drawn, it seemed to be alive. Miniature birds and beasts of exotic shapes frolicked among its various twigs and branches. Their colors leaped off the page. No wonder the Broomholm Abbot was anxious to please Finn.

She shuffled the page slightly to see what exquisite embroidery might lie beneath it. What she found on this page surprised her even more. Here, the border was barely sketched and not yet colored—hardly more than a design. But it was the text that shocked her. Not Norman French at all, but Saxon English! At least it was a kind of English: part old Saxon, part Norman French, stirred together with a few Latinate words for seasoning. Why would Finn, or any craftsman, waste talent and labor on an English text? French was the language of the noble and the rich—only they could afford the luxury of owning books.

"I trust you find my work worthy."

Lady Kathryn whirled around at the sound of Finn's voice, but feeling her face flame at being caught snooping, bent immediately over the desk once again, hoping that the trailing gauze of her headdress would hide her embarrassment. She determined to brazen it out.

"Your work, yes. Your subject, sir, less so."

Finn cocked an eyebrow. "You do not think Saint John worthy of illumination."

"Saint John requires no 'illumination.' It's what lies beneath Saint John I have reference to."

"Indeed? What lies beneath Saint John! I would have thought Saint John celibate."

In other circumstances she might have found his wit amusing. As it was, his bawdy misinterpretation merely annoyed her. Best to ignore his impudence. She picked up the English text and waved it in front of him.

"Oh, that," he said. "It's a poem by a fellow I met at court. A customs official, a bureaucrat for the king. His name is Chaucer. Mark it well. You may one day hear it again. He has some peculiar notions about language, but he's a fine poet." He retrieved the text from her and returned it to the desk, straightened the stack of papers she had disturbed. "He says *this* is the real language of England."

"This?" She pointed to the manuscript on the desk. "The real language of England?" She was sufficiently outraged at such a notion to forget her embarrassment. "There is no *language* of England. There's Norman French for the lords and Saxon and Old Norse for the common sort. Latin for the clerics."

Finn grinned, obviously enjoying the exchange. "Have you heard of a poem called *The Vision of Piers Plowman*?"

"A poem, you call it? Roderick—my late husband—brought it home. I think Colin has it, though I don't know why he'd want it. It's a dog's blend of sounds, difficult in meaning and in the sounding of it. Not flowing off the tongue—hardly worth the nibs it took to scratch it down."

"West Midland English," Finn said, "carries its own beauty, once your ear is attuned to it. In London, they call it the king's English. King Richard has proclaimed it the official language of the law and of the court. 'Tis hardly surprising, since the king and his uncles have an intense dislike for all things French—even the old northern French brought by the Vikings."

"I assure you that I, too, have no liking for France. I am loyal to young Richard. As I was to his father."

Even to her own ears she sounded defensive, protesting too loudly. His statement that he had been at court put her on her guard. Could he be spying for the duke of Lancaster? Roderick had made plain his allegiance to John of Gaunt. Was the duke using Finn to sound out his widow and sons to make sure that fealty was still intact? Or worse, what if Gloucester, John of Gaunt's brother, had sent the illuminator into her household to gather evidence against the day when he would win the power struggle between the young king's uncles? A familiar pain began to tread the borders of her left temple.

A straight beam from a low-slung sun shot through the narrow window, then fanned out, marking a path to the door. Finn stood in the light between her and the chamber entrance. As she spoke, she moved away from the desk, toward the door, closer to him, close enough to smell Agnes's perry on his breath.

"I'm just a poor widow who knows little about such things. My ear prefers what it's used to, that's all. Norman French or Midland English, it matters not as long as our Lord's words are read in Latin."

It had been a cast-off remark, said for the benefit of the abbot's ears—in case her new lodger carried tales back to his employer—meant to extricate her from the political turn of the discussion, but she detected a tightening of the muscle in the illuminator's jaw. He started to speak and then changed his mind. This confused her. But then, much about Finn confused her. He was commissioned by the abbot on a holy task, but she had noted a lack of piety in his manners and demeanor, a carelessness in his speech that treated holy matters lightly. He mentioned having been at court, yet there was a bluntness about him that belied the courtier.

"You're a simple widow and I'm just a simple artist whose pen is for hire—be it French or Latin, or Midland doggerel."

The curve of his mouth, the spark in his gray-green eyes mocked her. She should make some witty comeback, should challenge his tone that suggested she was something more than a 'simple widow," should question his connections with crown and abbey, make him define his own loyalties. But she said nothing. His eyes reminded her of the sea-green pools she'd bathed in as a child, when she had spent summers in her mother's little house by the sea, before Roderick, before her sons, before the dead priest had come calling, before she knew more than she wanted of intrigue and greed. They were the exact color of the initial *I* . . . In the beginning . . . It was as though he had dipped his brush into that pool of her childhood summers. Those had been happy times. Times when her mother was still alive.

"Lady Kathryn, was there something you wanted of me?"

Startled, she felt the blood rush to her face. Finn was waiting for her to explain her intrusion into his privacy, privacy the abbot paid well to secure for him. She attempted to gather her composure, cast about for some likely explanation, and then seized upon the truth as the best defense.

"You have caught me snooping, sir, and I beg your pardon. I had no intention to pry into your private affairs or the nature of your work. The truth is simply that I came looking for Colin, and I happened to see your manuscripts. I mean, after all, a mother is allowed some interest in that which robs her of a son. Is she not?"

"I'm flattered that you want to look at my humble efforts," he said. But his smile showed more amusement than flattery. "Colin has an eye for color and light. I think, with my tutelage—with your permission, of course—he would make a fine illuminator."

At the mention of her son's name she regained her composure, tore her gaze away from his eyes and focused instead on his paint-spattered smock. She nodded toward the desk beneath the window and smiled apologetically.

"Please don't misunderstand a mother's whining. I've seen your work. You have a great gift. If you are willing to teach Colin, then I am, of course, grateful. And I shall just have to find another companion for my quiet hours. Prayer and contemplation are always . . . profitable." Her teeth bit the inside of her upper lip.

"Yes. Good for the soul." He nodded, not smiling.

Was there a hint of mockery in his tone? She felt awkward. She moved once again toward the door. He moved with her. She said, "I might even take up reading poetry—dip again into *Piers Plowman* to find what you so enthusiastically recommend. Then, there is, of course, my embroidery."

She stepped a foot or two back, to give more space, so she could breathe better. This time, he did not move with her.

"I would not have thought the running of such an estate provides you many free hours. What about your other son?"

"Alfred? He was always more his father's companion. Anyway, he spends his days with the overseer. He will be of age soon. His sixteenth birthday is two days before Christmas."

"And you'll have plenty of time for prayer and contemplation, unless, of course, a young lord, like a boy king, requires a strong regent's hand."

Was that a veiled comment about Lancaster? The duke of Gloucester, perhaps? Or was he merely mocking her again? She couldn't see his face. He'd walked over to his desk, where he picked up a fresh sheet of vellum, a couple of quills, and a pouch of powdered charcoal. Her path to the door was unobstructed. Make your exit now, she told herself, while the hem of your dignity is still intact, and she had indeed almost gained the door when she heard his next words.

"You're welcome to join me in the garden," he said. "There are still a few rays of light left. I just came back here to retrieve my tools."

She turned to see that he had followed her to the door, once again closing the space between them. She looked up at him.

"I don't think . . . I wouldn't want to intrude on your inspiration."

"The company of a beautiful woman never intrudes, only spurs inspiration."

The angels must have lent him the color for those eyes. Or maybe the devil. And the smile, crooked and a little disdainful, still it warmed her.

"The roses are very fragrant. Come," he coaxed. "Bring your embroidery. We'll sit in companionable silence while you stitch and I sketch. We'll take advantage of the waning light together."

Like an old married couple, she thought and realized, with a sudden chill, how lonely she was. How lonely she had been for a very long time.

"Well, maybe just this once. I'll get my needle from the solar and join you in the rose garden."

Just this once, she promised herself.

⋇

The jays grew accustomed to the sight of Lady Kathryn sitting with Finn in the garden and no longer protested their presence. She looked forward to the afternoons they spent together. How at ease she felt with him. Each day, she loosened the strings bundling caution until it crept away, and she talked freely in spite of the fact that she had learned surprisingly little about her companion. But she had seen a glimpse of his soul in his art, and she found it trustworthy.

Today it was quiet in the garden, sultry with the heat of late August. A welcome breath from the sea disturbed the air and sighed against her moist skin, cooling it. Inspired by the red-breasted thrush perched on the sundial, she chose a scarlet thread from the basket at her feet and threaded the eye of her needle. Beside her, Finn's long fingers darted, sketching with swift, sure strokes the scrolling leaves and twining knots that he would paint on the morrow. She noticed that his gaze, too, flicked between the sundial and the paper. In three bold strokes the redbreast was captured forever on the page, a charcoal promise of future glory. His beak peeked between the leaves of what looked suspiciously like those of the hawthorne tree that shaded them from the dying sun.

"The days are growing shorter. These long twilights will soon be over," Finn said.

Was there a note of regret in his voice? She, too, hated the thought that these pleasant evenings would end, but she could not say so.

"Already, the harvest has begun," she said, stabbing at the cloth with her needle. "It's difficult to find laborers. Shameful. They go about from harvest lord to harvest lord seeking the best wage and have no shame to leave the rye and barley rotting in the field for the sake of a shilling."

"For the sake of a shilling? I'd say more for the sake of their families. For the sake of food and clothes and shelter."

"If they'd remained tied to the land where they belonged, they'd have no want of food and clothing and shelter. Ask Agnes. Ask John and Glynis and Simpson and my dairymaids and crofters if they want for the necessities."

"Aye, my lady, but a man must have more than necessities. He must have a dream. Besides, not all the rich are as beneficent to their tenants and servants as you."

"Rich. You think I'm rich. If you only knew how I'm squeezed between king and Church.

He waved his quill to indicate the environs of the manor. "You have land. You have fine clothes. You have servants. And all the food you can eat. The mother who doesn't have a crust for her hungry child can't understand such poverty."

She was not offended. She had learned it was his way to speak his mind bluntly.

"Sir Guy says there is to be a new tax levied by the crown," she said. She raised the scarlet thread to her lips and snipped it with her teeth, then tied a French knot in the end. "But at least this time it's a poll tax: a shilling per head. Mayhap, I can scrape up three shillings for Colin and Alfred and me."

"And Agnes and John?"

"They're to pay their own out of the wages I give them."

"You give them wages?"

She read approval in his smile.

"I had to start paying them after the plague took most of the able-bodied men. It seemed the prudent thing to do. I couldn't afford to lose them. I can't think Agnes would ever leave Blackingham, though John might. Anyway, the sheriff says they should pay the tax out of their own wage. Sir Guy said it's much fairer this way. A flat tax. Everybody pays the same. Rich and poor."

"And you call that fair! What about the crofters who get no wage? Only what they can scrounge out of the dirt they rent from you and the other landholders. A man with six children and a wife will have to pay eight shillings. He couldn't earn that much in a season."

Sir Guy had said nothing about that. She'd been so relieved that she had not thought to question him further. She felt a heaviness descend on her. She knew where her laborers and crofters would come when they could not pay. They'd come to her, and she'd have to find the money somewhere. But what about the others? she wondered. What about the ones who hired themselves out daily, who would pay for them? And the ones whose landlords could not be moved to pay, what would they do?

"Well, maybe it's not such a fair tax, after all," she conceded.

"Not fair, and it will not work. Even poor people have their limits. If you push them to the wall, where they have nothing left to lose, then they will become fearless. Already there is a rumbling against the archbishop of Canterbury."

"What has he to do with the king's tax?"

"He's been appointed chancellor by John of Gaunt. Be sure, it's the two of them who've cooked up this scheme to replenish a treasury plundered by the French wars. Otherwise some of the wealth of the abbeys might be siphoned off. But it's a devil's bargain. Too much greed there by half."

Was he talking about king or Church? To whom did his loyalty belong? But she did not ask.

"I know something of the greed of both," she said, thinking of her lost pearls—the ones that had disappeared into the priest's pocket—and wondering if they adorned the dainty neck of some French courtesan or that of the bishop's mistress. A little sigh escaped. Whichever, they were lost to her. And they had been her mother's.

They sat in silence for a while—the only movement in the garden the quick scratching of the quill against the paper. The breeze no longer fluttered the leaves on the roses. The light had shifted, casting long shadows. The hawthorne and the sundial painted dark stripes across the garden. She put away her needle. She did not want to squint at her work like an old woman.

"Will Alfred be harvest lord?" Finn asked.

He, too, was giving up, returning the manuscript and pens, the little pouch of charcoal to the leather satchel that looked something like a shepherd's scrip, only larger.

"No. He can't be harvest lord. It would not be seemly for him to have such direct contact with peasants. He is noble born."

Why did she not like the sound of her own voice as she said this?

"I see," Finn said.

"Simpson will be harvest lord. He will, of course, report to Alfred."

"And Alfred to you."

"Until he's of age."

Finn carefully stored his sketches and his nibs in the leather scrip. Kathryn, taking that as her cue, rewound the scarlet skein and replaced the needle in its case. Finn gestured toward the wide fields that stretched out beyond the hawthorne hedge.

"Blackingham is a noble heritage. Your husband did well by his heir."

"Blackingham belonged to me," she said, too quickly to hide her irritation. "Roderick did little but squander the income from it to impress his friends at court."

Finn's furrowed brow lifted to his graying hairline.

"I just assumed—"

"My father had no sons. My mother died when I was five. I cared for my father until he was old. One day he brought Roderick home and said that I should marry him. That Blackingham must have a master."

"Did you love him?"

"I loved my father dearly."

"I didn't mean your father. I meant Roderick. Your husband. Did you love him?"

The red-breasted thrush had departed. The sundial was now in complete shadow, its last mark having been passed.

"He gave me two sons," she answered.

"That's not what I asked you." His voice was husky. "Did you love him?"

She shrugged, got up from her seat and picked up her basket of thread.

"Love? What is love between a man and a woman? Groping, panting in the dark—the satisfaction of carnal lust." Like Roderick and his faceless doxies, she thought. Finn had gotten up, too, and was standing uncomfortably close. It was hard to get her breath in the still August air. She took a step back, then added, "Love is what a mother feels for a child. Love is what our Lord felt for us on the cross."

"Love is many things. Takes many forms. That greater love you mention, it's also possible between brothers, between friends. It's even possible between a man and a woman."

The garden was perfectly still in the gathering twilight. His voice was so low, it did not even disturb the small space of air between them. Was he talking to her? He might have been talking to himself, or some remembered other. It was hard to tell.

In silence, they crossed the small stretch of grass that separated the garden from the solar. As they reached the entrance, he looked thoughtful. "Would you like to come with me to my chamber?"

She didn't answer for a minute. He'd caught her completely off her guard. It seemed to be a gift with him. She felt flushed, as with the heat waves that woke her sometimes in the night or attacked her at odd times during the day. She was sure her face was flaming.

He grinned. "Colin or Rose will probably be there. Neither your virtue nor your reputation will be compromised. I would like you to see how my work progresses. You seemed to have taken an interest in it once before."

She was tempted to cut him off with a short remark for his smugness. But she was curious. She suspected he was up to more than Saint John. And she would like to see some of the sketches she'd watched him make colored in their brilliant hues.

"I suppose. As you say, no harm will come to my reputation. After all, I am your landlord in a sense, and therefore entitled to inspect your quarters at my discretion. As to my virtue? I can assure you, Master Finn, that it would not be cheaply bought."

The illuminator threw back his head and laughed with a rich, hearty chuckle. The wind from his laughter caused the rushlights in their sconces to flicker. Shadows frolicked around them for the briefest moment, breaking the gloom of the twilit staircase.

"My lady, I'm shocked that you might think I have designs on anything other than your companionship. At the current price of papal forgiveness, the sin of fornication far exceeds my purse," he said, pulling a clown's exaggerated frown that made her laugh. "Alas, celibacy—and platonic friendship—is all I can afford."

But as she followed him up the stairs, she reminded herself that friendship bore its own price, though in a different coin. Even the cost of that might strain her resources.

∽✦∼

There was something far too appealing about the illuminator. Kathryn decided this after she had spent a pleasant hour in Finn's chamber, watching while he shaded the sketched redbreast in brilliant hues of deep carmine. She had never met a man quite like him. She liked everything about him: the extraordinary patience he showed with his daughter, the tidiness of his work space, his quick intellect, and the sea-green color of his eyes and his easy laughter and the way his fingers held his pens and brushes, almost caressing them, as he plied his art with swift, curving strokes. Even the easy way he drew her out—too easily—sometimes causing her to reveal more of herself than she wished. All of this made him a very dangerous man. A man to be avoided.

And yet the more she tried to avoid him, the more he seemed to be in evidence, encountering her en route to her chamber, or on her way to the kitchens, or even in the kitchen garden, where she'd gone to gather fresh lavender for her bath.

"Agnes has favored me with one of her special cinnamon custard tarts. It's big enough for two. We could share it on this bench, here in the herb garden. A summer picnic."

The man was a devil. How did he know of her fondness for cinnamon custard tarts?

"I have no fondness for cinnamon, Master Finn. Thank you anyway." And she walked away, her mouth watering at the tempting smell of spicy sweetness, walked away from the invitation in his smile and left him sitting on the garden bench alone, with only his custard tart for company.

The next day he accosted her in the rose garden. His sudden appearance startled her, making her jab her palm on a thorn. He apologized prettily, lifting the injured part to his lips. She snatched her hand away hastily, feeling her face flame like a silly maid. He looked a little startled.

"I was on my way into the woods in search of berries for a particular shade of purple. It's such a fine day, I hoped you might lend me your company," he said.

Lend, as though it were something he'd have to pay back. And he carried no bucket or scrip for gathering berries.

"Thank you, but no, Master Finn. I shall . . . be far too busy." Did she stammer? She looked past him, trying to hide her embarrassment, trying not to be sucked in by the disappointment in his eyes. "I'll be busy for several days. Making an inventory of the buttery and the pantry."

But she felt guilty when he was gone. An occasional walk in the woods between friends, what harm could come from that? But she knew what harm. She could feel it in the heavy pounding of her pulse. Surely it was not healthy for a woman of middle years to have her blood rush through her veins in such a fashion!

His proximity, his popping up at odd times made her very nervous.

But his absence likewise made her nervous.

For the next four days she did not see him. She inquired casually of Agnes.

"He was in the kitchen yesterday for his usual glass of perry. But today, I think he took his daughter into Aylsham to the market. They left at dawn. Did ye need him for something? I'll tell him to seek ye out."

"No. No. Just curious. I had not noticed him about. That is all."

Agnes said no more but cocked an eyebrow in her direction and gave a little half-smile.

Kathryn decided to ignore the gesture.

By two of the clock face on the sundial, Kathryn felt very listless.

Ridiculous. It was almost as though she missed him. The house felt hollow. Her footfalls had a lonely, whispering echo she'd never noticed before.

She went into the solar and sat in the window seat, her embroidery in her lap. On a small round table beside the window someone, Colin probably, had left a book. *The Vision of Piers Plowman*. The English book. It reminded her of Finn. She picked it up and began to read, struggling with the awkward spellings. It did not flow like French. Why would anyone choose the West Midland dialect as a language for poetry? And the content. It reminded her of Finn, also, with its alliterative talk against pardon and penance and prayer.

A shadow crossed the lines of text. She looked up to find Finn standing in the doorway, watching her, the look on his face unreadable. Her heart danced against her ribs. She took a deep breath to calm it.

"My lady, how well met and fortunate."

She closed the book, covering the title with her hand.

"'Fortunate,' Master Finn? To encounter a lady in her own chamber? And how 'well met'?"

He smiled, but the smile was small and uncertain and did not reach his eyes. "Fortunate to find my lady not otherwise engaged. Well met because I am in need of another pair of eyes."

"Is there some problem with your eyes? Agnes can recommend a tincture of—"

He laughed. This time the smile crinkled the corners of his eyes. "No. My eyes are good enough to see beauty when it presents itself."

She felt the color creep up her neck and into her face. She would have willed it away if she could.

"I say *well met* because I am in need of your opinion. That is, if you can spare the time. My daughter usually advises me. But she ran off somewhere as soon as we returned from the market."

"Advises you? How so?"

"About the colors. If the hues are too bright. Or whether too subtle. But I should not intrude upon a busy lady's stolen moment with her book. It would be too great a sacrifice. Perhaps Rose will be back soon."

He turned to go.

"Wait."

She would regret it later. She knew she would. But she could not stop herself.

"Giving up such a book is no sacrifice at all. I find the English you so highly recommend a tedious language. It has little music to recommend it. I will look at your work with pleasure. Though I don't know of what value my uninformed opinion might be."

He wheeled around as though jerked by some invisible string on which she had just tugged. Or was it he who did the tugging?

"Shall I bring the pages to you here? I'm not sure that they are completely dry."

"Yes. No. I mean . . . I will look at them in your chamber. That way you will not have to risk damage to them."

Kathryn, Kathryn, you invite trouble, a small voice inside her head said.

But her heart said something else entirely.

※

By late September, the days had shortened. Finn now sat with Lady Kathryn in the warm sunshine of the garden at midday instead of late afternoon. In the late afternoon, they preferred the privacy of his quarters. She inspired his work—and much more besides. The golden light of autumn angled through the window, pouring over his worktable and slicing across the bed, where the pair lay tangled among the crumpled linens. How had he not thought her beautiful that night when he first sat at her board? Was it because she was so different in form and face from his Rebekka?

Finn disengaged himself gently from her embrace and got up from the bed. Her arms trailed off him like water. "I have to work now, my lady," he said, laughing, "while I still have strength enough to lift my tools."

She lay back on the feather pillows, her arms behind her head, in open invitation. All that silvery hair spilled in a mass across the pillow, its dark streak winding like a silk ribbon around the pink nipple of her breast.

"Your tool, sir, seems to lift itself," she said.

He laughed, feeling the hot blood inflame his face also. "Then I shall have to put it away and choose another," he said, pulling on his breeches. He bent to plant a kiss on her forehead. She arranged her mouth in a pretend pout as she wrapped herself in the crumpled sheet and followed him to stand behind his shoulder, watching, waiting for the light to fade.

She had been right when she said her virtue did not come cheaply, he thought. He had purchased it at a very great price. He had the sense that their union had changed him in some profound way that he had never before experienced with a woman, and that he would never be the same again. She had taken him inside herself, and now he was no longer himself but a part of her. She had swallowed him completely, consuming his body, mind, and soul with the fire of her own. But it wasn't just her passion—though he had been surprised by that, had not guessed at its depth and breadth until he kissed her that day she first came to his room to see his sketches—not just the way her body melted into his, but the way her spirit seemed to reshape to merge with his. Sometimes, it was almost as though she could read his thoughts and he hers. And his artist's gift, which lay at his core like a seed, he could not shield even that from the heat of her. On the illuminated page his lines and forms leaped from their narrow margins, the murky hues murkier, the brights more brilliant, the knotwork more intricate, twisting, twining like her female mind. His gift no longer his, but shared. And if he could not keep this from her, what of his secret? How long before she divined that, too? But he must keep it; he must protect her from it, for she had become the source of his creative energy and the object of a love he had not felt since he laid his wife in the grave sixteen years ago.

"You'd better dress, Kathryn. Rose and Colin will be returning soon." He was already at his worktable, the lined vellum spread out before him, its text transcribed in Rose's careful calligraphy.

"It will be a while. I saw Colin leaving with his lute. I asked him where he was going. He said he was giving lessons to Rose. As a *surprise* for you."

"So that's where they disappear every day." He wiped his brush on a rag and dipped it again. "Well, I'll try to remember to be surprised." He paused, trying to think how best to say this next. "I thought I saw Alfred talking to Rose the other day. Something about his manner seemed too familiar." He waited for her to read his thoughts, to reassure him, but she just looked at him, waiting for him to go on. "She's my daughter, you understand, Kathryn. I want to protect her from . . ." The pleading tone in his voice made him vulnerable, he knew. But he trusted her; he would not hide his softness from her.

"I understand." She bent to kiss him on the neck. "A child is a rare treasure, a gift from God, to be protected above all else." Then she nibbled on his ear and whispered. "I'll speak to Alfred."

Undone, he laid down his brush.

SEVEN

*Grete houses make not men holy, and only by holy-
nesse is God wel served.*

—JOHN WYCLIFFE

Bishop Henry Despenser paid little heed to the intricate carving in the Stone above the portal of Norwich Cathedral. It depicted a number of unfortunate souls roped together, dragged by devils toward a flaming cauldron while angels led only a few redeemed innocents in the opposite direction. Though this graphic reminder of the damnation awaiting sinners was not placed there for the benefit of the gatekeepers of Paradise like himself, nevertheless, had Bishop Despenser been less young, less arrogant—and more innocent—this sermon in stone might have occasioned some introspection into the state of his own soul.

But his concern was more for this world than the next. And right now he was concerned with the unsolved murder of Father Ignatius, a circumstance that was becoming an embarrassment.

The slap of his leather soles against the flint pavement scarcely disturbed the silence hovering beneath the graceful Norman arches of the cathedral's south side ambulatory. It wasn't that Henry was unimpressed by the grandeur around him. The great timber ribs of the vaulted roof spanning out like the skeleton of some mythical leviathan, then soaring ever upward; the paintings, the rood screens, the treasury of silver and gold plate: the sheer power and wealth of it all impressed him greatly.

Indeed, Henry's God dwelt here. But he was no humble Galilean carpenter. The bishop's God was the cathedral itself. And like all false gods, it demanded human sacrifice and ceaseless service. Not Henry's sacrifice—though, if asked, on some days, he might have said he'd rather be fighting the French, rather be wearing hauberk and helm into battle than the gold pectoral cross with its ruby-encrusted Christ—but the sacrifices of an army of stonemasons and carpenters, many of whom died before their work was done, only to be replaced by their sons and their grandsons and their apprentices. Some had labored for five decades to build the great cathedral and labored still to replace the timbered spire, damaged by a gale a quarter century past. The slapping of mortar, polishing of stone, the hissing of the carpenter's plane was as much a part of the cathedral sounds as the plainsong of the monks who lived in its priory.

To Bishop Despenser, the great stone edifice, gleaming golden in the sun, was a hymn of praise to human creativity, a paean to ambition, and his own soared as magnificently as the grand vault overhead. But of all the glory that surrounded him, Henry loved best the bishop's throne behind the high altar. The throne stood in unquestioned dominance over the eastern apse like a Moses Seat reincarnated from some ancient synagogue. It was this throne that sucked Henry's soul. To rule the cathedral was to rule East Anglia. The thousands of sheep that dotted the fields, the meadows golden with saffron, the fens and rivers teeming with fowl and fish and eels, even the willows and rushes along the streams: all might as well have been deeded to Henry Despenser. For the bishop of Norwich knew that he who has the power to tax has the power to destroy. And what was that if not ownership?

But it was a co-ownership with the king. That rankled. And that—along with the archbishop's reprimand—accounted for the foulness of his mood on this otherwise fine summer morning. He had just been informed about the king's new poll tax.

The ermine fringe of his heavy robe slithered behind him, gliding swiftly along the curving walk as he passed a scattering of monks who toiled, copying manuscripts, in the ambulatory that served as scriptorium. He did not pause to peer at their progress or even acknowledge their nervous shuffling of pens and papers. Books held little interest for the bishop even under ordinary circumstances, and today was no ordinary day. It was Friday. Today, the bishop had a special appointment.

He was grateful for the coolness of the cathedral, but even its skin sweated in the summer heat. Moisture stained the joints of the stone walls. It stained also the armpits of the bishop's fine white linen shirt.

He didn't enter the nave today, did not approach the chancel, did not genuflect before the golden chalice on the altar. Today, he hurried to the privacy of the rectory, where he could change his shirt and exchange the heavy robe for a shorter surcoat, which he would have worn anyway had he not been meeting with the king's exchequer and the archbishop. That aging worthy had loudly decried the current laxity of protocol in religious dress. The Council of London had even issued a decree reproaching clerics who wore clothing "fit rather for knights than for clerics." He'd complained that they frequented the rich clothiers of Colgate Street—where Henry bought his own fine lawn shirts—and strutted about "like peacocks." But the bishop was not about to give up his lawful right to ostentation. He was, after all, noble born and rather vain of his shapely calves. Still, in deference to his superior, he had donned the heavy robe of which he divested himself with relief as soon as he gained the privacy of his chamber.

Stripping away his stained shirt, he shouted for his ancient chamberlain. Old Seth, who was dozing in the corner, woke with a start, blinking open rheumy eyes with a questioning gaze, and then scurried forward, "beggin' his lordship's pardon" and presenting his master with a fresh shirt and doublet. Henry handed him the robe, and the old man began to brush it vigorously. Too vigorously. Henry knew the old dresser worried about being replaced with a younger man. But he need not have. Seth might be old and slow, but the bishop knew that he was loyal. And loyalty counted for everything in these perfidious times.

"Has Your Eminence had any dinner?"

"The archbishop fed us on oysters and fish stew with fritters and cherry conserve." He frowned and let out a loud belch. "My stomach rolls in protest. I fear the oysters may have been overripe. But you may bring me a beaker of wine. And then you may retire for the afternoon. I'm expecting a visitor."

Henry never even noticed as the old man bowed out of his presence. Nor did he hear him when he returned a few minutes later. The bishop poured his wine and sat down to think in the hour or so he had before the girl was to appear. Constance always came on Fridays for her confession. He had readily agreed to become her spiritual adviser. She was the daughter of an old friend, and he couldn't help noticing the firmness of her thighs and the way her young breasts thrust forward, begging to be squeezed.

But today, he almost wished she weren't coming. The heat and the archbishop's lecture about the laxity of morals among the clergy had dampened his ardor. The pompous old fool had gone to great pains to remind Henry of the scandal just four years ago, when ten priests in Norwich had been accused of unchaste behavior, one of them with two women. It had been all Henry could do to keep his tongue quiet. He suspected the archbishop kept his own mistress and knew he suffered the bishop of London to maintain a profitable and convenient brothel. Still, he wondered, had word of his Friday-afternoon adventures leaked beyond these walls? Not likely. But there had been no mistaking the warning in his voice.

About the murder of Father Ignatius, the archbishop had been more direct. "What news have you concerning the priest's murder?" had been the greeting as he extended his ring for Henry to kiss.

"We have not yet found the culprit."

"Try harder. This crime cannot be allowed to go unpunished. See to it."

See to it. Just like that. See to it. Didn't Henry have enough worries with raising money for his campaign to unseat the Avignon antipope? And now this new tax. Only so much juice in a turnip. The murdered priest was a loss to him, too; he had been the best at separating women from their treasures. He had been going to or coming from such a mission in Aylsham when he met his demise at Blackingham. That was it. The sheriff had said he questioned the lady of the manor there. Mayhap he should question her more closely. He would send for Sir Guy in the morning. Pass that hot coal on down the line.

Bishop Despenser sipped his wine. The cathedral bell tolled nones: three o'clock, three hours before vespers. His stomach was more settled now. The wine and the thought of Constance's cool white hands stroking him comforted him. Just once he'd like to spend himself inside her. Not have to withdraw. But that way lay risk and ruin. That had been what occasioned the scandal with the priests. Two of the women had turned up pregnant. Stupid.

Irresponsible. A grievous sin. He would exercise his usual control, and still he'd have full measure of his pleasure.

"The Virgin approves," he had assured Constance, the first time she reluctantly came to him. He had held her chin with his right hand, forcing her to look in his eyes. "In offering yourself to God's servant, you offer yourself to God." After that, she had been compliant, if not enthusiastic. But her lack of enthusiasm didn't really bother him. If truth be told, it rather added to his pleasure, affirming his power over her.

The girl should be here any minute. He could already feel her warm, firm flesh pressed against him, the touch of her skin, smooth and alive beneath his exploring hands, like the carvings in the chancel. Nothing like a little harmless romp, a little amour, on a summer afternoon to make a man forget his troubles. He sipped his wine, rolled it around on his tongue. The French should stick to what they did best and leave the pope to Rome.

~ ~

Sir Guy noticed gray smoke in the distance as he rode the twelve miles north from Norwich to Aylsham. A grass fire, he thought, started by some careless crofter burning off his field in the too-dry October air. Sir Guy had a sister at court, who complained of London's gray skies and dreary rain, but in East Anglia summer refused to give way. Each day had been hotter and brighter than the one before, and what few clouds appeared overhead scattered like washed fleeces of white wool. He was grateful for the breeze, never mind that it fanned the fire on the distant horizon. It cooled his skin beneath his leather doublet as well as his horse, which he rode hard.

Officially, he was on business for the crown, unofficially for the bishop. Jurisdiction was unclear in the case of the dead priest. Since the victim was the bishop's legate and ordained by the Church, the investigation could be carried out by the Church, but since the crime was committed on crown lands, it was decided that the investigation should fall to the sheriff. A sorry business. The world would hardly miss another greedy churchman, so why all the fuss? But the bishop had let him know that the murderer had to be brought to justice and it was the sheriff's job to do it, and sooner rather than later.

"The Church has been insulted and the king's law officer can't find time to catch the murderer? How hard can it be to ask a few questions, seek out a motive?" Henry Despenser had sneered when he delivered the slur. "You have the nose for it. Use that beak of yours to snoop out some answers."

Impertinent upstart. Ordering Sir Guy de Fontaigne about like a Saxon clod. Demanding he question Lady Kathryn of Blackingham. Still, maybe he could turn the bishop's suspicions to his advantage. He doubted Lady Kathryn was capable of murder, but there was something amiss there—the way her back had stiffened and her lips tightened when she denied having seen the priest the day they discovered the body. If she felt sufficiently threatened, she might reconsider her cold behavior toward him. If he handled the questioning just right, she might even welcome him as her protector.

His horse jerked to the right and stamped, threatening to rear its forelegs. The air carried a definite acrid odor. The dull smear on the northern edge of the sky had darkened and the color of the clouds on the horizon had changed from white to gray, more tethered to earth than sky. This was no grass fire. It lay off to his right, in the direction of Bacton Wood, northeast of Aylsham. If the wood caught fire, it might imperil Broomholm Abbey and burn miles of virgin forest, even threaten his favorite preserve for hunting stag and wild boar. He jerked the horse's reins, digging his heels into its side. The thickening air argued that the fire was closer than Bacton Wood, closer even than Aylsham. It could be a crofter's cottage or one of the several hovels scattered across the fields used for storing grain and carts or even a shepherd's hut. But that billowing smoke was more than just a shed. Indeed, as he neared his destination, he concluded that the source of the conflagration might well be Blackingham itself. Sir Guy spurred his recalcitrant horse hard in the direction of the smoke. He had an interest there, too.

EIGHT

Lully, lulley, lully, lulley
The fawcon [falcon, i.e., death] *hath born*
my mak [mate] *away.*
—FROM AN EARLY 15TH-CENTURY LYRIC

n the day the wool shed burned, Lady Kathryn was busy put-
ting out other fires. She had just come from a confrontation with Alfred, who
was complaining bitterly about being ostracized to "the shearing pens." She
put him off for two more weeks, urging him to stay until the harvest accounting and the rent receipts were collected, "to keep Simpson honest."
Also, there was still a pack of wool left to be sold to the Flanders merchant—
240 pounds, not sheared but pulled to make the finest thread—that she was
holding to exact a better price when the market was no longer glutted.

"In just two months your father's title will pass to you," she'd said and
promised a birthday feast worthy of a young lord.

She missed him, missed his easy laughter, his wit, his restless energy; but
she dreaded having him move back in. Finn would not be happy about it
either. She'd promised him she would keep Alfred away from Rose. But
Alfred was her son. Finn would just have to keep a closer eye on his daughter, prohibit the closeness he'd allowed between Colin and Rose. She'd seen

them working together to prepare Finn's manuscripts and playing tag in the garden, their laughter floating up to the window where she watched. Colin was always too serious and contemplative, so Kathryn had been pleased at his friendship with the girl. But once or twice she thought she'd seen a look pass between them that suggested something else, some more private, less innocent, knowledge. She'd even mentioned it to Finn. He'd told her to put it out of her mind. They were just friends, just children who knew nothing of the ways of the world. But Alfred? Finn was not so trusting of Alfred.

Merely thinking about Finn made Kathryn long for him. He had left for Broomholm Abbey three days ago with his completed pages wrapped securely in his saddlebags. She did not expect him back until tomorrow. She'd slept alone for two nights, and she missed his body wrapping her like a shawl, his breath warming her neck. Simply having him near gave her an odd sense of comfort. The heat inside her that had sometimes boiled over had settled into a pool of temperate calm. The headaches were better, too. She hadn't had a recurrence in weeks. Until today.

She had become a wanton woman, though, strictly speaking, they'd not committed adultery—Finn had pointed that out after that first time they'd lain together, the first time he'd unbound her hair and kissed her neck, the first time he'd caressed her breasts with the same graceful hands that brushed color into the sacred texts. His Rebekka was long since dead, he'd argued, as was Roderick. Even the Church acknowledged the needs of the body—it's not a *mortal* sin; it's easily expunged by a few Paternosters. Then he'd kissed her forehead and cupped his hand under her chin, tipping her face upward to look at his own. Their union was more, he'd said, than the appeasement of animal appetites; it was a spiritual union. It must be, had to be, sanctioned by God. And he'd called upon their shared joy as witness.

She'd pushed her guilt aside and taken his assurance as a sop for her conscience. He had become her confessor. Only he could take away her guilt. But now, in his absence, guilt revisited. The Virgin frowned on fornication, Kathryn was sure. Not that she'd communicated with her lately—without a priest to watch, she no longer even prayed at vespers, and too often, at matins she was otherwise engaged.

And she'd been careless in other ways. Although her woman's curse was irregular—heavy bleeding and then nothing for months—she suspected she was still fertile. And she had not cared. She'd even daydreamed about having his baby, had looked at his beautiful Rose and coveted a daughter of her own. A love child, born outside of marriage, shunned, a subject of pity and scorn. Holy Mother, she had been very, very foolish. Yet, knowing this, still she missed Finn, longed for his return.

After her confrontation with her oldest son, she had felt the old familiar tightening in her face, the sharp picklike pain piercing beneath her cheekbone. She'd lost her temper with him, shouted at him, called him irresponsible like his father. She would have to seek him out again, tell him she was sorry. She would make it up to him at his birthday. But now, she wanted a cool drink. She went to the kitchen in search of Agnes.

~ ⚑ ~

At first Kathryn hadn't noticed the smoke. The kitchen was always smoky with roasting meats and fats sizzling on the hearth. If the air inside the cavernous room seemed more blue than usual, Kathryn just ascribed it to the October sun pouring through the back door that now stood open to expel the kitchen heat. Light poured in and lit a blue haze hanging in layers above the long wooden table on which Agnes worked. The old woman had been a constant presence in Kathryn's life, and though, like all others of her class, she regarded the servant as mere property, still, like a child who clings to a tattered favorite toy or a worn-out blanket, Kathryn drew comfort from her. It was rare, she knew, to have a woman oversee the kitchen of a noble household, but Kathryn had held out for Agnes in her marriage contract. Blackingham was her dower lands, and with his wife gone it would be Roderick's. Poison was an ever-present threat when domestic life did not run smoothly. So she had taken great pains to make sure that her kitchen was loyal to her.

"Agnes, I need a cooling drink." She sank onto a three-legged stool beside the worktable, the same stool that Finn used when he visited the cook, less frequently now—his leisure hours were otherwise filled.

Agnes jerked her head in the direction of the scullery maid in the corner. "Get a tankard from that shelf over your head and fetch some buttermilk from the cellar for milady."

The girl, a skinny urchin of about fourteen, at first appeared not to hear, but then stretched to reach the tankard.

"Wait. Best wash those filthy hands first. I saw you fondling that mangy cur that yer always slippin' scraps to."

The girl went slowly over to the pewter basin at the end of the table and started to wash her hands. She didn't give them the cursory washing that most children do but stood as though she were in a daze, sliding one hand over the other, methodically, as the water dripped off them and splashed onto her ash-smudged shirt.

"That's enough washing now. Hurry up. Lady Kathryn can't be awaitin' all day. And carry it carefully."

"I haven't seen her before," Kathryn said as the girl left.

The portly cook sighed as she lifted a heavy pot onto the fire, then wiped beads of sweat from her face onto her apron. "She's a simpleton. Her mother begged me to take her. Said they couldn't afford to feed her anymore. But she's more trouble than she's worth. I may have to turn her out."

But Kathryn knew that despite Agnes's gruff manner, she would keep the child. The girl might get little praise from the old cook, but she would be well fed. Although Agnes fed many of the ne'er-do-wells around Aylsham from Blackingham's kitchens, Kathryn knew that the cook was a frugal manager and probably saved as much as she gave away. Besides, acts of charity were acts of contrition, and so by her silence, Kathryn considered herself a participant in Agnes's charity.

She looked at the bundle of rags in the corner by the hearth. A bed for a dog, not for a child, Finn would say, if he were here.

"Agnes, see that the girl has a straw pallet and a warm blanket. The nights are growing colder."

The cook's surprise showed in her face. "Aye, milady. I'll see to it right away."

Kathryn coughed. "The air is thick in here today. Has the chimney been swept lately?"

"Aye, only last month. But there's been wind in it all day, stirring the coals."

The girl came back with the buttermilk, handed it shyly to Kathryn, dropped what might pass for a curtsy. Kathryn noticed the pewter tankard was only half full, but she said nothing. The girl had either spilled half of it or hadn't filled it for fear she might spill it and then be beaten.

Agnes motioned to the girl with a heavy spoon. "Now go down to the dove cote and catch a couple of pigeons. It's the stone house down behind the laundry. You know where the laundry is. Behind the wool house."

The girl nodded mutely, then hesitated as if uncertain of her instructions.

"Two fat pigeons," Agnes said. "Now off with you."

"Do you beat her, Agnes?" Kathryn was surprised to hear the question come out of her mouth. But something about the girl touched her, reminded her in some unexplainable way of herself, unexplainable because she had been bred a child of privilege, yet she knew the fear of failing, the shivering uncertainty in the presence of authority.

"Beat her? Not unless you call one smack with a stirring spoon across her shoulder once in a while just to get her attention a beating."

"A light smack with a small spoon," she said. "She is built slight of body."

At just that moment the subject of her concern appeared in the doorway, minus the pigeons, her eyes wide with fright.

Agnes sighed. "What is it, child, can't you find the dove cote? I told you—"

The girl interrupted, her voice hardly more than a whisper. "B-beggin' your pardon, mistresses"—she looked at Lady Kathryn and then at Agnes, apparently unable to discern the class gap between them from her place at the bottom of the heap—"I c-come back to tell you."

"Tell us what? What are you blabberin' about?" Agnes asked.

" 'Tis f-fire. The wool house is a burning," the child whispered.

The wool house. And suddenly, Kathryn was aware of a stronger smell carried on the smoke. It was not the smell of dripping fat from the kitchen hearth but the smell of burning wool. Two hundred and forty pounds of wool—all profit. She pushed the girl aside and fled in the direction of the wool house. But all she saw where the building should have been was billowing black smoke and orange flames.

~❧~

By the time Kathryn got to the wool house, it was fully engulfed. Simpson and a few others, mostly Blackingham field hands and stable grooms, stood downwind from the heavy smoke, leather buckets dangling, empty and useless, at their sides. They watched as one corner of the roof sagged and, with a large pop, cracked and fell.

"No use now—she's past dousing," Simpson said, but Kathryn noticed that he'd scarcely broken a sweat, and he held no bucket.

"Aye, it'd be like pissin' in the sea." The speaker, whom Kathryn didn't know—probably one of the yeoman laborers hired by Simpson to prepare the sheds for winter—split his scraggly whiskers with a toothless grin.

At Lady Kathryn's approach, his grin vanished. He removed his grungy cap in a perfunctory gesture of half-hearted deference.

"Beggin' your pardon, milady."

Simpson stepped forward, pushing the laborer aside as if he were a sheaf of grain or a tree branch blocking the path.

"There was nothing we could do, milady," he said. "She went like a tinderbox. The floor planks, covered with years of wool wax, made good fodder. And then there was the wool sack."

She longed to wipe the smirk from his smug face. If only she had somebody, anybody, of his class and station to take his place, she would sack him on the spot. She clinched her teeth and sucked a heavy dose of the smoky air. This resulted in a fit of coughing, dealing a further blow to her temper and her dignity. Her eyes stung from cinders and frustration. Her left temple throbbed.

She'd been counting on the profit from this last wool pack to outfit her boys in new clothes. A surcoat alone could cost as much as three shillings, two days' wages for a yeoman. With their birthday approaching, she'd need the extra gold sovereigns for provisions. With a pound of cane sugar or a pound of spice costing five times a day's wages for a skilled laborer, it was getting harder and harder to keep up appearances. She'd been skimping, cutting corners, in order to meet the death taxes, but with the young lords of Blackingham coming of age, more and better hospitality would be expected of her.

"I don't understand how this could happen," she said, shouting above the roar of the fire and between coughs. "The wind fanned the flames, but what provided the spark? There's not been a thundercloud for weeks."

"Someone probably left a lantern too near the wool sack." His eyes shifted to Agnes and the scullery maid, who'd followed Kathryn and now stood on the periphery, watching. Simpson raised his voice so that it would carry. "Someone careless. Or drunk. You might ask the shepherd. If he ever shows his face."

The toothless man sniffed the air and rubbed a bald head as withered as last year's turnips. "If you be asking me, I'd say there's a nasty sweet smell in that smoke. More than burnt wool. Burnt flesh, more like."

He screwed up his mouth and spit. The spittle bored a hole in the wind and settled in a speck of foam at his feet. He continued, "You mayn't be missin' anybody, now, but if I was you, milady, I'd be doin' a head count of them what's important to me."

He said it casually, as though he were talking about a missing cart or cup. Kathryn smelled it, too, a pungency that clung to the smoke, seasoning the smell of burning wool and wood with charred fat and skin and hair. Her stomach clutched, threatened to dislodge its contents.

Alfred. Where was Alfred? Shouldn't he be with the overseer?

Simpson knows what I'm thinking, she thought. Still, he's waiting, enjoying the moment. He's going to make me ask. She tried to keep her voice from betraying her. "Simpson, do you know where Master Alfred is?"

"I saw the young master earlier. On his way out of the courtyard. Headed for the White Hart, I'd imagine. The way he was cursing his horse, I'd say he was looking for a pint to cool his temper. He was with milady earlier, I believe, was he not?"

Relief flooded over her, giving her grace to ignore the overseer's snide insinuation. Heat from the fire scorched her face. Wind whipped and a fountain of sparks spewed as the roof caved in with a whoosh and a roar. The group of watchers moved with one accord, upwind, away from the sparks. The flames, partially satiated, no longer gulped but gnawed at the charred bones of the building. The heat was too intense to get closer. She peered into the inferno in the center where the roof had fallen. A beggar, perhaps, seeking shelter from last night's cool wind, or some animal slinking under the ill-fitting door. A shudder quivered her stomach. Pity the poor wretch, be it human or beast, who lay under the burning timbers. But thank God it wasn't Alfred. And Colin would have no business in the wool shed.

"There's nothing more to be done here," she shouted above the sputtering and spewing. "Go on back to work." She turned away from the men. Her sigh rivaled the hissing of the fire. "Come, Agnes. There's nothing now but to let the fire burn itself out. What's lost is lost and no amount of wishing can bring it back."

The scullery maid bolted off like a frightened rabbit—probably to her bed of rags beside the kitchen hearth, Kathryn thought. But the old woman didn't move. She stared past Kathryn at the front of the building where the door had been. Then she started to run toward the fire, stumbling as her clumsy skirts twisted around her legs. She kept her footing and struggled on like a swimmer fighting a heavy current upstream. It seemed as though she were headed into the fire. Kathryn ran after her, calling.

"Agnes, come back. You'll catch fire if you go closer. Come back. Let it burn."

But by the time Kathryn reached her, Agnes had fallen to her knees and was keening a high-pitched wail that rocked her body back and forth with its rhythms. She clutched something to her breast, something she'd picked up from the ground. Lady Kathryn knelt beside her and gently pulled her arms open to see what she'd found.

It was a shepherd's scrip. The leather bag that John had carried. Kathryn didn't recall ever seeing him without it. The smell the yeoman had commented on, the smell of burning flesh—it was Agnes's husband burning inside the shed.

The heat from the fire was searing, but Kathryn knelt beside Agnes with her arms wrapped around the old woman. "We can't know for sure, Agnes. John may have gone to get help. He may be back any minute."

Minutes passed, years, and John did not appear. Simpson and the knot of onlookers drifted away, anxious, no doubt, lest they be called upon for some heroic action. But Kathryn knew there was nothing to be done. If it was John's body burning beneath the collapsed roof, they would find little of it left to bury.

The two of them huddled before this funeral pyre like ancient worshipers praying before a pagan sacrifice. Kathryn's legs and shoulders were aching from remaining in the same position long before Agnes stopped her keening and attempted speech. Her eyes were dry. There had been no tears, just that desperate, terrible moaning, more animal than human. For the first time, in all of her long association with her servant, Kathryn was aware that this person whose service she had taken for granted was more like than unlike the one she served. Agnes's grief for her John was as deep and real as any grief Kathryn would ever feel. Indeed, Kathryn had felt no grief for her own husband's death. But Kathryn *could* know that kind of grief. If not for her husband, for her sons. Maybe even for Finn. She felt a shudder of relief, once again, that it was not her son inside the burning wool house. And then guilt. Guilt because she was glad that, if it had to be someone, it was John and not Alfred.

"If it is John, I will buy masses for his soul, Agnes. And when the fire is cooled, we will claim his poor body and bury it on chapel grounds."

"You would do that for John, milady? After what Simpson said?" And then, before Kathryn could answer, "He was wrong, you know, my John never drinks in the day. Only at night, when the longing overcomes him. He never touches strong drink when he works."

"I know that, Agnes. Put it out of your mind. I know that John was a good servant, and that you and John are loyal to Blackingham."

"Aye, loyal, yes. But John wouldn't have stayed, wouldn't have been here to die, if 'tweren't for me." And then her shoulders began to shake with dry sobbing.

Kathryn knew what she was talking about. She'd known for a long time that it was Agnes's loyalty that kept the couple from seeking the freedom of the open road and a yeoman's wage.

"Come." She half-lifted the naturally heavy woman, made even heavier with the weight of her grief. "There is nothing we can do for John." And then she added lamely, "If it is John."

She took the leather bag from Agnes and lifted the flap, looking for some clue. There was the usual tar box, some twine, a knife, and a bit of bread and cheese and onion wrapped in waxed linen. Agnes cried out loud when she saw the contents.

"I packed it for him, before he left this morning. He said he would be in the far field and might not be back 'fore even." Her voice broke.

Kathryn pulled out a leather flask, removed the wad of cloth that served as stopper, smelled the contents. The sharp smell of alcohol made her nose wrinkle.

"Look, Agnes. It's still full. Not one sip. If John went into that shed, he went in for a good reason. The way his bag lay beside the door, like it was thrown there in a hurry. He saw something. Maybe he saw the fire, threw down his bag and rushed in to put it out." She hugged Agnes against her. "Maybe your John died a hero, Agnes."

Agnes looked up at her mistress, her face a crumpled mask of sorrow.

"He *lived* a hero, milady. And I never told him."

By nightfall the charred remains of what had once been Agnes's husband were recovered from the smoldering rubble. Sir Guy had come just as Kathryn and Agnes arrived back at the main house and, at Kathryn's request, quickly marshaled a cadre of firefighters—even the surly overseer would not let the sheriff see his reluctance—to squelch the flames sufficiently to salvage John's body. Dusk was crawling in when the men summoned the women back to the site. They carried the shepherd out, wrapped him in a clean blanket, and presented him gravely, first to Lady Kathryn, and then to his widow. Agnes emitted a small choking sound, strangled words that Kathryn could not decipher, but their intent was made clear by the frenzied movement of her hands. Agnes wanted the blanket pulled back so that she could see her husband's face. Kathryn understood the need for certainty.

"Milady, I would not advise—" Sir Guy started, but at a brusque nod from Kathryn shrugged his shoulders in acquiescence and, kneeling beside the body, opened the blanket to reveal the dead man's face.

Kathryn had to turn her head away to fight the cresting nausea, but she put her arms around Agnes when she felt the weight of the widow sag against her. John's bones and burnt flesh no longer resembled anything human. The skin on his face was burned away. Two gaping, melted sockets, where the eyes should have been, stared out of a hairless skull covered with strips of black, peeling flesh. Still smoldering. But one plug of familiar stringy gray hair still adhered behind the left ear that had not been burned.

Kathryn allowed the weight of Agnes's body to sink gently to the ground beside her husband. As she began to sob, Kathryn didn't try to cajole her into silence, but let her spend her grief. Finally, when Kathryn thought she could endure no more, and Agnes was too weak to resist, she half-lifted, half-pulled the new-made widow away.

"Take John's body to the chapel," she said. "We'll follow." Then, turning to Sir Guy: "I would be much in your debt, sir, if you would go to Saint Michael's and fetch the priest. John's soul must be shriven. Tonight. For Agnes's peace of mind. I'll send someone of my household with you."

She scanned the clot of onlookers for her sons and saw Colin, pale and stricken, standing at the edge of the crowd. This is too much for him, she thought. He looks ill. But she did not have time to tend him now.

"I would be pleased if you would allow Colin to accompany you, Sir

Guy. My younger son has a gentle spirit. And occupation is balm for a troubled mind. I would send him alone but with night coming on—even Father Benedict will feel safer traveling in your company."

"Father Benedict? You have no confessor of your own?"

She read disapproval in his expression. Why was everybody so concerned about the state of her soul?

"He died of a bloody flux last spring." She tried to keep irritation out of her voice. "I have yet found no replacement, but I maintain a schedule of private devotions."

Not exactly a lie. Although she didn't keep to the canonical hours, she counted the beads on her rosary daily and sometimes visited the small brick chapel attached to the back of the main house. She and Finn had even gone there twice together, sat on the first of the four benches provided and prayed before the small gilded statue of the Virgin, which sat on the altar. His devotions were less traditional, but somehow more personal than hers. He had said no prayers, counted no rosary, merely sat in contemplation while she mouthed the Ave Marias.

Sir Guy said nothing, as if waiting for more explanation.

"We rely on the priest at Saint Michael's. Father Benedict serves Blackingham well. We have contributed generously, from the wool profits, to the building of Saint Michael's."

If he had any further thoughts on the subject of Blackingham's religious conformity, he kept them to himself. The look of disapproval vanished, swept away like words written in sand, and was replaced by that secretive, closed-off look that was his more habitual countenance. Kathryn did not particularly like Guy de Fontaigne. She thought him pretentious and cunning—maybe even dangerous, but for all that she was glad he was here.

And when he clicked his heels together and said, "As you wish, my lady. I will not come back without the priest, and I will attempt to divert your son's mind from the horror it has just witnessed," she felt almost warmed by his smile.

With the matter of the priest and Colin seen to now she could turn to the task she dreaded. She thought fleetingly of calling Glynis to assist Agnes with the body, but the vacant look on the old cook's face told Kathryn that she herself would have to direct the washing—if indeed a charred corpse could be washed—and laying out. Agnes's grief had rendered her incapable of action. Thank God I have a strong stomach, Kathryn thought. If only the pain in her head would be so agreeable.

She took Agnes to the kitchen, sat her before the fire, and held a cup of ale to her lips. "Drink this," she directed. Agnes opened her lips and swallowed, her movements jerky and wooden, like a mummer acting in a Christmas play.

"Agnes, if you feel you cannot prepare John's body, I will call Glynis to help me."

The old woman shook her head, a short, jerky movement. "No. It's my duty. It's the last thing."

Kathryn patted her shoulder to reassure her. "We will do it together, then."

She had a sudden image of what Roderick would have said about her touching the body of a servant, and this was followed by a flood of longing for Finn. For his strength and confidence and compassion.

Simpson shuffled through the kitchen door. "The body is in the chapel, milady. If you have no other need for me, I will return to my supper. My servant had just served it when Sir Guy requested my assistance."

"By all means, Simpson. Go. It would be a sin for your supper to get cold."

His face reddened to the color of a boiled ham. He turned to go but flung a parting shot over his shoulder.

"By the by, milady. If you wish to investigate the burning of the wool shed, you might start by questioning that son of yours."

Scurrilous dog. To fling such an insinuation and then retreat before she could respond. Could Alfred have burned down the shed, started the fire in carelessness? Or worse, in an angry rage? They'd had words only that morning. But that was lunacy. It was his loss too. Still, who could fathom the temperament and illogic of youth? She would confront him when next she saw him, provided he was sober enough to give her a straight answer. As for now, she had work to do.

While Agnes sat like a wooden image beside the kitchen fire, watched over by the wide-eyed scullery maid, Kathryn went in search of a clean linen sheet. She selected one of coarse weave, then, sighing, dug deeper into the chest and brought out a finer one. She ferreted through the silk flotsam of her sewing basket for thread of sufficient weight and strength and collected her needle case.

On her way back down the stairs to the kitchen she found Glynis and instructed her to lay a table in the solar. She would have to pull together proper victuals later. Sir Guy and the priest and her sons would all have to be fed. But she couldn't think about that now.

She returned to the twilight gloom of the smoky kitchen and approached the cook as gently as she could. "Come, Agnes. Let's do this one last thing for John."

Together, they walked to the chapel to sew the dead man into his shroud.

NINE

*The night-raven under the eaves symbolizes recluses
who live under the eaves of the church because they
know that they ought to be so holy in their lives that
all Holy Church, that is Christian people, may lean
upon them. . . . It is for this reason that an anchoress
is called an anchoress and anchored under a church
like an anchor under the side of a ship to hold it so
that the waves and the storm do not pitch it over.*
—ANCRENE RIWLE
(13TH-CENTURY RULE BOOK FOR ANCHORESSES)

inn enjoyed his trip to Broomholm Abbey. It was a fine day, warm
for October, at least for the dreary Octobers that he was used to in the moun-
tains that formed the spiny border between England and Wales. Even in
London the winter rains would have set in. But here, it was sunny, summer at
dalliance, and there had been no rain for days. He passed the night as a guest
of the abbey, not like the pilgrims and travelers who sheltered in the hospitality wing, but as a special guest of the abbot. He dined well and slept
soundly. Surrounded by centuries of silence absorbed into the stone walls, he
dreamed of Kathryn and awoke with a smile on his face and dampened
sheets—a circumstance he had not experienced since his youth.

He broke his fast that morning with the abbot, who squinted at the intricate knotwork and the interlacing gold crosses of the mulberry carpet pages. "These endpapers are exquisite. Very complex. The real test of an illuminator's skill. Perfect symmetry! You know how to use a compass as well as a brush. We'll be hard-pressed to make a cover to equal them."

Finn took an artist's satisfaction in such praise, making his breakfast of the abbot's excellent ham and bread and cheese taste all the better. The abbot shuffled the pages of the first five chapters, carefully examining each, tracing the tempera drawings with a beringed forefinger. "Excellent work. Couldn't be more pleased."

He handed the pages to Brother Joseph, who hovered at his shoulder, eyeing Finn suspiciously. On his initial journey from Broomholm to Blackingham, the monk had been an amiable escort, and Finn had greeted him warmly yesterday, only to be rebuffed. Ever since, he'd been trying to figure out in what manner he had given offense.

"Your art is worthy of its text," the abbot said. "And I have commissioned a goldsmith of some renown. The cover of the book will be beaten gold encrusted with gems."

"Your Excellency is also to be commended on the work of your scriptorium. They provided me with well-spaced text." The monks had done the tedious work of copying, leaving only the large square capitals, and of course the borders, for him. "My Latin is not as fluent as it should be, but I know a good transcription when I see it."

Finn was uncomfortably aware of Brother Joseph's look of disdain. What was it? Something about Scripture and text. That was it. Translation. Wycliffe and his English translation of the Bible. Finn suddenly had a vision of Brother Joseph leaning across the table in Blackingham's great hall, his little mouth screwed into a tight little line at something Finn had said. The talk had been of Wycliffe and his Lollards, and Finn vaguely remembered that he had made a half-hearted defense of the beleaguered cleric. Unwise of him, considering the circumstances.

"Careful, Brother Joseph, don't smudge them," the abbot said sternly over his shoulder. Then, turning back to Finn, who sat across from him at table, he pushed back his chair and rested his interlocked fingers across his chest, covering the ornate cross that hung around his neck. He looked like a man well satisfied with himself.

"Finn, your reputation is well deserved."

"I am glad that you are pleased."

"Pleased. I'm beyond pleased. Such work deserves a bonus. Rich pigments . . . and so much gold in the carpet pages . . . I know that doesn't come cheaply, my friend." He motioned for Brother Joseph, who seemed to understand his wordless commands. The monk returned quickly with a carved casket, placed it carefully in front of the abbot and then stepped back. The rigidity of his posture showed his disapproval, which the abbot ignored, as he fumbled among the keys on his belt, opened the lid, and counted out six gold coins. He handed them to Finn.

"I thank you for your generosity."

"You've earned every farthing."

"I'm pleased to be a humble servant to the abbey."

The abbot then took several silver coins and, placing them in a small bag, pulled the drawstring to secure it, then handed it to Finn also.

"And this is for the lady of Blackingham. Would you be so kind as to see she receives it?"

"I shall place it in her hand myself." Finn smiled and tucked the little purse inside his own larger one, which hung around his neck and just inside his shirt.

"I trust you and your daughter are comfortable at Blackingham."

"I assure you we are."

"And your spiritual needs are being seen to as well as your physical?"

Had the dampness of the abbey walls suddenly created a tempest in Brother Joseph's nose, or was that a sniff of disdain?

"Brother Joseph, please go to the scriptorium and collect the pages of text which have been prepared for the illuminator to take with him."

Brother Joseph bustled from the room, his head held at an indignant angle, obviously aware that he was being dismissed.

"Now we may continue," the abbot said.

"Lady Kathryn and her household are devout. My daughter and I have often shared her devotions."

The abbot hesitated ever so slightly.

"We are glad to hear this. There has been some concern, since she has no confessor. Father Ignatius, before his unfortunate death, expressed strong concern that the souls of Blackingham might be imperiled."

Finn imagined that Brother Joseph had also contributed to the abbot's concern.

"I assure Your Excellency, that is not the case. Lady Kathryn's coffers have been sufficiently impoverished to insure her soul."

Almost immediately Finn regretted the remark. The abbot was his patron. He started to apologize.

"Your Excellency, please forgive—"

"No need. Perhaps, if the king's taxes were less onerous . . ."

"Perhaps," Finn agreed.

"Deliver our high regard to her ladyship and convey our gratitude and friendship."

The gravity of his tone belied mere ceremonial chatter. The abbot, Finn suspected, was a man who knew which way the felled tree would fall.

When Brother Joseph returned, Finn's host stood, indicating that their meeting was at an end. Finn stood also. Brother Joseph handed him the newly transcribed copy and a sealed packet.

Of the latter, he declared, "A messenger brought this for you last week with instructions to hold it for your coming."

"Thank you," Finn said, taking both packages from him.

"It has an Oxford seal." Brother Joseph's gaze challenged him.

"Yes, so it does," Finn said and tucked both packages under his arm, showing the inquisitive monk that he did not intend to satisfy his curiosity. "Your Excellency. Brother Joseph." He nodded to each in turn. "I've taken enough of your time. Thank you for your hospitality and your patronage. I serve at your pleasure. I'll return with the next illuminated installment as soon as I can."

"I'm gratified that you and your daughter will be safe and snug at Blackingham. Our roads sometimes become impassable when winter sets in. Winter enters East Anglia abruptly. An impatient husband who takes his bride without courtship or ceremony."

Hearing such an incongruous metaphor from a man whose only company was that of holy men, Finn wondered briefly in what waters the abbot had sailed before running aground at Broomholm.

The abbot held out his hand. "God go with you," he said.

Brother Joseph said nothing.

The sovereigns were more than enough to purchase the superior pigments needed to finish the manuscript. It was Thursday, market day in Norwich, and Finn reached the city in time to squander some of his windfall. He bought a new ladle for Agnes, who complained that the old one was warped, and presents for Rose and Kathryn: fine leather boots, glove-soft; not stitched cowhide slippers such as they usually wore, and of the newest fashion, straight from London, where the new silver fasteners called "buckles" were a fashion statement. Of the fit for Rose, he was reasonably sure. For Kathryn he was certain. He had held her foot in his hand, his palm caressing her instep, his fingers massaging the heel, the ball, between her slender, perfect toes.

He was eager to get back to Kathryn and to Rose, eager, too, to get started on the new packet delivered to him at Broomholm, the codex from Wycliffe. It would be a different kind of challenge. He'd agreed to the commission at the urging of John of Gaunt, for whom he'd done a Book of Hours last year, though he'd not been aware of the controversy that swirled around the cleric.

He'd been intrigued by Wycliffe's use of English as a translation for the Holy Scriptures, and he liked the idea of a less ostentatious, cleaner artistic expression. Surely a more appropriate illustration for the Gospel story than the gem-encrusted, gaudy display the abbot envisioned. And he'd been impressed by the cleric's forthright, honest manner, plainspoken, equally plain in dress and demeanor. Finn had enjoyed the lack of pretension, having found a surfeit of sophistry and pretense while in the employ of the duke. All in all, he was not sorry he'd taken on the commission, though he now knew enough to be discreet, enough not to open the packet in the presence of the abbot.

He was glad to see that the Oxford seal had not been tampered with.

It was late afternoon when he left the market and mounted his horse. He felt a twinge in his shoulder. The abbot had been right. They were in for a change in the weather. The summer was about to be routed, but that was as it should be. Everything in its natural order. It would be good to spend the cold winter days in the warm cocoon of the redbrick manor house, nesting with his art and the two women he loved. But he had one more stop to make before returning to Aylsham. He turned his horse toward the little church of Saint Julian.

Julian recognized the man who tapped at her visitor's window as soon as she pulled back the curtain. "Finn," she said. "How good to see you." She still held in her hand a sheet of the parchment she was working on.

"I knocked at Alice's door and there was no answer, so I came around here to this window. Now I see I've interrupted your work. I'm sorry."

"You have interrupted nothing but my frustration. And that interruption is welcome. I wish I could offer you refreshment, but Alice did not attend me today."

"I have already eaten. But I've brought you a fresh loaf and a treat besides."

He pulled a parcel from inside his doublet and handed it to her through the narrow window. She unwrapped it with a small cry of delight. The crusty loaf was welcome, but the small brownish brick beside it was a treasure indeed.

"Sugar. Oh, Finn, there must be at least a pound here. Too much for one person, surely." Mentally, she calculated. It would take 360 eggs to barter for a pound of sugar. An egg a day. A whole year's worth. "You must take some back."

"The abbot has paid me generously, and Blackingham Manor feeds me well. You have many visitors. I'm sure you will find a way to share the sugar."

His voice was like a reed pipe pitched low. She felt herself relaxing, soothed by its undulating rhythms. He tapped the crusty loaf lightly with his long paint-stained fingers, an artist's hands. She wondered if she would like his work. Somehow, she thought she would.

"The bread is still warm from the oven," he said. "Eat some before it gets cold."

"Only if you will join me," she said, feeling her spirits suddenly lighten. "Come around through Alice's chamber. Alice hides a key beneath the second stepping stone in the garden. We can share a meal through the window into her room. It's much larger than this skinny little portal."

"It would be my pleasure to break bread in such holy company."

As she listened for the sound of the key in the outside door, she cut two slices, releasing the yeasty aroma into the close room. She scraped a few precious grains of sugar onto each. By the time she had finished he had already entered and pulled a stool beneath the window.

"I have fresh milk. Alice brought it before she left." She pulled her own stool over to sit opposite, poured two pewter mugfuls and set them on the window ledge in front of him. Then she poured a saucerful and set it on the floor at her feet. A gray shadow separated from the deeper shadows in the corner and whipped across the room.

Finn laughed and pointed to the smoke-colored cat, who lapped daintily at the milky offering. "I see you have acquired a boarder since last we met."

"This is Jezebel," Julian said, breaking a few crumbs into the cat's saucer, stroking its ruff. "Half-Tom brought her to me. He said he found her in the market, half-starved and choking on her own fur."

"An unlikely name for a companion to a holy woman."

"Father Andrew, the curate here, named her in a fit of temper. She knocked over the communion wine."

"And he let you keep her after such a sin?"

"When I pointed out to him the line in the *Ancrene Riwle*—that's the rule book for anchoresses—that specifically says a holy woman may keep a cat within the anchorhold. That—and the fact that she's an excellent mouser—convinced him."

They laughed together. It was good to laugh. She'd had little cause of late.

They talked as they shared the milk and the bread: about Half-Tom, about Jezebel's grooming habits, about Julian's Revelations. He asked about the bowl of hazelnuts on the wide ledge of the window.

"I give them away to my visitors. As a reminder of God's love. How He loves the smallest thing He has made. Please, take one with you when you leave. It will cost you less than a holy relic. Like grace, it is free."

She noticed Finn's gaze wander to the manuscript that she had hastily pushed aside. Though the sparse cell was furnished with a small scrivener's desk, she used the window ledge as a shelf.

"You say your writing does not go well?"

She swallowed before answering. "Most of that, my Revelations concerning my visions, was done months ago. I have written little of late."

"Not since the child," he said.

"I cannot get past the mother's pain. My failure to comfort her. To show her His love in spite of the death of her little girl." She picked up a few grains of errant sugar with the tip of her finger.

She was grateful that Finn offered no empty words of condolence, no admonition that grief disavowed faith and was thus a sin. His own grief showed in the tightening of his jaw line as she told him how the little girl had been doing better, her leg healing, until the fever came; how the mother would not be consoled, but railed against a cruel God who would take her child; how she cursed the Church and the pig and the bishop who owned it.

When Julian had finished her story, they sat in silence for a minute, then he asked to see her work.

She pushed the pile of papers toward him, chewed the sweet bread in silence as he scanned the scattered pages of vellum. Jezebel, having licked her bowl clean and washed her face with her pink tongue, bounded into Julian's lap and watched Finn warily, her green eyes half-closed as he read. She purred as Julian scratched between her tufted ears.

Minutes passed. Julian felt uncomfortable. The realization that she craved his good opinion both surprised and alarmed her. Jezebel, as if sensing her disquiet, leaped down and padded toward her shadowy corner. Finally, Finn straightened the pages into a neat stack, neater than when he'd found them, and set them down.

"I'm not a pious man, but I can see how this, your teaching of a loving God, a Mother God, could move some to a truer understanding of the nature of God. This is a text worthy of illumination."

Despite his disclaimer, she suspected he was very much a pious man, though not in the self-righteous sense that too many displayed with their elaborate rosaries and ornate crosses. And, in spite of the fear that it was a prideful feeling, she was pleased that he liked her work and a little embarrassed. He must be used to eloquence.

"The writing is mostly for my own understanding. To help me understand the true meaning of my visions. I am not learned enough—my Latin is poor. I do not write for others. I cannot write in the language of the Church."

He smiled, a slightly crooked, enigmatic smile.

"Tell me about your visions," he said.

She told him about her sickness. It was so much easier to talk about than to write about. He was a good listener, leaning forward intently as she told him how, as a young woman, yearning for salvation, she'd asked three things of God.

First she'd prayed for a true understanding of His passion, desiring to behold His suffering—like the Magdalene who stood beneath His cross—to see, to know, to share His agony, to hear His cry to the Father, to see the bright fountain of His cleansing blood when the Romans pierced His gentle flesh. It was not enough to hear the Scriptures intoned in a language she only half understood. She had to see, to know, to really *know* His passion before her soul could drink from that fountain.

He nodded encouragement as she told him how she prayed for some bodily sickness, a great suffering so that she would be drawn closer to God in patience and understanding, so that her soul would be purified. She told how she begged for three wounds: true contrition, true compassion, and a true longing for God.

She paused to sip from the cup. She could hear herself swallowing.

Finn listened—she'd never seen a man sit so still—whilst she told him about the malady that attacked her body, how she lay three days and three nights at the point of death, how her mother propped her up on pillows so that she could breathe after she became dead from the waist down, and how, when the priest came to offer the last rites, her sight began to fail so all she could see was the light from the cross her curate held in front of her. Only the cross. Only the light.

"It was six years ago, before I came to the hermitage of Saint Julian. I was thirty years old," she said.

As she told her story, the light in the room was fading, too. She stood up and got a candle and placed it on the windowsill that separated them. Its light illumined his face—the graying beard, the high brow where his hair had thinned. She waited for some signal—a gesture of restlessness, a scraping of his chair—that he was growing impatient with her story. Some did. He asked no questions. Simply waited for her to go on. The bread lay in front of him half-eaten.

"Then suddenly, as I beheld the cross, all my pain, all my fear was taken from me. It simply ceased as though it had never been. I was as right as ever I was before. I felt whole, alive, as I had not felt in weeks. I wanted to get up. I wanted to run. I wanted to sing. I knew immediately that this marvelous change could only be a secret working of God."

He shifted his weight, leaned slightly closer. "And the visions?" he asked.

"I saw the red blood running down from under His garland of thorns.

Hot and fresh. And lifelike. Just as it was in the time that the crown of thorns was pressed on His head. It was a great agony to watch Him thus, but it was great joy also. A surprising great joy, a joy like, I think, there shall be in heaven. And I understood many things. Without any intermediary, no one between my soul and His. I saw and understood by myself. With no one to interpret or explain."

"Without the help of a priest, you mean. I've heard such doctrine before from—well, never mind. Go on. What other visions did you have?"

"The last thing He showed me was His Mother, our Lady Mary. He showed her to me in ghostly likeness, a maiden, young and meek, little more than a child."

He gestured toward the pages of vellum. "And this is what you're writing?"

"This is what I'm *trying* to write. But I find my gifts are insufficient."

He picked up the pages, weighed them in his hands. "What I see here is a wonderful beginning."

"But that's just it, I've finished. I've written all the shewings, and it isn't enough. My scribblings are not worthy of the joy that He revealed to me. I cannot show the overflowing nature of His love. My words—any words—are . . . insufficient. There are not words enough to tell." The candle flame flickered with the force of her breath. "I can say it is the kind of love that mothers show for their children, that my own mother showed for her sick child, but it is more. So much more. Such words are inadequate, empty—when I remember the warmth in which He wrapped me. The closest I can come is to say His love is like—but oh, so so much greater than—a mother's love. He is a perfect mother with a perfect love for an infinite number of children."

"A perfect mother? But He was a man."

She shook her head. "I do not deny His maleness. Only that God the Father is our maker, whilst He, the Son, is our Nurturer, our Keeper, our Protector. His blood feeds us like mother's milk. The love He shows is best modeled in a mother's sacrifice. That's the only way I can explain it."

Finn's face softened, like clay warming beneath a sculptor's hand. "I know something of that kind of love. I have a daughter. Her name is Rose."

Julian nodded, indicating that she remembered, thinking it an odd name for a Christian child. Fanciful. But lovely the way he said it.

"My wife died giving life to our child. But you know the last thing she said to me before she died? Rebekka, my wife, held our Rose against her—this tiny new-formed human being whose birth had caused her such pain—and whispered, 'There is such joy here, husband, I wish that you could know it.'"

Rebekka! A Jewish name? A Christian and a Jewess? No. A man would have to be a fool, and she knew the illuminator to be no fool. Unless his Jewish wife had bewitched him. But a Jewess would not want to defile herself with a Christian, would not want to take such a risk for her own life. In France, a Jew could be beheaded for relations with a Christian. The Jews were charged with poisoning wells and causing the plague in '34. Julian had prayed for their souls when she heard hundreds of them had been herded into buildings and burned alive in the areas along the Rhine. She had wept, too. Some within the Church argued for tolerance, pointing out that the plague had occurred in places with no Jews, and in the communities heavily infested with them, the plague had passed by without exacting its death toll. Finn would probably be one of those tolerant ones. But tolerant enough to defy his Church and king by taking a Jew to wife?

She watched the way Finn's jaw muscles twitched, tasting the bittersweet memory of his wife. She waited for him to say more. When he didn't, she reached out to him, touched his hand as she said, "I know one thing, and one thing only truly, Finn, and that is that *whatever happens in this world, our Mother God will see that all is well.*"

He looked at her in disbelief. "Anchoress, in the face of the child's death, having witnessed the grieving mother, how can you still believe with such surety?"

"I believe it because He told me so. My Mother God told me so. And my Mother does not lie."

"I envy you such certainty," he said. He tapped the pages of the manuscript with his fingers. "Let me take this first section, the part that tells of your illness. I will illuminate it for you. While you rewrite the rest."

"I'm glad for you to read it, but the language is unworthy of illumination. It should be in Latin."

"The language may make it more widely read. Have you heard of John Wycliffe?"

"Enough to know the bishop does not like him."

Finn's frown made her laugh. She dropped her voice to a conspiratorial whisper. "You think that alone should be sufficient to recommend him."

He answered with his crooked smile. "Mother Julian, you are a woman of great perception." He stood up, gathering her manuscript in his hands. "John Wycliffe is translating Holy Scripture into this same tongue in which you write. I have a couple of apprentices who could learn on this, if you have a mind to trust me."

"By all means, take the manuscript. I know my words will be safe with you, Finn. My only request is that the illustrations be simple, such as would befit humble words, not overblown or gaudy."

"Mother Julian, you have more in common with John Wycliffe than you know."

By now, the long East Anglian twilight had fled and the room was lit only by the single candle in the window. As Finn moved toward the outside door with the manuscript under his arm, Julian's gaze followed him to the threshold. A slice of night sky showed through her window as he opened the door. No breeze stirred in the cool October night and a full moon picked out blue-green patches of herbs beside the path.

"The frost will get these soon," Finn said as he paused at the open door.

His horse whinnied, restless to be gone, having heard its rider's voice.

"It will be a cold ground to camp on tonight," Julian said. "And it is All Hallows' Eve. Not a night to be abroad. It's a long ride to Blackingham. You might stay with the monks at the cathedral."

Finn laughed. "I'll get a pallet at the inn beside the hearth. It'll be safer there among the vagabonds. The bishop has little liking for me. He thinks I deprived him of his property."

"Thank you for your gifts," she called to his good-bye wave, "and next time you come, bring your daughter."

But he'd already shut the door. She heard the key grate in the lock, then the sound of it being replaced beneath the stepping-stone. She poured the last of the milk from the pewter cups into Jezebel's dish, brushed away the crumbs, and carefully wrapped the bread and sugar in oiled paper. She blew out the candle—candles were almost as precious as sugar—and made her way in darkness to her corner cot. Jezebel leaped onto her bed. A wriggling of the coverlet, and then a ball of fur curled into the warmth of her knee.

Rose had never felt so alone, not even when she was with the nuns at Thetford. Her favorite dress—her blue silk, the color of the sea on a sunlit day—didn't make her feel better, either. She'd worn it for Colin and he wasn't here. Lady Kathryn had said he was "resting" and would not join them for dinner in the solar. Lady Kathryn apologized that the board was not laid in the great hall. The sheriff said it was "cozy." Rose found it stifling.

She distrusted the long-nosed sheriff, hated the way he looked at Lady Kathryn, hated the way he looked at her, too—his beady little jet eyes made her skin crawl. If only her father were here. When she was little, her father had never left her with strangers. Though Rose had to admit Lady Kathryn was hardly a stranger. She was Colin's mother. Might some day be her mother-in-law. That thought sent her heart racing.

Maybe she should ask to take Colin a tray. Nobody would tell her anything. They treated her like a child when it suited them to shut her out. All she knew was that the wool house had burned and John, the shepherd, had been killed in the fire. Burned up, like a soul in hell. A horrible thing. And now they were all supposed to sit here eating a stew of pigeons and leeks, as though nothing had ever happened. She and Colin had been together in the wool house last evening. Had they lit a candle? She couldn't remember. Sometimes they did. But they would have been careful to extinguish the flame. Wouldn't they?

Lady Kathryn smiled at her across the trencher she shared with the sheriff, a tired smile. Rose had helped her pull together the meal for the sheriff and the visiting priest. It would have been cruel to ask Agnes to do it. Agnes who'd been kind to her, Agnes worn out with grieving over the poor burnt body of her husband. Rose shuddered and reached for the little silver cross at her throat. Her hand touched only bare skin. She'd taken the cross off to wash the cord and forgotten to put it back on. She felt vulnerable without it. Naked. As though she'd forgotten to put on her shift or her shirt.

A greasy smear, a bit of fat, gleamed on the sheriff's beard. The smell of the stewed pigeon mingled with wood smoke from the fire they'd lit against the chill and the lingering miasma of the wool-house fire.

The door of the solar where they were dining opened into the courtyard. Rose barely gained it before she started to retch.

TEN

〜〜〜

If he defiles a vowed virgin, he shall do penance for three years.
—THE PENITENTIAL OF THEODORE (8TH CENTURY)

In the darkness of the cavernous kitchen, the perpetual fire in the giant stone maw had gone out. No smoke issued forth from its great chimney for the first time since the plague in '34, when Lady Kathryn's father was master of Blackingham. But the scullery maid, shivering on her bed of rags, knew nothing about that. She knew only that the hearth on which she lay was cold. Even the hound that sometimes curled into a ball beside her on the stone hearth had deserted her for a warmer bed.

But Magda had no other bed. It was two miles to the village where her family of eight existed in a squalid one-room hut, miles across fields where demons lurked in shadows, past the shell that had been the wool house where a man had died today in the devil's fire. But she could not have gone back if there were no shadows, no fresh-made ghosts. She could not face her father's temper, her mother's disappointment. Her father had cursed her for being stupid and beaten her when she pulled up the vegetables instead of the weeds in the pitiful patch of garden the family tended. Her mother, in desperation, had brought her here. "At least, you'll be warm and fed," her mother had whispered. "Do whatever they tell you." She hadn't said, "You can't come home," but the child had seen it in the slump of her mother's shoulders, hunched over to protect her swollen belly, as she walked away without once looking back.

So Magda accepted this turning as she accepted the changes in the season, as she accepted her father's drunken tantrums and her mother's yearly birthings, as she accepted all the things in her life over which she had no control. Nor did she expect any. She knew she was a simpleton. They had told her often enough—even a simpleton could understand. But they didn't know about the gift. "The Lord giveth and the Lord taketh away," her mother had said when her oldest son was crushed by an overturned cart. Maybe the gift was from the Lord, in return for making her simple. She knew that others didn't have it. Else why would they do and say such stupid things? Like the time her father traded their only pig for a cow that sickened and died the next day. Magda had known the trader was not to be trusted. His eyes showed his greed and so did the too-quick way he made the bargain. But her father had not guessed. So, she concluded, it was a gift that not everybody had, this ability to see inside people, to hear what they didn't say.

She knew other things, too. Like the color of their souls. The tall lady with the white hair, her voice was proud but her soul was blue, not the color of the sky but a greenish blue like the color of the river. The river, yes. A shady pool, reflecting willows weeping on the bank, white tufts of cloud floating in a sun-blue sky. And Cook—her soul was rusty brown, like wet earth, the kind clay pots were made from. It was sad about her husband. Magda had seen the shepherd only once or twice, and he'd seemed nice enough. His soul was brown, too, only lighter, the color of grass in winter. But the one Magda liked best was the girl who'd helped the tall woman make the pigeon stew. Rose and Lady Kathryn—she had learned their names. Said them over in her mind as she'd said the words to a song she'd heard the minstrels sing on May Day, said them over and over and over, until she remembered. From her corner she had stared at the strange color of Rose's skin, a pale fawn color, not pink and white like her own, and her hair, as dark and shiny as coal. But it was the two colors of Rose's soul, blending, glowing, one inside the other, a golden yellow like sweet butter inside a rosy rim, that fascinated her. She'd only seen one other with two colors. Her mother's soul was violet, and it had sometimes had a golden center. Not always. Just sometimes.

Magda shivered and scratched the scab of a fleabite on her leg until the blood trickled. Maybe she could stir the embers, find some fuel at the stable. It wasn't far to the stable. She'd scrape courage enough to venture there. She picked up the huge poker with both hands and scratched among the dead coals until she found sparks in the ashes. The ostler's boy had laughed at her, called her "girlie," but his soul was green, and she'd never known anyone whose soul was green who treated her unkindly. He would help. Agnes would be glad in the morning that she had kept the fire from going out—and she would not sleep cold.

⚬

Finn had made his bed on a pallet by the hearth in the inn's common room rather than risk sharing a moldy mattress with two strangers in one of the closetlike cells at the top of the twisted stairs. He listened in disgust to the snores of the six or seven travelers, pilgrims on their way to Canterbury, sleeping on the floor around him. The one closest looked as if he hadn't washed his beard and hair since last year's wheat harvest. Clumps of suet and crumbs hid out with God only knew what else among the stringy mass of matted hair. Finn pulled his blanket closer and wondered just how far a flea could jump. He wondered, too, how many cutpurses lay among his sleeping companions. He adjusted the heavy pouch tucked inside his shirt so that it would not reveal itself whilst he slept. But, alas, he shouldn't have worried. Sleep did not come. His general fastidiousness conspired with his sense of unease to keep him awake.

The day that had started so auspiciously for him—the abbot's generous payment, his shopping trip among the colorful market stalls, his visit with the anchoress—had rapidly deteriorated after he left the little Church of Saint Julian. He'd been tempted to follow King Street outside the city walls and head for Blackingham, but that would have put most of his journey in darkness. Instead, he followed the Wensum River a mile or two north to Bishop's Gate. There, in the shadow of the great cathedral, he was sure to find an inn.

He'd been forced to wait at Bishop's Gate while a great entourage entered the city. Most of the other travelers had dismounted in a show of obeisance to the Church's seal, which was affixed to the scarlet drapery of the touring wagon, but Finn had remained astride his horse, which snorted impatiently as the gaudy carriage lumbered by. This put him eyeball to eyeball with the worthy inside the carriage.

Henry Despenser, bishop of Norwich.

Finn looked away to avoid eye contact, but it was too late. Recognition flickered between them. The great carriage creaked to a halt. The crowd murmured its surprise as the wagon disgorged a footman in scarlet livery. He approached Finn.

"His Eminence, Henry Despenser, bishop of Norwich, would speak with you," the footman intoned, jerking his plumed hat in the direction of the carriage.

Finn had a sudden inclination to refuse and simply ride away. But stupidity was not one of his faults. He dismounted and handed the reins of his horse to the splendidly garbed attendant, who looked somewhat abashed but nevertheless stood by the horse, holding the reins as though he had something nasty between his gloved, ringed fingers.

"Guard this horse well," Finn said. "He carries valuable manuscripts from Broomholm Abbey." Glancing nervously at the Oxford packet, Finn approached the parted curtains of the window. "Your Eminence," he said to the haughty face framed therein.

The crowd pressed slightly forward, silent now, as if listening with a collective ear. The bishop murmured something to another footman and the door to the carriage opened. A fringed and brocaded footstool was placed in the dust of the road.

Finn didn't move but looked at this second, this equally splendored, attendent quizzically.

"My lord the bishop will speak with you privately." His tone clearly said that he thought this simply robed horseman not worthy of such distinction. The crowd sighed as Finn parted the curtain and entered the drapery-covered wagon.

Once inside the equipage of Holy Church, this palace on wheels, Finn was at an immediate social disadvantage. Did he sit without being asked, or did he remain hunched over in this awkward position, his height putting him in a decidedly clumsy and uncomfortable position? The bishop's smirk showed that he was aware of Finn's discomfort, and after a pause sufficient in length to reveal Henry Despenser to be a man who enjoyed the discomfort of others, he waved toward the velvet-covered bench opposite. "Sit, please."

Finn sat. He said nothing.

The silence lengthened as guest returned the even gaze of host. From this close perspective, and in the facing light, the bishop looked even younger than Finn had remembered. Young in age, mayhap, but his arrogance was ripe. Despenser spoke first.

"You are the illuminator who has been engaged by the abbey at Broomholm."

"Yes, Your Eminence."

"The one who has a taste for pork."

Finn did not rise to the bait. Did not acknowledge the veiled reference to their last meeting. Despenser continued. "Since our last meeting under"—he smiled cattily—"unfortunate circumstances, I have inquired about the nature of your work. The abbot informs me that I was wise in my generous forgiveness of your irreverence for Church property. He sings your praises."

Finn still did not acknowledge the former meeting and accepted the compliment with only a nod and a smile. What was this about? Was the bishop just playing with him? A smile like the anchoress's cat, he the mouse caught between her dainty paws.

"You are a man of action, it seems, rather than words," the bishop said. "Well, then, I'll get right to the point. I may have a commission for you. I wish you to paint a reredos, an altarpiece, for me." He paused as if just now giving thought to the subject of his commission. "To depict the Passion, the Resurrection, and Ascension of our Lord."

Well, here was a surprise. Was this some kind of a trap? Was Despenser plotting revenge for the butchered pig?

The bishop continued, "I know what you're thinking—why do I not go to one of the guilds?—but I'm a man of certain aesthetic standards, and your superior ability, so the abbot assures me, is not easily found."

High praise, and from a high patron. This should have made him comfortable. It did not. The close interior of the wagon with its heavy drapery was too confining, almost like a prison. The bishop, in spite of his youth and his ermine-edged robes, didn't smell all that sweet; his body carried the distinct smell of old garlic and stale perfume.

"You do me great honor," Finn said carefully. "But I'm afraid that I must plead incapacity at the moment. The abbot has given me much work, and he has proved himself to be a generous patron. I would not want to disappoint him."

Almost before the words were out of his mouth, he knew they were wrong.

The bishop's face flamed. "You would choose to disappoint a bishop rather than an abbot, then? Broomholm is not even an abbey of great distinction. I must wonder at your ambition, Illuminator. And your wisdom."

"Not disappoint, Your Eminence. Merely postpone, until such time as I could do the altarpiece justice."

Despenser's thin lips tightened. That had been the wrong thing to say, too. He should have seen that the bishop would not appreciate being put behind the abbot. Was that why he'd said it? An unconscious desire to needle this upstart of a churchman who represented everything he hated about the Church? He tried again.

"I am truly flattered at the confidence of so noble and esteemed a patron, but, as I'm sure Your Eminence would be the first to concede, in serving the abbey I serve the same Lord that I would be serving if I carried out your commission. To choose one over the other for personal gain would be a sacrilege against the Holy Virgin to whom I have dedicated my art."

"A pious and circumspect answer, to be sure. And a shrewd one." But his tone indicated that neither piety nor shrewdness was what he desired in an artist.

Finn pleaded that he worked in miniature, that the scale of such a work was outside his ability. "I suggest, with your permission, that your altarpiece might be better served by one of the Flemish artists."

The bishop had fidgeted at that answer, just as Finn fidgeted now on the hard floor of the crowded inn.

"Well, of course, if you're incapable, I shall look elsewhere," he'd said sharply, then waved impatiently at the footman who stood outside the window. The door opened abruptly and Finn backed out of the carriage into the settling chill of early evening, barely getting clear before the coachman whipped the horses and the wagon lurched forward.

I botched that bit of business. I may have made a powerful enemy, he thought. But for now, he was more bothered by the snores and farts of the sleeping flotsam of humanity around him. Give it up, Finn, you'll not sleep tonight, he told himself. So, before daybreak, he went out to roust the ostler and claim his horse. By the time the first bleak morn of winter had shown its grayed underskirt, he was outside the walls of Norwich, headed for Blackingham.

⌁

Finn's early-morning journey was not as pleasant as yesterday's promise. He was filled with a restless anxiety, the kind of loneliness and foreboding that usually comes at the close of day rather than at dawn. Even the weight of the gold florins around his neck and the thought of the gifts in his saddlebags did not lighten his mood. His eyes were grainy from lack of sleep and his back ached. He was getting too old to sleep on the floor. Or maybe he was spoiled by his comfortable quarters at Blackingham. Blackingham. That gouged too. Like an ill-tied knot in his braies. He knew about the cost of love.

What would be the price for his brief respite from loneliness? And brief it would have to be. Indeed, if it were known that he and Kathryn had relations . . . but his past was well behind him. And when his work was finished, he would move on. Not because he wanted to. But because he had no choice. As long as their affair was secret Kathryn's position would not be compromised. Still, perhaps he should rein himself in, lest the price for this short-lived happiness be exacted in a coin he could not afford.

A pall of cloud stole the sun's warmth as he paused to let his horse drink from a marsh pool. Maybe it was the weight of the Scripture carried in his saddlebag that burdened his natural optimism. Or maybe it was the weight of the secret he carried buried so carefully that sometimes even he forgot. Was it right to keep it from her? But ignorance would be her only defense.

He peered at a nonexistent horizon. Gray sky washed into marshland and marsh washed into sea like a seascape painted by a somber child with only the color gray in his paint box. A landscape so flat, it seemed one might walk off the edge of the world—not one little hill, not even a bump on the watery landscape to shelter him from the wind. How had he found this flatness, this huge, unsettling sky beautiful? The long summer with its clear golden light had beguiled him, but he had a sense that the long summer had ended. The cold north wind, rushing down his neck, confirmed it.

Blackingham loomed before him, its red brick face a relief from the pall that had settled on his spirit. Only a thin spiral of smoke snaked from the kitchen chimney, hardly visible against the gray sky, but Finn read a welcome there and spurred his horse toward Rose and Kathryn. Rose and Kathryn.

Colin spent the night prostrate on the cold floor of the chapel where morning found him, agonizingly conscious, as he'd been all night, of the shrouded body laid out before the altar. Its charred smell made the vomit rise in his throat. Its pale linen shroud reflected a ghostly light from the lone torch left burning in its sconce, keeping watch over the dead man until morning came and the shepherd could make his last journey. Colin kept watch, too. *Pater Noster, qui es in caelis, sanctificetur nomen tuum. Adveniat regnum tuum . . .* How many times had he said the Our Father? His throat was parched, his tongue thick with saying it. *Libera nos a malo, libera nos a malo, libera nos a malo.* Deliver us from evil. But in his heart he feared it was too late. It was all his fault. Why had he not seen it sooner? The devil had used Rose's beauty to tempt him into mortal sin. He had seduced a virgin, and now the shepherd's blood stained his soul and hers.

Had they put out the lamp? He couldn't remember. But it didn't matter. God spoke through the fire. The wool shed was God's judgment against them. *Et dimitte nobis debita nostra,* he mumbled between sobs into the cold silence of the chapel. No white dove perched on the narrow slit of window; no angelic vision of light promised redemption. Only a rat rustled across the floor. He'd really not expected any supernatural manifestation. His sin could not be so easily expunged. It would take a lifetime of Paternosters to save his soul, and Rose's, too—Rose, who'd been the first to call what they did a sin.

Hadn't he always known he belonged to God? He'd denied his calling, and the devil, not content with such small booty, had snared him. And now there was blood on his hands. And Rose's, too—beautiful, innocent Rose, tarnished by his lust. He'd spend his life in prayer for her salvation. But it would not be as he had imagined it. There would be no music. There would be no chorus of harmonious voices. No glorious hymns of plainsong praise offered to heaven. He would choose a tuneless abbey, maybe Franciscan. He would take a vow of silence, spend what was left of his youth and all the days of his life in unbroken stillness, praying for the Rose he'd soiled, growing old without the solace of his music. He would atone.

His skin felt hot despite the chill of the chapel. Maybe he would catch an ague and die. Escape. But he could not wish for death outside a state of grace. Besides, there was Rose. Her soul needed him.

The bell in the courtyard tolled prime, calling the faithful to morning prayers. Calling him. This sniveling in front of an altar that had seen too few prayers bought no grace. With dawn's gray light, the room appeared even more ghostly, but it no longer frightened him. He rose stiffly, like an old man. He would dress himself in sackcloth and ashes and follow behind the cart as it transported John's body to Saint Michael's. He would himself lift it from the cart, carry it through the lych-gate into the holy ground where it would be received. And then? He felt a weight shift within him, not removed, just shifted, to be better borne.

Then, he would confess his sin to the father at Saint Michael's, and his life as Colin, youngest son of Blackingham, would be over.

~ ❧ ~

Sir Guy de Fontaigne also rose with first light. He'd no wish to tarry at Blackingham. He'd slept badly after eating a scant portion of cold pigeon stew provided by his apologetic hostess. So the cook's husband was the lout who'd died in the fire. So what? She was a servant. Her first duty was to the household she served. If he were master of Blackingham—an idea of which the sheriff was becoming more and more enamored, especially since he had lately learned that Blackingham had been Lady Kathryn's dower lands and by rights reverted to her at her husband's death—such laxness would never be condoned. Not that he would deny the woman her grief. Even peasants and villeins were entitled to that, he supposed. She could use her tears to flavor the victuals. But victuals there would be. And served in a timely fashion. Duty, like one's station in life, was ordained by God, else Sir Guy's ambition would have seen him king. That might be out of his grasp, but Blackingham Manor was not.

But first, he must woo Lady Kathryn, and just now, with a gnawing in his belly and no fire laid in his chamber, he was not in a wooing mood. He'd fetched the priest last night, as she'd requested, and tried to *divert* her petulant son—also as she'd requested. Roderick had often brought the other twin hunting. Alfred was more to the sheriff's liking, a merry lad, full of fun and occasional mischief. This pale one of the silken hair and pretty features had come hunting with them only once and cried at the sight of a wounded stag. Roderick had mocked him and sent him home. "He's sucked too long at his dam's pap. He'll never make a man."

Well, by God's Body, he'd made a poor companion. He may as well have been a deaf mute for all the response he gave to the sheriff's determined attempts at diversion. They'd returned within an hour, priest in tow, to this inadequate hospitality. All this over the death of a shepherd. Blackingham truly needed to be taken in hand, and he itched to do it. The proud widow was a bonus. If he should marry Roderick's widow, her dower lands would come under his control.

He dressed quickly in the first chilly dawn of winter, cursing briefly that there was no water in his ewer, then quickly tied on his sword and dagger. As he strode across the deserted courtyard to the great kitchen, nothing stirred in the sepulchral house. He entered the smoky cavern hopefully: mayhap there was a fat sausage sizzling somewhere after all. But no sign of life was here, either, just a scullery maid sleeping before a half-hearted fire.

He clanged the flat of his dagger among some overhead pots. The sleeping girl jumped like a kicked dog, her body involuntarily scrunching, as though trying to make itself invisible.

"Look to, wench. Where's your mistress?"

The girl only blinked large sleep-encrusted eyes.

"God's Body, girl. Are you daft? What must a man do to get a crust of bread here?"

The girl leaped up, like a cat on all fours, her eyes suddenly alert. She grunted something unintelligible, but she scampered to a cupboard. She brought him a half-round loaf, covered in a moldy cloth, and stuck it out to him.

"Bread," she said. Then she laid the loaf on the table between them and cringed back into the shadow.

"She's offering you the food from her own hoard. It would be churlish not to accept."

Sir Guy spun around at the sound of a man's voice behind him. He held his dagger at the ready, lowering it only slightly as he half recognized the grinning man behind him.

"More churlish to eat rotten food, I would say." He returned his dagger to his belt but kept his hand upon the hilt. Recognition nagged. "You were here the night the bishop's legate was killed. You're from the abbey, an artist of some kind."

"An illuminator. My name is Finn. And you're the sheriff. I remember the occasion well. You frightened Lady Kathryn with your untimely display of the priest's corpse."

Sir Guy's spine stiffened. His thumb traced the carving on his dagger hilt. An arrogant tone for an artisan. The fellow's demeanor didn't fit. And anything that didn't fit irked him. He remembered some exchange between then, some disagreement at table, but he could not quite summon the nature of it. The only thing he could remember for certain was that he had disliked the fellow then. And he disliked him now. "And I remember that you are a lodger here, not a member of the household, so it's hardly your business to notice if Lady Kathryn is frightened or not."

The interloper appeared to ignore the remark but looked around the kitchen, now empty except for the two of them. The scullery maid had fled, leaving her insulting offering behind.

"Where's Agnes?" Finn sniffed the air. "By this hour she's usually baking bread."

The illuminator's familiarity with Blackingham, the fact that he not only remembered the cook's name but used it as though they were old friends, further irritated Sir Guy.

"*Agnes* is at the funeral of her husband. And for that we are all made to fast." He was rewarded with a look of genuine shock on the illuminator's face. Here at least they could be in sympathy. But the shock was not for an ill-run household, as Finn's next words revealed.

"John? Dead? But how—"

A noise behind, a cold gust of wind, a rustle of skirts and a raven-haired girl rushed toward Finn, throwing her arms around him. Sir Guy, at first taken aback by the affectionate display, searched his memory. Ah yes, the daughter. But so familiar. None of the formality, the respect that he would demand from a daughter. This silly girl needed to be taught her place.

"Father, it's too horrible. You should have been here. I could not bear it."

The sheriff watched as Finn gently disengaged his daughter's arms from around his neck and brushed a tear from her cheek with a paint-stained forefinger.

Odd, he hadn't noticed before how exotic the girl looked. Coloring much unlike her father. Probably the by-blow of some dark-skinned slut.

"Shh, Rose. Calm yourself. Now tell me."

The girl glanced around, apparently noticing for the first time that they were not alone.

"It was the wool house, Father. It burned. And John was within." Her voice was scarcely above a whisper.

The illuminator looked shocked, even distressed. What was the shepherd to him? Sir Guy wondered.

"Poor John." Finn shook his head in what looked like a genuine expression of grief, muttering, "Poor Agnes." Then: "A great pity."

The sheriff was becoming more confused by the minute.

"It was a great loss to Lady Kathryn as well, Father. She was counting on the wool."

Well, here, at last, was an emotion that made sense.

The girl continued. "She didn't say much, but she was distraught. I think she wished you were here."

She wished you were here! She? Lady Kathryn? Tiny grains of uncertainty and irritation gritted against the smooth surface of the sheriff's plans.

"I'll go to her right away. Now dry your tears. What are you doing here so early in the morn?"

"I've come to help. When they return from the burial, they will need food. Lady Kathryn, and Colin, and Agnes."

Agnes? This girl, a guest of a noble house, was going to act as servant to the cook? Was the divine order of things suddenly reversed?

"I can help," she said proudly. "I helped Lady Kathryn last night. We cooked a pigeon stew."

The sheriff's stomach growled at the memory.

"Then I shall help, too," the father said. "It will be like old times. And Lady Kathryn and Colin and Agnes will return to the comfort of a warm kitchen and hot food."

The sheriff turned on his heels and departed, cursing under his breath, fully aware that Finn and Rose, busy with stoking the fire, took no notice of his leaving.

~ ✸ ~

Alone with a bit of bread and cheese at the Beggar's Daughter, an alehouse in Aylsham where the proprietor regularly fed the sheriff gratis (and also whatever minions might accompany him), the sheriff chewed on something else.

"I'll go to her right away," the illuminator had said. And he'd said it in a proprietary way. As though something lay between Lady Kathryn and this Finn, something like friendship. Sir Guy chewed and swallowed. Such a friendship would possibly be an obstacle in the way of his goal. If she already had a protector, then she was not as vulnerable as he needed her to be. Or maybe it was not something that lay between them but that they lay together. Maybe they were lovers. No. The idea was preposterous. A woman of nobility and an artisan. Besides, it would be fornication and, though Lady Kathryn, as Roderick had talked about her, was not an overly pious woman, yet, she was a prudent one. And if Roderick were to be believed, a cold one as well. No. He rather suspected that the illuminator's role was one of friend and adviser. Still, he'd wormed his way into her best graces, and who knew what might come of that. One thing was sure: friend or lover, the illuminator was an obstacle that needed to be eliminated. But first things first.

First, he had the matter of the dead priest to reckon with. It had been three months. The bishop, initially, had other things on his mind; he was busy converting the old Anglo-Saxon cathedral ruins at North Elmham into a manor house and hunting lodge. But now that the archbishop was growing impatient, the bishop was demanding action. So now it was the sheriff's problem. Sir Guy downed his last drop of ale, pinched the wench who served him as payment and, without so much as a nod to the innkeeper, took himself and his horse off to investigate the scene of the crime.

The river Bure was just one of many veins that bled the peat bogs of East Anglia. A shallow, lazy stream that often overspilled its narrow verge on its meanderings to the sea, it ran north and east of Aylsham and bordered the south pasturelands of Blackingham, where black-faced sheep grazed peacefully. Here there was a fording place, where the river crossed the main road that led south to Aylsham and beyond to Norwich. Here was where the priest's body had been found, in the shallow fringes of the stream among the reeds—on Blackingham land. The priest must have been on his way to Blackingham—not returning, since Lady Kathryn said she had not seen him—or maybe farther north to Broomholm Abbey. So this was the area to which Sir Guy returned this somber day to renew his investigation, though what he expected to find there he couldn't say, since the marshy nature of the area would probably have long ago obliterated any evidence of the crime. A cold trail, but nevertheless, a trail. His men had scoured it only days after, and reportedly found nothing. But, under this renewed pressure from the bishop, he needed to assure himself.

His horse picked its way reluctantly along the marshy edge, disturbing a sheldrake feeding as it paddled among the reeds. The sheriff's keen eyes noticed nothing unusual. Of course, any sign of bloody violence would long have vanished; there was only a spot of recently cleared turf where the reed cutters had been harvesting. They'd left behind an abandoned sheaf half-hidden where it had fallen among some taller grasses. No stone unturned. Sir Guy was nothing if not thorough. But not wishing to dismount, he speared the bundle of reeds with the blade of his sword. The sheldrake, interrupted once again, honked and, beating its wings in a splash of frustration, was airborne.

The sheriff, finding nothing beneath the bundle of reeds, pitched it away, and using the flat of his sword like a scythe, probed among the uncut reeds. Nothing there either, as he had suspected. He pulled his horse's rein sharply to the right. Its hoof disturbed the bundled reeds once again. This time, a squarish brown packet dislodged and fell away. Probably a bit of sacking from the reed cutter's lunch. Still, it was worth investigating.

His curiosity was sufficiently piqued to motivate him to dismount. He retrieved the fallen object, which was amazingly dry, protected from the wet by the heavy bundle of reeds. It must have caught among the grasses and been bound up into the sheaf after the reeds were scythed. Closer inspection showed it to be a small leather-bound slate with a stub of chalk tied to it by a cord. His breath quickened when he noticed the seal of the Church embossed on the outside of the leather cover. Heedless now of the moisture seeping into his fine leather boots, the sheriff examined with acute interest the scribbling on the slate. His Latin was sufficient to allow for a halting translation.

"2 gold florins," followed by what looked like the initials "P.G." He could just make out then: "for the soul of her mother."

"1 goblet silver plate," then followed by the initials "R.S., for the soul of his dead wife."

"2 pence Jim the Candler for the sin of avarice."

These three were linked together by parenthetical markings and the word "Aylsham." It dawned on the sheriff what he'd found. It was the inventory of goods claimed for the Church on the priest's last run. It even had the date scratched at the top: "July 22, the Feast Day of Mary Magdalene."

There was more. One other entry. The last. "1 length of pearls. L K for the sins of Sir Roderick." The entry beside it said "Blackingham."

Lady Kathryn had said the priest had not yet been to Blackingham. Yet here it was, in the dead man's own hand: proof that Lady Kathryn had lied.

❧

The morning was well on when Alfred spurred his mother's palfrey in the direction of Saint Michael's, in search of his mother. Earlier he'd gone looking for Lady Kathryn to make amends. Glynis had told him that his lady mother and brother had joined the funeral procession. She would probably be mad that he'd taken her horse without her permission, but he should have his own mount. His father had promised his sons fine stallions when they came of age. His mother, pleading poor, had put them off. Colin had agreed. What did a girl like him care, anyway? He was with their mother now, as usual. Currying favor. Alfred should be there, too, because it would please her, and just now, he was anxious to please her.

He shivered beneath his linen tunic, wishing he'd worn a heavier one, and breathed the damp air heavy with smoke from the cookfires of Aylsham. The smell of burning fat reminded him that he'd not eaten. He could see the squat little steeple of Saint Michael's just ahead. What a terrible way to die. He wished he had been there when they brought the shepherd's body out. Were the eyeballs melted? Was the flesh peeled away? He would wager a crown he would have been man enough to look at the corpse and not retch. If Colin was there, he was probably green and puking. He was such a milksop. Probably never even had a girl.

Simpson said John was drunk and burned the wool house down with his carelessness. Alfred doubted it. He had learned enough watching the overseer to know that his mother was right: he couldn't be trusted. True enough, John had enjoyed his ale, but he was not irresponsible. He wouldn't be drunk in the middle of the day. No, for some self-serving reason, or maybe pure meanness, Simpson wanted them to think John burned the wool house down.

But it was not just about Simpson's accusations that Alfred wished to talk to his mother. He had something that belonged to her, something he'd found at the overseer's house. Yesterday, he'd stormed out, sulking because she wouldn't let him return to the main house. He'd wearied of playing spy. Simpson had seen through his lord of the manor act and found several ways to trick him into doing menial chores. It was hard to play the knight when you were up to your rump in sheep dung. So yesterday, after his mother lashed out at him, he'd ridden first to Aylsham, to the White Hart to douse his own temper and bruised ego in a couple of pints. Then he'd gone to Simpson's house to settle a few things with him. If he had to stay two more weeks until his birthday, he wanted some things made clear.

Finding the house deserted, he'd seized the opportunity to make a thorough search of the overseer's cottage—heretofore he'd always found the door to Simpson's chamber locked. He'd found no evidence of embezzlement, but he'd found something else, something she could hold over the overseer's head. The threat of a charge of theft would keep Simpson in line. And Alfred would offer this evidence to his mother—a kind of peace offering, and a kind of bribe. He'd made up his mind. He was born the eldest son of Sir Roderick of Blackingham, and he was not going to spend another day as a lackey.

But if his mother wouldn't let him come home, he had another plan. His Viking blood on his father's side craved action, and he had an idea where he could get it. There'd been talk, complaints, among the lads at the White Hart about the bishop's ambition to raise an army to restore the Italian pope. If that was true, the bishop would need more than gold to raid Avignon. He'd need brave English soldiers. Noble English soldiers. Thing was, Alfred would need his own horse. Another reason to get on his mother's good side. When he'd last tried on his father's armor in the spring, he'd been tall enough. The helmet and leggings had fit, but the mail was loose in the chest, the hauberk clumsy. Still, withal, he was sure he'd bulked up during the summer. He would try again.

He spurred the reluctant palfrey harder, forgetting about the cold and the damp. In his mind the sun was shining in a cloudless sky and he could feel the wind teasing his hair. Dreams of battlefield glory courted his fancy. Flying silk banners. Heralds' trumpets. And he himself riding triumphantly into the French court whilst all the ladies chirped behind their fans about the brave English youth whose armor glinted in the sunshine. (Unmarred by any blemish of mud or taint of blood.) He might even make Knight of the Garter, an honor that had escaped his poor father.

He pulled up short some distance from the churchyard lych-gate. The burial must be finished. Only the old cook was left weeping over the new grave. There was no sign of his mother or Colin.

For one brief minute Alfred considered dismounting, going over to offer his condolences. But he wouldn't know what to say to a serf.

ELEVEN

Dirige, Domine, Deus meus, in conspectu tuo viam meam.

Direct, O Lord, my God, my steps in your sight.
— THE DIRIGE (DIRGE) FROM
THE OFFICE OF THE DEAD

Lady Kathryn stood alone in the churchyard at Saint Michael's. The handful of crofters and their families who had attended the funeral mass nodded at her timidly as they left.

"Good day to ye, milady."

"It be a good and gracious thing for you to come to the shepherd's burying, milady."

Good and gracious? Or just plain foolish? She had watched with half an eye to—yes, admit it—envy, as they crowded around Agnes offering their condolences, their heartfelt sympathy. A strong sense of community existed among Blackingham's serfs and leaseholders that she'd never really noticed. But what occasion had she to notice? They had first dealt with her father, then her husband, neither of whom had been known for their largesse. Now, it was Simpson who hounded them for tardy rents, confiscated their livestock, and took their strongest sons as indentured laborers when they could not pay. And as Roderick, and now Simpson, had represented her to them, she could only wonder in what ill light they must hold her. They cast furtive, self-conscious glances in her direction.

" 'Tis unseemly to take the Holy Eucharist with nobility," one of them whispered.

He looked familiar, but she couldn't call his name, couldn't call any of their names. She looked around for Simpson, conspicuous in his absence. This irritated her. He should have been here to pay his respects, and he could have acted as liaison between her and her crofters. She pretended not to hear their whisperings or notice how uncomfortable her presence made them, but she felt as obtrusive as a gargoyle trooping with seraphim.

She paid the monks who chanted the Office of the Dead, but lingered long after the final psalm, after the last *misere nobis* had been said, after the shrouded body had been removed from its processional coffin and deposited in the grave and mounded with its peaty covering. Even after the others had drifted away, she lingered, reluctant to leave Agnes alone in the churchyard. Agnes knelt beside the grave, raw and ugly, like a new scar stretched over proud flesh. Kathryn waited beneath the mossy roof of the lych-gate, watching for her sons. She'd sent for Alfred, and he had not come. Even Colin had left. He'd insisted on walking in mourner's procession behind the two-wheeled cart that carried the body, but he must have slipped away before or during the mass. That surprised her. Colin loved the liturgy.

Kathryn sat on the bench where, less than an hour gone past, the little procession had rested as they waited for the coming of the priest. A mourning dove called plaintively to its mate. She shivered. She should have worn her cloak. Agnes didn't seem to feel the cold, slumped there on the ground next to the mound of dirt. But everybody knew that peasants were hardier than gentlefolk. What was it like to lose a beloved husband? She'd not lingered over Roderick's grave lest relief, not grief, should show itself in her face.

The wind had shifted to the north and blew a rattle of dead leaves across the dead grass. Hadn't Agnes enough of grieving? And then Kathryn thought about Finn. Not her husband—he would never be her husband because the king would never give permission for a noblewoman to wed a commoner—and yet how hard she would find it to leave him in the lonely churchyard, ringed with its black yew trees, like lonely sentinels. She wrapped her shawl tighter, and blew on her hands to warm them.

When she could endure the chill no longer, she approached Agnes gently, put her arms around her shoulders, tried to lift her, much as she had done the day of the fire.

"Come, Agnes. We've done all we can for your John, this day. I'll buy masses for his soul. It's time to go now. You need some warm food."

"You go on, milady. If it please ye, I'd like to be alone with John for a little while. When I come back I'll see to yer needs and that of young Master Colin, and the illuminator's daughter."

Kathryn had little choice but to walk the two miles home alone, leaving Agnes in the graveyard, but she was determined that they would see to their own needs. Surely, this once she could put the needs of this woman, who shamed her with her loyalty, before her own and let her grieve in peace. At least they would not have to feed the sheriff. Kathryn had seen Sir Guy leave just after dawn, feeling much slighted, no doubt, that Blackingham's hospitality had been lacking, and he would lose no time in noising that fact abroad. She'd noticed how he turned up his nose at the dinner she and Rose had prepared. Now, she had to scrape something together for Colin, Rose, and herself. Had the lackeys remembered to keep the great kitchen fire stoked in the cook's absence? Probably not. She'd have a cold hearth to contend with as well. How tiresome it all was. She longed for the comfort of her chamber fire.

As she approached the house—why had she not worn sturdier shoes; the rough clods of earth in the rutted road bruised her feet—she saw smoke curling from the double chimneys. Thank God that was one chore she'd not have to do.

As she crossed the courtyard, she heard a man's familiar voice. The sound of it made her forget her weariness and her sore feet. She picked up her skirts and ran into the kitchen. Rose was there, and so was Finn, breaking eggs onto a smoking iron griddle.

"You're back," she said, feeling stupid, wanting to rush to him and fling her arms around his neck, and knowing that she should not—not in front of Rose.

"My condolences, my lady, Rose has told me about the fire," he said, but she read something else in his face, some secret language that lovers speak with their eyes and not their mouths.

Suddenly she was ravenously hungry.

"Have you enough eggs to share?"

He laughed his honey-graveled laugh. "We prepared them for you; however, we will be honored if you invite us to share."

But halfway into the meal of bread and cheese and eggs—whenever had such simple fare tasted so good—Rose turned green and rushed outside to disgorge hers on the ground of the courtyard. Finn rushed after her, held her head, and when she had done retching, wiped yellow-speckled spittle from her lips with his lawn handkerchief.

"I think I'd like to lie down awhile, Father, I feel faint," she said when she had emptied her stomach of the offending eggs.

Lady Kathryn held the back of her hand to Rose's forehead. "She is not fevered. It is probably just her reaction to all that's gone on in your absence. She's been a very brave girl and a great help to me. A true daughter of Blackingham could not have served better."

The girl smiled wanly at this praise delivered in front of her father, but she was still a sickly shade of green.

"Take her to your quarters and put her to bed. I'll bring her a soothing tea, a physick I used to make for my father whenever he was bilious."

Finn led his daughter away, looking for all the world like an old mother hen, while Kathryn tried to make good on her promise. After a cursory search—she was becoming more acquainted with the innards of this kitchen than a lady should be—she found a mortar and pestle and pounded anise, fennel, and caraway seeds to a powder. By the time she'd taken the seed tea upstairs, Rose was already in bed. Her father clucked over her, tucking the coverlet under her chin, unhooking the heavy tapestry over the window to shut out the early-afternoon light.

"I feel better. I think I can get up now. I should help Colin mix the colors. You'll be wanting them now that you're back, Father."

"Colin is resting, too." Kathryn held the pungent tea to the girl's lips. "I haven't seen him since the burial. It has been an ordeal for us all. I've instructed Glynis to take a tray to his room, and left some bread and cheese and a glass of wine for Agnes." She glanced at Finn, sent a signal with her eyes. "I'll be seeking my own respite soon." But he was too preoccupied with Rose to read her invitation. If invitation it was. Even she was no longer sure. She thought she could sleep forever. Rose drank her tea and when her eyelids began to droop, Kathryn tiptoed from the room. Finn was sitting beside Rose's bed and didn't appear to hear her leave.

~ ◦ ~

A sluggish fire had been laid in her chamber and Kathryn was poking this back to life when she heard a knock at her door. Probably Alfred. Come to make amends after the fight. He always did. Would he have to be fed, too? Or had Simpson's housekeeper given him breakfast before he left? More like, he'd drunk a morning repast in a friendly Aylsham alehouse. Wearily, she pulled a robe around her—she'd stripped down to her shift.

"My lady, may I come in?" A throaty, husky pleading. Not Alfred.

She moved to the door, lifted the bar but opened it only slightly.

"Shouldn't you be with Rose?"

"She's sleeping like a babe. My presence would only disturb her. As you said, it's probably just a girl's nerves. Open the door. I have something for you."

Temptation. Just to be held. To be able to forget the grinding-down abrasion of the last two days. "Not now. Not in my chamber. Colin or Alfred might come."

"Would that be so bad?"

She remembered how circumspect he'd been with his own greeting in the kitchen, how he'd not embraced her in front of his daughter. The blood rushed to her temples. She should just send him away.

"Come on. Open the door. We'll just talk."

~ ◦ ~

Kathryn was warmed at last, less by the neglected fire on the hearth than by the sinewy body curled around her. The room was pungent with smoke from the sputtering embers and the smell of their lovemaking. A delicious lethargy covered her like wool. If she could just stay thus forever, her limbs entwined with his like tangled skeins of silk thread; her lips touching the smooth crown of his head where the hair had thinned to a perfect O.

She was aware of every rhythm of his body when they lay together, his breath matching hers, long after their passion had burned itself out. There was a great mystery in the way the "two became one flesh." It seemed no less a miracle than the Holy Eucharist, the transformation of the bread and wine into Christ's blood and bone. That miracle she was only told about, having never experienced the taste of flesh and blood n her mouth—was that because she was unworthy? In her mouth the wine remained wine and the bread, bread. But this sacred rite, this communion of two souls, she experienced for herself. It had never been like that with Roderick. In her marriage blessed by Church and king, she had been nothing more than a brood mare, and her husband a stallion, copulating according to their natures.

"I brought you a present from the market at Norwich," Finn said.

"I don't need a present. Having you here with me is present enough." Each word was a feathery kiss against that perfect O.

"Ah, having me here. I understand. The abbot sent your fee for 'having me here.' And a heavy purse it is. Must be a burdensome task indeed."

His words were teasing, and he smiled and chucked her under the chin when he delivered them, but she bristled. She knew he judged her to be selfish, thought her uncaring of those not of her own noble estate. She remembered their discussion about who should pay the poll tax for her servants. As he kissed her throat and lifted a strand of hair to expose a bare breast to his tongue, she pushed him away—gently—and pulled the coverlet up, securing it under her armpits.

She propped herself up on one elbow, facing him. "Don't mock me. That's not what I meant by 'having you here.' I merely meant your presence. Though I'll not deny I'm glad enough of the abbot's generosity. Especially now that I've lost the wool house. Not to mention the profit from the wool sack." Why did she say that about the profit? Because she knew it would annoy him?

Because his tone had held an unpleasant insinuation. He'd practically called her a whore—not something to joke about.

"You didn't mention the shepherd."

"Well, of course the shepherd. He'll not be easily—or cheaply—replaced." Might as well feed his low opinion of her greediness.

He lay back, arms crossed behind his neck. He wore a hazelnut mounted in a pewter casing on a leather thong around his neck. She had asked him about it, and he said it was a gift from a holy woman. Suddenly she found it annoying, as though it represented some hidden part of him withheld from her. She pushed it aside, tracing the outline of his breastbone with the tip of her finger, lightly, teasing. But he was no longer smiling and had stopped looking at her, frowning instead at the ceiling as though he watched demons cavorting in the recessed shadows of the tarred roof timbers.

"Is that the only reason?"

"What do you mean, 'the only reason'?"

"Profit. Is *profit* all you think about?"

"Obviously, not all," she said, indicating the disheveled bedcovers with her hand.

Where was he when she was bathing the shepherd's corpse? Where was he and his overblown notions about charity when she was comforting Agnes? He was hobnobbing with bishops, discussing philosophy with holy women. Dining on wine and cakes in the fine luxury of the abbot's quarters.

"I have the welfare of my sons to think of. I have their inheritance to protect. You, on the other hand, are an artisan." She saw his eyebrow lift and regretted the heavily inflected "artisan." "I mean, you can depend on your skill to support your daughter. That's not something that Church or king can wrest from you."

She sensed a quickening in his blood, a tensing of his limbs, the muscles in his face, his whole body as taut as a harp string newly tuned. She touched the hollow beneath his rib cage where the skin was loose, the muscles slack but not gone to fat. No slackness now.

"I depend upon my skill as an 'artisan' because I have no choice. King and Church have already stripped me. As clean as a willow wand."

Her hand remained on his stomach, her fingers weaving tiny whorls in the hairs surrounding his navel.

"What do you mean?"

"What I mean, Kathryn, is that you're not the only person to feel the heel of tyranny pressing on your neck. Ask the crofter who cards your wool; ask the yeoman who tills your fields for a pitiful wage; ask the villein whose labor you own. But for them it's *your* dainty foot that presses their faces into the mud."

Her hand ceased its exploration.

"You may be a fine dabbler in paints, Master Illuminator, but you know nothing of what it takes to run a fiefdom the size of Blackingham."

His hoot of derision resonated with righteous indignation and wounded pride. His eyes were not smiling. He was genuinely angry, his pride wounded.

"This little brick enclosure with its few acres of sheep! I'll have you to know, *my lady*, that I once was heir to a holding—a stone castle with motte and bailey, a retinue of my own retainers—that makes Blackingham look like a . . . like a guild master's house."

Had she heard him right? Her hand flew to her throat to still the jump of pulse.

"Do you mean to say, Finn, that you are of a noble house, and you never told me? Do you realize what this means?" The hand that had lately made whorls in his chest hair cradled his chin in its palm, turning it to face her. "If you are of noble birth, we can petition the king to be married!"

He said nothing. Conflicting emotions—irritation, consternation, and dismay—played tag across his face. She waited. The joy leaked out of her with each second of silence. A heat that had nothing to do with passion seared her skin. What if he'd kept quiet precisely because he wanted no alliance with her, thought her beneath him? All this time he'd been laughing at her, watching her play the great lady. Now that she'd flushed this information from him in a spurt of pride-filled arrogance, he'd be forced to reveal the fact that he'd only wanted to bed her. Was it possible that for her what had been a grand passion was for him a mere dalliance—a dalliance for which she was paid?

She felt like Eve after the fall.

She couldn't look at him. She sat up, moved to the edge of the bed, pulling the sheet with her.

He grabbed at the edge of the linen and held it in place before it exposed him completely. "I said *was*, Kathryn. *Was* heir. I am as you have said. Nothing more than an artisan," he said miserably. "My lands and title are forfeit to the king."

Forfeit?! That could only mean one thing. He was a traitor, and she was harboring him—literally—in her bosom, in the bosom of Blackingham. She had betrayed her children's birthright. Maybe even endangered their lives.

"You should have told me," she said. "You should have told me if you have committed treason."

She could not look at him. By not telling her, he had betrayed her trust, betrayed their intimacy. And yet, she still wanted to hold him to her and comfort him for his loss. What could be worse than losing his land? And she knew him well enough—or thought she knew him well enough until now—to know that he would grieve that loss for his daughter if not for himself.

"If I had betrayed the king, I would have been hanged, drawn and quartered," he said from behind her. "My head would be on a pole and the crows would have long since pecked out my eyes."

Those eyes the color of the sea that read her soul, those laughing eyes whose lids she even now longed to turn and kiss, not laughing now.

He sat up in the bed, leaned across her shoulder, touched her cheek. "My land was forfeit because I loved a woman too much. That seems to be a weakness with me."

Some misunderstanding then, some minor offense that might yet be forgiven, and if his lands were not restored, what did she care? Blackingham, despite his disparagement of it, would be enough.

"Where was your castle?" she asked over her shoulder. She still sat with her back to him, unprepared to meet his gaze.

"In the Marches. On the Welsh border."

"And the woman? Is she—"

His eyes reassured her. "She was Rose's mother."

Kathryn felt a great weight lift. She knew how he'd loved his wife. She loved him the more for it. Though some part of her envied the dead woman.

"And the king did not approve."

It was not a question. An old story, really, easy enough to decipher, Kathryn thought. Finn had been young and in love, had shown his rebellious streak, had imprudently disobeyed the king, married in haste, maybe turning his back on the wife King Edward had chosen.

"The king did not approve," he repeated.

He paused. She waited, anticipating, with relief, a romantic tale of love requited and against great odds. She wanted to turn back to him, but she would wait a moment longer, wait for further reassurance, punish him for giving her such a scare. She sat upright, her spine stiff, and looked at the ceiling instead. She heard a sharp intake of breath and then a quick exhale.

"I married a Jew," he said.

At first she thought she had not heard right, but the word hovered up near the rafters. It seemed to write itself in the air, each one writ larger than the last. Jew. Jew. Jew. She sat very still, frozen like a rabbit cowering beneath the shadow of a hawk. Even her breath would not come.

Jew, Jew, I married a Jew, he'd said. She had taken a man to her bed who'd had intercourse with a Jew. A Christ killer.

He reached out to her, touched her shoulder.

"Kathryn, if you could have known Rebekka—"

She cringed, felt herself pulling away and could not stop until she sat, barely teetering on the edge of the bed. *Rebekka.* And Rose with her olive skin and raven hair, the girl she'd first compared to the Holy Virgin. But how could she have known? She'd only ever seen one Jew, and that an old money lender in Norwich her father had once pointed out to her. She tugged violently at the sheet until it came away. She wrapped herself in it and stood up, her back still turned. She would not have one who consorted with a Jew see her naked.

"I need to go back to the kitchen to see if Agnes has returned to her duties. The household has to be fed." Her voice sounded small, squeezed tight.

"Kathryn, don't you think we—?"

"You'd better go back to Ro— your daughter. One of my sons may come at any time."

Alfred and Colin. What if they knew their mother had fornicated with a Jew?

She pulled her shift over her body. She heard his heavy sigh, the whisper of his linen braies as he pulled them over his thighs. As she wove her hair into a thick braid, she felt his breath on her back, a brushing of his lips in the nape of her neck. Her skin prickled.

"Kathryn, please—"

"Another time, Finn. There'll be time, later."

Would he not guess her repulsion and despise her for her small-mindedness? But she was not like him—did not have the great well of mercy and compassion inside her as he did.

She heard him moving away, his hose rustling against the rushes scattered on the floor. *Call him back. Tell him it changes nothing.*

"Later, Finn. I promise, we will talk later." She fumbled with the fastenings on her bodice. There were her sons to consider. It was unlawful to consort with a Jew.

No answer. She turned to call him back, to lead him back to the bed. But she was too late. She was alone in the room with the sound of the bar slipping into its iron latch as the door closed.

And on the table beside her bed glittered the silver coins the abbot had sent.

❧

Alfred did not come to his mother's chamber that afternoon as expected. He'd already been there, arriving in time enough to see the door close on the back of the person entering. A man's back. He'd listened at the door only moments. But long enough. He went straight to the illuminator's quarters, his father's old chamber—how dare she—to confirm his suspicion. It was, as he suspected, empty. He peeked behind the curtain separating the antechamber, only to see the sleeping Rose, a sight which at any other time would have excited his imagination to mischief. But not today. Not with his mother defiling his father's memory and her chaste widow's bed with this interloper.

He fingered the pearls in the pocket of his tunic, the pearls belonging to his mother that he'd found in Simpson's private chamber. No doubt, the sly overseer had pilfered them when Lady Kathryn's back was turned, thinking she would assume she'd lost them. Alfred had looked forward to returning them to her as proof of his competence, had anticipated her smile of pleasure when she saw them. It would be like a gift to her, something she could hold over Simpson's head. But she'd been otherwise engaged, and now his gift was spoiled.

That was why she'd sent him away. All that pretense about spying on the overseer. She'd just wanted him out of the way so she could fornicate with a stranger. She probably figured Colin was too stupid to know what was going on under his very nose. God's Blood! They'd probably even done it in his father's bed. The thought sickened him. His own dam! It was as though his father had been erased. Alfred suppressed a desire to shove, with one fell swoop of his hand, the neat little paint pots from his father's desk—the desk that this . . . this *shriveled little cod* had dared to appropriate. But no. The noise might waken the sleeping *princess* in the next room. Sure to bring down his mother's wrath on his head. Instead, he picked up a couple of quills and crumpled them in his hands, poking their nibs into the flesh of his palm until he winced.

A leather book bag hung, open, on a peg. A bag that once held his father's books. He shuffled through the loose pages of illuminated script. Hasty examination showed the sheets on top to be John's Gospel. And underneath, more pages, these crammed into the bottom as though less valuable or half-forgotten. He recognized some Saxon words, English words. Unimportant scribblings. Not so angry as to endanger his soul by desecrating a Holy Gospel—especially now that a seed of an idea had occurred to him—he returned Saint John carefully to the bag. Then he took the pearls from his pocket and arranged the strand in the bag, covering them askance with the loose pages from the bottom, so that if one looked with only half an eye, the pearls would be visible while still having the appearance of an attempted concealment.

Having vented his frustration in this petty act of revenge, Alfred tiptoed out of the room, but not before pocketing a thin sheet of gold leaf—one didn't have to be an artist to know it was costly—and strode down the stairs with a smile on his face. Once outside, he laid the gold leaves onto a pile of dung, smiling to himself at the result. He thought briefly of putting the gilded cow pile in the illuminator's bed, but not wanting to dirty his hands with the fresh dung, shrugged off the urge. Just the thinking of it was enough to satisfy him. Let his lady mother find her pearls in her lover's room. Let him explain that.

⚜

Alfred rode straight to the Beggar's Daughter to celebrate his mischief. And to drown his grief. He bought the first pint himself. Sir Guy de Fontaigne bought the second. And the third. And then Alfred began to talk.

Sir Guy, listening attentively, gave the boy an avuncular pat on the back, a sigh of commiseration, and motioned for the publican to pour another pint.

⚜

Agnes lingered by the grave, oblivious to the cold. She couldn't leave yet. Not until she said her piece.

"I reckon ye were a good husband to me, John. Except fer the drink. And God'll forgive ye that. He knows 'tweren't yer fault."

She plucked a long strand of hair from her head—when did it go so gray?—wound it around her index finger in a perfect circle. Then she slid the ashen ring of it from her finger and patted it into the loamy earth. The crows would probably steal it to line their nest, but she had nothing else to give him.

John had wound such a ring for her on their wedding day, a bright circlet of his own brown hair. She'd cried when a spark from the cook fire had singed it from her finger, cried more for the loss than the pain. He'd laughed at her, then held her to him and said he would shave his head and braid all his locks—his brown luxurious locks—into jewelry if 'twould make his bride happy.

[145]

"Ye're free now, husband. Long last and untimely so. I know ye had no love fer Blackingham, and it right pleases me to know ye'll not lie in Blackingham ground. But Lady Kathryn did right by ye, John. She doesn't blame ye for the fire. I canna blame ye either."

She sat beside him a long time. A veiled sun struggled to show itself but could not penetrate the mist. The dove ceased its plaintive mourning calling. The only sound now came from the rustle of dry leaves overhanging the roof of Saint Michael's.

"I have to leave ye now, John. I've me duties to attend."

She stood up and turned away before his ghost could wrest from her lips the one reproach she did not wish to say. The one thing she could not forgive. She was well beyond the lych-gate, well past his spirit's hearing, when she muttered the words. And the saying of it squeezed the last drop of bitterness from her heart.

"Ye gave me no children, John. Ye've left me alone."

She walked the two miles back to Blackingham along the same hard path that Lady Kathryn had taken earlier. She did not feel the cold. The calluses on her feet within their ill-made clogs served her well. The redbrick house loomed ahead, calling her to task. It was too late to roast a joint, she could tell by the position of the weak sun playing hide-and-seek with the mist. Maybe a brace of partridge on the spit. If she hurried, there might be time enough to make a custard tart.

A thin stream of smoke curled from the kitchen chimney. Thank the Holy Virgin for that. She'd been afraid that, without her there to oversee, the groom who fed the fires would make himself scarce. He was a yeoman's son but a lazy, loutish boy, marked by the pox and not fit for the wars or he would have gone with all the rest.

She entered the silent kitchen and put her back to the oak-planked door to shut it behind her. How had she never noticed it was so heavy? Suddenly, it gave with a creak and the metal bar slammed into its latch as if pushed by an unseen angel.

"Oh, 'tis only ye, Magda. Hiding behind the door again," she said as she hung her coarse wool shawl on the peg. "More devil than angel if cleanness be a virtue."

She'd meant to make the scullery maid bathe once Lady Kathryn had said she could stay. She'd not have such filth in her kitchen. The wench smiled at her as if she'd been paid a compliment, her eyes wide with pleasure, her hand raised close to Agnes's head, stroking the air as though 'twere a piece of fine silk flowing between her fingers.

The girl was daft, pity be. Agnes peered at her more closely. Daft, surely. Yet, there was something about her, mayhap even an intelligence behind the downcast eyes.

The girl pointed to the fire, then to herself, nodding her head vigorously. "What are you trying to tell me, girl? Just say it."

"Magda." She pointed to herself, then to the hearth. "F-Fire."

"Ye kept the fire going?"

Smiling broadly, the girl nodded. "Asked b-b- asked boy for logs."

"Well. Well. Ye kept the fire. Ye may not be as simple as they said."

The girl rubbed her crossed arms together. "Magda, cold," she grinned.

The warmth of the fire felt good to Agnes, too. She hadn't noticed how cold she was 'til now. *Cold. Was John cold in the churchyard? Better not to think that way. There lay grief past bearing.* She looked at the girl with an appraiser's eye. She reckoned the stable boy would see cause enough to make him come to the girl's aid. The girl was small, but beneath her rags could be seen the budding breasts of a woman.

"Food. For you." Magda pointed to a dish of fried eggs.

"Did you cook the eggs, too?"

The girl hung her head as if disappointed that she could not confirm the deed as hers. "No. A m-man and the lady." Then, almost defiantly: "But I can cook eggs."

"Can ye indeed?"

Lady Kathryn, bless her. And a man. The illuminator must have returned. And right glad of it she was. The eggs were a blessing. Not just because she needed food—though grief had dulled the blade of her hunger—but because it meant that the others had been fed. They would still need supper, but not so much.

With a dirty hand, the girl handed her a piece of bread. Agnes looked at it and frowned—bread baked before the fire, when her John was still with her—but she took it and scooped up a bit of congealed yolk with the crust the girl had not touched. As she chewed she looked at the scullery maid thoughtfully.

"Put some water on to boil, Magda. Ye're going to have a bath."

The girl shook her head, fear widening her eyes.

"It won't kill ye, child. And once ye're rid of fleas and lice, then ye won't have to sleep with the dogs."

Magda's look of fear abated only slightly, but she poured the water into the swinging kettle. She had filled the water jar from the well that morning, but she poured it stingily, as if each drop were poison.

"Fill it full up. That's right."

For the first time since the fire, Agnes felt the weight on her chest ease ever so slightly. She went into the cupboard, collected a bar of lye soap and frayed wool rags. But when she came back out, the girl had vanished. The only sound was from the hissing of the boiling water. Then a slight movement beneath the heavy oak table, hardly more than a chimney sweep's brushing wing.

"Come on out, child. I'll not hurt ye and ye'll not melt."

The girl came out, as she was bidden, but cringed when she saw the soap and rag. Agnes took her arm gently and pulled her toward the hearth, seated her on its raised stone end. The girl stood obediently but poised for flight as Agnes filled a bowl with steaming water. Then Agnes took Magda's upturned face and began to scrub until pink skin showed.

"Tonight, ye'll share my bed," Agnes said. "It'll keep us both from the cold."

~·¤·~

Kathryn heard Colin praying in the chapel as she passed on her way to the great hall for Simpson's monthly reckoning. *"Misere Nobis, Kyrie Eleison."* Prayers at prime with the rising sun, more prayers at terce and sexte and none, and then again, when the evening shadows came creeping at vespers. No matter what time of day—even as the bell tolled curfew at compline—when she'd passed the chapel lately, she'd seen her son at prayer. And no perfunctory priestly offerings, either, but sincere supplication.

Were the sins of Blackingham so great that her beautiful boy, wan and gaunt with fasting—when had she last seen him eat?—must mutter these incessant pleadings for mercy? Did he whisper his entreaties here in the cold chapel even at matins, when the rushlights danced with demon shadows on the wall, and again at lauds, when Saint Peter's cock crowed in the blackness of pre-dawn? While the sinners at Blackingham slumbered, while his mother slept with a Christ killer—a "Christ killer" with more Christ in him than any priest she had known—her child, surely the most innocent among them, kept prayerful watch.

She paused at the chapel door, poised to go in, to interrupt, pull him away from his pious devotions into the crisp sunshine of the November day. She could not think when last they'd talked. Not since the shepherd's death, surely, a week gone. Finn had not come to her either, not since that afternoon she'd sent him away. Seven nights she had waited, listening for a knock at her door. On the day after, Glynis had brought a message from him: "A gift of appreciation for my lady who gives shelter to a poor artisan and his daughter," attached to a parcel. *Artisan.* The word slapped her in the face. She unwrapped the package to find shoes of soft suede with a buckle fastener like none she had seen before. She'd heard the buckles were the latest fashion. She'd not seen one until now. The boots were beautiful. Why had he not given them to her himself?

Domini Deus. Colin was crying in the chapel. His pale hair gleamed like a halo around his fine-boned face, now gaunt with too much piety. The light from the crimson cross of the chapel window played upon his hair, a sign that painted its sacred cruciform across the crown of his head and down his shoulders like a monk's mantle. Saint Margaret's window. Roderick had paid handsomely for its brilliant hues depicting the patron saint of childbirth. When she was carrying his sons he'd burned candles, changed the chapel from Saint Jude's to Saint Margaret's—how easily he disposed of saints, as easily as he disposed of favorites. All this trouble and expense—not for her, she knew. But for his issue, "the pride of his loins," as he called the lusty male twins the midwife had presented to him, though from the beginning he seemed to find more pride in one than in the other.

He'd handed the smaller, sleeping infant back to Kathryn, and held the screaming red-faced one that he'd named Alfred up into the air, one-handed, like a trophy. "This one. This one," he'd said, "is destined to be a fighter." She'd shuddered when she'd heard those words. Shuddered and prayed to Saint Margaret to protect both her sons. Saint Margaret, who now conspired with her sunlit cross to woo Colin away. What would Roderick say if he saw his youngest son mewling before the altar day and night? Roderick had no penitential leanings, though heaven knew his sins were great enough to give him cause.

Colin remained immobile, kneeling before the altar, his hands clasped, eyes closed: the classic penitential posture. Surely he could feel her presence, had heard the rustle of her skirts. He gave no sign.

"Colin." Softly, almost a whisper.

He might have been carved in stone, except for the gentle movement of his lips as he mouthed the prayers.

Sighing, she turned away. Unable to save his brother, she had stolen this younger one from the malediction of his father's affections, but she would not struggle with that other Father. Not even for a son. Lest she endanger not only her soul but his as well.

"*Christi Eleison.*" Fainter now, his voice pleading as her footfalls fell away.

Christ have mercy on us. Yes, and especially for you, Colin, for my beautiful boy child. Mercy for you. She mouthed the words silently. "*Christi Eleison.*"

Mercy for me, too, she prayed. She could feel the throbbing begin beneath her cheek. Soon the headache would come. Her monthly time was late. Should she be worried? It wasn't the first time. She'd put it to her time of life. But that was before. Could Finn's seed even now be seeking some still-fertile niche inside her womb? He *had* pulled out, hadn't he? Every time? He'd never spoken of it, had not invited her to enter into sinful conspiracy, but she'd learned to wait for him to spend his passion against the soft of her belly. Like spilled wine.

Coitus interruptus.

She massaged her left temple, willing the pain away. There was this reckoning with Simpson to get through.

Coitus interruptus. Christi Eleison. She took a deep breath and exhaled, her bosom moving with the heaviness she felt. Too much Latin in her life by half.

⁂

Kathryn entered the great hall where the steward would attend her; its portable banqueting tables and benches had been cleared away after the last great feast—feasts were few and far between since Roderick's death. The hall's only furnishings now were the heavy tapestries that lined the walls, filtering the cold that seeped through the bricks, and one lone table and chair, which she was to occupy in her various dealings as lady of the manor. This saddle-shaped chair built of sturdy English oak had fit her husband. Roderick had been a large man, filling up the space, a master on his throne, but even with her voluminous velvet kirtle tucked inside the chair's curved arms, there was extra space. And when she tried to rest her elbows on its arms, she felt like a wounded falcon with its wings stretched unnaturally beyond their span.

She'd given orders that the chair be moved from the dais to the center of the room, thinking it would be less threatening. She preferred conducting her affairs in the warmer atmosphere of the solar and had only decided to use the great hall in this one circumstance to remind the surly overseer of her position. Now she thought that moving the chair from its elevated position had been a mistake—she needed Simpson to have to look up to her, and besides, she felt very small in the middle of that great expanse of emptiness—but the chair was much too heavy. And her head ached horribly.

She closed her eyes to exorcise, or gather strength to endure, the familiar pain, and to await the overseer's coming. Why did she let the man bother her so? He was servant. She was master. She should let him go, but where was his replacement? She heard the shuffle of feet across the floor, then the murmur of voices. She opened her eyes to see not only Simpson but her son as well. Of course, why had she not assumed Alfred would be with him? Alfred— when had he grown so tall and handsome?—stood beside Simpson. The dread shifted, eased. She straightened her spine and raised her chin.

Alfred reached for her hand, brought it to his lips as he dropped to one knee in a courtly gesture.

"I trust my lady mother is in good health."

He's practicing his court manners, she thought. How like his father he is in some—too many—respects. But he belongs to me. He suckled at my breast. That bond is strong. And he'll make a strong master for Blackingham. She smiled to think how her father, the first lord of Blackingham, would have been pleased with his sturdy heir.

There was much she needed to say to Alfred—she'd put it off too long— but she was mindful of Simpson, who stood behind him in a posture, but not an attitude, she noticed, of submission.

She motioned for Alfred to stand.

"I am well enough, considering. It is good that you've decided to finally attend your mother. Your absence has been conspicuous during this recent misfortune"—here she glared at the overseer—"and your absence as well. You should have attended mass."

Behind Alfred, Simpson smirked. She could read what he dared not say: a funeral mass for a common peasant was an affectation and beneath him.

Alfred colored slightly, his eyes flashing resentment.

"My lady mother, it was not my intent to be neglectful. I have been busy about the task you assigned me."

Pretty words, but the tone she was less sure about.

"I came to my mother's chamber the afternoon of the shepherd's funeral, thinking to lend what support a dutiful son may lend in troubling times, but I found the door closed and my lady mother closeted with another. Not wishing to intrude, I departed."

The overseer was smirking, but she scarcely registered it, so taken aback was she. The afternoon of the shepherd's funeral, he'd said. The last time she and Finn had been together. She felt the blood drain from her face.

The door had been barred. She was sure of it. He could not know whom she entertained or the intimate circumstances. She decided to brazen it out. The best defense was an offense. At least that had always been Roderick's strategy.

"You should have knocked. I'm sure I was alone. My sons are always welcome. I needed to speak with you. I have some questions concerning the fire, or any activities you might have had that took you into the wool house prior to the fire."

Was it her imagination or did Simpson fidget? If he'd lied about Alfred, now let him explain it.

"The fire?" Alfred looked puzzled, then his flush deepened. She recognized the color of his temper. "Surely you aren't going to blame me! I was there only once, maybe twice to . . . to help John lay out the fleeces."

"It's just that someone saw you go in the morning of the fire, I thought you—"

"Thought I what? Started the fire? I'll wager you didn't ask Colin about his whereabouts."

Another glance at Simpson showed him to be suddenly interested in the vaulted ceiling of the great hall, but he was listening, she was sure, gloating on every word. He made no attempt to hide his smirk.

"We shall discuss this in private, after the accounting," she said.

Simpson stepped forward, handed the pages bound with leather lacings to Alfred, who handed them to Lady Kathryn. She perused them carefully enough to see that the balances were in line with last year's harvest reckoning, which she had already studied in preparation.

"These seem to be in order." She placed the account book on the table that separated her from her son and Simpson. "Well done, Alfred. Your supervision seems to have had an efficacious bearing on Simpson's figures. This time there is no shortfall."

This wiped the smirk from the overseer's face.

"You may go now, Simpson. I will speak with my son in private."

His bow was as abrupt as the slam of a coffin lid.

As his footfalls receded, Alfred maintained his businesslike posture, reluctant, Lady Kathryn thought, to relinquish his grown-up mantle.

"We are alone, now, Alfred. Don't be so sullen. Come, give your mother a kiss to settle our quarrel."

He made no move to render the requested kiss. If anything, his posture became more rigid. He reached into his doublet and drew out a parchment tied with a silk cord.

"I have a petition for my lady mother."

There was about him a new reserve. She thought of Colin lying prostrate before the altar in Saint Margaret's chapel, and stifled a sigh. Her boys would soon be men. Already, she could feel them slipping away.

She nodded sedately, determined not to undermine his newfound dignity. "You may present your request."

He handed her the parchment. She recognized the seal. Sir Guy de Fontaigne. Curiosity mingled with unease.

"This is the seal of the sheriff," she said. "I thought you said it was your petition."

"The request is mine. In the absence of my father, Sir Guy stands as sponsor to me in my request."

"I see," she said, running her fingers quickly under the seal, breaking the wax. "You have made a formidable alliance."

"An alliance formed by my father and in accordance with his wishes, as you will see."

She scanned the contents, then riffled the pages frantically, reading incredulously. Dread pressed her into the chair. She wanted to go to him, wrap her arms around him, crush him against her bosom, but she feared she could not stand.

"Alfred, are you sure this is what you want?" was all that she could manage.

"It is what my father wanted for me. It is what I would have done if he had lived."

"But is it what *you* want?"

"It is what I want. In the service of Sir Guy I will learn to be a knight like my father. I have already tried on my father's mail. It fits me well. I shall take it with me and Sir Guy will provide me with a mount." Then, stonily: "With your permission, of course."

She felt suddenly old. The great hall loomed larger than ever around her. In the high expanse of the rafters a crow flew in under the eave and pecked at an abandoned wren's nest. She examined the parchment again, Sir Guy's scrawling signature, sharp and angular as the man himself, above the official seal of the high sheriff. She knew she could not refuse. Sir Guy would only petition the boy king and his regent John of Gaunt. They could turn her son against her, maybe declare Blackingham, even the part that was her dower lands, under Alfred's control. She would be shunted off into some desolate abbey to eke out her life under the "protection" of the king. With only Colin to speak for her.

Christi Eleison.

No, she could not afford the enmity of Sir Guy de Fontaigne.

"I will miss you," she said in a small voice.

"I'm sure you will find other company to take my place. You were glad enough of my absence before."

"It is not the same. I knew you were close by. I could see you whenever I wanted." She pointed to the accounting ledger. "Your absence was a necessary sacrifice for Blackingham."

His only answer was a tightening of his jaw muscle, a firm-jutting jaw, Roderick's jaw.

"You will come for the Yuletide feast? It is to be a birthday celebration for your brother and you."

"If Sir Guy will give me leave."

His young body stood before her at attention, rigid, unyielding. She knew if she put her arms around him, embraced him, he would remain so. She would not invite that kind of rejection. "Go with your mother's blessing, then," she said, her voice hardly above a whisper.

He bowed slightly, turned to leave.

"Not even a kiss, Alfred?"

He bent across the table that separated them, a mere brush of her cheek with his full lips. She had a flash of that same mouth, his infant bow-shaped mouth fastened on her breast, greedily sucking. So reluctant to let go then, so anxious now.

She resisted the urge to call him back as he strode toward the door. She had no power to order him. He had gone into the world and made other alliances. She would only make herself look foolish.

"Take one of the grooms with you to serve you. I will not have you go to the sheriff's household in poverty. You will go a man. Have your father's armor polished."

He turned to her and for a moment she thought she saw in his eyes the boy who'd hidden his tears in her skirts when his father beat his sons "to toughen them." But it must have been her imagination, for there was no mistaking the swagger in his walk when he saluted farewell from the doorway.

She had not asked him the other question that had been nagging for so long: where he was on the day the priest was murdered. Months had passed. It probably no longer mattered—except to her. She was already mourning the loss of her son, and a warning bell sounded in her mind. By entering into service with the sheriff, Alfred brought him into the circle of their affairs. And while she had never ridden to the hunt with a falcon on her wrist, she knew a predator when she saw one.

Kathryn sat for a long time in the silence of the great hall, pondering her double loss. Within the space of seven days, two of the three most important men in her life were absent from it. And the third was pulling away. *Christi Eleison. Lord have mercy.*

The crow sat still as well, perching on the ceiling rafters, its beak poised over the nest, as if waiting for the return of the wrens. The slant of afternoon sun pierced the narrow windows, turning its wings to giant shadows that hovered over Kathryn, small and alone in her great oak chair.

TWELVE

She knelt upon him and drew her dagger with broad
bright blade to avenge her son, her only issue.
—BEOWULF
(8TH-CENTURY ANGLO-SAXON EPIC)

pon rising from his bed, skins piled on the floor of hewn poplar (a dirt floor would not harden in the fens), the dwarf poked his banked fire into life, then went outside to relieve himself. Early morning: the smell of hope aborning, the world stretching, not yet fully awake. Here and there, a tentative peep penetrated the hush of nocturnal creatures, yawning into day sleep. He breathed deeply of the mist rising over the swamp. A young ghost of a sun struggled to form itself behind the fog. Half-Tom had seen enough such mornings to know that the sun would win. The day would emerge a fine one, a rare gift for mid-November—Martinmas, the Feast of Saint Martin, November. But Half-Tom kept no saints' days. Neither did he go to church, not even to the splendid new Saint Peter Mancroft, the market church in Norwich, with its raucous bells. He reckoned his calendar by the changing phases of the moon.

With the notches he marked on a willow wand, he kept track of market days, not holy days. A glance at his notched wand showed the second Thursday in November, market day in Norwich. If he left now, there was still time to make it by noon, time to catch the tag end of the trading day. The signs augured a harsh winter; it might be his last chance until spring. He could treat himself to a pint or two. There would even be time for a visit to the holy woman. He thought about the long trek home at night. If need be, he could take shelter in some cotter's haywain until the waxing moon came up. Then he could pick his way home across the white wetlands.

He went inside to get a flat cake and a dried fish for the journey. He'd built his one-room hut from a wind-bent poplar, thatched the roof with reeds from the Yare River. The hut was surprisingly tight, providing protection from the winter winds that swept out of the east. It provided sanctuary, too. His tormentors lacked the courage to follow him into the heart of the swamp. The muddy throat of the fens could swallow horse and rider in seconds, sucking its pleading victims beneath the sand.

The peaty fire, smoking on the hearthstone in the center of the room with its comfortable chair in front, argued against his journey. That chair fit his child's stature perfectly, cleverly fashioned as it was from a curve in the tree where the wind-chiseled trunk looped back on itself. But there would be plenty of time during the long winter nights to sit in front of his fire, plenty of time for weaving his baskets—beehive, stoppered eel, fish kiddles, pole carriers—from the willow rods he'd cut in spring, stripped in summer. Plenty of time for dreaming, too. Time for singing to himself the songs he'd heard from the wandering minstrels who came to the monastery where he'd spent his childhood, songs of the heroic exploits of the mighty Beowulf.

In these winter reveries, Half-Tom's own soul inhabited the great warrior. After he'd eaten his bit of dried fish and drunk his turnip broth, the dwarf would leap about the room challenging the flickering shadows with his willow-stick sword. In his imagination, Half-Tom *was* Beowulf. It was Half-Tom who swore fealty to the Lord Hrothgar, Half-Tom who wielded the flashing sword against the monster Grendel, Half-Tom who sighed with satisfaction when the dagger plunged into the yielding throat flesh of the huge sea troll. He could almost feel the hot spurt of blood. Did it smell like pig's blood? It was Half-Tom, tall, a giant among men, and brave—the scops sang his fame—who tracked Grendel's vengeful monster mother to her swamp lair. It was Half-Tom who "thrust at the throat, broke through the bone rings" of Grendel's mother. It was Half-Tom who watched the steel of his sword melt in the poison of her blood.

In more thoughtful times (for when he was not dreaming wild and wondrous deeds from this other life, he had time for thinking), he spared a care, a bit of human understanding, for the monster. Had not the fickle hand of Wyrd given Grendel a craving for human flesh? Was the monster not, then, blameless? Did fate not make monsters of them all? Monsters did not make themselves. And then there was the mother, fierce in her vengeance, fierce in her love. He envied Grendel such a mother.

"Devil's spawn," some called Half-Tom, and "begotten of a goblin." His soul had been abraded by such words until it was a polished brilliant, hard and gleaming. If God, never the devil—he knew this with certitude because the holy woman had assured him that the devil could not create—if God had left him unfinished, there had to be a reason.

"God hath made all that is made; and God loveth *all* that He hath made," the anchoress had said. She had been so reassuring, so motherly in her affection, in her surety, that he'd come to believe it too.

He grabbed his trident-shaped eel spear and headed down to where the Yare spilled its shallow waters into an oxbow lake. With one thrust of a muscular forearm, he pinned a great pike through its gill to the shallow bottom, then heaved it, tail flailing and splashing, into a willow kiddle. A fine fish for his friend. A fine gift for the holy woman.

❧

At the end of market day, after his second pint of third ale—he was not so rich as to afford first pouring—and after his visit to Julian of Norwich, Half-Tom didn't head west into fen country and home, but north toward Aylsham. He had a message for the illuminator, *his* Hrothgar. This time, he would not give his message to a servant. He'd promised the holy woman that he would place the pages, carried inside his tunic, in the illuminator's hands only.

It was out of his way, a longer journey than from the market home—twelve miles to Aylsham and then two more to Blackingham Manor, all in the opposite direction, and the light was fading. But it was the least he could do. He owed a great debt to the illuminator.

And Mother Julian had been kind to him, too. She understood his needs in the way of no other. She knew about his aching loneliness. What was more, she celebrated his smallness. The first time he went to see her, he'd poured out his bitterness against a God who'd made him half a man in a world that demanded giants. She'd looked at him with compassion in her eyes—so unaccustomed was he to it that he didn't recognize it at first. She'd plucked a hazelnut from a bowl sitting on the window ledge between them.

She leaned forward, held it up before his eyes. "See this, Tom?"—for she seldom called him by the slur that was his name, given him by the monks who found him at their door. "It is a hazelnut. Our Lord showed me a little thing, no bigger than this, which seemed to lie in the palm of my hand; and it was as round as any ball. I looked upon it with the eye of my understanding, and thought, 'What is this?' "

Here, she opened his callused palm and pressed the hazelnut into it, then continued. "Understanding came to me thus, 'It is all that is made.' A thing so small. All creation. A world no bigger than a hazelnut. Safe in Christ's keeping hand. I wondered how long it could last. It seemed as though it might suddenly fade away to nothing; it was so small. And I was answered in my understanding; 'It lasts, and ever shall last; for God loveth it. And even so hath everything being—by the love of God.' "

That had been three years ago, and the hazelnut Half-Tom carried in a fox-skin pouch strung around his neck was as firm and hard and round as when she'd first pressed it into his palm. Miracle enough for him. Let the rich abbots cradle their bones of saints in gem-encrusted reliquaries of hammered gold. This was the only holy relic he needed.

The sun set clear, but cold, as he trudged north, the road almost cleared of pilgrims now. Most had found their journey's end in Norwich, and those few who had not, had sought shelter and would resume their pilgrimages on the morrow. It took a brave heart, or a fool, to be on the road after dark when the brigands and outlaws came out to claim their rights with daggers and garrotes. It was with considerable relief that he saw the last rays of the dying sun glinting off the redbrick face of Blackingham.

He eyed the huddle of outbuildings with a thought to shelter. His nose wrinkled as he passed the tan yard, where the fresh pelts of slain livestock cooked in vats of urine. After he'd delivered his package, he would bed down near the smithy, where the heat from the forge would linger into the cold night. From Aylsham on, the air had been heavy and pungent with smoke from the crofters and yeomen smoking their winter meats, the closer to Blackingham, the stronger the smell. Best to enter through the kitchen. As a messenger for a guest of the house, the cook would be bound to give him victuals. There would be an abundance of meat from the winter kills, maybe he could score a rich mutton stew or a pork pie.

As he approached the kitchen yard, last light picked out a dead tree, its gnarly oak fingers and twisted hollow trunk silhouetted against an indigo sky. A good bee tree, he thought with a sigh, but the honey would have been robbed in late September. There might be mead in the Blackingham kitchen. Sweet-spiced and heady, fermented from the honeycomb wash. Mead and a meat pie.

He patted the packet inside his jerkin and made resolutely for the kitchen door. But he was stopped dead in his tracks. A whisper from the region of the tree. Tuneless, and yet musical. Humming of the bees, perhaps, about to swarm. In November? He approached the tree to investigate. On the hill the heavy twilight softened to light-streaked lavender and the wind had died to that absolute stillness that sometimes comes when the day fades. He seemed to be alone beneath the tree; no other person—at least that he could see. Yet the formless tune grew stronger, more melodious. Angel song. Music such as only the Lord would hear in Paradise. The voice of the Holy Mother? A quaking terror began in his toes and swelled to his head, making it bob foolishly like a jester's mannequin. He moved closer to the tree, drawn forward by the floating music that beckoned, undulating and soft, like a woman's body, that forbidden fruit he'd never tasted except in his dreams (for it was only the overripe or the rotten that would be accessible to the likes of him—and he would have none of them).

His eyes scanned the purple twilight, searching the knoll and the tree. The sound seemed to come from the interior of the great oak trunk. He circled, like a deer approaching the verge of the forest. He touched the rough bark of the tree. Song, undoubtedly a woman's voice, but younger, a girl's perhaps, rose from the bowels of the tree. Not the Holy Virgin. Her voice would come from loftier heights, surely. A witch, then? Some evil spirit, possessing the tree? Half-Tom was not easily frightened. He'd seen predator and prey, witnessed the treacheries of field and fen and violent weather, encountered what he thought might have been the occasional fairy, or was it a dragonfly—who could ever say for sure? But even in the marvels that the dwarf encountered in his childlike acceptance of his natural world, trees did not sing. And this one was undoubtedly singing. In a woman's voice, that in itself a cause for anxiety.

He jerked back his hand, faster than from a hot griddle. Then he turned and fled toward the kitchen, as though the devil nipped at his tired heels.

※

Magda sat, cross-legged, inside the great hollow oak, humming softly to herself. This was a sound that pleased the bees. She didn't know how she knew this, she just knew it. The bees were her friends. The tree was a favorite retreat. She liked its quiet. She liked its small secret room, hidden from the world. She'd entered through a hole at the base, squeezing herself to half-crawl, half-slide between the gnarly roots. Carrying her offering with her, she'd twisted her body into a seated position. This is the way a baby feels inside its mother, she thought. No wonder they all came crying into the world.

Magda liked most small things, small spaces, small creatures. She missed the two little ones that she'd watched at home. On cold nights such as this, she'd hugged her little sisters under her arms in the hayloft where they slept, like a chicken sheltering its chicks beneath its wings. She wondered who warmed them now. And who cared for the ferret for whom she'd filched morsels from her father's table.

It wasn't that she was unhappy at Blackingham. The work was hard, but no more than she could do. And Cook was good to her, even let her sleep with her in her bed on cold nights. She'd plenty to eat and a warm shirt of wool that smelled of herbs. Her old ragged one had smelled like a privy. And wicked bugs lived in it, devil bugs that tormented her. She was glad when Cook had burned it. Now, her skin was pink, and her hair smelled nice, like lavender. And all her scabs were healed. (She couldn't remember when she hadn't had scabs to pick.) Still, sometimes the bigness of the place—so many people, so much emptiness, so many colors—confused her. And sometimes, in lonely moments that sneaked up on her, she ached for the little ones. She had nobody to take care of.

In the shadowy interior she could scarcely see the bees clinging to the wall of the tree-room, a seething mass, a living tapestry, the wings of the outside bees stirring, making body heat, to keep the others warm. She knew that when the outside bees grew cold, they would swap. Such a perfect unity, working together to ensure the survival of all during the winter. Why couldn't people work like that? Probably some reason that she was too dull to understand. She was, after all, a simpleton. Her father had said so.

From the bowl on the ground in front of her, she took two sticks, soaked in honey water, and inserted them gently into the living mass so that the bees could feed. The interior of the mass was as warm as the bed-brick Cook placed in their bed on cold nights. The smell of the pulsing bee tapestry mingled with the earth and wood. But there was no hint of rotten sweetness inside the tree. The worker bees had swept it clean.

The hive was growing. Soon, the tree would be too crowded. Next year, they would drive out the old queen and another hive would be born. She remembered the feel of the bees, gathering on her arms and shoulders like soft wool, when she'd taken the honey last September. That was when the blacksmith had come to kill the bees to rob them of their treasure, but she'd convinced him, with a violent shaking of her head and Cook's help, to let her gather the honey. And save the bees.

"Let 'er have a try," Cook said. "That 'un's got a surprise or two up her sleeve."

The blacksmith had backed away, a gentle giant, smiling and nodding. She knew him well. All the children knew him. He suffered them to hang around his forge, watching his pounding hammer flashing sparks against the anvil. If one of them got a sty around the eyes, he would say, "Come 'ere. Hold this iron rod while I hammer t'other end. When I've finished here, I'll fix yer peeper."

The heat from the forge would force the pus and then the smithy would make a great fuss of wiping it away with some magic incantation.

"She has the gift of charming, all right," the smithy had said, when she gentled the bees and produced the dripping comb from the interior of the tree.

Magda hadn't known it was a special gift, but she'd always known how to take the honey without killing the hive. The bees, like all God's creatures, owed tribute, and they paid theirs in sweet gold. Now, she brought the sleeping workers her tribute in return: a bowl of sticks soaked in water, honey, and rosemary so they could feed during the winter.

She sat with the bees while the evening gathered, thinking about how fortunate she was to have found this hermitage. The thickening gloom reminded her it was time to return to the kitchen to help Cook. It was Magda who carried the meals to the illuminator and his daughter. Lately, the last week especially, they no longer came to the solar to eat with Lady Kathryn. The illuminator seemed cross, out of sorts, and the girl was sick a lot, green and retching. Not really sick. Her father should not worry so. Magda knew why Rose could not keep her victuals down. And she'd figured out why the illuminator's daughter was surrounded by two colors, the pink with an inner rim of light and that light growing brighter, more distinct, as Rose grew sicker. The sickness would be over soon. It never lasted long.

When Magda could no longer see the bees clustered on the brown velvet of the tree wall, she took two honey-soaked sticks from a waxed linen pouch tied to her belt and placed them on the spot where she'd been sitting, a sweet tribute for the bees. Then she hushed her singing and crawled backward from the tree.

She stood up just in time to see a white light, flying low and fast, skimming the ground, headed in the direction of the kitchen. From her position on the hill, Magda could see the kitchen door open, see Cook standing, outlined by the kitchen firelight, gesturing to someone in the purple twilight shadows. As she started down the hill, Magda smiled to hear Cook's shrill voice, her bark always so much worse than her bite.

"I don't care who be chasin' ye. Ye'll not be coming in my kitchen with muddy boots."

Magda's curiosity outweighed her natural shyness, and her feet fairly flew across ground that night cold was already hardening into spiky clumps. She almost burst out with glee when she entered the kitchen. There was a delightful little man, a perfect little man, gulping for air, gesticulating wildly, right there in Cook's kitchen. And he had the most beautiful aura she'd ever seen.

THIRTEEN

inn stood as he worked, easier to catch the ephemeral December light through the slit of casement. From his position, leaning over his desk, he spared a glance, now and then, for the curtain that served as door to Rose's antechamber. He'd ordered his daughter to bed shortly after nuncheon. The kitchen maid had brought a bowl of pottage and a cup of hot spiced cider, but Rose had refused to eat, pleading interest in her work. When the girl had placed it in front of her, like a sacred offering before a goddess, Rose had pushed the bowl away as though the aroma of sage and rosemary offended her.

"My daughter's appetite is fickle," Finn said to appease the serving maid.

The girl withdrew tentatively. She seemed about to reply. Her lips parted and she gathered her breath for speaking, but exhaled silently without utterance. Finn picked up the bowl, warming his fingers against it, wishing his daughter had taken a few bites of the rich, sustaining broth.

"You may take it back to the kitchen," he said, "but tell Agnes it's not the fault of her cooking." He moved his own to the other side of the great desk, out of offending range. "I will enjoy mine later."

The girl took the bowl in one hand, curtsied and dropped her head, then moved to the door with soundless dignity. Hard to believe this was the same dirty urchin he'd seen hiding in the shadows beside the hearth. Finn would have liked to coax her out of her shyness, explore the flash of animation he'd seen in her eyes, but not now. Now, he was more concerned with his daughter. He'd noticed a greenish tinge slide over Rose's face. And he didn't like her pallor, or the smudges darkening the skin beneath her eyes. Maybe it was some mysterious female thing. He wished that he could discuss it with Kathryn.

"Maybe a nap would do you in better stead than victuals, Rosebud." He'd not called her that in a while. He hoped to get a protest of the childish nickname, but she said nothing. "Go on," he said. "I heard you up late last night. I know you didn't sleep. Besides, I've work to do you cannot help me with."

"Yes, Father," she said without protest.

That was unlike her, unlike her, too, to be so quiet or so pale. A malady of the body or of the spirit? He watched her draw the heavy tapestry that separated their chambers—a woman's modesty, too—just one more sign that she was approaching marriageable age. How much longer could he protect her from the implications of her parentage?

From behind the embroidered curtain, he'd heard muted noises, movement, coughing, then silence. Judging by the slant of light, that had been an hour ago. He resisted the urge to peek behind the curtain.

He would use this time to work on Wycliffe's Bible. He had been careful not to involve Rose in this work in any way. He would not add to the burden of his daughter's heritage with his own indiscretions. Even though he could have used her help, for in this instance, he had to be calligrapher, illuminator, and miniaturist all. The former was an art that he'd neglected. Most of the manuscripts he illuminated were scripted by monks in scriptoriums or by copyists in the great Paris guilds. At least, by doing his own calligraphy, the text would be free of the sloppy work done by the Paris artisans. Moreover, the completed work would have an artistic integrity, a balance that was harder to achieve by work done piecemeal.

He tidied up the manuscript Rose had been working on—a Psalter, a New Year's Day gift for Lady Kathryn. It had been his daughter's idea. She much admired the mistress of Blackingham. Finn had noted the wistfulness in her eyes at even the slightest praise from Lady Kathryn and had hoped for a friendship there, at the very least, for his motherless child. How could he have been so besotted?

He forced his thoughts back to the chore at hand. It would be better if he made his own ink for the calligraphy. He'd already bought as much as he dared without calling attention to his illicit project. Though it was not Wycliffe who cautioned secrecy. Wycliffe was, if anything, too bold in his confrontations with the Church. Sometimes caution was the better part of valor.

From beneath the table, Finn pulled out a leathern bucket filled with blackthorn bark that he'd been soaking. This knowledge of inkmaking, like his other artist's skill, was a gift passed on to him by his Flemish grandmother. What a chuckle it would give her, who hated Wales and all things Welsh, to know the arts she taught him as a child would someday constitute his living. She'd been a strong woman, proud and not sparing with her tongue, not afraid to speak her mind, not unlike Lady Kathryn.

Except in this one instance, Kathryn had held back, had not spoken to him of her hatred for his Jewish alliance. Some better angel restrained her tongue. Or perhaps she was too horrified to find voice for her prejudice. But he'd not needed words. He'd read it in the way she averted her eyes, the way she could not bear to look at him.

He carefully strained off the water from the bark, carried it into the garderobe and poured it down the privy, where it combined with the castle wastes that migrated to the Bure River and out to sea. He took the black residue and carefully mixed it with gum from the cherry tree in the garden. He'd tapped the tree in autumn, when the light was warm and golden. Afterward, he and Kathryn had gone to her chamber and made love during the long afternoon. In the garden, the sap dripped from the wounded cherry tree. This image he later juxtaposed in miniature with the crucified Christ onto the pages of Saint John. Cherry-red droplets, flowing from His pierced side. Blood drip, drip, dripping from the wounded tree.

He warmed the glob of cherry gum over a candle flame until it was of a consistency to grind with the blackthorn residue. He tried not to think about Kathryn, tried not to remember that afternoon. Or the afternoon three weeks ago when she'd sent him from her bed. She'd tried to pretend, said she'd send for him after her sons had come and gone. But she had not. He'd seen little of her since. He'd not wanted to see her at first. His sore pride needed a chance to heal, his anger time to cool.

Upon their brief and accidental encounters, she would mumble a formal greeting, avert her eyes and plead busyness: the coming Yule, the feast day celebration for her sons. They would have time together, soon, she'd promised when last they'd met, a chance encounter outside the chapel. *When boars suckle,* he thought. He'd not go to her like a starveling, begging on his knees. To resolve else would be less than manly.

He stirred the ink, then put the mixture aside. His hand was not steady enough today to draw the fine letters. It could wait for a better day, a day when his patience was not stretched threadbare. He would work on something that took less finesse—the gilded background for the border of the text he'd already transcribed.

Somebody had moved his paint pots again. A quick shifting among the colors. Where were the gold leaves? He'd brought the gold back from the market the day he'd bought the pretty shoes with the silver buckles. Had Kathryn liked them? She'd sent him a polite note of thanks. Formal in its wording; "Master Finn, your generosity is gratefully . . ." It was a note such as a great lady might send one of lesser birth. Hardly a billet-doux to be carried near the heart. Hardly the language of love. Had she worn the slippers? With this new coldness between them, he had not the temerity to playfully lift her skirts to see.

His frustration increased as he picked up and rearranged, picked up and rearranged the same color pots, over and again. Still, no gold leaf. Maybe Rose had put it away in the book bag hanging on the peg.

He removed the carefully placed pages of the Gospel of John that he'd already finished. Burrowed deeper past the fragment of English Scripture last worked on, carefully hidden from prying eyes, until his fingers encountered . . . not the leaves of gold, something, several somethings, smooth and round as stones. He pulled his find from beneath the rustling papers. A waist-length string of perfect pearls gathered the meager light in the room and glowed up at him.

From behind, he heard the swishing of the tapestry. He turned to see Rose, her cheeks pinker, smiling.

"I'm sorry to be such a slattern, Father. You must think me a lazy daughter, truly." Her teeth flashed white, the color of the pearls he held in his hand.

"Feeling better now, I hope?"

"Fit as a summer day. I don't know what came over me. Some silliness, I suppose. Don't furrow your brow so. I'm fine. Now, what is this mysterious project from which you banished me?"

She had moved closer now, and was standing on her tiptoes, peering over his shoulder into the book bag. When she saw the pearls in his hand, she gasped. "Father, they are beautiful. Are they for me?" She was already reaching for them. "First, the shoes with the little silver fasteners and now this wonderful necklace. Was ever a girl so blessed to have such a father! Here." She lifted the heavy braid that swung just above her waist, "Fasten them around my neck."

He was so tempted. The excitement brought a bloom to her cheek. She almost glowed.

"I hate to disappoint my beautiful daughter, but I'm afraid—"

"Oh." She let her hair drop. "They're not for me, then."

Her full lips twitched with trying to hide her disappointment. She has her mother's mouth, he thought. He'd never noticed that before. The more woman she became, the more she reminded him of Rebekka.

"Are they for Lady Kathryn?"

"Lady Kathryn? And why would I buy such an extravagant gift for our landlady?" Did she mark the bitter edge to his voice?

The pink in Rose's face deepened. She dropped her eyes. "Well, then, if not for me or Lady Kathryn, why did you buy them?"

"That's just it. I didn't. I was looking for my gold leaf, which seems to have gone missing, when I found this necklace among my manuscripts. I don't know how it got here or who put it here."

His mind groped for possibilities. Some servant had stolen the pearls, maybe, and about to be apprehended, hidden them among his things, hoping to retrieve them later. Or another possibility. He looked at Rose hard.

"Could it be, Daughter, that you have some lovesick swain on the string, some suitor that you haven't told me about, who has made you this extravagant gift?"

"No, Father. Of course not."

So far-fetched was the idea of a lover that she could not even look at him, he thought.

"I . . . I know nothing about the pearls. But I might know something about the gold leaf. Though I'm not sure."

"What do you mean, you're not sure? You either know something about the gold leaf or you don't."

"I think there might have been an intruder."

"You think there might have been an intruder." He tried to rein in his frustration; he did not want to upset Rose. "Well, of course there has been an intruder, if neither you nor I know anything about how the necklace came to be in my possession."

"No, I mean I think I *saw* an intruder."

"You think? Did you *see* an intruder, Rose?"

"Yes. But I thought it was a dream. I saw Alfred going through your things."

"Alfred?" She had his full attention now. "Alfred has been here and you never told me?"

"Only once. And I wasn't sure. I mean, I was asleep. It was that day I was taken ill. About three weeks ago. Lady Kathryn made me some tea, remember, and I took to my bed. I awoke from a deep sleep. I thought I heard a clanging noise, and then footfalls, heavy footfalls, then a door slamming. The curtain was open."

She paused as though she was re-creating the scene in her mind. He waited, nodding encouragement, watching her as she fiddled with the filigree cross he'd given her on her sixth birthday, telling her it had belonged to her mother, telling her to wear it always, thinking it would protect her—not from the devil but from as great an evil.

"I couldn't see anything, but I got up and went to your worktable. Your paint pots were all over the floor. I ran to the door and looked out into the hallway. I saw Alfred, at least it looked like Alfred from the back—tall, broad-shouldered, red hair. I called out to him, but he just stalked away. I felt dizzy, so I went back to bed. When I awoke, the pots were all neatly put away, so I thought that maybe the seed tea Lady Kathryn gave me had made me dream the whole thing. But now I'm thinking it was no dream and that Glynis came in and cleaned up while I slept."

Alfred? What possible reason could Alfred have to plant the pearls? Unless he was doing the bidding of his mother. But surely Kathryn was not angry enough or frightened enough of him that she would try to rid herself of him by accusing him of thievery. What to do next? Should he return the pearls, confront her with Alfred's activity or her treachery? To do so would put a quietus to their already troubled relationship. And what if he was wrong? He would have created an unbreachable gulf between them.

There was a false bottom in the small traveling chest that he kept with him. That was where he kept the Wycliffe papers. He would hide the necklace there until he could think what to do. He must not act in haste. Tomorrow would be time enough.

～※☞

Agnes was sorting through the last of the Norfolk biffins, the little red apples that John had loved so much, when Magda left to take the nuncheon trays. The old cook breathed a silent prayer of thanks to the Holy Virgin for the girl. She was not a great talker, but she was a goodly companion, anxious to please, and one of the few folk Agnes knew that didn't have to be told what to do. Simple she might seem. Simple she was not. The girl had a mind of her own.

The smell of the apples was musty and cidery, overripe. Agnes placed one in her pocket, for later, an offering to be placed on John's grave, when she had time to visit. But that would not be today—nor tomorrow, from the looks of things. The apples should have been brought up from the cellar long before now. Some of them had already gone to rot. So much work to be done, especially with the approaching Yule season. It made her feet hurt and her back ache just to think about it. But 'twould not be as bad as when Sir Roderick was alive, she reckoned. Lady Kathryn would not be expected to entertain so lavishly. She was, after all, still in mourning: Sir Roderick had only been killed in the spring of this year. (Fighting for the Duke was what was said. Agnes had her doubts about that pretty story. More like, he met his death brawling over a woman.) But mourning or not, there would still have to be the usual day of open house for the servants and the crofters, and for the yeomen who served the manor on a paid basis. The board would have to be laid in the great hall with souse and smoked fish, and saffron cakes and mince pies, and of course the little dried biffins.

Such as that was nothing she couldn't handle herself with a little extra help from the village at Aylsham. Not like last Christmas, when Sir Roderick had entertained the duke of Lancaster. Her kitchen had been invaded by hordes of men, barking orders and preening in their green-and-scarlet livery, grinding their pride against one another like knives on whetstone. There had been a prancing caterer in charge of all the brewers and bakers and yeomen of the buttery and pantry and ewer, as well as the two spit boys, who had been hired to roast an ox and a boar and five suckling pigs.

"I'll not be humiliated before the duke with a woman ruling Blackingham's kitchen," Sir Roderick had said. "The fat old cow can confine herself to a corner and cook my lady's dainty morsels."

It had been a part of Lady Kathryn's marriage contract that she would eat no food except that prepared by Agnes. A smart move that was, for many a noble bride had been poisoned for her dowry, especially after producing an heir. Surprisingly enough, most of the time Sir Roderick had been content to have Agnes cook his food, too, and brew his ale without even so much as an extra serving boy; content, too, to be served with the extra hands she could hire, usually women's hands, in exchange for food. Why would he not fear poisoning? She herself had been tempted more than once to flavor his hunter's sauce with nightshade. Was he so sure of his lady's loyalty? Or was it just another token of his arrogance that he considered himself too strong to be brought down by women? Mayhap, having Agnes run Blackingham's kitchens allowed more money for gaming and sport? Except before his noble friends. No. There, he must play the great lord, leaving Agnes responsible for everything, but in charge of nothing.

Sighing for the waste, she pitched two apples into the slop bucket for the pigs. Another she put aside in a growing mound. With the rotten patches cut away, half could be saved and mashed for pies. The firm unmarked ones she cored and placed on a heavy oaken plank, to be pressed with a weight and dried whole in a cooling oven. She looked over her shoulder when she heard Magda returning with the nuncheon tray. The cook pursed her mouth into a frown at the sight of the still-full bowl of pottage.

"Wholesome victuals wasted when the road to Aylsham is full of beggar-women who'd trade a day's labor for something to warm their children's bellies."

"The girl dinna eat," Magda said.

Agnes harrumphed. "Well, I'd be surprised if 'twas the Welshman's empty bowl. Nothing wrong with his appetite. Come to think of it, that Rose has been looking peaky lately." She crossed herself. "God help us she's not carryin' the plague. Ye canna be too careful with foreigners."

Agnes had lost a father, mother, and three older brothers to the plague thirty years ago, but it seemed like only yesterday that the corpse carts came calling, "Bring out your dead." She'd been spared, the only one left alive in her family, because she was in service at Blackingham. That devastation had been brought by foreigners, too. Some said 'twere a group of traveling players; others said 'twere an old Jew what brought the scourge in his carpetbags. For a long time after, there'd been a ban on troubadours, and the old Jew and his family had been burned out, fleeing only with their lives and the clothes on their backs.

"No p-plague," Magda said, stingy as always with her words. "She is with child."

"The illuminator's daughter? Don't be foolish. The girl is a virgin, sure. It's the way of gentlefolk, child. Their women don't go around beddin' the first barnyard lout that comes at 'em with a stiff——"

The girl was staring at her with large round eyes, gray, serene, like a deep cistern of clear water.

Agnes continued, "What I mean to say is she's had no opportunity." She flung another apple into the slop bucket. "That father of hers watches her like a broody hen." She gathered the pile of salvageable biffins into her apron and transferred them to a chopping block, then began to whack away the rotten parts. "Why ever would ye say such a thing?"

"But 'tis true. Her soul has split."

"What nonsense you talk, child."

"Her soul is two colors. Like Mum's, before she births."

What a thing to say! To claim that a soul could be seen, like a hat or a cloak. Two colors, indeed!

"Rose's soul is p-pink." A wistfulness softened the girl's face, making it almost pretty, Agnes thought. "The wee one's soul is like b-butter, all warm and melting around the edges."

Melting around the edges! Still and true, there were more things under heaven than could ever be explained. Mayhap, Magda had a gift. Or a curse.

"Don't ever say that to anybody else, ye hear me, child?" Agnes said in her sternest voice. "Women have been burnt for such careless talk. Whatever it is ye think ye've seen, keep it to yerself. 'Tis probably nothin' save yer own silly imagination."

That was all. The product of a child's imagination. Girls on the cusp of womanhood were known to harbor all sorts of fanciful notions.

Magda picked up the knife laid down by Agnes and began chopping the half-rotten apples. Sighing, Agnes reached for the knife.

"Here, I'll finish the apples. You go fetch the laundress. Tell her I need to see her right away."

⁓⁂⁓

Kathryn awoke and threw back her bedcovers. She took no notice of the cold stone flags against her bare feet as she pulled her shift over her head, stepped into her skirts, and scavenged in her clothing chest for stockings. Glynis scarcely had time to pour water into her basin before Kathryn splashed her face.

"Just run a comb through it, Glynis, and leave it loose. I'll wear a cap. I've no time for elaborate braids." She snatched the comb out of the girl's hand. "You're too slow. Here, I'll do it. You run to the kitchen and tell Agnes to prepare a basket of victuals for the tanner's wife. Tell her I'll need it right away."

"Run" was not a word the girl understood, Kathryn thought as the maid ambled to the door with a sullen expression on her face. No good to chasten her; it would just slow her further. And today Kathryn was in a hurry. There were the household matters to see to, a charitable visit to be paid to a sick tenant—she must not neglect good works, especially now, with so much to atone for—and then she would seek out Finn in his chamber.

Kathryn called to the maid's back, "Come right back. My boots need tending to. They're caked with mud up to the ankles."

Yesterday, she had made her confession. Alone, she'd trekked the two miles to Saint Michael's in the mud and the wind—more penance that way than riding her palfrey—sought out the curate, and told him in the fewest words possible of the sin of carnality (that had been the priest's term, not hers) between Finn and herself. She'd chosen her confessor carefully, confident of his discretion. After all, it had been the tithe from the sale of Blackingham wool that built Saint Michael's. The priest would be reluctant to betray so generous a benefactress over a venial sin.

Her penance had been light enough: twenty Aves and ten Paternosters, followed by an act of contrition—hence the basket of food for the tanner's wife. But it wouldn't have mattered if she'd been told to crawl to Walshingham Shrine on her knees in the dead of winter to kiss the relic of the holy cross. She knew that nothing short of the flames of hell licking at her hem would kill her desire. She feared that even in purgatory she might seek her lover's company and follow him, if such should be his punishment, to the very gates of hell. Would she follow him inside those gates? That was a question she hoped to avoid, though if ever there was a passion worthy of a soul's peril, this was one.

It had been three weeks since she'd sent Finn from her bed, and each time that she'd passed him on the stairs or in the courtyard, she'd seen the question in his eyes; and when she could give no answer, she'd felt the chill growing deeper between them. It wasn't just lust—though she could not quench that fire with prayers no matter how hard she tried. It was his whole self: his easy laugh, his wit, his understanding, the way he seemed to read her thoughts. Each time she saw him now, the cloak of intimacy they'd shared seemed to stretch more threadbare, and the mantle of aching loneliness settled more solidly on her shoulders. When she could bear the loss no longer, she had gone to the priest seeking absolution—and not just for past sins but for those she was bound to commit in the future.

She had confessed to the sin of fornication and nothing else. Not to consorting with one who'd consorted with a Jew. But was not the Saviour Himself a Jew? And would He not take offense that she should spurn one so like Himself? And if our Lord extended His perfect grace even to the Jews, would it not be a sin for her to do less?

And she was entitled to some happiness.

Upon entering the kitchen, Kathryn went straight to the breadboard, cut herself a slice and, placing it on a toasting fork, approached the cook fire.

"Let Magda do that, milady," Agnes said, looking up from the basket she was filling. "Ye should not have to break yer fast by gettin' yer own victuals. I was about to fix a tray, but I stopped to do your bidding. Glynis said you—"

"I'll toast it myself. Like old times, Agnes. Remember when I was but a chit of a girl? You were quick enough then, to hand me a crust and a fork."

"But ye be mistress now. And it's not fittin' for ye to toast yer own bread."

Agnes nodded at the kitchen girl, who tentatively reached for the fork and turned it carefully, browning the bread evenly. When it was golden and crusty, Magda smeared it with currant jam and presented it to Kathryn on a clean napkin. Kathryn noticed that her hands were clean, too.

"This girl turned out very well, didn't she, Agnes?"

"Well enough."

Kathryn chewed the toast in silence and considered the particularly taciturn response from a woman whom she'd never known to be parsimonious with words.

"Are you out of sorts today, Agnes? If you're not well, maybe we can hire the smithy's wife to come in, and you can take a rest."

But not too long a rest, Kathryn was thinking. Not too long, at a penny a day.

Agnes glanced over her shoulder, jerking her head sideways, indicating the door. "Go out to the smokehouse, Magda, cut a rasher of bacon," she said as she placed a crusty loaf of black bread in the alms basket.

"Two rashers," Kathryn said. *Good works. Atonement for sins past. Sins yet to come*. "And cut them thick."

A blast of cold air stirred the ashes on the hearth as the girl shut the heavy oaken door behind her. Agnes chewed on her upper lip. Kathryn chewed on her toast. Finally, Agnes spoke.

"I'm not ailin', milady. But I do 'ave somewhat on my mind."

Kathryn drummed her fingers impatiently on the handle of the alms basket. "If you have a problem, Agnes, tell me about it. If it's about the poll tax, you need not worry. I've already decided I'll pay your tax. It's only fair. You are a good and loyal servant."

"Ye're kind, too good to me, milady, and grateful I am fer it. But it not be about the taxes." She pushed the basket aside to wait for the last offering, the bacon from the smokehouse. "Ye know I'm not one to carry tales . . . gossip being the devil's tongue and all, but . . ." Agnes wiped her hands on her apron, fluttered her hands nervously.

"If it's something I need to know, then it's not gossip, Agnes. Tell me."

Kathryn swallowed the last bit of toast, licked the sweet crumbs from her fingertips. Probably some squabble between the yeomen and the serfs. Rancor was always breaking out over wages paid the former. But maybe whatever it was this time, Simpson could handle it.

"It's about the illuminator's daughter," Agnes said. "She's been finicky lately, and yesterday she sent back her victuals."

Kathryn felt herself relax.

"Oh, I wouldn't worry, Agnes. She *was* ill, but I think she's better now." Poor Agnes, every snotty nose was a herald of the plague. She had an unreasoning fear of the black death. "You know young girls. Probably the vapors. Or maybe Eve's curse."

Agnes pursed her lips, shook her head. "Nay, milady. 'Tis not Eve's curse. The laundress says she's had no bloody linen from the girl in three months."

Kathryn poured herself a beaker of ewe's milk. "The girl may not be regular in her courses. Some are not in the beginning. You know how gossip spreads among the—"

"Aye, I do. That's why I questioned the laundress meself. Regular as the sun sets for three months and then nothing."

"Are you suggesting . . . ?"

"I'm only saying what the laundress says. I thought you should know."

There was the sound of the door scraping open, and Agnes took the smoked bacon from the girl, wrapped it in a clean linen rag, and placed it in the basket. Kathryn picked up the basket and nodded to Agnes.

"This is information best kept between us for now."

"Aye, milady. Ye have no reason to doubt my loyalty." And then, to Kathryn's retreating back: "Give my good wishes to the tanner's wife. Tell her to try the marrowbone broth in the bottle. It'll strengthen her."

Once outside Agnes's discerning eye, Kathryn paused on the other side of the door, leaning for support, hugging the alms basket to her, conjuring an image of Rose, teasing with her father or with Colin, the enchanting smile that reached to her eyes. Was there a woman's knowledge in those flashing eyes? No. Rose was an innocent. She'd bet a bale of wool on it. There had to be some other explanation. After all, hadn't that been why she'd sent Alfred away? At least she thought he'd stayed away. But what if he'd been meeting the girl all along? Meeting her in secret places? "Ask that son of yours," Simpson had said when the wool house burned.

Holy Mother of God.

⸙

Kathryn found Rose alone in Finn's chamber, so engrossed in her work that she didn't even look up. The door was half open to let in extra light from the passageway that joined the master's bedchamber with the garderobe and smaller rooms. Kathryn stepped across the threshold with only the slightest rustle of her slippers against the stone.

Rose sat on a high stool at one end of the desk. She leaned slightly forward, her mouth pressed in a pout of concentration, her hand moving swiftly across pages spread in front of her. Kathryn recognized Finn's sure, light strokes, but executed by his daughter's dainty hand, made to appear even daintier by puffed sleeves and beribboned cuffs. The girl looked as cosseted as any Norman lady. She wore a gold brocade skirt and matching bodice that flattened her bosom until it rose in two gentle swells above the square neckline, a virginal promise of a woman's fuller cleavage. A shirt of fine French lawn matched white horizontal inserts banding the skirt. A flowing scarf of the same finely woven linen covered her head and played peekaboo with her dark hair. Elegant dress for an artisan's daughter. Elegant dress for a Jewess. And there was the cross she always wore. She said her father gave it to her, a gift from her mother. A cross from a Jewess? Or a clever ruse by Finn, a Christian talisman to protect his daughter?

As Rose worked, she hummed a tune under her breath, a melody familiar to Kathryn, floating somewhere on the verge. That and the scratching of the nibs against the vellum were the only sounds in the room. Suddenly, Rose left off singing, heaved a sigh, and gazed out into the middle distance, her quill poised above the paper. Her face looked thinner, almost gaunt around the wide-set eyes; yet otherwise, the girl looked hearty enough. A watery sunbeam, brushing through the leaded window glass high above her, painted a bloom on her cheek. Except for the heightened cheekbones, there was about her a glow of youth that a woman of Kathryn's age could envy—if envy were not a sin.

A draft from the flue drew a current of air across the room from the half-open door where Kathryn watched. The draft stirred the ribbons hanging from Rose's cuff, brushing them against the paper, smearing the carefully drawn letters. She gave an exclamation of dismay and, one-handed, fumbled to tie up the offending streamers.

"Here. Let me help with that," Kathryn said, moving forward.

Rose looked toward the door, a startled expression rounding her mouth.

"My lady," she said. "I'm sorry I didn't know you were there. I mean, I didn't hear you." Rose got up from her stool and went to meet Kathryn halfway. "Please. Come in." She dropped a little half-curtsy, a teasing smile lighting her dark brown eyes. Minx. She knew how uncomfortable Kathryn was with noble pretensions.

"You're hard at work. I can come back later."

Put off finding out the truth. Ignore the problem, and it might go away. But Kathryn was already drawn in, already tying the blue ribbons into perfect bows above Rose's wrists. She gave the last one a little pat.

"There," she said, seeing through a teary haze her own mother making just that same gesture, a mother whose face she could not conjure up even in memory, but whose hands she remembered—long, slender fingers tying blue ribbons into bows.

"Thank you. It's hard to tie them by myself. I'd have to be a contortionist."

"Of course it is. When a girl reaches a certain age, she needs a lady's maid to help her dress. Tell your father that. He can afford a girl from the village. The abbot pays him well enough."

"I've thought about it, but I'm not sure . . . It's always just been Father and me, and I wouldn't want to hurt his feelings. Sometimes Magda, Agnes's girl, helps me. Other times I just keep wriggling until I get everything hooked and tied." Rose laughed, glanced at the cuffs. "Well, almost everything."

She had Finn's high forehead. But the wide mouth, the dark eyes, Rebekka's? Beautiful eyes. How could her son, how could any woman's son, not be tempted?

"Please do come and sit," Rose said, taking her by the hand, drawing her a few feet forward before releasing her. "It is a treat to have your company." A sudden dimming of the smile, like a shade put over a flame. "Though I suppose you came to see Father. I'm afraid he isn't here. He has gone to Norwich market to buy gold leaf. He said he would be back before sunset. Will you sit with me until he comes? I would be glad of the company."

Perhaps she wasn't pining for a lost lover after all, Kathryn thought, but merely suffering from loneliness. Kathryn remembered what that was like, how like a sickness . . . before her children, before Roderick, even, when she had been the only female in her father's household, the only woman, with naught but Agnes for company. Illness, even loneliness or anxiety, could throw a woman off her cycle. It was a fickle and mysterious thing. Especially in one so young. Or in one as old as she. She'd heard stories how women in convents matched their courses so that the whole company would suffer at one time. How in other convents, once they'd married themselves to Christ, the courses ceased altogether.

"It's you I came to see, Rose, not your father."

There was such gratitude in the sparkling smile, it broke her heart.

Kathryn looked for a place to sit. She paused at the foot of the bed, smoothed her skirt in preparation, then stopped herself. Her marriage bed. Roderick's bed. Finn's bed, now. The hangings were pulled back, the coverings neatly arranged. He was the cleanest man she'd ever known. Everything about him, his clothes, his surroundings, even his mind reflected order. So unlike the former occupant of this bed who'd had discipline in nothing. A chill started at her ankles and crept up her spine, raising the hair on her neck. A seam in time's curtain split, the merest glimpse, but she saw for a second, like a flash behind her eyes, the bed as she had last lain in it with her husband: hangings closed, sheets tangled about her limbs, binding, stifling, the pressure of his weight stealing even the stale air, as she lay corpselike beneath him. Her body remembered, too—the violence with which he'd thrust into her and then, cursing, thrust her from him.

"My lady." Rose's voice, bringing her back. "You look unwell. Here, sit on Father's bed. He'll not mind."

The bed was once again benign, neatly made, curtains drawn back, tassel-draped to their carved posts. The air smelled of clean linen, linseed oil, and turpentine, a smell that Finn carried in his clothes, overlaid with a bit of peaty smoke from the fire. She breathed deeply.

"No, I'm fine. Your father might not like me to sit on his bed. I'll choose his work stool, instead."

She pulled the stool across from Rose's own, and they sat facing each other with the scattered sheets of calfskin between them. Kathryn noticed the writing. Something to talk about. She couldn't just blurt out the question that was making her mouth dry, not without dishonoring the girl.

"What are you working on? I see it's what your father calls English."

Rose blushed and hastily shuffled the papers, covering up her work. "Oh, it's nothing to see. A bit of fancy. A Book of Hours for a . . . friend."

Or a present for a lover. Please, Holy Mother, let it not be for my son.

"I'm glad you have your work," she said. "You must get lonely here."

"Well, sometimes. Just a little. When Father is gone." Rose dropped her head and added hastily, "But I like it here. Sometimes, Colin brings his lute and sings for me. He's a good scribe, too. Father says he has a gift."

The familiar melody Rose had been humming. One of Colin's songs.

"I'm glad he's pleasant company for you and your father," she said. "I also enjoy his music."

"I've . . . we've not seen him much of late."

"And Alfred is gone now, too," Kathryn probed.

"Alfred? I hardly ever saw him. Though I'm sure I would have liked him." She added this last apologetically. It was touching how anxious she was not to offend. "It's just that he was always so busy, or with the overseer."

A reassuring answer. It was hard not to like the girl, regardless of the circumstances of her birth. She had her father's charm.

"Well, I rarely see either of my sons. I miss them both. Alfred has gone as page to Sir Guy, and Colin . . . well, I don't see much of him either, I'm afraid. He spends a lot of time in the chapel since the shepherd's death. He talks in riddles, about forgiveness and atonement, as though he carries some guilt that somehow he was to blame. But he won't talk about it. At least not to me. Has he spoken of it to you?"

Rose averted her eyes, raised a trembling hand to her throat. The corners of her mouth worked. "He doesn't have time for anything anymore, not even the music. Not since the fire."

"He'll work it out. He must have been closer to John than I knew. I guess a mother can't know everything about her sons. What about you, Rose? Are you feeling well? Your father has been very worried ever since the night you were so sick. The night I brought you the seed tea. Remember?"

Rose blinked and nodded. "You were very kind to me. Yes, I think I'm better. Though I still get dizzy sometimes. A kind of weakness comes over me, but most of the time I feel well enough." A light little laugh crinkled the corners of her mouth.

Someday, she'd have laugh lines there, like her father, Kathryn thought.

"For weeks I couldn't eat anything, and now I'm making up for lost time. Last night, in the middle of the night, I woke up and I suddenly had the strongest urge for pickled herring. I don't even like pickled herring. It puckers my mouth."

Suddenly, Kathryn's own mouth felt dry as ashes. And it had nothing to do with pickled herring. The girl had cravings. Was she so innocent that she couldn't know what that meant? But of course, what female company, what female counsel had she had to grease her way into womanhood? Kathryn knew what that was like. When her woman's flow—flowers, some called it—had first come upon her, she had seen the wine-dark blood and thought that she was dying. Had thought so for months until she'd gone to her father and told him. He'd grown red-faced and summoned the midwife, who had explained the mystery to her in terms that did not make her welcome her passage into womanhood.

How much had Finn told his daughter? He was gentler than her father had been, but might he not, like her own father, have avoided that counsel usually given by a mother or female relative? After all, he had been willing to ignore the implications of his Jewish marriage for Kathryn and her sons.

"Let us talk frankly, Rose. Woman to woman." She might have said mother to daughter once, but could not bring herself to say it now. "Have your moon cycles been regular?"

Rose looked at her uncertainly.

"Your monthly bleeding, child. Does it come every month?"

Outside, the sun went behind a cloud. The light in the room dimmed, tinting everything gray, except Rose's blush.

"It has been three months," she said. "But there were other times when it did not come. When I was younger. I thought it might be because I was sick."

Silence lay between them for as much as a minute. The sun did not reappear and the room grew cold in spite of the peat fire sputtering on the hearth. Kathryn's temple began to throb. This was not a conversation she wanted to have. This should have been Rebekka's duty. Not hers. Did Jewish mothers handle such situations differently? What advise would the dead Rebekka have given her daughter?

"Rose, it may be tied to your illness, all right, but not in the way you think. It may be the cause and not the result."

"I don't understand." Almost the whining voice of a child, the child the girl had been a too-short time ago.

"You may be . . ."

How else to say it? "You may be carrying a child. The bleeding stops when a woman becomes with child."

The girl looked ready to swoon. She dragged a trembling hand across her face. Kathryn stood up and walked over to her, bent over slightly, touched the girl's chin and tilted it up so that she had to look at Kathryn directly.

"Rose, have you been with a man?" Each word soft, but clearly and slowly enunciated.

The girl said nothing, just chewed on her upper lip, her chin trembling.

"Answer me, child. Have you been with a man?"

Kathryn tried to keep her voice low, so as not to frighten the girl, but it was hard. After all, Alfred might be off the hook, but this was Rose.

"Only Colin."

"I don't mean like that. I mean have you had intercourse with a man? Some knave who may have seen you walking in the garden and taken advantage of you? Even forced you to let him have carnal knowledge of you?"

Rose started to cry, large tears falling in a fountain over the rims of her eyes, running in little streams, seeking their own grooves, pooling in the corners of her quivering mouth.

"Only Colin, my lady."

Colin?

"Rose, do you know what carnal knowledge means?" Kathryn said in exasperation.

Rose nodded, her hands covering her face.

"Does kissing count? We only kissed. Most of the time." She paused. Her trembling fingers began to worry the pretty little cross she wore around her neck. "In the wool house."

The wool house! Kathryn felt the muscles around her heart tighten.

Ask that son of yours about the wool house.

Rose stood up, her skirts knocking the stool over with a clatter, overturning a bucket of steeping hawthorne bark. Both Kathryn and Rose ignored the inky stain creeping across the floor, soaking into the wooden boards. Rose paced, the back of her hand pressed tightly against her throat. She began to sob. Kathryn had to calm her down or she would make herself sick. She put her arms around her and led her gently over to sit on the bed.

"Rose," she said evenly, as calmly as she could, "kissing doesn't count. Now, is that all you did? Did you and my son do anything besides kiss in the wool house?"

Kathryn could hardly understand her. The word was carried on a little sob that escaped around her hand.

"Twice."

"Twice? Did Alfred have carnal knowledge of you twice, Rose?"

She started to cry even louder, nodding her head. "We only . . . twice. But it wasn't Alfred." More sobs, ragged breaths. Rose sniffled into the ribboned cuffs.

"It was Colin." Her son's name sailed out on a hiccup. Kathryn could not have been more surprised if Rose had named the pope. She struggled for breath. Beside her, the hysterical girl rocked back and forth, moaning, "Don't . . . tell . . . Father . . . please," each word jerked out of her by ragged breaths. Kathryn wrapped her arms around the girl.

"Hush, you'll make yourself sick, and that won't help any of us," she whispered as she rocked the girl back and forth, all the while thinking *Colin*. Why had she not seen? But she had. She'd thought them only children at play. "We won't tell anybody, just yet," she said. "Mayhap we are wrong. It's possible, even though you've . . . it's possible you're not with child. We'll wait and see. If you are, well then, there are certain things . . . For the time being let's just try to stay calm."

Kathryn's reassurance had a soothing effect on Rose. Her emotional storm subsided into intermittent whimpers and ragged hiccups, but Kathryn's mind whirled with the implications of the predicament. She knew her reassuring words were as empty as hell's cisterns. She knew, too, there was no time to lose. She would go to the midwife right away. There were special concoctions . . . but first she must speak to Colin. Colin!

She'd promised Rose she would not tell Finn. Better that way. Less complicated. He would be in a rage to learn that her son had deflowered his daughter. Would probably insist that the marriage banns be published immediately. After all, he'd given up everything for the sake of a Jewess; would he not expect her son to do the same? But a son of Blackingham would not marry with a Jew. Not as long as she drew breath.

She pushed the disheveled girl away, held her at arm's length.

"Dry your eyes, Rose. Go to your room and rest. Unbind the curtain lest your father come in and see his pretty daughter in such a state."

It would never do for Finn to see his daughter so upset. He would worm the truth out of her as easily as a fat friar breaks wind.

"I'll send you up a soothing cup. Try not to worry. We'll think of something."

FOURTEEN

Foreasmuch as the Bible contains Christ,
that is all that is necessary for salvation;
it is necessary for all men, not for priests alone.
—JOHN WYCLIFFE

inn approached Norwich from the north. From his vantage above the city, the market unfurled like a corded ribbon streaming from Norwich Castle, massive, hulking, ugly, no longer a military fortress but a prison where souls languished in dungeons. In spite of its creamy veneer of Caen stone glowing golden in the sun, it cast a menacing shadow, looming over the colorful market stalls like a buzzard hunched on a hill. Finn shivered and drew his woolen cloak tighter.

The lower end of the castle bridge led to an outer courtyard where the livestock market was held. A knot of onlookers had gathered there, beneath a scaffold. Finn knew what the attraction was. Such events were always timed for market days, when they could be sure to draw a crowd. Even from this distance—he would venture no closer; he had no stomach for such things—he heard raucous laughter. If he'd only been a few minutes earlier, he could have missed the spectacle altogether. But now it could not be avoided. He'd already seen the rope being placed around the doomed man's neck, and now

Finn, try as he might, could not avert his eyes. The faceless crowd moaned with one voice, a moan that rose to a keening crescendo. The trapdoor opened. Finn held his own breath as the crowd exhaled in one great collective sigh of near ecstasy. He felt the muscles in his own torso twitch as the body arced, then jerked intermittently before coming to swing at the end of the rope like a side of meat. Thank the Holy Virgin he was not close enough to see the bulging eyes, the purple lips protruding from the swollen face. He pulled his horse's bridle to the right and turned his own head away, too late to avoid the rising nausea.

Poor sod, he thought, as he wiped his mouth on the back of his hand and urged his horse forward. Probably some rebellious peasant who'd spoken too loudly and too articulately against John of Gaunt's new poll tax, the second in three years. Strong price to pay for speaking naught but the truth. His severed head, eyes pecked out by birds, would soon adorn a pole at a city gate, a warning to others. Truth-telling was a hazardous business.

With the castle behind him, Finn's gaze now rested on the city's other architectural wonder, east of the market. Norwich Cathedral, like Castle Prison, glowed mellow in the afternoon light, and to Finn it was only slightly less menacing. However, he had to admit it was a more pleasing structure to the eye. Its Norman square crossing tower was imposing, though spireless. A hurricane had smashed the wooden steeple to toothpicks in 1362, destroying a portion of the apse in the process. Finn smiled, remembering Wycliffe's calling the hurricane "God's wrathful breath."

The cathedral's apse had been rebuilt by Bishop Despenser's predecessor, but other priorities superseded the building of the spire. The cloisters needed rebuilding, too, and a wall to protect the Benedictine monks from rioting villagers. The monks had been burned out earlier, in 1297, by a mob of villagers angry at the Benedictines, whose priests sometimes withheld services, even the Eucharist, pending an offering. *They sold the body of our Lord for a penny so they could purchase permits to keep their concubines*, Wycliffe had told him. Not much had changed in the almost hundred years since, Wycliffe had said. Finn had agreed with him there.

Rebuilding the cloisters was an ongoing process. As Finn's horse picked its way along Castle Street and up toward Elm Hill, he saw stonemasons laboring there, heard the slapping of plaster and the scraping of stone as they dressed the sturdy Norwich flint with the more pleasing imported stone from

Normandy. Their curses—against the plaster hardening too soon in the frigid air, against their own blue fingers numb inside their open-fingered gloves—mingled with cries of birds flushed from their nests inside the stone ribs of the cloisters.

When he reached Elm Hill, Finn dismounted in front of the Beggar's Daughter, with its sign promising a frothy tankard—God's Blood, how he could use a frothy tankard. He flicked the reins of his horse to a beggar boy he'd seen before.

"A ha-penny and a pork pie if my beast is here when I come back."

The ragged urchin scooted forward, grabbed the horse by the bit and led him to shelter in the narrow space between the buildings.

"Old Scratch hisself couldn't get him from me, milord." He saluted smartly with a vigor and energy that belied his circumstances.

"It's not Old Scratch I'm worried about," Finn said.

He admired the boy's enterprise. He'd seen him hustling before—running errands, cleaning up for the vendors in the market, anything to earn a bit of bread. There were dozens of such boys, in spite of the fact that it took a lot of ingenuity for a beggar to stay out of the stocks. Even someone giving charity to beggars was subject to imprisonment. They were mostly runaways from the leasehold, living on the city's refuse, hiding within its walls until they could become free. And there was plenty of refuse here. Elm Hill was the narrowest street in Norwich. An open sewer running in a gutter down the center of its cobbled street made trafficking treacherous for man and beast. But aside from the weekly market, it was Norwich's premier commerce section. Rich wool merchants and Flemish weavers lived in some of the larger town houses, with their warehouses spreading out behind them down to the river. At the street's other end, the houses of shopkeepers and guild masters perched on top of businesses and shops, leaning higgledy-piggledy into the street, giving it the feel of a labyrinth. It was a labyrinth a boy and a horse could disappear into if the temptation should offer.

Inside the tavern, Finn sat next to a grimy window that afforded him a view of the lad and his horse. The boy saluted him again and gave a cheeky wink. Finn saluted back. His horse would be there when he wanted it, Finn was certain.

Finn had come to Elm Hill to buy pen nibs. But first, he'd have a little something to warm his bones and wait for Half-Tom, who was to meet him there with a packet from Wycliffe. He didn't have to wait long. From the farthest corner of the bar he heard drunken laughter from a group of five men, huddled together in a circle. The ringleader, the man closest to Finn, with his back to him, wore the livery of Castle Prison.

"We could string him up, see if 'e'll swing as wide as t'other one."

"Naw. 'E's too short. No sport in that. He'd just twitch like a little piece o' fish bait."

General laughter.

"Well, then, let's see how high we can pitch 'im."

A flash of an arm and then a ball of rags hurtled toward the ceiling, bounced off one of the beams, and somersaulted through the air before landing. It came down just outside the circle, flattening out as it landed, then bounded up onto two legs, miraculously undamaged. Half-Tom. The dwarf ran for the door but an arm reached out and grabbed him, drawing him back inside the circle.

Finn reached for the dagger in his boot. Moved toward the circle.

Inside the circle, Half-Tom flailed and cursed and attempted to bite the arm that held him.

"Blimey, 'e's a tough little whelp. But a twopence says 'e'll splatter this time."

Finn approached the circle. By and large, they were a motley lot. Playing to the bully more out of fear than love of the sport, and some blood lust maybe brought on by the execution. He'd seen it before: ordinary men, who might at other times be caught in an act of kindness, turned into wild dogs sniffing a scent. Feigning interest, he looked over the shoulder of the prison guard, drawing back ever so slightly as he saw a louse making its progress through the man's greasy hair. Finn pressed the point of the dagger to the man's back, just below the rib cage, pushing hard enough that it would penetrate the leather jerkin.

"Why not let the dwarf go, friend?" he said pleasantly enough, but pressed a little harder so the guard would feel his intent.

The man's head jerked around to see his assailant, his body going rigid as he felt the dagger pierce the coarse linen of his shirt. His grip on Half-Tom relaxed just long enough for the dwarf to twist free and sprint for the door.

Finn put one hand on the shoulder of the guard, while he held the dagger firmly in place with the other.

"Your friends here probably feel like celebrating that they're not the ones swinging at the end of Castle Bridge."

"What business be this of yern?"

But there was a false bravado in his tone, and Finn saw the furtive gazes of his companions as they tried to assess this new development. He would make it easier for them.

"Publican, bring a round of good ale for my fellows here and put it to my account."

A tall, weary-looking yeoman shrugged and moved away first. Then, one by one, they began to drift away to claim each a tankard from a tray offered by the landlord, who looked much relieved. The tenuous bond was broken and the circle of dwarf-baiters drifted apart, avoiding one another's gaze. But it's not over yet, Finn thought as he eyed the burly knave at the end of his dagger whose sport he'd spoiled.

"How about it, friend? There's a tankard there for you."

Before he'd even gotten the words off his lips, the man had twisted around and grabbed for the knife, but he miscalculated and grabbed the blade instead. Screeching like a scalded cat, he drew back his bloody hand.

At just that moment, Half-Tom appeared in the doorway with a bailiff in tow, wearing the scarlet insignia that marked him as one of the sheriff's minions.

"The little man here says ye're breaking the king's peace." Frowning, he surveyed the room. "Should've known ye'd be in the middle of it, Sykes."

Reinforcements. But still, they could all wind up in the stocks. "No trouble, bailiff," he said. "I assure you the king's peace is as intact as ever. I was just showing my new dagger to the guard here when he dropped it, and trying to keep it from falling, he cut his hand."

One by one, the other revelers gulped their drinks and sidled toward the door. One of them had the courtesy to raise his empty tankard to Finn on his way out.

"See. Everything's in order. Just ask the landlord."

The landlord nodded. No doubt, he'd reason enough to be wary of the king's justice. The bailiff, apparently not completely convinced, kept his hand on the hilt of his small sword.

"I was just telling Sykes here that he'd better see to that cut before it goes putrid," Finn said, as he cleaned the guard's blood from his dagger.

"I'll be seein' to it awright. I'll be seein' to it. Ye can count on it."

But despite the glowering looks and implied threat, Sykes wrapped his injured hand in a bit of rag the landlord provided and stumbled for the door. The bailiff moved aside but only slightly, forcing the guard to turn sideways to get past him.

"Every bloody time there's a hangin'. Never seen it fail. And usually Sykes is right in the middle of it. I'd stay clear of him fer a while if I was you. The man's got a mean streak as wide as an old fat whore."

"Thanks, but my friend and I"— here he nodded at Half-Tom, noting the surprise on the bailiff's face—"my friend and I will be gone before Sykes is in any shape to make trouble for us."

After the bailiff left, Finn ordered food for himself and Half-Tom.

"Are you sure you're unhurt? That was a pretty hard fall."

Half-Tom's wide grin split his round face into two half-moons. "I've learned a trick or two in me time." He tore off a chunk of bread and stuffed it into his mouth. Chewed vigorously, then continued, "Mostly I stay out of places like this, or I run, but when all else fails, I curl myself into a ball and draw my head inside my jerkin. See, like this."

Immediately, the little man's head seemed to shrink inside his body so that he resembled a large tortoise just emerging from its shell. Finn couldn't help but laugh. Far from being offended, Half-Tom seemed to enjoy the joke himself. He took a bite of onion, another bite of bread, and swallowed before adding, "And I allus wear two shirts when I'm coming to town. Makes good paddin'."

"Very resourceful."

"Yeah, but don't always work. Once I got three broke ribs. By my reckoning I'd not have come out so easy this time if you'd not been there to save me bacon."

Finn waved his hand as if to say no thanks needed. "If I'd been there at the agreed-upon time, your bacon would not have needed saving. Do you have something for me from Master Wycliffe?"

Half-Tom reached inside his shirt, untied a strap, and pulled out a leather-covered packet. "This was another bit o' paddin'. The papers are in here. Master Wycliffe suggests that you should be discreet." He said the unfamiliar word gingerly, rolling it around on his tongue first. "He says the archbishop has painted a target on his back."

"You spoke with him, then?"

"Aye. He was at Thetford to speak to the synod of bishops, just like you said. I sneaked in with a troupe of players who entertained them at meat. A couple of cartwheels, a handstand or two. Master Wycliffe pretended to send me on an errand and then gave me this packet like it was my pay."

"Did you give him the completed pages?"

"Aye. That was the errand he supposedly sent me on."

"Was he pleased with my work?"

"He only gawked at it real quick-like. He offered a purse."

"Did you tell him what I told you?"

"Aye. I told him that you said the work was . . ." He paused, rolled his eyes back in his head. "Gratis," he said with a swagger, obviously proud of his new vocabulary.

"And his response?"

"That you would get your reward in heaven."

"That's good enough, I guess. Did you tell him, too, that I would try to make an extra copy of his translations as time allowed?"

"He said . . . I can't remember what he said, but the gist was that the more people who read the Holy Word for themselves, the more they would see how the Church is fooling them."

Finn nodded. He'd read the translation as he worked on it, and found it fascinating. He'd never read the Gospel of John in Latin. He'd only gotten its meaning from sermons and plays and snatches of memorized Latin. He'd believed it because he'd been told to believe it. But Wycliffe's translation showed a different Lord from the one the priests talked about. Oh, the suffering was there, but so was joy and love, so much love, the kind the anchoress talked about. *For God so loved the world* . . . That was all there was, Finn thought. But that was enough. If you believed it.

"Can you read, Tom?"

"Monks tried to teach me, but I couldn't understand the Latin. If I could read the Bible for myself, well, might be worth the trouble." He grinned. "Now that I'm a messenger, it'd be easier than having to remember all them fancy words you're always sending."

From outside the window, Finn saw the boy who held his horse stamping his rag-wrapped feet to keep them warm. It was time to go. He ordered a pork pie and bought a warm blanket from the landlord, saying he might need it before he got home. If the boy didn't have a bed, he'd at least have a blanket this night.

✧

Finn was not to be spared the death mask of the hanged man, after all. Who was the dead man? Poacher, petty thief? Or maybe truth-teller. All hanging offenses. So easy for a man to lose his head—cross the Church or cross the king, he thought. A caution sign for him. Did the fact that he was illuminating the Wycliffe texts make him part of the Lollard movement? Not illegal. Not yet. What angel or devil had prompted him to align himself so hastily? And for what purpose? He didn't think about heavenly rewards that much. Or the flames of hell. It just seemed the reasonable thing to do. He liked the idea of it, every man reading the Scripture for himself.

As he left the city by Wensum Street, there, on the pole at Cowgate, was the wretch's head, or what was left of it.

✧

Kathryn mounted the three stone steps—one for the Father, one for the Son, and one for the Holy Ghost—leading to the thick-flagged roof of the crypt, which also served as the chapel porch. The living prayed above the bones of the dead. Her first task was to find Colin and see if Rose's story was true. And where else would he be but in the chapel? It all made sense suddenly: the incessant prayers, the unseemly grieving for a serf's death, the porcelain face gone thin and hollow-eyed.

It might have been a lamp kicked over in the heat of passion. Or a guttering candle they left behind. Or Rose and Colin might have had nothing to do with the fire at all. But Colin had always been devout. Had the carnal sin he'd committed with Rose festered in his innocent soul until his own guilt heaped on an extra measure of blame?

She listened at the chapel door. Silence. The door creaked on its iron hinges. Inside, the air was stale as though the room had been sealed for hours. The altar was empty. A sense of dread crept down her spine when she saw that the sundial on the wall indicated time for vespers. Colin had always kept vespers, even before the fire.

She left the empty chapel, and closing the door behind her, leaned on it for a minute to get her breath, to think. Colin was just worn out with praying, that was all, and was probably sleeping in his room, his blue-veined eyelids twitching in troubled dreams. She would go to his room, wake him, find out if his story matched Rose's. If it did, then she would tell him everything would be all right. She would send him on some errand, maybe to Sir Guy, with a message for his brother. That would divert him and buy her time to think. It wasn't that Kathryn didn't understand the need for atonement. But her cherished child, with his angel's voice and his gentle ways—he should not be the one to pay. He'd never hurt anyone in his life, had not even torn her when he was born, slipping from her womb in his lustier brother's bloody wake, like an afterthought.

Her father, and the mother who died when she was only five, slept beneath the chapel porch on the place where she was standing, next to Roderick—opposing, not beside. And opposing both, at the head of a triangle, a place waited for her. She'd planned it carefully: Alfred and his family completing Roderick's side, Colin and his bride making the line to her parents. Now, even that was spoiled. But Kathryn was resolved. When the trumpet of Judgment sounded, no Jewess, with the blood of Christ dripping from her shapely hands, would rise from Blackingham to indict her son.

Colin would not yet know about the baby. Whatever guilt he suffered was for his carnal act, that, and the shepherd's death as the assumed consequence. Rose could not have told him; she had not known herself. If confronted with the fact of the child now, she knew what her son would say. Thinking he could take Rose for his bride, he would answer any charge with protestations of love. And when he learned the truth of Rose's birth, would he do what Finn had done for Rose's mother—give up everything because he was bewitched by a Jewess? Bewitched. Maybe the girl wasn't as innocent as she professed to be. There were stories aplenty about Jews who practiced the black arts—if they could turn lead into gold, it would be a simple art to seduce her Colin. Then she remembered the look in Rose's eyes, a frighted fawn stumbling into a peopled meadow. No. The girl was no enchantress, just a maid whose innocence had failed to protect her. But innocence never did. Innocence was flax for a devil's loom.

Laughter, easy banter from the stable boys warming their hands by a courtyard fire drew her attention. Finn was back. She'd hoped he wouldn't return until the morrow. She needed to talk to Colin before Rose blurted out the truth to her father. She wasn't sure the girl could be trusted not to tell him, despite her agreement to wait, especially if she saw him now, with the new knowledge of her condition smarting like a fresh wound.

"Finn," Kathryn called.

He looked up and around, searching for the source, then fastened his gaze on the chapel porch.

"Agnes baked today," she shouted as she hurried down the three stone steps, her skirts whipping around her. "Your favorite. The *pain demain* you like so much." White bread, made with finest flour. A nobleman's taste. There had been so many clues she'd overlooked. "You should get some while it's still hot from the oven."

They were still a few feet apart. Her pace slowed, preserving the distance. He looked up at her, shielding his eyes from the dying sun with his hand. She had a momentary longing to rush to him, be comforted by him. But she'd find little comfort there if he knew the truth.

"I think I need to wash the city from me first," he said.

Her mind whirred like a mill wheel. He would go to his chamber. Rose would be there, fresh tears still staining her cheek. If Kathryn could just detain him, the girl might be abed by the time he went to his room, and they might be able to buy another day. A day to visit the old woman who lived in Thomas Wood, maybe secure from her some concoction—or even a spell—well, no, not a spell, too dangerous, but a mixture of some wild herbal substance, some virginal restorative for Rose.

"Go to the kitchen and tell Glynis that I said to heat some water for a bath," Kathryn said. That should be incentive enough. He bathed more than any three men she'd ever known. Was that something his Jewish wife had taught him? The ostler had gone inside the barn, leading Finn's horse. She lowered her voice. "Tell Glynis to carry the water to my chamber. I'll join you there after vespers." Would he wonder at her sudden piety, her desire to pray alone in a chapel where no priest said the office? "You can chat with Agnes over a mug. Tell her I said to pour the French wine she's been hoarding."

He hesitated, ran his fingers through his gray-streaked mane that her own fingers twitched with wanting to touch. Had she lost the power to charm him?

"We need to talk," she said.

"I'm too weary to do much else, Kathryn."

There was hurt in the look he turned on her, and mistrust. She felt a momentary pang for the deception, but had not he deceived her first? She reached for the leather satchel.

"You don't need to go to your chamber. You might disturb Rose. I think she's resting. She's been working very hard on some task you've set her. My husband kept a change of clean linen in my garderobe." She heard a vestigial longing in her voice. She hoped he heard it too, and would read a promise there.

"*Pain demain,* you say? With honey?"

"With honey. Still warm."

"Don't pray too long," he said, a bit of the old tease returning.

"Here. I'll take that satchel and place it on your worktable." She touched his sleeve in a half-stroke before taking the scrip from him.

"Now, go. Before your bread gets cold."

She passed his chamber on the way to Colin's, tiptoed in and placed the leather satchel in the center of the worktable. The curtain to Rose's alcove was drawn. No sound. The soothing tea she'd sent up was working.

Now, for Colin.

But Kathryn saw, to her dismay, that Colin was not in his chamber, and his bed had not been rumpled. He could not have gone far. His lute lay on the lone chair in the corner. She'd never noticed before how plain he kept his quarters, how cell-like. She lifted the lute and strummed it. He'd taught her a few notes, once, a long time ago. But her anxious fingers would not hold the strings.

Finn would be waiting for her, might become impatient and seek out his daughter—she returned the instrument carefully to its chair. A piece of parchment fluttered to the floor. She stooped to pick it up. She recognized Colin's fine script.

She had to read it twice before her mind could comprehend its meaning.

Her first thought was to go after him, bring him back. She could send Finn. She could guess which way he'd taken. Not to the Norwich monks, or even Broomholm. These would be too close to home. West, maybe, to Thetford, but more probably north to Blinham Priory, to the Benedictines, the wild lonely cliffs of Cromer, desolate, isolated.

But, if she brought him back, he would find out about the baby, and he would marry Rose. It wouldn't matter that she was a Jewess. That would just make his atonement more complete in his eyes.

No, better this way, she thought, as the tears began to flow. Better this way, for now. She might not have the strength to send him away, even for his own protection. This way he would never have to know about the baby, would never have to make a choice. He was too young to take a monk's vows; he would be a novitiate for years. Time enough to bring him back after she'd sent Finn and Rose away. She would keep Blackingham safe for him. For Alfred, too.

One day they could both come home.

She sat for a time on the floor, rocking herself back and forth until the room grew dark. In his note, he said he would dedicate himself to God, his hours to prayer. He said he was going to take the vow of silence. Little Walshingham and the Franciscans? It would help if she could just know where he was. The music in his voice hushed forever. She could not bear it. The room was almost in total darkness now. She must pull herself together.

She tucked the note carefully inside her bosom and stood up. Finn would be waiting for her.

FIFTEEN

He (God) suffereth some of us to fall more hard and more grievously than ever we did before, and then we think—for we are not all wise—that all we have begun is brought to naught. But it is not so.
—JULIAN OF NORWICH, *DIVINE REVELATIONS*

inn lingered over his supper to give Lady Kathryn time to return from vespers. He chatted with the cook, telling her of the hanging at Castle Prison, of the tension building in the city. She complained of the poll tax.

" 'Tis the second one in three years. Thank the Holy Virgin, Lady Kathryn agreed to pay mine, but now there's me girl to pay for." Agnes waved a stirring spoon in the direction of the scullery maid, who was scouring a kettle with as much concentration as he would have given the mixing of a crimson wash.

"If Lady Kathryn paid your husband's head tax," he said between bites, "she'll be no more out of pocket for the girl's."

Agnes nodded, doubling her ample chin, but the creases on her brow showed she was less sanguine. "Aye, but that was before she lost the wool in the fire. Last time, she paid for crofters as well. But there's only so much juice in a turnip, and I'm afeared when the king's uncle has squeezed all the juice, there'll be a riot."

"The threat of a noose is a powerful silencer."

"Not when ye figure a rope is quicker than starvation."

Finn agreed to the simple wisdom of that statement and pondered it as he made his way up to Kathryn's chamber, though he soon banished it for more personal thoughts. He'd had enough of crime and punishment for one day.

He tapped softly on the door of Lady Kathryn's chamber before letting himself into the empty room. The room was dimly lit against the gathering gloom by a sputtering fire and two rushlights, and in front of the fire sat a tin tub whose bottom was barely covered with water, no more than five fingers' worth. Finn tested the water. Tepid. Not enough to chase the cold from his bones but sufficient to remove the travel stench. He disrobed and folded his body into the tub. A draft from the flue caused him to shiver, and he winced as his back touched the cold tin. He rubbed his arms for warmth and looked down at his shriveled manhood. Maybe this wasn't such a good idea after all. His body had never yet failed him when desire was awakened, but there was always a first time, and he was no longer a young man.

As he scrubbed his gooseflesh with Saracen's soap, he heard the clatter of horses' hooves and the raucous barking of stable curs drifting up from the courtyard, muffled by the heavy wall hangings of Kathryn's chamber. Pilgrims, probably, seeking hospitality against the frigid December night. He knew they would not be turned away, but would be allowed to spread their bedrolls—some in the great hall, some in the stables—depending on their social standing. The Norwich beggar boy who'd held his horse outside the tavern stalked across his mind, giving him another cheeky salute, another wink and grin. Who would pay his head tax? What could the king's bailiffs extort from him—the ragged shirt off his back, the blanket Finn had given him—and where would he sleep tonight?

The soap was fragrant, mingling its own lavender scent with the earthy smell of the peat fire. It reminded him of Kathryn, the smell that lingered in her clothes, her hair, the enticing hollow between her breasts. Thoughts of Kathryn awakened a familiar stirring. Good. The blood was warming. If he'd read her right—and one could never be totally sure when a woman was concerned—there had been a promise of reconciliation in her eyes. She must be as eager as he to end the coldness between them. She had made the first move.

One of the dogs in the courtyard below yelped as though it had been kicked. Loud voices, unintelligible words, muted by the tapestries and closed window, followed by raucous laughter. Then, pounding on the door as though with the hilt of a broadsword. Boisterous, for a company of pilgrims.

He sluiced the lather from his shoulder with cupped hands, dried himself with the scrap of linen, and stepped out of the tub. Kathryn had said something about her husband's smallclothes. He eyed a chest in the corner but reached for his own mud-stained garment. He'd not stoop to wear Roderick's clothing. Frowning, he brushed at a spot on his tunic.

"Open up! We demand to see the mistress of the house!" Voices loud enough even the dead sleeping in the crypt could hear them.

"Open by command of the king! Serjeant-at-arms."

Kathryn's softer voice, her words not clear but her tone indignant, carried up the stairs.

Finn hitched up his leggings and pulled his shirt over his head as he headed for the door. He did not stop to pull on his boots and was halfway down the steps when he remembered that he'd left behind his dagger. For Kathryn's sake, he could ignore the cold floor on his bare feet, but the dagger was another matter altogether. He turned back, leaping the twisting stairs two at a time.

≈≈≈

Sir Guy rode into the courtyard just as Lady Kathryn opened the door. Well-timed—he'd known he could depend on his lout of a serjeant to conduct the business churlishly. All the better. That meant he could play the mediator and not the perpetrator.

The serjeant was shoving the widow roughly aside. "We don't need your permission. We have orders to search this place."

Sir Guy pitched his reins to a stable groom, dismounted and rushed forward, barking at his men-at-arms, careful that his voice would carry to Lady Kathryn's ears. "Clumsy fools! You insult this noble house and its lady at your own peril."

He jerked his head sharply left, indicating that his men should wait outside, and inserted himself between Kathryn and the serjeant. He reached for Kathryn's hand—"Please pardon their insolence, my lady"—and placed her hand to his lips. He held it thus a moment too long, tried to keep the temper from his countenance when she withdrew it abruptly.

"Sir, by whose authority is the peace of Blackingham broken?" She stared first at the serjeant, then at Sir Guy, as though she knew his gambit all too well.

Her posture irritated him. He'd noticed that arrogance in her demeanor before and wondered why Roderick had suffered it. He would not when he was master here.

The serjeant, his perplexity showing in his face, answered. "By authority of the king and his lordship the high sheriff." This last trailed off in a question. Sir Guy ignored the uncertain glance directed at him.

"I beg your pardon for this intrusion, my lady. It seems this business is being ill-conducted. I thought as much. I left a meeting with the bishop to attend you."

"You are well come, Sir Guy. But your words, and the arms your men would bear into a lady's house, suggest this is not a visit between friends."

"A visit, alas, no. But friendship, truly, on my part"—here he bowed stiffly—"if I may be so bold as to presume." He started to reach for her hand again, but thought better of it. He closed the door, shutting out the cold and the serjeant. "As the widow of my dear friend, I feel a certain responsibility toward you, my lady. I hope you know that I can be relied upon to look after your interests in this and all matters."

"And just what *matters* might these be?" The voice, a man's voice, came from behind him.

The sheriff recognized the illuminator as he stepped out of the shadowed stairway to his right. A pesky fellow. A horsefly buzzing about the ear. Best not to swat him now. Let him settle so that he could get a square blow.

He directed his answer to Kathryn to imply that the illuminator was not worthy of a response.

"Something easily satisfied, I assure you. A mere formality."

"Please, sir. Speak plainly," Kathryn said.

The sheriff nodded. "It is the matter of the dead priest."

Was it his imagination, or did her spine stiffen even more?

"Dead priest?"

"Father Ignatius. The bishop's legate found at the edge of Blackingham last summer with his head bashed in. You almost swooned when we brought the body into your courtyard. Surely, you have not forgotten."

"Not a sight easily forgotten. It pains me to remember it now."

Indeed it seemed to. She had gone quite pale.

"Pain the lady should be spared," the illuminator interjected. "Lady Kathryn assured you at the time of the body's discovery that she had not seen the priest. I heard her say it. It was the day I arrived at Blackingham."

"Ah, was it indeed? I had not remembered. Thank you for reminding me."

This scrivener was like a horsefly circling a dung heap. Patience. An untimely swat, and the sheriff might end up with excrement on himself.

He directed his remark to the lady. "As I was about to say, the priest's unsolved murder weighs heavy on the bishop's mind. It has been six months. An inventory has been found that would suggest the priest visited Blackingham. In spite of my lady's denial."

He chose his words carefully, well enough to frighten her so that his intervention would be that much more appreciated. She held one hand—the hand she'd withdrawn from his lips—at her white throat. She gave no response.

He continued. "Although I've done my best to assure His Eminence of your complete innocence in this, the bishop demands a search. My men will do a cursory inspection of your outbuildings and kitchen. Whilst I, with your permission, my lady, will accompany you on a tour of the manor house."

To punctuate his words, he gave her his sincerest smile: the one in which he arranged his face to say, *You can trust me for I am loyal and not self-serving;* the one he'd practiced before the bishop that very morning, the one he'd used to gain his lucrative position as sheriff of Norfolk. He touched the ribbons on her shoulder, ignoring her recoil.

"Together, we can easily satisfy the bishop."

He tried, too, to ignore the fact that she was looking past him, at the illuminator, as though asking him what she should do. He wanted to put his hand on her jaw and crack her skinny neck like a chicken bone. The illuminator nodded at her. God's Blood! If only the cursed insect would light within range.

She said, "Very well, you may proceed. But you will understand if I do not offer you hospitality, since the nature of your visit is official."

He remembered the day of the fire and the shepherd's death. Blackingham hospitality was something he could forgo. Still, he marked the slight, tallied it in a mental ledger to be settled at some later date.

"And please, ask your men not to treat other members of my household with the same discourtesy to which they subjected me."

Another tally mark in the ledger.

"Your household must be questioned, my lady. The bishop would settle for no less than a thorough investigation. You must understand, with no one to speak in my lady's behalf, the cloud of suspicion—"

"Innocence needs no advocate but the truth."

"If one wishes, like our Holy Saviour, to be martyred for truth. But you have two sons. Would you have them martyred also?"

Color flooded her pale face, and he knew he had shot home.

By now they had entered the solar. He was aware of Finn following on the periphery. Still there. Buzzing, just out of reach.

The sheriff opened a chest that served as table, stool, and storage, rifled through the plate and linens, ran his sword between the wall hangings and the bricks they covered.

Kathryn stood rigidly by, like a sentinel at an unpleasant post.

"Just a quick look in the sleeping chambers, and then we're done," he said.

She waved her hand toward the stair passage that led to the private rooms. "My chamber is at the top. My guest and his daughter occupy the room you will remember as Roderick's chamber. My sons' rooms are at the other end of the passageway. If you need to question my steward, I will send for Simpson . . . ?"

"That will not be necessary. The item in question is of a personal nature. But if you would be so good as to call Colin. I will speak with Alfred at my leisure."

He thought he detected the briefest hesitation before she said, "Colin is not here." She paused for a longer breath, then, maddeningly again, shifted her gaze to the insect illuminator. Obviously, Kathryn was no longer addressing him.

"Colin has gone on pilgrimage," she said to Finn. "He joined a band of pilgrims who came through earlier in the day. Just an interlude, a respite, he said, to pray for . . . he feels responsible for the shepherd's death. He and Rose had been using the wool house to . . ." Her gaze wavered as though she was in distress. "To practice the lute. It was to be a surprise for you."

The sheriff might as well have been an empty suit of armor propped against a lintel post. There was a pleading quality to her tone, a softness that suggested intimacy between the lady and the artisan. They were lovers. He'd suspected it before, but had thought she would not stoop so low. It simply was not to be tolerated. The prospect of Lady Kathryn—or any lady—with such a simpering pretender disgusted him. Yet, knowledge of this despicable alliance might give him leverage to use against her in future.

"I shall speak with Colin later, or I can send my men after him now," he said. "But perhaps neither will prove necessary. Now, if we can proceed. We will examine Master Finn's quarters first so that he shall be free to continue his work."

"But why his quarters if not Simpson's?" she asked.

"I'm only carrying out my orders. As Master Finn reminded me, he was present at the time of the priest's murder. But what was it you said about innocence needing no advocate? I'm sure your illuminator has nothing to fear."

"My daughter is resting. She has been ill," Finn said. "I will not have her frightened by your rogue's tactics."

"Rogue's tactics? You misspeak, sir. The sheriff of Norfolk is not ungentle with *gentle* women and *innocent* children. Please, precede us into the room, if you wish, to prepare your daughter."

He had no real suspicions that a search of the illuminator's quarters would turn up anything, but it was pleasant sport to harass him.

As they followed Finn into Sir Roderick's former chamber, now transformed into an artisan's workroom, Sir Guy was struck by the neatness of it. The girl, the illuminator's daughter, stood in one shadowy corner of the room. She was pretty, he thought idly, but not of Norman blood, he noticed again—probably a by-blow begot on some infidel—and her eyes were red and swollen as though she had been crying. Lady Kathryn went to stand beside her. An enigmatic look passed between them.

The sheriff pulled back the covers of the large carved bed, used his sword to empty out a large chest, as though its contents might be dirty, leaving Finn's carefully pressed linen lying in a rumpled heap. He rifled through a few paint pots, leaving them also in disarray, carelessly overturning one, then apologizing with a variation of his practiced smile, glancing at Finn to measure his discomfort.

"The pigments are expensive and paid for by the abbot of Broomholm," the illuminator said.

Sir Guy tried not to laugh, but the irritation in the illuminator's voice was so gratifying. In an attempt to provoke him further, Sir Guy stirred the neatly stacked pages. The candles in the wall sconce above the tables cast a flickering light across the sheets of calfskin. "You do passing work, Illuminator. I might allow you to do a book for me."

The illuminator said nothing.

Sir Guy measured the width of the chest with his eye, tapped it on the side with his sword. Ah, a hollow sound, then denser. The chest had a false bottom. He nodded to the serjeant, who turned it upside down and pounded. The wooden lining slipped out, emptying its contents onto the floor. Papers fluttered down in a shower.

"Please, sir, my father's work—"

The illuminator shook his head to silence his daughter. Sir Guy bent to retrieve some of the papers from the top of the pile, more out of curiosity than courtesy.

"Hmm. What's this? A text from Saint John? Not very colorful. I thought you did better work than . . ." He stood up, moved closer to the wall sconce to examine the papers in the light of the flame, his eyes squinting with the effort. "Saint John in English! The profane text of Wycliffe." The smile that broke out on his face was not contrived. "Master Illuminator, the abbot would be interested to know he is not your only patron." Then, more to himself: "The bishop might be interested as well."

The horsefly was buzzing closer, hovering, almost in reach.

He shuffled the papers beneath the light. "*The Divine Revelations of Julian of Norwich*. And in Midland doggerel, too. The bishop should also know how his holy women spend their time."

Sir Guy knelt to explore the rest of what was turning out to be a treasure trove of useful information, information he could trade for the bishop's favor. Henry Despenser's goodwill had lately been withheld because the priest's murderer had gone unpunished, and the bishop was probably feeling the archbishop's wrath. This little morsel might distract him. Henry Despenser hated John Wycliffe and his Lollard preachers with a visceral fury. Mayhap there was more to be mined in this innocent-seeming pile of script.

His hand touched something hard and smooth and round beneath the pile of papers. He picked it up and, gloating, held it up to the light, where it glowed creamy and luminous.

The insect had landed.

It was a string of perfectly formed pearls, the same pearls listed on the inventory of the dead priest.

SWAT!

Lady Kathryn stared at the necklace. It was the one that had belonged to her mother. The same one Father Ignatius had squeezed from her on the day his skull was cleaved in twain.

"My lady's pearls, I believe," the sheriff said.

He held the sword out to her, the necklace dripping from its tip. How did he know it belonged to her? And why the look of exultation? Was he so eager to gain evidence against her? His eyes, usually the dead gray of lichen in winter, gleamed like wet stones.

"'One string white pearls, perfectly matched, one black pearl in center clasp.' That's what the dead priest's inventory said. I believe these are they."

"Mine, yes. I don't deny . . . but, how came they to be . . . ?"

"Exactly so, my lady. How came they to be indeed?" His voice was low, each word drawn out in menace. "How came a string of pearls listed on a dead man's inventory to be in the possession of Master Finn? That's a question our illuminator will have to answer for the bishop."

Rose emitted a small cry. Finn drew his distraught daughter into a half-embrace. The sheriff gloated. The necklace had been the object of his search all along, and to find them in Finn's quarters, a man for whom he nursed an obvious antipathy, was gratifying indeed.

"Truly, there is some mistake. I know Fi—— I know the illuminator well. He has not the temperament of a *murderer!*" She reached for the pearls, more to assure herself that they were not an illusion than to reclaim them.

The sheriff retracted the sword just out of reach and caught the pearls in his left hand. They drooped between his fingers. The black pearl, in its gold-filigreed clasp, glinted in the torchlight. No one moved.

A slice of moon rose through the narrow window behind them. A small cloud floated over it. No one spoke for a long moment until voices, loud, gruff, from the men below, set them back in motion like players in a mystery play.

Sir Guy unlatched the mullion pane and shouted down, "Call off the search, Serjeant. We've run our fox to ground." With a serpent's grace, and just as swift, he flashed the tip of his sword at Finn's throat. "Come on up and bring the shackles."

"No! You can't." Rose clutched at Finn's sleeve with fingers white at the knuckles. "My father would never hurt anyone! Let him go!" Her face was the color of whey. Kathryn feared she might swoon.

"She's right, Sir Guy," Kathryn said, her voice rising. "In spite of how it looks. There's a mistake, I tell you. This man is no murderer. There's another explanation. There has to be."

"My lady, your affection, dare I say *ardor*, makes you shrill. Of course his daughter pleads his innocence. What other explanation can there be? Here is the evidence that offers proof. Proof, too, that your ladyship was less than honest in former testimony. But that's a fact which, now that we have our culprit, need not gain scrutiny."

His condescension and his insinuation infuriated and frightened her.

Finn cleared his throat loudly. "There is another explanation," he said. "The pearls were planted in my bag by an intruder. I found them two days ago."

The sheriff hooted in response. But Kathryn grasped for this explanation as readily as a child grabbing for a silver rattle. He could not be so calm with the sheriff's sword at his throat unless he could prove his innocence, could he? She wanted to ask him why he had not mentioned finding the necklace, but held her tongue lest drawing attention to his silence contribute to his appearance of guilt.

"It's true," Rose insisted, her pallor even more ashen. She held on to her father with both hands, tugging at his arm, seemingly oblivious to the threat of the blade should either of them make any sudden move. "Somebody else did place them there. I saw him."

"Him?" the sheriff asked.

She glanced at Kathryn and then at her father before answering defiantly.

"It was Alfred. The young lord of Blackingham."

Did she say Alfred? "Alfred! Rose, why would you even suggest—"

"Let the girl finish. I will not have it said that the sheriff of Norfolk rushed to judgment."

"It was the night I was ill. The night of the shepherd's burial. I was sleeping. I awoke to the sound of someone in Father's chamber, going through his things. I pretended to be asleep because I was afraid. I knew it wasn't Father."

"How did you know it wasn't your father? And with your eyes closed, how did you know it was Alfred?" the sheriff asked.

"He walked with the gait of a youth. My father's footfall is more steady. As he passed my entrance, I saw through a crack in the curtains that he—" Rose paused, tossed Kathryn an apologetic glance. "He had red hair."

Kathryn could tell by the way Sir Guy screwed his features into a mask of concentration, as though testing the weight of her testimony, that even he was half-inclined to believe her. If Kathryn was frightened before, now she was terrified. First Finn, now Alfred. Surely God would not make her choose between the two. To choose between a man she knew to be innocent and a son whose innocence she was less sure of.

Had Alfred in his youth's intemperance killed the priest because she'd complained about his greed? Was her son capable of such a thing? He was Roderick's son too, a thought that did not plead his innocence. He could have planted the pearls in Finn's room as a prank or out of jealousy.

But how would he have come by the pearls if he'd not killed the priest?

"When I heard the intruder leave, I got up and ran to the door." Rose had stopped crying, reassured by the sheriff's attention to her story or by the need to concentrate. "It was Alfred that I saw retreating down the hall. I came back into the room and saw that my father's paints had been disturbed, and that his worktable was in disarray."

"Did you cry an alarm?" Sir Guy was all interrogator now. He had lowered the sword. Although it still pointed at Finn's midsection, it no longer made contact with his body.

"No, I felt dizzy, so I lay back down to wait for Father. I must have gone to sleep. When I awoke, the room was back in order, so I thought that I had dreamed it all until Father found the pearls in the bag." She blushed, bringing two unnaturally bright spots to her ashen cheeks. "I thought he'd bought them for me."

"But you didn't actually see Alfred put the pearls in the bag," Kathryn interjected.

"Perhaps I have been hasty," the sheriff said. "Lady Kathryn, as chatelaine of Blackingham, have you knowledge of any intrusion into the illuminator's quarters? Do I need to question your son in this matter?" He looked at her directly. "Or can you give surety for his movements during the time in question?"

He knows what he's asking me, Kathryn thought. Give testimony against the one and the other goes free. He's delighting in it. She hated the hawk-nosed sheriff.

Kathryn heard heavy boots on the stairs, the sound of the shackles dragging against the stone steps. She read the pleading in Rose's eyes, felt the same pull to sympathy as when she'd learned of Rose's dilemma. Her dilemma, too. Finn's arrest would buy time. Time to question Alfred herself, time to let him escape, if he'd murdered the priest to protect his mother. Time, too, to purchase some concoction from the old woman in the woods to uproot the seed that Colin had planted.

If Rose's story was true—Heavenly Mother forbid—if Finn had found the pearls two days ago, why had he not come to her? It was not up to her to decide his guilt or innocence. It *was* up to her to protect her sons. And the bishop would not condemn an innocent man. She would pray daily, hourly, to the Holy Mother in his behalf. If Finn was innocent, he would be freed in time. And time was what she needed now.

She could not look at Finn or his daughter as she betrayed them both. She looked out the window at a piece of cloud eating the moon. "I'm sorry, Rose, but you had to be dreaming. Probably brought on by the seed tea that I gave you as a physick."

The serjeant crossed the threshold, pausing inches away from Finn.

Kathryn heard the lie as it slipped from her lips. Her words. Her voice as in a dream. "Alfred was with me the entire evening. I was upset by the loss of the wool and the barn . . . and a valuable servant. Alfred stayed to comfort me." It had not been her son who gave her comfort—such a brazen sinful lie—but she could not think of that now. "He slept on a cot in my chamber."

A grin cracked the sheriff's face. He nodded at the serjeant, who stepped forward and began to place Finn's wrists in irons. Kathryn opened her mouth to call back her lie but nothing came out. Rose gave one long shrieking "No" as the serjeant peeled her arms from her father's neck.

"Rose, it will be all right. Don't worry," Finn said. "It will be all right."

The serjeant shoved Rose, and she sank onto the bed. Kathryn wanted to go to her but couldn't move. She could feel Finn's gaze on her, his eyes burning like blue flame, charring her flesh, melting her bones until her lying, shriveled soul lay exposed like the hideous black lump that it was.

Outside the window, the wedge of moon had disappeared, eaten by the cloud. The night was as black as pitch.

SIXTEEN

*Westron winde when will thou blow? The small raine
down can raine; Christ, if my love were in my arms,
and I in my bed again.*
—14TH-CENTURY ANONYMOUS LYRIC

Blackingham hosted no celebration for its sons to mark their sixteen years in the year of our Lord 1379. Nor was the remnant of last year's Yule log brought out to kindle a new one. "'Twill bring ill fortune upon our house," Agnes said, "not to hang the green and light the Yule fire."

Her mistress merely looked at her and hooted in derision. "Ill fortune, you say. What have we left, you and I, old woman, that we should fear ill fortune?" Agnes liked neither the bitterness in Lady Kathryn's voice nor the fierce look in her eyes, liked even less the unkempt manner of her dress.

It had been twelve days since the sheriff took the illuminator away in chains, twelve days without word of his fate, twelve days in which her mistress had not changed her clothes or bound her hair. Glynis reported that she had been barred from milady's presence, "after she threw a hair brush at me, nearly blacking me eye." The slattern told the tale to all that would listen, in spite of Agnes's warnings that she should keep her trap shut. People in the village were talking enough. In answer to nosy inquiries about the lack of Yuletide festivities, Agnes retorted, "My lady is suffering from the ague and is too ill to preside over open house, but has instructed her kitchens to provide a feast. 'Twill be held in the great hall as usual and all are welcome."

That preening overseer would be more than happy to preside. He loved putting on airs and playing lord of the manor. That would hardly make a festive atmosphere, but what else was to be done? It was unworthy of a noble house to be niggardly at Yuletide. Even during the plague, Kathryn's father had spread an adequate if doleful board for his serfs and yeomen and crofters.

But Lady Kathryn had no interest in preparation for a feast of any kind. She had ridden off into the woods for the third time this week whilst Agnes labored in the kitchen, trying to plan a semblance of a Christmas banquet out of ordinary fare. Each time, her mistress had come back hours later with some noxious concoction stirred up by Old Gert—never mind that it was heresy to consult a witch. Not that Agnes believed the old woman was a witch, just an aged crone selling her herbs and potions to eke out a meager existence. Herbs and potions that usually didn't work. At least they hadn't worked for Agnes. Not a twit. Twelve years ago, she'd scraped together enough courage to go to Old Gert for something, a spell, a potion—she didn't really care—anything to open her plugged-up womb. The only thing she'd gotten from the devilish brew was a noisome biliousness.

'Tweren't working for Rose either. Crying and retching, crying and retching was all the poor girl did. Either from fear for her father, or the burden in her belly, or as a result of the crude pills the girl choked down to please Lady Kathryn. "You want to be healthy when your father returns," Lady Kathryn would say.

"Do ye know what's in that?" Agnes had asked last time when Rose had gagged on the odd-shaped pill. " 'Tis as big as a robin's egg and as stinky as a rotten 'un."

Kathryn had shot her a warning glance. "Just a physick of ordinary herbs."

Ordinary herbs, Agnes thought. Mixed with hazelwort and birthwort and larch fungus and spikenard and heaven knew what other vile thing Old Gert might have thrown in. Agnes knew what her mistress was up to. She wondered if Rose did. But so far, the girl had not expelled the contents of her womb—only her stomach.

Lady Kathryn would be back from her ride any minute. Agnes checked the boiling pot on the hearth, then glanced out the window. The great hollow oak—Magda's honey tree—was casting its cold shadow halfway down the hill, all the way to the cisterns. A groan of metal hinges as the door opened—the inside latch was never placed until vespers. That should be Lady Kathryn now. Good. There was enough hot water for whatever noxious brew she might demand.

Lady Kathryn slammed the door shut behind her, as though punishing the oak and the iron. She had so much anger in her. Agnes had only seen her that way once before, when her father had forced her to marry Roderick. That time, she had not eaten for two weeks but had eventually given in for the love of her ailing father. These last few days, Agnes had pondered over the source of the present anger, pitying the poor wretch who might feel its full force. At first she'd feared it might be the girl. But though Kathryn had sometimes been impatient with Rose, she'd seemed to exercise a gentle restraint.

"Agnes, grind these into a fine powder and mix with boiling water."

Agnes took the small basket of marsh-mallow roots mixed with milfoil, fennel, and dwarf elder.

"How much water? Is it to be an elixir?"

"No, just enough water to make a plaster."

Agnes sighed. Poor Rose. She would sleep tonight—or not—with the malodorous plaster blistering her belly and her privates.

Pacing, Lady Kathryn covered her face with her hands, massaged her forehead. "I'm at the end of my tether. If this doesn't work, she'll just have to bear the child and then we'll see what is to be done."

Agnes didn't even want to think what that might mean. She crossed herself and shivered, noticing for the first time that the woman she'd tended since a slip of a girl was growing old. Her white hair—turned thus when she'd not seen thirty summers—had never made her seem old. It was usually bound into a halo of light around her head. Now it lay in a tangled, ratty mass down her back, dragging down the muscles in her face. The skin on her cheekbones was stretched so taut it looked as though the bone might prick through its thin white tent.

"My lady, 'twould not be the first child at Blackingham to be born on the wrong side of the blanket. And I dare say mayn't be the last. What's the harm? The girl is pleasant enough, not lazy, and she could be company to ye. She and her babe could stay on."

"It's not that simple."

"Well, nothing ever is, is it?" Agnes ground the herbs in her mortar and pestle. The effort punctuated her words with little puffs of air. "She could at least stay until her father gets out. Can't think why they took 'im in the first place. I know human nature. And Master Finn is no killer." She ladled water from the simmering pot on the hearth. "Have ye any word from him?"

Kathryn shook her head.

"Does Finn know who the father of the baby is?" Agnes asked, trying to sound matter-of-fact, as though it were not a matter of grave importance.

Lady Kathryn dropped the metal bowl with a clang.

"That is not your concern, now, is it?"

Never mind. Agnes knew who the father was, all right. Who else but young Colin? The two of them were ever together, playing like children. Now Rose was breeding and young Colin had gone "on pilgrimage." The ways of nobility were hard to fathom sometimes. Why couldn't he just marry the girl?

Lady Kathryn put the bowl on the table. Agnes spooned the hot paste into it. The paste would need to be applied before it cooled and set.

"Be careful not to blister the girl's skin."

Kathryn gave no response, but threw other words over her shoulder as she exited the kitchen through the butler's pantry, "I have sent word for Alfred to attend me. He'll probably come here to your kitchen first. They all do. When he does, send him to me immediately."

As fading footfalls echoed on the stairs, another thought occurred to Agnes. Could it be that Finn didn't know about the babe? That would answer in part for Lady Kathryn's urgency. If Gert's potions worked, the illuminator might never have to know. Women's plots—too tangled for most men to unravel. She chewed on that for a minute, and then another, bleaker thought intruded. If 'twere to be the hangman's noose for the illuminator, it might even be a kindness to let him go to his grave in ignorance of his daughter's plight.

❧

Alfred did not come to Blackingham that day. But the dwarf did. Like everybody else, he always came to Agnes's kitchen first, but she knew it was not for something warming on her hearth. There was a simmering of another sort going on—she'd noticed it in the sly glances he gave her Magda and the funny little way the pointy end of his nose glowed pink whenever she was around. Thank the Holy Virgin, this day she was not. She'd gone with a basket of victuals to tend her broody mother.

It wasn't that Agnes didn't like Half-Tom, but she wanted more for Magda than a dwarf from the fens, and that made her unusually brusque.

"Be ye not a little far from yer swamp on this wintry day, Half-Tom? If ye've come to Blackingham with a message for the illuminator, he be'int here."

She didn't offer him a drink, as she had the first time he appeared at her door, looking for the illuminator with a message from the holy woman. If he hoped to find hospitality here now, he would find it of a grudging sort, only in kind and proportion as Christian charity demanded. She busied herself with plucking a brace of partridge and did not look up.

"I know," he said, shaking his head with a doleful expression. "I heard talk in Aylsham. A wicked business 'tis, too. They've not the brains to find the priest's killer, so they pin it on an innocent man."

Agnes responded only with a harrumph that communicated nothing. She'd learned long ago to keep counsel with herself in dangerous matters. Besides, she didn't want to encourage him in anything that might lengthen his stay until her Magda returned. Her girl so needful and eager to return love.

The dwarf warmed his hands at the blazing hearth.

"You go on, Agnes, I've a packet for Finn from Oxford. And I'm pledged to put it only in his hands. That being the matter, I thought I'd stop to see if Blackingham has any message for him. All upon the occasion, of course, that I can get into Castle Prison."

Yes, and then ye can carry it back, she thought. And soon enough, ye'll have excuse to traipse back and forth, back and forth from Castle Prison to Blackingham on the pretense of carrying messages. It was well out of his way from the fens. He had to turn left at the crossroads and go north to come to Aylsham, when he could save daylight and shoe leather by going straight to Norwich. She watched his eyes, set wide in his full-moon face, as they searched the corners of the cavernous kitchen. She knew what he was looking for.

"There'll be no message from Blackingham going to the prison," she said.

"Shouldn't that be my lady's decision?" His voice was deep, husky, like his powerful shoulders, all out of proportion to the rest of his body.

"You're an impudent fellow. Mistress already told me." Her fingers plucked the feathers from the birds so fast they bunched in her hands. "She's angry with the illuminator for causing her to harbor a fugitive."

"But she cannot think him guilty!"

"His guilt or innocence is not a matter for her to decide. If the law says he's guilty, then he's guilty."

"Well, what of his daughter? Surely she——"

"The illuminator's daughter is too ill with grief to see anybody."

The lies piled up like the feathers that she swept into a great sack hanging beneath the table to be saved for ticking. "If 'tis news of Blackingham ye wish to carry, ye may tell Finn his daughter is being cared for by Lady Kathryn herself and that no harm will come to her because of him. Now, ye'd best be off, little man, ye've a long trek to Norwich. Here. Take this for yer journey." She slid a pasty filled with pork and mashed turnips down the length of the long deal table. "I'd not take time to eat it here if I was ye. The light will not last in winter."

He looked at her with eyes that seemed to read her—too well. Then, picking up the pasty, he nodded his thank-you and waddled to the door. He walks like a fat-breasted bird, she thought. He'd already lifted the bar and put his shoulder to the heavy oak—she'd be rid of him before Magda came back—when, to her chagrin, she heard words that made him pause in his leave-taking. Words coming out of her own claptrap mouth.

"When you see the illuminator, tell him Agnes will say a Paternoster for him." 'Twas more than was prudent to say. But she couldn't stop herself. She remembered with a pang how Finn had sat in her kitchen last, telling her about the hanging, how it had sickened him. She remembered, too, how he always seemed to be worrying about the plight of common folk. Then there was that quick grin he'd give her in that flirty way whenever he asked for some special treat or an extra glass of ale. She an old crone and he a man still in his prime. A kind man. A rarity.

"Tell him that, for what it's worth, old Agnes knows he's no priest-killer."

A broad grin split the dwarf's face.

"If I've any news, I'll report it to ye on me way home."

Agnes brought the meat cleaver down hard on the back of the birds, making the brace a quadruple in one powerful stroke. The heavy door slammed shut, creating a draft that raised a lone brown-tipped feather to float in the air. It landed on the hearth and, singeing, released its acrid odor into the air. With a practiced hand she gutted the birds and flung the entrails into the slop jar.

Colin had been gone four days, and he wondered if he was any closer to Blinham Priory than when he left. Sun on the right at daybreak, he reminded himself each morning when he set out, but for the last two days there had been no sun, only a cold, gray dawn with no redeeming stain of pink. He'd taken the byroad through the forest, thinking that if his mother pursued him, she would take the high road, probably south to Norwich. He half hoped she would follow him, bring him home to Blackingham, home to Rose, assure him it had all been a bad dream: that the fire had never happened, he had never sinned, never deflowered a virgin. But he knew his mother would not think to seek him on this bracken-pocked trail marked by criminals and feudal refugees.

Colin knew about the dangers of the road from eavesdropping on Agnes and John. As a small lad, he'd been often in the kitchens, underfoot, ignored by Agnes except when he got in her way. He went to the kitchen for the marzipan the indulgent old cook gave him. He lingered to hear the stories John told his wife about the camaraderie that existed among these outlaws of the wood. "It's not the hard life ye might think, Agnes. There's a kind of brotherhood. And 'twouldn't be forever. A year or so in the woods until Blackingham gives us up, another year and a day inside a town, and we'll be free, Agnes. Free."

Colin had known what he meant, even then. But he'd not told. He knew the shepherd would be punished. He didn't want to see him whipped or put in the stocks. And now John was dead and Colin was on the outlaw road. All because of the fire that he and Rose had caused. They had not meant to leave the lantern in the wool house; he wasn't even sure they had. But there was no other explanation. Unless the fire was a sign from God that they had sinned in that place and God had breathed His fiery breath on it as He had done on Sodom and Gomorrah. Either way, the fire and John's death were his fault. Not Rose's. He'd been the seducer. He'd be the one to atone. So, if he was lost and alone in the forest while she slept in her feather bed, if he fasted while she feasted, then that was as it should be. His suffering would buy her redemption. Still, it was hard to pray for her here, hard to beg for John's soul, hard even to think about God when he had to think so much about finding a place to sleep.

He'd been lucky last night. At twilight, he'd stumbled upon a rough plank shelter hunched beneath a big oak tree like a giant mushroom. An abandoned hermit's hut? An outlaw shelter whose inhabitant might return at any moment, accusing him of trespass? But John had talked about the brotherhood of the forest. Maybe the rightful owner of the shelter would take pity on him and offer him hospitality, maybe even share a crust with him. Finally, Colin had fallen asleep on the rush-strewn floor, grateful to be out of the wind.

He dreamed of Blackingham.

He dreamed of Rose.

He woke at daybreak to the sound of a lone calling bird, brushed bits of rush straw from his clothes, then, when all the straw was gone, kept right on brushing for the warmth, stamping numb feet to start his curdled blood flowing. A hen, sitting a nest in the gable of the rafter, set up a loud ruckus, clucking and fluttering down from the low crossbeam. Colin reached up over his head and swept the nest. One egg. While the hen clucked her outrage, he cracked the egg and sucked its contents, careful not to spill a drop. It gave a pleasant, albeit too brief, respite from the gnawing in his stomach. He eyed the hen with purpose, but she flew up to the top of the rafter just out of reach. Just as well. To steal an egg was one thing, the producer of the egg quite another. Though he hoped the hen would stay out of reach to remove temptation. He'd not eaten since yesterday, when he'd gleaned a withered apple from beneath a pile of leaves. And he'd encountered no members of John's brotherhood. Indeed, although he often felt as though he was being watched, he'd met no other soul on this road.

It had snowed during the night, two inches, judging from the size of the white stripes that drifted between the thatch and the rough boards. He emerged from the hut and surveyed his surroundings. The world looked new. He stretched and breathed deeply; it smelled new, too—and so silent he fancied he could hear the breathing of the foxes sleeping in their dens. Time to go. But which way? No footsteps in the virgin snow, and now the half-trail had disappeared. Sun on the right at daybreak. But there was only a pearly, silent mist. The boy shrugged and headed south—in the opposite direction of Blinham Priory.

When he came to a main road several hours later, it was well past midday and he'd seen no other soul. His footfalls made no sound in the snow, except for the occasional crunch of a brown twig or cone that echoed alarmingly in the quiet. The whole forest slept beneath a down blanket. The numbness in his feet had spread into his calves. He inhaled the sharp smell of bruised pine and wiped his dripping nose on his sleeve. It had begun to snow again, and he longed to sit, but feared if he lay down in the snow he might not get up. So when he came to the wide road, although he knew it meant that he was off course, he almost cried with relief. To his dismay, he soon found this road to be as empty as the forest—no pilgrims or peddlers abroad on this wintry day—but at least, if he kept trudging, he might come to a barn where he could rest. And, if he was lucky, there might be another nesting hen.

At mid-afternoon, although he saw no signs of civilization, he smelled the smoke from a peat fire. The snow was falling harder now, and he didn't know how much longer he could go on. He was almost past it—the landscape was erased by the swirling snow—when he saw a long pole extending from the header of a cottage door. The sign of an alehouse. He'd once been to such a place with his brother. There would be food and drink for sale, he thought excitedly, before he remembered he'd not a farthing to his name. At least, he could warm himself by the fire.

As he crossed the innyard, he heard boisterous laughter. A gaudy wagon loomed, larger than life, in the small yard. He'd seen that kind of wagon before, a flatbed cart tented with colorful awnings that could be removed to form a stage. It probably belonged to a troupe of players who had gone inside. All the better. He could slip into a crowd, unnoticed, maybe glean a scrap of bread. The discarded trenchers the dogs ate would stop the gnawing in his belly.

Colin opened the door tentatively to shouts of "Shut the door. Y'er lettin' in the bleedin' cold."

He fastened it quickly. "Sorry." He ducked his head, so the publican would not see how young he was. Alfred would have bluffed his way. Colin was too self-conscious of his boyish, and unkempt, appearance.

"Over here, landlord," a voice shouted from the dim interior.

Grateful for the diversion, Colin leaned against the door, took a minute to get his bearings. The air was thick with peat smoke and the smell of birds roasting on the spit. His stomach clutched with hunger pangs. He squeezed behind two jugglers, one slight and wiry, one more muscular, who were arguing good-naturedly among a knot of brightly clad performers. As he warmed himself by the fire, trying to ignore the sensation the smell of the roasting meat created in his belly, he listened with half an ear.

"The dowager made me a gift of this velvet tunic. 'Twas to show 'er appreciation for my *silken voice*." This from a preening dandy who sported a plumed hat to match the crimson tunic.

"Well, I'll match that and see you better: his lordship gave me a gold purse," the muscular juggler said, flexing his forearms.

"I can best both of you. Her ladyship gave me more than a gold purse." The wiry fellow wiggled his eyebrows and gave a lewd grin. "She expressed a particular partiality for my *contortions*."

Guffaws all around.

"Better'n gold, I'd say."

"Nay. Not really. Not nearly good as Maud there." The contortionist raised his voice and his goblet as he winked at a serving wench across the room, who was pretending to ignore him. "Just one more thing us common folk do better, right, Maud?"

Maud didn't answer, but the muscleman did. "I'll raise a glass to that. Never did see a nobleman could scratch his arse and pick his nose at the same time." He took a swig of beer and frowned. "All them lords and ladies, puttin' on airs, gorging themselves on swans and hummingbird tongues while poor men starve and their wives go mad from eating moldy rye. They strut around like fat pigeons in their fine clothes, ignoring the ragged beggars at their door. It's like that preacher John Ball says. I heard him preachin' after mass at Thetford. Remember that name. John Ball. Ye'll likely be hearin' it again. Ball says God created all of us outa the same clay dirt."

"Sounds like one of those Lollard preachers to me."

"It may be Lollardy, but there's a lot of truth to it. Who needs a priest anyway? Let every man be his own priest, I say."

"Aye and spend his own tithe." The plume on the feathered hat bobbed in enthusiasm.

"What do you know of tithes?' The muscular one grinned, his good humor apparently returned. "Whenever the summoner comes around to collect the tithe, you're always pleading poverty."

"I guess he could give the summoner that fancy velvet sleeve for a tenth," the contortionist said.

"Yeah, and you could give him one tenth of what her ladyship gave you." The feather shivered with mirth. "If he's willing to search between the sheets."

Everybody laughed.

Colin, who was not used to such ribald humor, hoped his red face would be attributed to his proximity to the fire.

As Maud made her wide-hipped stroll among her customers, Colin watched her. Her womanliness—the way her bosom strained at the lacings on her peasant bodice—ignited his now-informed boy's imagination as much as the crude humor. He wondered what her soft thighs would feel like wrapped around him. This thought disturbed him. It reminded him of that part of himself that had led to what he now thought of as the great sin. And it reminded him, too, of all that he was giving up.

Maud approached the jugglers with a tray of full mugs. The muscular one retrieved one from her tray. The contortionist reached out and pinched her breast. She slapped his hand and twisted skillfully away.

"If it's fool's gold ye're looking for, ye can go back to her ladyship. I've no *gold* to squander on fools. I've naught but beer to give ye," she said as she emptied a full glass over his head.

The others applauded and hooted in derision. Colin, too, had to suppress a smile at the expression on the miscreant's face.

"I guess ye've been baptized right enough." The plumed hat shivered again.

"Aye, and by a fairer hand than any cleric." The victim stuck out his tongue and licked his lips. "Tastes better than holy water, too."

Their merriment made Colin feel even lonelier. He was finally warm, so he moved away from the gathering in front of the fire, away from the smell of the roasting meat. One of the players had left a lute lying on a bench in a corner. Colin picked it up and began to strum it softly, singing under his breath.

"You've a pleasing voice, lad." It was the wiry contortionist. Colin had not been aware that he'd followed him. He laid down the lute, felt himself flushing. "I'm sorry. Is this your lute? I was just looking at it. I meant no harm."

"No harm done."

Colin didn't know what to say. He hoped the fellow would go back to his companions. But instead, he motioned for Colin to move over and sat down beside him.

"Are you from here?"

Colin didn't know how to answer that. He didn't know where "here" was.

"I'm from Aylsham," he said, before he had time to think that his mother might have someone out looking for him.

"Aylsham. That's about twenty miles north of here. What are you doing way down here? You're south of Norwich."

South! Sun on the right at daybreak, but there'd been no sun. Colin felt his heart sink into his toes. His feeling must have shown on his face.

"Where're you headed?"

"I was headed to Cromer, to Elinham Abbey. I'm going to join the brothers there. I got a little turned around."

"You don't look good, lad. When did you last eat?"

Colin studied the rushes on the floor. "Not in a while."

"Landlord, half a pint and a joint of meat here for my young friend."

"I don't have any money."

"You can sing for your supper. Anybody want to hear a song?"

"Aye." A voice from the back of the room. "A love song. No hymns or dirges. We'll have enough of those soon enough."

Maud brought him a trencher of victuals and while he wolfed down the food, the wiry contortionist explained. "We're cycle players on our way to Fakenham for the Easter Cycle. We'll probably wind up in Cromer come early summer. We can always use a singer and a lute player. If you don't mind a little face paint, you're welcome to tag along. No pay, but all you can eat." He motioned for Maud to refill Colin's mug. "And you'll pick up a little pay on the side. A pretty blond boy with a sweet voice—the ladies will ply you with gifts. We'll play at a few feast days and banquets along the way. Makes for a nice change from the Bible stories. After Ash Wednesday, we'll start the miracle plays. We should make Blinham easy by Pentecost."

Colin didn't have to think about it very long. What choice did he have? After a week on the road, he'd wound up hungry and cold and farther away from his destination than when he started. He could either go with the mummers or go home. And if he went home . . . His mind conjured a vision of Rose, quickly replaced by the dead shepherd's burnt face. If he went back to the warmth and safety of Blackingham, he would gain no atonement. Not for himself. Not for Rose.

"Do you go through Aylsham?" he asked.

"Aye, but we've no plans to linger there."

That was good. He could get a message to his mother to let her know that he was safe. He knew she would be worried. He could still make it to Cromer. It would just take a little longer.

Colin stripped the last bit of flesh from the chicken bone and wiped his hands on his breeches.

"Well, what say you, boy? Are you going to join our little band?"

"I have to eat," Colin said. "And it's a long way to Cromer."

The contortionist laughed. "Well said. It's settled then." He picked up the lute and handed it to Colin. "Now, it's time to pay for your supper."

Colin strummed the strings of the lute. "I know a love song," he said, and he began to sing, his throat tight and nervous

I live in love-longing
For the seemliest of all things
Who may me blisse bring,
And I to her am bound.

Just another love song, he told himself, hardening his heart against the memory of the scent of her hair, the softness of her lips. But a hush fell over the players, and they nodded their approval as they listened to the plaintive sound of his voice.

≈

Finn remembered the dagger in his boot. They did not search him but merely pushed him down the stairs, still shackled, into the black pit beneath the ancient castle. He thought he recognized the blackguard who handed down his pail of slop on a pole. No recourse there.

He must be patient, he thought, scratching the days on the rock that was his bed. Hard to wait, hard to be calm, remembering Rose's stricken face, but wait he must. Some robed lawyer would come—sent by Kathryn—to plead his innocence, to restore justice. These things take time, he thought on the second day, remembering Kathryn's eyes when she'd lied. There is some misunderstanding. Kathryn will sort it out. Alfred will explain why he planted the pearls. On the third day, he screamed his anger, his righteous protest and threats—sometimes answered with rough laughter, or, more often, answered not at all—until he lost his voice.

When there were seven marks on his stone, he briefly entertained an idea of attacking his jailers. He need not wait to be rescued like some helpless maiden imprisoned in a tower. But to escape would mark him as an outlaw and mark his daughter, too.

In the end it was the filth that made a coward of him. It was not the darkness of his dungeon cell, not the cold; not the hunger, not the thirst that his daily ration of fetid water with its film of mutton grease could never assuage; not the raw despair that tormented his mind—more frequently with the passage of days—a despair that bespoke certain knowledge that he should never escape this oubliette, into which he'd been cast like Satan into hell. It was not even the fear for his abandoned Rose or the pain of remembering Kathryn's betrayal. (This last had swirled around in his head until he vowed not to visit there again, only to find his mind besieged by those very same thoughts— why? why? why? The words screamed inside his head like a grand inquisitor's litany.) It was none of these It was the squalor: the lice he picked from his body and his beard—day by day, hour by hour, second by second—and, cursing, cracked between dirty fingernails, the pus-filled scabs that crusted over his vermin bites; the mildewed slime coating the rock ledge that was seat and bed and table. It was the stench of his own excrement—this was his undoing.

He couldn't even pray. What god would hold congress in such filth?

There was little difference between night and day, just a thickening and thinning in the smothering blackness, but he had marked the passage of days by his daily ration of slop and scratched the tally on the rock. Now he traced them with his hand. Twenty-one marks. Twenty-one days. How could a man be reduced to a beast in so short a time? He was too weak to drag his shackles even a few feet to stab at the night vermin who beaded the dark with their eyes. What could the dagger avail him now, unless he wished to fall on its point like Saul falling on his sword? One quick thrust up and under his rib. A sound, a scraping of a rat's teeth against a well-gnawed bone of uncertain origin quelled that temptation. That and the thought of Rose.

In fitful dreams, Kathryn came to him, sitting beside him in the autumn garden. *There is the smell of succulent fruit in the air, and the smell of roasting meat from the smoking shed. Her head is bowed over her own art, her little bone needle gliding in and out, marking a curved path on the fabric. One half of her face hides behind her silver hair, the other in the shadow of a hawthorne branch. He kneels beside her. He touches the ribbons on her sleeve, parts her hair and whispers into the porcelain trumpet of her ear. She laughs, like clear water bub-bling in a stream, clean and pure and sweet. She lifts her face to receive his kiss. A flash of arm and she stabs his eye with her little bone needle. He sees nothing but white-hot pain.*

He always woke to lick salty tears from the corners of his mouth.

To fight the demons in his living nightmare, he painted bright pictures in his mind, laying out the colors and the miniatures of Saint John, conjuring a Book of Hours. He painted enough pictures on the canvas of his eyelids to fill a lifetime's work. Not the luxurious Gospel the abbot had commissioned, certainly not the plain illustrations of the Wycliffe text. A Psalter, as glorious as the God that David and Solomon celebrated, all in azure and crimson, bordered with acanthus leaves in gold leaf and bound in hammered gold set with a coronet of rubies. A book to make the bishop of Norwich drool with greed. A book to rival the legendary Herimann's Gospel commissioned by the duke of Saxony in 1185, the great *Aurea Testatur,* witnessed in gold. His eyelids hurt to dream it.

And then there came the day when he had not even the strength to hold this bright vision. There was only the cold, and the gnawing in his belly, and the smothering darkness, and the stench.

It was on such a day the bishop summoned him.

SEVENTEEN

*I saw his (the monk's) sleeves were garnished at the
  hand
With fine grey fur, the finest in the land,
And on his hood, to fasten it at his chin
He had a wrought-gold cunningly fashioned pin.*
—GEOFFREY CHAUCER,
    THE CANTERBURY TALES (14TH CENTURY)

inn lay curled on the stone slab of his cell in the half-sleep half-stupor when he was awakened by the guard's foot in his stomach. It prodded his belly, thrusting upward. For a minute, Finn's breath fled and then returned abruptly, bringing with it a tearing pain. The guard fastened wrist irons on him and dragged him to his feet. He tottered like an old man. A shaft of light spilled through the opened grate above his cell, stabbing him in the eye like Kathryn's little bone needle. He squinted at his tormentor, who laughed.

"Ye don't know me, do ye? Don't recognize Old Sykes, the one what ye ill-treated over a bit of harmless dwarf-baiting?"

Finn had recognized him, all right. That first day. But he had hoped Sykes had been too drunk to remember their encounter in the Beggar's Daughter. Vain hope, that. Sykes remembered and was here to exact his due. Finn said nothing. Best to let the fellow spin himself out. Less sport if his antagonist met no resistance. Finn didn't have the strength to resist anyway. He hunched forward, elbows in, to provide support for his hurt ribs.

"Not such a fine gentleman now? The smell of ye makes me sick. We'll have to clean ye up, else the hangman won't come near enough to noose ye. Not so tough now without that pretty little dagger, are ye?"

The dagger. Maybe here was the chance, after all. Finn wriggled his left foot inside its boot. Flat leather where the dagger should have been sheathed. He'd a vague memory of throwing it at a pair of glittering eyes in the dark. He'd not troubled to put it back. It would have meant groping on the slime-caked floor with his hands, and to what avail?

The guard shoved him toward the stairs. He stumbled against the first riser. He still wore the leg irons—had worn them so long they were like a part of his body, even the chafed skin around his ankles had toughened into a protective scar.

"I can't climb with the shackles on. You'll have to loose them." He had to speak low because of his hurt ribs. Breath cost too much to squander.

"I don't have to loose anything. I can just kick ye up the stairs, like the sack of dog shite ye are. But that might overwork me kicking leg and I might want to use it later, mightn't I?"

He loosed the iron cuff from one leg so that the chain and the loose cuff clanged behind Finn as he climbed.

"If ye've any idea o' running, I'd advise agin it." To prove his point he stepped abruptly on the chain. Finn lurched forward, stifling a groan.

When they reached the bare dirt yard outside the dungeon, Finn stumbled again. The light blinded him and caused his head to throb. The noise was deafening to a mind wrapped for weeks in silence—neighing horses, squawking barnyard fowl, angry shouts, barking dogs and clanging guardsmen—an assault on his senses. He had an almost religious longing for the insulated quiet of his cell.

It was a cold bright winter day and he wore only his filthy shirt. He started to shiver uncontrollably.

"What ye got there, Sykes?" This from one of the men hanging around the stables.

"I got me some crow meat. But got to scrub him up first or e'en the buzzards will have naught to do with him."

"Need any help?"

"Wouldn't want to share the pleasure."

Finn lurched blindly, goaded by Sykes, until he stumbled against a wooden trough and felt himself pushed in. The water was a shock, numbing even the pain of his ribs. He struggled to get out, his free leg thrashing against the lip of the trough, his body half out, but a brutish hand held his face down. So the hangman was to be cheated after all. He forced himself to cease struggling, to go still like a possum in a hound's mouth. Knowing he was no match for his assailant, he resisted an urge to fight. Dissenting voices were muffled by the water rushing in his ears.

"God's Blood, Sykes. Ye've drowned 'im. The bishop ain't going to be pleased. Haul 'im out."

A second longer and his lungs would burst.

"Now, I said."

The hand moved from his forehead, and Finn's head lunged upward sputtering water. Sykes grabbed the fabric of his shirt, bunching it when it tore, and pulled him out. Another guard came running forward and wrapped him in a blanket.

"Despenser wants him alive, you fool."

"I had to clean him up, didn't I? Couldn't have the bishop's delicate nostrils offended. Wouldn't be seemly now, would it?"

"Seemly. I'll show you seemly, you idiot's spawn."

By now, Finn was standing, streaming water, wrapped in a horse blanket, which, if not altogether clean, was an improvement over the one he'd left behind. He couldn't stop his body's shaking, but the cold water—there was a broken crust of ice on the horse trough where he'd been pushed in—had helped to clear his head.

The bishop had summoned him. So at least he was to have a hearing. He'd better start to prepare his case. He stood in the courtyard, shivering, listening to them argue over him as he tried to rebuild the broken scaffolding of argument he'd constructed in his mind early in his confinement.

Sykes skulked back to the stables as his captain took charge of removing the shackles. Finn rubbed his ankles. They felt light, alien, without the irons.

"What day is this?" Finn directed his question to the newcomer. His teeth chattered, cracking his words. He couldn't stop shaking.

"January seven. Yesterday was the Feast of Epiphany."

Blessed Redeemer. He'd been in that cesspit for over a month. He started to tremble more violently, each shiver jarring his broken ribs.

"Come on. We've got to get ye thawed out and cleaned up proper for the bishop." The constable looked at Finn as though the latter was going to be a burdensome and difficult task.

"I am to have a trial then?"

At last someone had sounded an alarm. Lady Kathryn had finally brought some influence to bear. His ill treatment was only the fault of the scoundrel Sykes.

"I don't know about a trial. Only that the bishop has summoned you to the tower chamber." The constable motioned for Finn to follow him.

Once inside the keep that served as guardhouse, Finn warmed his exterior by a charcoal brazier and held a cup of broth between his hands as though it were the Holy Grail. His gorge seemed to rise if he risked more than tiny swallows. At least the trembling had subsided. And if he held his upper body perfectly still, the pain was tolerable.

"Has there been anyone else asking for me? A lady, the mistress of Blackingham, or my daughter? Her name is Rose."

"Not that I've heard. And I would have heard. I'm the constable in charge."

Then, as if to prove it, he turned to shout orders for a bath to be drawn and placed in front of the fire. Finn's last bath had been in front of Kathryn's chamber fire. Before she had betrayed him. He would never be clean again.

"Now that I think on it. There was one came asking for the illuminator. That's you, right?"

Finn nodded.

"Said he carried a message from Blackingham. A dwarf. Funny little man. I sent him to your jailer."

His jailer. Sykes. So they had not abandoned him completely. Kathryn had probably sent Half-Tom and Sykes had stopped him.

The guard stood up, his keys jangling, and threw Finn a scrap of towel.

A clean towel. Finn's eyelids smarted. Surely, he was not going to cry in front of the guard over the sight of a clean towel and a chunk of soap.

"I've got rounds to make," the constable said. "This castle holds some noble *guests*. Frenchies, mostly. Being held for ransom. They pay me a little extra for a few luxuries." He winked at Finn. "There's a duke from Bordeaux has a special fondness for blondes with big arses."

He pitched Finn some clean breeches and a shirt, not fine lawn, but good English broadcloth.

"Sorry, no razor, of course. But here's a comb for your head and beard. Use the fine-toothed end. The bishop has no liking for lice."

Finn took the comb, added it to the pile, which he held away from his body so as not to contaminate the clothes with his filth. "One more thing. If I might ask, though under the circumstances I'm not able to offer you immediate recompense for services."

The constable grinned. "You can ask."

"I think Sykes has cracked my ribs. If you could bring me a length of strong cloth to bind up my rib cage, I will remember your kindness."

"I think that can be arranged for a special prisoner of the bishop."

"A clean one. If it's not too much trouble?"

The constable laughed and Finn realized he might have given the man more insight into himself than might be prudent under these circumstances. He was so overcome with the thought of being clean again that he'd only half heard the constable's response. Had he said the "bishop's special prisoner"? That had an ominous ring to it.

"A clean one it shall be. And I'll send a boy to help you bind it and some poppy juice for the pain. Then the constable will take you to the bishop." Then, all laughter gone, he added, "If you've any notion of trying to break away from one of my lads, I wouldn't. The castle is secure and this meeting you have with Henry Despenser may be the only chance you have. Do the best you can to please. I've known men of high birth to disappear from within these castle walls."

⚜

Henry Despenser sat tall in his high-backed chair, his ears alert, like those of the greyhound tethered at his feet. It was a considered pose, calculated to intimidate by forcing his supplicants to kneel fully. (Bishop Henry Despenser scorned the perfunctory bow.) The beringed forefinger of his beefy, square-palmed left hand fondled the dog's ear. His right hand rested on the arm of his chair. The signet ring on his middle finger tapped, tapped, tapped against the carved oak. Such pleasure in the exercise of power. To bend a man to his will, especially a man like the one he had summoned, could deliver a shock of ecstasy almost equal to that of carnal release.

He surveyed the room. All was in readiness. Those who served him knew well his attention to detail. The dog's ears pricked. Then he heard it, too— the dragging of a long sword on the lip of each stair, followed by a pair of footsteps.

He spread the edge of his robe to broaden the circle of its furred border. So much energy expended to trap a dabbler in paints, a dabbler in heresy too, mayhap. Worth the trouble, anyway—the man's insolence should not go unmarked; besides, there was the matter of the reredos, the five-paneled retable, he wanted painted for the cathedral altar. Why pay for that which he could get for nothing? He'd seen the illuminator's work, the bold strokes, the opulent colors, and envied him that talent. But if he did not own the talent, he would own the man who owned the talent.

He dug his fingernail into the bitch's fur, deep into the soft juncture where ear meets skull. The dog quivered but remained still. Not even a low growl. A well-bred beast and well-mastered. That was the kind of obedience he inspired.

There was a tentative tap on the door. Henry stroked the hound's head. She whimpered low in her throat and gave the tiniest shiver before settling her head on her front paws.

"Benedicite."

"Your Eminence." The constable strode across the threshold and dropped to one knee, his long-sword clanging on the stone flags. The illuminator, standing behind him, inclined his head in a token bow, but he held his torso erect.

"Your prisoner does not kneel in the presence of Holy Church?"

The constable tugged on Finn's arm, forcing him to his knees with a clunk. But it was not a voluntary action and there was insufficient humility in his posture to suggest that his weeks in the dungeon had improved his attitude. All right. Sweeter still the triumph that was hard fought.

"The prisoner has been injured, Eminence. His ribs are tightly bound. It is difficult for him to pay due homage."

"This injury occurred while he was in our custody?"

"An accident, Eminence. He tripped on the stairway."

"I see." Henry smiled. "You should be more careful . . . Master Finn, is it? You may rise."

Pain flickered across the prisoner's face as he struggled awkwardly to his feet. Henry continued to stroke the dog's head.

"You may leave us, Constable."

"But Eminence, the man *is* charged with murder."

"I'm aware of the charge. I repeat, you may leave us."

As the constable backed awkwardly out the door, the bishop turned his gaze on Finn. Lesser men in his position fidgeted beneath such scrutiny. Despenser admired, albeit grudgingly, the man's discipline.

"Are you a priest-killer, Master Finn?"

"I am no killer, Your Eminence. I am greatly wronged, as you will see once you hear the evidence. If you will interview my daughter, you will——"

Henry waved the words away.

"A daughter who would not speak for her father is poor issue. Besides, such testimony would be premature. The shire reeve is still gathering evidence. Gathering evidence takes a long time. Sir Guy has matters other than this one to resolve. Or so he keeps reminding me. In the meantime, I'm sure you can understand that Holy Church cannot allow one who may be a priest-killer to go free."

Especially one with your heretical connections, he thought but did not say aloud.

He watched as anger worked the muscles of the prisoner's emaciated face. Amazing how quickly the face takes on a starved, hunted look. He'd seen the man twice before: the first time when he'd boldly confessed to killing the sow and a second time when he'd refused the bishop's patronage. Both were memorable occasions. Yet Henry would not have recognized him, except for his cocky posture. Five weeks in Castle Prison dungeon had scarcely dented that—a not unworthy adversary.

"We can't grant you freedom, but we can provide more comfortable quarters while you're waiting trial. The dungeon is hardly a place for a man of your talents. Of course, such an arrangement would require your cooperation. But I forget my manners. You look quite unwell. Have you been ill?"

No doubt, the succulent aroma coming from the draped table in front of the fire was having its desired effect. Henry clapped his hands and his aged servant appeared from outside the door.

"Seth, prepare the table and assist Master Finn to a chair before he faints. Pour him a glass of wine."

Henry rose from his own chair and walked across to the table. He picked up a breast of roast quail, dipped it in a black ginger sauce, and nibbled at it daintily.

He watched as Finn averted his eyes. He recognized the mix of desire and nausea that the man was fighting. He knew how, after an extended fast—and this man's fast was significantly longer than those rare and short holy days during which he fasted—an indulgence in rich food could overwhelm the senses with unpleasant results.

"Please. Be my guest. You must be weary of the meager fare of the common prisoner."

Finn shook his head. "Just bread—to soften the effects of the wine. My stomach has become accustomed to the dungeon's humbler rations."

So. He was to be denied the gratifying sight of the haughty illuminator falling on his food like a beast and being humiliated by his own vomit. But Henry nodded consent and his servant cut a slice of bread and placed it before Finn.

"Maybe a bit of the applesauce," his prisoner said as he took a minuscule sip from his cup. "And a sliver of plain cheese, please." He pushed his chair away from the table, edged it closer to the fire.

Seth measured a wedge of cheese with his knife. Finn shook his head and the servant halved it; again, then quartered it.

Henry frowned, but he had to admire the man's willpower. "I trust you have found your cell to be reasonably comfortable." He sat down across from the illuminator, watching closely to see the effect of his irony.

"It is a habitat created by the devil for his vermin." He dipped the bread in the applesauce and chewed carefully.

Henry helped himself to a sugared tart, spooned clotted cream over it. "This is delicious. You really should . . ." He swallowed, licked his fingers. "I'm sorry if you've found your cell unpleasant. We do have other quarters. This chamber that we're in, for example, is furnished . . . less Spartan than the cellars."

With a sweep of his hand he indicated the bed with its clean feather mattress, the pegs on which hung clean linen shirts and breeches, the low worktable laid with paint pots and brushes.

"The bishop's chair, of course, doesn't stay. But there is a comfortable chair and the worktable is a generous size. The room is high enough in the tower that it has a rare window where a man could see a patch of blue sky. I would think that might be important—a patch of blue sky—to a prisoner. He could stand at the window and look down at the river, watch it flowing past. Such a cell might even become a refuge to one dedicated to his art."

The prisoner said nothing. He sipped his wine, took a small bite of the cheese, then inspected it as though it were some rare delicacy, but his glance lingered on the paints and brushes. Henry noted how the fingers of Finn's right hand made involuntary grasping movements as though holding a sable brush.

Henry smiled, drank deeply from his own glass. "A fine wine. The French should stick to making burgundy and leave the pope to Rome. Now, concerning the matter of your trial. Of course, you could appeal to the king, but it would avail you nothing since the king has no jurisdiction in ecclesiastical matters. The Holy See passes judgment. The king's authority only becomes involved at the execution phase."

He pointed to a small chest. "There's clean linen there. The occupant of this cell will be supplied with clean linen once a week." He inspected his fingernails, twisted his signet ring. "If it's a speedy trial you're pressing for, well"—he shrugged his ermine-caped shoulders—"a speedy murder trial usually ends badly for the accused. It's best to take one's time, to forge alliances . . ." He nibbled again, wiped his mouth and looked around. "There's enough light here for an artist, wouldn't you think? If you moved that worktable, over there, directly beneath the window?"

The prisoner set down his wineglass and got up abruptly. He walked to the window and gazed out. He dared turn his back on his bishop! Henry considered, then decided to ignore this act of rudeness.

"Of course, we could offer you Trial by Holy Writ. That would be swift. You could be free by nightfall."

"Or dead by nightfall," Finn answered, not turning around.

"Exactly so. Depending upon the text my finger lights upon."

"Or your interpretation of that text," Finn said, turning around to meet Henry's gaze.

"Exactly so." This was more fun that he'd had in a while.

"And exactly what would be expected of an artist in return for this exceptional treatment?"

So, now we are to negotiate in earnest, Henry thought. "Only that which you did before your unfortunate arrest. You may recall I mentioned to you once before that I wanted to commission a paneled altarpiece depicting the Crucifixion, Resurrection, and Ascension of our Lord. Do you remember that conversation?"

"Some vague remembrance," Finn acknowledged.

"As I recall, you declined the commission, pleading that you did not have enough time to do such a large work justice." Henry smiled. "Well, suddenly it seems that Fate has conspired to give you time enough." Now he was really enjoying himself. "Wouldn't you agree?"

There was a pause. The muscles in Finn's face worked as though he were chewing something hard and bitter, but his voice was steady as he said, "Such a piece as you have described would require talent and concentration. What would be the compensation?"

"Compensation! You are bold to speak of compensation from such a weak bargaining position." The room was close, overheated. He felt sweat popping along his hairline. His prisoner, however, appeared not to notice. He had even moved closer to the fire. "You would have a clean supply of linen once a week, a servant would be supplied to look after your chamber, purchase, prepare, and serve your food."

"It is written man does not live by bread alone."

Finn extended his hands to the fire, almost touching the flames.

God's Blood. If the man got any closer, he'd be sitting in the fire. "You may well be too clever for your own good, Illuminator. If by your choice of Scripture you seek to cast me in the role of the devil, I would remind you that you are hardly fit for the role of Jesus Christ. Look to your own soul. You've much to worry about in that quarter, even if you don't have the priest's blood on your hands as you claim. Sir Guy told me of the wicked translations found in your papers. You're keeping the devil's company, Illuminator, with John Wycliffe and John of Gaunt. These men are not the kind of friends you need now. Maybe by dedicating your art to that which is holy you can find some redemption for your soul."

"I thought I had dedicated my art to that which is holy. But it's not my soul to which I had reference. I have a daughter. She depends on me for her living."

"What use will you be to her dead?"

"I'm not dead yet."

Henry was growing weary of this game. He removed a silver dish of minced meats from the table and placed it in front of the greyhound and then returned to his high-backed chair. He tapped his signet ring against the wood. The dog cocked her head and looked at the bishop. When he ignored her, she whined. He nodded. She began lapping greedily at the minced fowl.

"Your daughter will be provided for."

"Will she be allowed to visit me?"

The hunger in the man's eyes was thinly disguised. Ah, at last, here was the weakness. How best to exploit it? No rash promises. Keep him off his guard. Play him like a fish. Henry might get more from this catch than art for the cathedral apse.

"I will return in a week. In the meantime, paint for me a set of playing cards—four suits: cardinals, archbishops, kings, abbots. Do you know the kind I'm talking about?"

"I played at such cards at court: kings, queens, knaves."

At court. So the fellow was seeking to parley a little influence of his own. Good. Good. Court connections—valuable information that just might lead straight to the duke of Lancaster and his nest of Lollard heretics.

"Paint the backs, too, with my coat of arms. A bishop's miter and Saint Peter's keys flanking a cross of gold on a field of crimson."

He kicked the silver bowl away from the hound's muzzle, gathered her tether and walked to the door. "Call the constable to carry my chair," he shouted at Seth, who was dozing in the hallway.

"I will need a special wax to stiffen the vellum," Finn said.

Henry undid the purse hanging at his belt and extracted a shilling. "Send the attendant to buy whatever you need. If this is not enough, just say it's for the bishop. If the vendor refuses, take his name."

"Will my daughter be able to visit me?"

"We'll see. If the playing cards please."

"They will be ready in two days."

"I'll be back in a week. No need to hurry. You've plenty of time." He drew the string tighter on his velvet purse. "By the by, do you play chess?"

"I have some small knowledge of the game."

"Good. Good. I'll bring a board when next I come."

Henry smiled as he closed the door behind him. A very productive afternoon. And he'd still make it back home in time for vespers.

Tomorrow, he would question the anchoress.

EIGHTEEN

*The mother's service is nearest, readiest and surest;
nearest, for it is most of kind; readiest, for it is most
of love; surest, for it is most of truth. This office no
one might nor could ever do to the full except He
alone. . . . Our true Mother Jesus, He alone beareth
us to joy and to endless living . . .*
—JULIAN OF NORWICH, *DIVINE REVELATIONS*

hen Rose wasn't throwing up, she was on her knees before the little altar to the Virgin. What would her father say if he could see to what use she'd put his worktable? He wouldn't approve—she'd heard him often enough bitterly commenting on "the pious ones" who "wore their religion like fancy surcoats over filthy shirts." But she knew he would not deny her. When had he ever denied her anything?

The little statue of the Madonna and Child was her only source of comfort now. There was Agnes, and the little kitchen maid—they were nice to her, saw that she had wood for the fire and food, but they were in the service of Lady Kathryn. And Lady Kathryn Rose no longer trusted. The little alabaster statue of the Holy Virgin in her blue robe seemed her only friend. The perpetual candle Rose kept burning on her makeshift altar reflected the painted eyes, making them glow with compassion whenever she prayed to the Queen of Heaven: prayed for her father, prayed for Colin, prayed for the babe growing inside her. When she woke in the middle of the night with visions of Finn being dragged off in irons, the candlelight illumined the face of the infant Jesus, making it blush with color. Like a living child, she thought, kneading her stomach, like the child Colin had given her.

As she recited the Ave Maria—some of the words were difficult; her religious instruction had not been a priority—she wondered if her father prayed too. She hoped so. It would comfort him as it did her. She did not possess a rosary, but with every Ave, she stroked the cross on the silken cord tied around her neck. She'd never wondered about the necklace before. But now it struck her as odd that her father, who wore no signs of ritual piety upon his person, had instructed her always to wear the cross. It was her protection, he'd said. She needed that protection now. Her lips moved with each prayer, but the only sound in the room for a long time was the occasional rustle of her satin skirt against the stone flags and the shifting of the coals in the grate— Rose was always cold in spite of the blazing fire.

A shuffle of footsteps interrupted her devotions.

"It's stifling in here, Rose." Lady Kathryn opened the shutter, letting in a blast of cold air. The candle flame danced. Shielding it with her hand, Rose hurriedly moved the candle away from the path of the breeze. "And it's not healthy for you to spend so much time on your knees. Colin never should have given you the Madonna. You're turning into a religious fanatic."

Rose shivered. "Like Colin, you mean. Maybe I should go live with the sisters now that Colin has gone to be a monk." It was an exploratory remark, meant to gauge Kathryn's reaction.

"It's a soupçon too late for you to become a bride of Christ, don't you think?" Kathryn frowned as she held out a cup. Rose had gotten up and was sitting on the bed. "Here. If you drink it quickly, it won't taste so bad."

Rose gathered her shawl and her courage closer. "I'm not going to drink it at all."

"What do you mean, you're not going to drink it?"

"I'm not . . . it's not healthy." She took a deep breath. Where would she go if Lady Kathryn turned her out? "I know what you're trying to do." Her voice was defiant but she was trembling inside.

"And what am I trying to do?" Lady Kathryn asked, her voice low and even, her gaze direct, challenging.

"You're trying to poison my baby so . . . so it will go away. You want to punish me because I accused Alfred." Then, with less confrontation, more pleading in her voice, pleading for her child, for Colin's child: "But I only told the truth."

She half-swallowed the last word. Her throat was dry, sticking together, and her eyelids pricked, but she was determined not to cry in front of Lady Kathryn. "You hate me because Colin ran away. If his baby dies inside me, then you can send me away, too."

There. She'd said it. Her greatest fears given voice.

Kathryn was standing beside the makeshift altar, holding out the cup like a poisoned chalice, her other hand resting on the Madonna. She didn't answer immediately. She traced the outline of the Jesus Child with a finger, like one who noodles an object in deep study. Rose couldn't read her expression. She looked thinner and frail, and Rose would have pitied her had she not felt so threatened by the wreck of a woman who towered over her, shadowing her. Lady Kathryn stood between her and the window. The cold light filtered through a veil of gray cloud, highlighting her pallor.

"I could send you away anyway," she said quietly, almost as if she were talking to herself. "Colin doesn't know about the babe. Would never have to know."

Rose thought she was going to faint.

The candle flame on the altar danced erratically. Thunder rumbled in from an unseasonal storm born far out at sea, miles from Blackingham. Lady Kathryn moved toward the window. With another gust of wind, more thunder growled, like the gut of a hungry man. Lady Kathryn paused, looked down at the contents of the cup in her hand, then looked up at Rose as though she were seeing her for the first time. Rose said nothing. What was there to say? Should she beg for the sake of the child? Would it make a difference to this woman she no longer knew?

A chilly breeze blew a strand of hair across Kathryn's face. With her free hand, she pushed it back, combed the tangled mass with her fingers. Something—a dried bit of leaf—fell onto her woolen kirtle. She brushed it away, then, with a puzzled expression, picked at a dried stain. When she looked back at Rose, she had the look on her face of one who was awakening from a troubling dream.

She lifted the cup and flung the contents out the window.

Rose jumped at the sudden movement as though she had been slapped.

"You need not drink it anymore," Kathryn said, then added, with a shrug of her shoulders and a bitter little laugh, "it wasn't working anyway."

Rose pulled her shawl tighter. She could not stop shivering. "My lady, I only want—"

Lady Kathryn held up her hand to stop her. "Nobody is going to send you away, Rose. Nobody is going to hurt you." She glanced down at the empty cup dangling from her hand. "No harm will come to your child."

The words rang in Rose's ears like prophecy.

"You can go back to praying if you want." Lady Kathryn's hand went to her mouth as though she was holding back a cry. She reached up to shut the window, her back to Rose, and added in a small voice, "You might pray for me as well."

Rose exhaled, her breath coming in a heavy, ragged sigh. "Thank you, my lady," she said. "Thank you. I will pray for us all."

She wanted to embrace Lady Kathryn, who was a pitiable sight with her disheveled hair and stained clothes, a shadow of the proud woman she had been. But the older woman held herself straight and withdrawn in posture, as if to say that too much raw feeling had passed between them already.

As Kathryn started to leave, she paused at the door and said without looking back, "I'll tell Agnes to send Glynis with something nourishing, a posset made with milk and eggs." Then, almost as an afterthought: "When she comes, tell her to bring me clean linen and ointments. I need a good washing."

❧

Julian heard the evil tidings about Finn from her servant, Alice.

"Ye remember that Welshman that brought ye the babe that died? Well, he's in Castle Prison." She pushed the news through the window with a steaming bowl of pottage.

Julian could not hide her shock. "On what charge?"

"He's charged with murder. A *priest's* murder!" Alice made the sign of the cross, as though the evil of which the illuminator was accused might rush into the room and grab her by the throat. "I told ye there was something sly about him. All that Welsh anger bottled up behind those cloudy green eyes. Never trust a Welshman, that's what I always say."

Murder! Alice had to be wrong. Idle gossip she'd picked up in the marketplace. Julian's mind whirled with questions, but out of habit she admonished her serving woman for her prejudice. "For shame, Alice, the way you rush to judgment. God created the Welsh out of the same earth he created your own Saxon flesh."

Alice's head bobbed, ignoring the reprimand, rushing to offer details for which Julian had not asked. "He's guilty right enough. I knew he would come to no good the first time I ever laid eyes on him. In spite of all his comely manners. Mark my words. He bashed that poor priest's skull in, just smashed it like a rotten turnip." She shivered and crossed herself again. "Brains and blood splattering everywhere."

Julian was alarmed as she watched the violent image in Alice's mind contort her pleasant round face into a mask of ugliness. Mild-mannered Alice, who tended her so carefully! Who knew what horrors lurked in the human heart? How much we all stood in need of grace.

"Alice! Enough! Calm yourself before you scare yourself witless. We will pray on Master Finn's behalf. I'm sure of his innocence; there is some mistake, some case of wrongful identity, perhaps, or false witness. *All will be well.*"

There were no more conversations with her servant about Finn's guilt or innocence, but it had not been idle gossip. Julian made inquiries through Tom. The evidence appeared damning, at least what she heard, something about pearls found in Finn's possession that the mistress of Blackingham had given to the dead priest. But no evidence would alter the one thing she knew. The man who had cradled the wounded child in his arms as tenderly as any mother, the man who had taken the blame upon himself for killing the bishop's sow to save Tom: that man was not capable of cold-blooded murder.

Tonight, as every night, the anchoress knelt in the flickering candlelight before her altar and said the compline prayers from the Book of Hours. As she recited the Hours of the Virgin, followed by the Hours of the Cross and the Hours of the Holy Spirit tonight, as she had for a fortnight, she prayed an intercessory prayer for Finn. Her lips prayed in Latin: *Domine Ihesu Christe . . .* Her heart prayed in English: *Lord Jesus Christ, Son of the living God, interpose Thy Passion, Cross, and Death between Thy judgment and me.*

But as her mouth formed the ritual pronoun, in her mind she called Finn's name. She prayed on through matins as the midnight shadows gathered. Her body grew stiff and began to ache—*Deus in adiutorium meum intende. God come to his assistance*—substituting the masculine pronoun in place of her own.

The Book of Hours lay open on the altar to the picture that was her inspiration and her comfort. She saw it with her eyes closed, her Suffering Saviour, the bleeding Christ. At first, it was the artist's flat rendering that painted itself behind her eyelids; the image of her Lord on calfskin vellum, skin ashwhite, thinly streaked with crimson paint from the wounds. The corners of the suffering eyes drooped; the body sagged; the head slumped slightly forward. But as she concentrated on the mental picture, the body began to pulsate, slowly at first, then more rhythmically, transforming and reforming itself in the light it generated, until it became three-dimensional, life-size. The head lifted. Blood trickled, tiny pearl-like drops: drip, drip, dripping from his brow, then flowing more freely from a crown of thorns so true, if she dared touch it with her own hand, its thorns would prick her fingers.

This was her Christ. The Christ of her vision, the vision her Mother God had granted her as she lay dying—a Christ whose blood flowed so freely from the Crucifixion wounds, from the scourging, from the pierced side, from the bleeding brow, until it rushed in a veritable fountain, gushing, pulsing not with death but life, enough life to nourish all the souls of hungry humanity that He would gather to his breast.

She recited the prayers from memory, transfixed before the glory of her Lord, eyes closed against the flickering candle flame, her mind transported, her body denied. The candles guttered out, and the nightingale signaled lauds. It was the purest part of the night, rich and deep, like the blood, like the love of her Jesus. She and her Christ, her Friend, her Lover, her Mother God—alone together while the rest of the world slumbered. Exquisite pain. Sublime joy. Her mind was bathed in peace—peace and warmth and light, her body transcended, until her soul was free to touch His.

I shall make all things well.

And she knew it to be true.

⸙

Shortly before the bells tolled prime, a sound penetrated Julian's trance. It was the sound of the great oak door, the door that sealed her tomb, creaking on its hinges. She was suddenly alert, acutely conscious of the darkness around her, the hardness of the floor beneath her body, the film of moisture forming between her open palms and the floor. Would some outlaw dare to violate the sanctity of her anchorhold? Some angel sent from God? Or some demon come to torment her? She stood up and turned away from the altar to face the door.

With one great groan, it opened. The morning sunlight sliced through the door, almost blinding her. She closed her stinging eyes, then opened them, squinting. Her cell had not been filled with so much light since the day she had been sealed within its walls.

She could just make out the bishop silhouetted in her doorway.

She was so exhausted from her night's devotion that when she bent to kiss his ring, the room began to whirl, and she would have fallen against him had he not reached out his hand.

"Forgive my unsteadiness, Your Eminence. I have spent the night in prayer and it sometimes leaves me unsteady on my feet."

"But firm in your faith, is that so, anchoress?"

His accusing tone, a tenseness in his manner, the way he scowled at her signaled displeasure, as though she had in some way given offense. And why had he chosen to break the seal of her enclosure? He sometimes visited her, but on such times they communicated through her visitor's window or through Alice's window. This was not a routine visit. He always came much later in the day and sent a servant ahead with his chair, a basket of cakes, and a saucer of milk for Jezebel. He sometimes brought her books from the library of Carrow Priory. Today he was empty-handed. The rigidity of his posture, the way he absently fingered the ornate cross hanging at his breast as he frowned at her eye-level-to-eye-level—she was a tall woman—told her he had not come to discuss theology.

"My soul is much refreshed, Your Eminence. It is only my body that is weak." She looked at him evenly, answering the challenge in his words, in his gaze. "Do you question the faithfulness of my devotion?"

His fingers massaged the heavy chain holding the cross. "Not the faithfulness of your ritual, anchoress. But something has lately come to my attention that causes me to question your faithfulness to your Church."

He went over to her writing table where he perched on her stool. She sank gratefully onto the edge of her cot. It was nerve-racking to have him inside her cell, a violation of her vows. He of all people should know that. The only other human that she'd been this close to since her enclosure was the wounded child.

From the high stool, he towered over her, so close that the ermine fringe of his bishop's robe touched the hem of her own plain linen garment. His jeweled fingers rifled through the pages strewn on her desk. It was as though he was looking for something. He shoved the papers aside, his mouth still molded into a hard line.

She did not answer his charge of unfaithfulness, did not know how. Protestation of her piety would be empty unless she had proof. How does one prove the contents of one's heart?

"Why do you not write in the language of your Church?"

Was that the source of his disapprobation? That she did not write her Divine Revelations in Latin, but in English? But surely, that was hardly enough. "Is the language of Rome the language of our Lord? Latin, Aramaic, English: what does it matter if the truth is told?"

"Had you chosen French, I could better understand. But this Midland dialect, this English is the language of common villeins."

"Have common villeins not need of the truth?"

"Have common villeins not priests to instruct them in the truth?"

"Many among the guild classes can read. Would their faith not be strengthened if they could read about His love, even the Holy Scriptures, for themselves?"

His eyes narrowed. "I see the influence of evil reaches even into the anchorhold. The devil must surely laugh to have a holy woman make his argument."

Anger was an emotion she had almost forgotten until now. "But surely you cannot think—"

He held up his hand to stop her protest. "Know this, anchoress, that so common a translation profanes Holy Writ. Furthermore, the laity has neither the wit nor the wisdom to interpret Scripture. They would only use it to dispute with their more learned betters to the detriment of their souls."

Was that a slur, a warning intended for her, or just an observation? Either way his statement was an inaccurate one. Many of the clerics from whom the masses gained instruction were not learned at all; they could scarcely read and write beyond a few rote Vulgate phrases. But she thought that was better left unsaid. Instead she said, "English is widely used in London. It is not just the language of the commoner. It is the language of the court."

"At court, you say. I know of one at court, John of Gaunt, the king's regent, who would agree with you. But the duke is no friend of Holy Church. He is a supporter of John Wycliffe, who sends his mumbling Lollard preachers out across the countryside with his *English* pamphlets, haranguing the bishops and the priests with false charges of corruption and apostasy." He punctuated his words by pounding his fists on her writing table. "Stirring up the rabble with false doctrine, false notions of equality." The eyebrow just above his left eye had developed a tic. "He writes in English also. Anchoress, I hope you have not come under his influence. He preaches heresy. And heretics will not be tolerated!"

Finn had talked of Wycliffe. Was that why he was imprisoned on false charges?

The bishop reached inside his sleeve, pulled out a sheaf of papers and, leaning forward, waved them under her nose. "Do you recognize these?"

She took the papers, glanced at them briefly. "They are my writings, my Divine Revelations. But how came they to be . . . ?"

"We have arrested a man on suspicion of murdering a priest. These, along with a profane copy of the writings of Saint John the Evangelist, Wycliffe's English translation, were found in his possession. And I wonder, anchoress, how you can explain the fact that these writings bear your name."

"They are mine," she said simply, "and I gave them to him."

"Your own the writings then. You admit giving them to him."

"Yes. He showed an interest." She did not say that it was the illuminator who first suggested that she should publish her writings in the language in which they were written precisely because it was a language for the masses.

"It seems this Finn has an interest in many seditious writings."

Had she heard him right?

"Your Eminence, are you saying that my Revelations are seditious?"

He snatched the papers from her. "I would hardly call this orthodox theology." He slapped them against her writing table. "This talk of a Mother God. What is this, anchoress, some kind of pagan goddess cult?"

"No, no, Your Eminence. If I may be so bold as to say, you misunderstand my meaning . . . if you would but read the rest."

" '*And the second person of the Trinity is our Mother in kind . . . For in our Mother Christ we have profit and increase*'—Jesus Christ is not a woman!"

He rose to his feet, knocking the stool over.

"*'He,'* Your Eminence," she said, lowering her voice in an attempt to tamp down the rhetoric, "if you will read on, I said, *'He is our Mother of mercy.'* Motherhood, the gentle, loving, caring mercy of motherhood is like the love of our Lord Jesus: that is all I'm saying. The quality of love, the quality of Christ's infinite mercy is most like a mother's love for her child. *That* is all I'm saying here."

He slapped his free hand hard against the table. Her inkpot sloshed, spilling precious drops onto clean vellum.

"It is not well said. And it is in *English*."

She hastily blotted the ink. "I am sorry if you do not find my simple language to your liking, but I'm not writing for priests and bishops who I assume already know the depth and breadth of His love. I'm only trying to explain God's love, His infinite mercy in a way that was revealed to me so that the unlearned can understand. What difference does it matter what language I use, if I speak the truth?"

"It calls your loyalty into question. It is a matter of alliances. Alliances and appearances."

And if that's all it comes down to for you, bishop, then my heart fears for your soul. She pinched her lips together to hold back the words.

He had tortured the sheaf of papers into a scroll-like roll during their exchange. He stood for a long moment tapping them against his knee, apparently weighing her comments. At least he seemed calmer after his outburst.

"What do you know of Finn the illuminator?"

"I know him to be a good man," she said, a little taken aback at the abrupt shift.

"Do you accuse me of falsely imprisoning an innocent man?"

"I accuse you of nothing, Your Eminence. Those were your words, not mine."

He scanned the room. "Where is your cat?"

"My cat?" Had she convinced him? Was that why he was changing the subject? She tried to smile at him, reluctant for him to see how violated she felt to have him standing inside her anchorage. But he was her bishop. Perhaps he had the right. "Jezebel has been gone for about a week. It's not the first time. She'll come back when she's ready."

"I miss seeing her on your lap." A bit of a smile. Mayhap the storm had passed. "I will send a servant with some curds to coax her back. And something for you as well," he said.

"You are kind, Your Eminence." She sighed with relief as he laid the rolled-up papers on her desk. Thank the Holy Virgin his visit was coming to an end.

"In the meantime, if you wish to maintain fellowship with Holy Church, you are to write an apologia for this deviation from orthodoxy. Explain your understanding of the Godhead and Holy Trinity. It must state your loyalty to Holy Church doctrine and must be appended to any published copy of your English writings. Since your Latin is deficient, you may transcribe a copy of the apologia in Norman French for my keeping."

He might have been reading off a list of supplies, his tone was so detached. Was she hearing him right? Was her right to the anchorhold threatened?

"Until such a document is in my hand, you will abstain from the Holy Sacraments."

Even her right to the Eucharist!

"I warn you to be circumspect in your associations and careful in your language. Heresy is a serious charge. It can bring eternal damnation to your soul and death to your corporeal body."

He moved to the door. She had risen when he did, so as not to be sitting in his presence, and now her head was spinning. She dropped to her knees in a half-curtsy, half-swoon.

"I will send for the document tomorrow, and I will send also writings on the Holy Trinity. Church-sanctioned writings, which I admonish you to review for the instruction of your soul."

He extended his ring for her to kiss. Trembling, she raised it to her lips.

"I will not visit you again," he said.

She stayed on her knees, not out of reverence, but because she lacked the strength to face him. She heard the heavy scraping of the door, the bolt being shot with the dead finality of the first time, leaving her alone once again in the smothering darkness of her cell.

⁓⋇⁓

Father Andrew was preparing to celebrate Candlemass at Saint Julian's. It was the feast of the Virgin's Purification. The candlemaker brought the candles to be blessed early in the day and grumbled as he handed over his merchandise. The vestibule was so cold you could see the man's breath as he spoke.

"If all my customers were as tight in the purse as you, Father, my children would go hungry."

He was right; of course. The Church set the price, not the chandler, and Father Andrew knew that it was scarcely enough to pay the cost of the beeswax.

"The candles are used in the service of the Holy Virgin. Your sacrifice will not go unrewarded. Your soul will profit."

It was an answer he gave by rote. He knew full well it meant little to the man who wanted honest pay for honest goods. As a young priest, he'd tried to communicate his own sense of honor at being allowed to serve his God, hoping it would inspire others. It never did. Now, he just delivered the official Church response for services rendered, never thinking about the words. He delivered the mass in like manner.

The chandler mumbled something about the Church being rich enough to pay a poor man proper wages. Father Andrew only smiled and nodded as he shut the heavy doors, shutting out his complaints with the frosty air. These days, nobody seemed to understand how important it was to maintain the house of the Lord. Just let the plague come calling to Master Chandler's house. He'd be begging to donate his wares to the Holy Virgin for free, the curate thought as he stored the candles in the cupboard behind the altar.

He opened the left side of the double doors and put in the candles, neatly stacking them one by one, placing the half dozen or so left from last year aside to be used first—they had already been blessed. While he was there, he would get a fresh stole for the mass. He opened the right side. The door sagged on its hinge; the iron bolt had worked loose. Now he would have to find a carpenter. No easy task when most were busy rebuilding the steeple on the cathedral, and the ones who were not did inferior work. Even these found excuses to put him off, looking for more lucrative employment. Filthy lucre. The contaminant of the soul.

The acolytes were careless, too. Where the folded, newly mended vestments should be there was a pile of rumpled linen. He picked up the altar cloth to fold it and saw that it was stained. Mildew, probably, a perpetual problem in the dark interior of the chapel. But even in the winter-dim interior of the chapel, he could see it was not mildew. It was darker—and stiff. It looked almost like a bloodstain. His pulse quickened. A bloodstain? He unfolded the cloth, held it up to the light from the window. He squinted his eyes. The stains were in blotches and spots, broken, but there was no doubt about it. The spots connected in the shape of a cruciform. *Domine Ihesu Christe*. The Holy Rood! It was the Saviour's blood. A miracle. A miracle, here, at Saint Julian's Church. On his watch. The Church of Saint Julian had an anchoress, and now it had a miracle. God was smiling on this church. God was smiling on him.

He looked at the great crucifix hanging above him, half-expecting the blood to begin dripping from the ivory legs, but there was no sign of life, no tears flowing from its painted eyes, no drops of blood. No matter. The Saviour had granted them a miracle. This was the blood of Christ on the altar cloth. He, Father Andrew, curate of the Church of Saint Julian, would take it to the bishop, who would pronounce it authentic and commission a gold reliquary. With great ceremony—in which he already saw himself playing a significant role—they would place the holy relic on the altar. Pilgrims would come from as far as Thetford and Canterbury, maybe even London, to see it. Saint Julian's would be famous for its miracles.

His heart was hammering so fast he could almost hear it. No. That was not his heart—unless his heart shuffled more than beat within his chest. The noise was coming from the back of the cupboard. They sometimes had trouble with rats, but not lately. That's why he suffered the anchoress to have a cat. He carefully folded the stained cloth, pressed it to his lips and placed it gently on the altar. Then he reached his hand back into the cupboard to retrieve the rest of the vestments to make sure they had not been soiled with mouse droppings. His hand encountered something soft and wriggling, a tongue rough as pumice licked his fingers. He jerked his hand out of the cupboard and reached for his crosier. He swiped its crook once against the back of the cupboard and drew it out.

A pair of kittens, their eyes barely opened, lay curled and purring within its crook.

Disappointment carries the taste of bile, and it filled Father Andrew up, spilling into his mouth bitter as quinine. Here was his miracle. The she-cat that the anchoress sheltered was responsible for this. That devil's familiar had profaned his altar, daring to drop her unholy spawn beneath the image of the Saviour.

By now the kittens had discovered their new environment and begun to explore, tumbling over the shepherd's staff with wobbly legs. His crosier would have to be reconsecrated and the whole altar cleansed. There would be three of the things now and the next litter would be larger. Jezebel—an apt name. The whore of Babylon, she was out whoring now, probably, satiating her evil nature, abandoning her babies.

In a fit of resolution, he went to the vestry, where he prowled in a closet. Muttering imprecations inappropriate to his calling, he came back shortly with a rope, a grain sack, and a large stone. In a matter of seconds he had scooped up the kittens, thrown them in the sack with the stone, and secured the top. The sack writhed, forming and reforming into little bumps of desperation. So much crying and mewling for such small beasts. He had a moment's—just a moment's—pang, and then he looked again at the soiled altar cloth, his non-miracle.

He slung the bag over his shoulder and was headed toward the door when he heard a hiss behind him. He turned in time to see the mama cat fling herself at his face, claws outstretched for his eyes. He grabbed her by the neck, but not before she had torn a bloody gash in his cheek (which scar he would bear into old age). He wrung her neck as though she were a chicken, then opened the sack and threw the dead mother in with her kittens.

He flung the lot from Bishop's Bridge into the Wensum River.

⚘

"Father Andrew, have you seen my cat?" the anchoress asked after she finished her confession. "She's been gone almost three weeks. She's never been gone that long before."

Julian watched him as he fingered the bandage on his cheek.

"Not for many days," he said.

There was an abruptness, almost an irritation in his voice when he addressed her, and a disengaged look in his eyes. It had been thus ever since the bishop's visit. Had the bishop spoken to him about her? Maybe he had instructed him to deny her the right to communion? She had wondered this daily, each time the priest had offered her the Body and the Blood in the same distracted way. Mayhap it was just her imagination. Perhaps the bishop had relented or merely forgotten to instruct the priest that she should be denied. Each time she took the host onto her tongue, she did so with great relief.

"Father, if you will come around to Alice's window, I'll dress your wound. It has been three days since we changed it."

A few minutes later he entered through Alice's room and sat opposite Julian on the other side of the window. His shoulders slumped forward. He didn't seem to want to look at her. What was so interesting about her floor? Or was it that he couldn't look at her because he knew she was about to be charged with heresy or driven from her anchorhold? She retrieved her sewing scissors to cut away the dressing.

"It's healed nicely," she said, leaning through the window to examine it. "It no longer needs a bandage."

"It still smarts."

"The bishop sent me some books from the library at Carrow Priory last week." She tried to keep her tone light, conversational as she traced a line of ointment down the scar with her finger. "Did he send you some too?" she asked, even though she had never known Father Andrew to be a student of theology. They had never really talked of spiritual matters. Not talked about anything, really. He was her confessor, that was all. He appeared daily at the chapel window through which he celebrated the mass. Their relationship revolved around the ritual.

"The bishop does not often seek me out," he said.

"He visited me Tuesday week past. I thought you might have seen him then."

"I was called away to Castle Prison Tuesday past, to say the Office of the Dead for a hanged man."

Her hand froze on his scarred cheek. Dare she ask the name?

"Last rites for the condemned? Is that usual?"

"When the criminal asks to confess, the Church tries to comply."

"Was this man . . . was he . . . what crime had he committed?"

"He poached the king's deer."

Not Finn, then, but some poor peasant, some father, or husband, or son, had died because he dared get meat for his table. Her hand resumed its ministrations.

"I will pray for the poor man's soul," she said as she replaced the stopper on the ointment jar. "Take this with you. Put it on your wound daily. I'm afraid you may be left with a narrow little scar as a reminder to be more careful when you are pruning thornbushes."

"Thornbushes? Oh. Yes. I will. Be more careful."

"You were blessed in that the branch missed your eye when it snapped back."

"Yes, I was fortunate," he said, and then, as though it were an afterthought:

"I have an altar cloth that needs mending. The embroidery threads have been snagged . . . careless acolytes. I will leave it in the chapel window for you to mend. After you've finished reading the books the bishop sent, of course."

"I'll do it right away."

He rose as if to leave, then hesitated. Was he going to say something about the bishop? Was he gathering the words to approach her on matters of orthodoxy?

"Anchoress . . ."

"Yes?"

"About your cat."

"Oh, my cat. Jezebel. Yes?"

"She will probably not return after so long a time." A pause. He seemed to be looking past her, through the communion window into the shadowy chapel interior. "I will get you another cat."

The next day, an old tom appeared at her garden window. He was fat and slow and lazy, a retired mouser fresh from the kitchens at Carrow Priory. He spent most of his time dozing in the garden window, ignoring the mice that scurried in the chapel.

NINETEEN

Eleven holy men converted all the world into the right
religion; The more readily, I think, should all manner
of man be converted, We have so many masters,
priests and preachers, and a pope on top.
—WILLIAM LANGLAND,
PIERS PLOWMAN (14TH CENTURY)

Half-Tom had tried twice in the last two weeks to get to Finn. Each Thursday, he'd made the difficult trip to market, not because he had much to sell—buyers and sellers alike were rarer in winter—but he persisted in the hope that he could see his friend. Each Thursday, he'd been turned away, once by the surly guard who had tormented him in the Beggar's Daughter (the time that Finn had come to his rescue), and once by an impatient bailiff who said he knew nothing of the prisoner. Neither had any patience with a dwarf from the fens.

This time he was determined, and he had a plan. On Wednesday, he made the long trek to Blackingham, and for more reasons than to eat the old cook's pottage—lately she'd taken a dislike to him—or to catch a glimpse of the pretty kitchen wench who'd frighted him so with her singing in the bee-tree. He could not add inches to his stature, but he could add inches to his status by wearing the livery of a noble house. A ducal house would have made him a giant. But since he knew no dukes, he'd have to settle for a knight's household.

"A *short* groomsman," he'd said to Magda as they conspired together to steal the uniform from the laundry at Blackingham.

Now she'd returned with her stolen trophy, and they were alone in the cavernous kitchen, cozy with the great fire and the smell of simmering stew on the hearth. She laughed at him when he draped the blue tunic over his head. But he didn't mind her laughter. He waved his arms in the air, flapping the excess fabric about like a jester, to inspire more of it. To him, her laughter was as heady as mead—and just as rare, for she seldom bestowed it on anyone.

"Ye'll snare no respect looking like a scarecrow," she said, tears of mirth spilling down her cheeks. "They're like to toss ye in the dungeon with Master Finn."

That was more words than he'd ever heard the girl string together. He hopped about on one foot, tripping over the too-long leggings, hoping for more. Instead she screwed her mouth into a pout of concentration and, reaching for a kitchen knife, commanded him to climb upon a stool.

She slashed at the excess fabric: first the sleeves, then the legs. "Stand still. Ye don't want to be gettin' blood on Lady Kathryn's livery."

He stood motionless, as if he were watching deer feed in the forest, afraid to breathe lest he startle her and break the spell of her closeness. He wanted to reach out and touch her hair, but he dared not. He'd already heard the sound of the heavy oak door groaning on its hinges—Agnes returning. She would not welcome any sign of affection from a half-man for the girl she treated like a daughter.

"What foolishness are the two of ye up two?" Agnes asked as she set down a basket of turnips.

Magda paused in her tearing and slashing. "'Tis cold. Ye should've sent me to cellar to fetch those."

"What's he gussied up for? Yule's well past. Season for tomfoolery's over." She picked up the torn rags of cloth from the floor, peered closer. "Lands, that's Blackingham livery you're destroyin', girl! What are ye thinking? That fine blue cloth don't come cheap. Lady Kathryn will have all our hides— though at least one amongst us wouldn't be worth much." She glared at him.

Half-Tom explained his plan.

Arms akimbo, her brow puckered with frowning, she considered for a long moment. Half-Tom grinned at her. He didn't doubt, despite her gruffness—and who could fault her on that score for wanting to guard her treasure—the goodness of her heart. " 'Tis the only way," he said.

"I'll fetch my needle to hem the edges," the cook said. "Save them pieces, Magda. Cloth's too fine to waste."

～❧～

The next day Half-Tom presented himself before the head constable at the castle keep.

"I've a message from the lady of Blackingham for the prisoner Finn."

The constable looked him up and down without getting out of his chair. Half-Tom waved a rolled-up parchment in front of the officer's nose—not a letter at all, but an old purchase order for goods for the Blackingham kitchen. Magda had helped him reheat the seal so that it appeared not to have been broken. The constable reached for it. Half-Tom pulled it behind his back.

"Lady Kathryn says the seal is to be broken only by Finn. Private matters between a man and his daughter. Lady Kathryn asks that I be allowed to visit the prisoner so his daughter will know that he is not being ill-used."

The constable appeared to be considering, but did not move.

"Lady Kathryn is a friend of Sir Guy de Fontaigne," Half-Tom said.

"The sheriff has given his approval?"

"If she has to ask, she would have to explain that you refused her request, wouldn't she?" He heaved an exaggerated sigh. "And that might make the sheriff angry."

The constable grinned good-naturedly. "You negotiate like a full-grown man." He stood up. "Follow me."

Half-Tom followed the constable up two flights of curving steps, where he opened an iron-grated door with the large keys on his belt and ordered Half-Tom to wait in the hallway. "He's a particular favorite of the bishop. If they're playing at chess, His Eminence would not like to be disturbed."

"The bishop?"

"Aye. He visits at least once a week. They have animated discussions about theology."

Half-Tom didn't understand the meaning of "theology." Why would a bishop visit a prisoner—unless it was to question him? A sense of dread settled over Half-Tom's shoulders like a monk's hood. He'd heard stories, horrible stories, about racks and pulleys and spiked cages and brandings. He must be crazy to meddle in such. But he owed the man. At least the illuminator was being kept aboveground, way aboveground, judging by the number of steps they had climbed.

The constable came back shortly, motioning with his head for Half-Tom to enter the room at the end of the hall. There was no iron door there, and the wooden door stood open to the hall. "Just bang on the grille here when you're ready to leave. There's a guard at the bottom of the stair."

Half-Tom almost cried with relief as he peeked over the threshold. The room was clean, warm, furnished with a bed and a worktable, and filled with afternoon light pouring through the high window onto the worktable. He recognized Finn immediately, thinner and more stooped than he remembered. But it was Finn, sitting at his worktable, brush in hand, as though he were not imprisoned at all.

Half-Tom cleared his throat. The illuminator looked up and smiled broadly.

"Half-Tom! Old friend, come in." Finn got up stiffly. "Are you a sight for these sore old eyes! Have you news from Blackingham? Come in. Here, take my chair. I'll stand." He dragged the chair closer to the small coal fire, wincing as he did. "Lady Kathryn has sent you. I can tell by the livery."

Half-Tom squirmed, then laughed self-consciously. "Uniform is just a ruse. I tried to get in to see you before and couldn't, so I *borrowed* the uniform. With a little help."

"Oh, I thought . . ."

There was a haggard, gaunt look in his eyes, disappointment in his face.

"But I'm going back to Blackingham. They've asked for a report."

Finn smiled weakly as if to say he knew Half-Tom was only being kind. "My daughter? Is she well?"

"I have not heard otherwise. Except I'm sure she misses her father." He sat on the floor, careful of his new livery. "You take the chair. Where does the bishop sit when he visits?"

"The bishop brings his own chair."

"Are you in pain, Master Finn? You favor your side." Half-Tom was remembering the instruments of torture his imagination had conjured earlier.

"A little going-away present from Sykes. You remember the blackguard from the Beggar's Daughter?"

"I am much in your debt."

"You owe me only what debt one friend owes another. But I do have a scheme whereby you can come to my aid."

"An escape? I'm for it."

"No, old friend, no escape. That's not possible. But first, let me offer you refreshment. My serving lad brought enough victuals to share, let's see what's here." He removed the cloth from a basket resting on the hearth. A savory odor of beef broth and vegetables filled the room.

"You have a servant?"

Finn's low laugh was filled with bitterness. "My circumstances have much improved in the last two weeks. It seems I am a valued slave."

Half-Tom surveyed the worktable—the paint pots and brushes, the tall wooden panel propped in a corner on which a ground of azure had already been laid. "You're painting for the bishop?"

"Henry Despenser wants a five-paneled reredos for the cathedral. That altarpiece is the thread that holds my life. I intend to spin it out until it is as fine as the gold wire in a lady's snood."

Half-Tom shook his head, declining the plate of food the illuminator held out to him. How did he know this wasn't the only hot meal Finn would have for a week?

"Come on. Eat it. I can have whatever I want. The bishop feeds his pets well."

"Are you sure?"

"I'm sure. I frequently pitch the leftovers out the window to feed the fish in the river. I think they are disappointed with the scraps. They keep expecting something warm and living."

"River is deeper there. A man might live after such a jump, if he could swim," Half-Tom offered.

"I have my daughter to think about," he said. "I cannot place her in danger. That's where you come in."

"Anything."

"If you could just act as messenger between my daughter and me. Assure her that her father is still alive. I've a letter for you to take to her." Something like the closing of a shutter passed across his face. "And one for Lady Kathryn. They're already written. I've been hoping for a messenger I could trust."

He rummaged in the chest that held a variety of paints and brushes and brought out two tight rolls of parchment. Half-Tom accepted them, and as he placed them inside his fancy belted tunic, he was gratified to find a small slit in the lining for just such a purpose.

"They will be delivered today."

Finn closed his eyes for just a moment. The muscles in his face relaxed. "There's more," he said.

"You've but to say it."

"The Wycliffe papers. I'm convinced of the importance of an English translation. God is not something the bishop and his ilk have a right to keep for their exclusive use. See if you can get me a copy of Wycliffe's Gospel of John and bring it to me—"

Half-Tom grinned, reached inside his blue tunic and handed Finn a wrapped parcel. It bore an Oxford seal. "Master Wycliffe gave it to me when I delivered your last," he said.

"Good. Now I can fill my days with something more worth the while than the bishop's whimsy. But I can't afford to have the translations found. My cell is subject to search at any time. So if under the guise of carrying messages to and from Blackingham you could pick up the illuminated text, you won't have to make the journey to Oxford but once. I'll make plain copies that you can give to any Lollard priest for dissemination."

"Dis——?"

"Spreading. The priests will give them out so that people can read the Scriptures for themselves."

"What if the bishop should surprise you with a visit and find you out?" Half-Tom had a sudden vision of torture racks and pulleys.

"His servants always precede his coming. But I need to warn you, my friend. This work will be dangerous for anybody connected with it. The bishop is anxious to charge Wycliffe and all his followers with heresy. Wycliffe has the protection of the duke. You do not."

"I've enough wits to stay out of the bishop's way," Half-Tom assured him.

"I know that to be true. You're here, aren't you?"

"Aye. And I'll be back. I promise " He stood and patted his tunic, feeling for the letters in the lining.

Finn stood too, and extended his hand.

"I'll be waiting, old friend."

A blackbird landed on the casement of the window, pecked at a crumb, then took wing. Half-Tom watched Finn watching the bird, and felt his longing for freedom as though it were his own.

～✹～

The play wagon was well out of Norwich and on its way to Castle Acre when Colin spotted the contortionist sprinting after them. "Slow down, driver," someone shouted, and the muscleman held out an arm and swung his partner into the wagon. As he settled himself onto a pile of blankets, he slapped Colin on the knee and told him he'd delivered his message.

Colin had been trying for a month to get a message to his mother. But the players had found a venue to their liking and tarried. Their schedule was nothing if not flexible.

"Nice house, lad. Generous, too. But the place was a bit deserted. I had to go to the kitchens to raise anybody. The old cook gave me this."

He unfolded an oiled cloth, and Colin recognized the familiar smell of Agnes's yeasty bread. His throat tightened with longing. He should have delivered the message himself, or better yet, he should have gone home, told his mother he'd changed his mind. But John's ghost tapped him on the shoulder. He closed his eyes to the vision of the shepherd's empty, blackened eye sockets, a vision that had not visited him since joining the troupe.

"Was anybody else in the kitchens?"

"Just a dwarf on his way out and a pretty little blond maid coming in. She was friendly, too."

Glynis. Colin felt his face burn in the darkness of the covered wagon. He knew what "friendly" meant by the jovial, leering way it was delivered. Colin pinched his flesh, hard, to chase the devil's temptations away, the familiar unwanted stirrings.

"You left my letter?"

The wagon rocked and jolted along the rutted road. Someone next to him spilled his beer and shouted, cursing, to the driver to watch out.

"Aye, lad, I left your letter. Your poor mum is probably crying her heart out right now that her baby boy has run off with a troupe of players. But never you mind. We'll take good care of you and deliver you to the monks come spring, hale and hearty."

"And a whole lot wiser," one of the party volunteered.

The band of mummers didn't seem to mind the cold as they passed around a jug of beer. Colin had never had beer before, only watered wine and ale. No wonder Alfred had been so fond of it. It tasted bitter, but it warmed the belly and made his fellows jovial. From the back of the wagon, someone began to blow on a recorder. Someone else picked up the high sweet notes and started to sing. Colin liked the music. Like the beer, it softened the hard edge of his homesickness.

❧❦

Kathryn was alone in the kitchen, where she'd gone to request a physick of Agnes for Rose's swollen ankles. Finding both the cook and the scullery maid absent, she was preparing it herself when she heard the door open behind her. She whirled around, expecting Agnes. A dwarf, resplendent in Blackingham's bright, ill-adapted livery, bowed low. The tassel on his peaked cap brushed the floor. "I have a missive for her ladyship." The dwarf reached in his tunic and held out a rolled fragment of parchment.

She'd seen the dwarf before. At least once or twice, he'd brought messages to Finn. And she wasn't really surprised to see him in Blackingham livery. Agnes had explained to her about the missing uniform. Kathryn had not voiced approval, though she was glad enough to hear it. She had made discreet inquiries of the sheriff, who had informed her brusquely that the prisoner was still alive and waiting judgment in Castle Prison. But that had been two weeks ago, an eternity.

The dwarf coughed as if to remind her he was still there. She took the parchment from him, but did not open it. It bore no official seal. A notice of execution would have a seal, surely. Her whole body trembled. She braced her hips against the table behind her for support. The little man's peaked cap danced as he fidgeted before the fire—a blue flame jumping among the yellow. Why couldn't he stand still? Her fingers clutched the parchment in a tight coil. Such a simple task to open it. To read its content. And yet she could not.

"This is . . . this is for me?"

Who else? Unless it was for Rose.

"Aye, milady. And there's one for the lady Rose as well." He reached into his pocket and drew out another roll

So. This was it. The word she'd longed for, the word she'd dreaded.

"From Castle Prison?" The words clotted in the back of her throat.

"Aye, milady. From Master Finn, hisself."

"You've seen him?"

"That I have. With mine own eyes."

"Is he . . . is he well?"

"He has endured much these weeks. But he is alive, and his lot is above the common prisoner's."

She realized that she had been holding her breath. She exhaled heavily, then asked, "How does he look?"

The dwarf paused in his fidgeting, blinked owl eyes at her. "He looks like a man who has endured much."

"Are there . . . are there marks upon his body?"

"Marks?"

"Scars, burns?" she asked in a raspy whisper.

"Nay, milady. He is stiff in the ribs and winces when he walks, but the ribs will mend. Though I'll be saying he is very thin."

"Did he ask . . . ? Did he ask for his daughter?"

"Aye, milady. His worry for her causes him much pain. He requests that—"

The door opened, pushed by a blast of cold air, and Agnes bustled in carrying two headless pigeons in her right hand. Blood dripped from their wrung necks into a bowl that she carried in her left. The scullery maid closed the door behind her, smiled when she saw the dwarf standing in front of the fire. A look passed between them. Kathryn remembered the maid's role in the purloined uniform. Magda, that was her name. The girl curtsied to her prettily. Kathryn acknowledged her with a nod.

"Agnes, it seems Blackingham has another groom in its employ. Provide him with refreshment and send word to Simpson to billet him for the night." Then, to the dwarf: "If you are to wear my livery, I should at least know your name."

"I am called Half-Tom."

"Well, Half-Tom, it would please me if you would quarter here for the night." She weighed the parchment in her hands. Its lightness belied the heft of the words within. "The message you have brought may require an answer. I shall consider it in the privacy of my chamber." She reached for the other parchment "And I shall deliver this to the illuminator's daughter."

She suddenly remembered her errand. "Agnes, the girl is poorly again.

Send Magda up with the seed tea as soon as it has steeped." Then, to Half-Tom: "You will be able to gain access to the illuminator again, is that so? To carry an answer on the morrow?"

"Aye, milady. Thanks to the badge of your household."

※ ※

When Kathryn reached her chamber, she sat on the bed, clinging to the hangings to quiet her trembling. The two rolled parchments lay beside her on the counterpane. The scroll bound with a blue cord, that was the one the dwarf had said was hers. Rose's was tied with scarlet. She picked up neither of them. Her hands smoothed, instead, the heavy brocade of one of the bed curtains tied at the four posts with silken ribands. In another time, a happier time, the curtains had been untied to give privacy to its occupants. A great sadness welled up inside her at the memory. "I never thought to find such happiness again," he'd said, breathing into her hair, his body spooning hers. That had been the first time. She could not bear to remember more.

With trembling hands she picked up the parchment tied in blue, unrolled it, held it beneath the wall sconce that had been lit against the late-afternoon gloom. The pen stroke, though not so bold as she remembered, was unmistakably his hand: the downward thrust on the vertical lines, the graceful flounce of the capitals. She traced the heading with her fingers, held it briefly against her lips, then, feeling foolish—did she hope to divine its meaning with her lips?—read the words.

Castle Prison
2nd Month, Year of Our Lord 1380
My lady,

(Was her name so hateful to him that he could not bring himself to write it?)

I'm writing you in direst straits, wounded by the betrayal of one who was formerly the object of my heart's most ardent desire.

(Formerly. He said formerly. She did not want to read more, yet she could not tear her eyes away.)

Mortally wounded by the dagger of treacherous words, I'm yet forced to endure an existence made hateful by the abandonment of all hope. I shall not offend my lady's ears with the tedious details of my suffering at the hands of my jailers. Since there has been no inquiry or intervention, no timely protestations of my innocence from the lady of Blackingham, I can only construe her negligence as indifference to my fate, or worse, belief that I am guilty of the crimes of which she bears witness against me. Either is a greater source of pain than any my tormentor could inflict. I have left to me only one reason to cling to this miserable existence. I would not have my child be an orphan. Therefore, I beseech you, Kathryn, in the name of that love which we once shared (here the letters wavered, was it because of her tears or his hand?) *that you grant shelter and support to my child until such a time as I may make other arrangements on her behalf. I am not without resources even in these circumstances and will recompense you for her keep.*

I would ask one other thing of you, yes, even beg it of you in my desperation. I ask that you provide Rose with an escort and a horse so that she may visit me. I must see her with my own eyes and assure her that her father has not abandoned her.

And then there was only his name like a slash across the paper. No benediction, no term of endearment. Just *Finn the Illuminator*, scrawled so hard he surely broke the nib of his quill.

Kathryn rolled the scroll back up, retied the blue riband, laid it down beside its twin. Neither bore a seal. She reread the letter. How it hurt to think that he thought he must pay for Rose's upkeep. "Is profit all you think about?" he'd asked the last time they were together, the time he'd left silver coins beside her bed, the time she'd sent him away because he'd loved a woman who was a Jew. She smoothed the coverlet with shaking hands. She would not send him from her bed now, not if he'd slept with a thousand Jews.

She picked up the other scroll, fingered the scarlet cord that bound it. Rose would be sleeping now. Kathryn's trembling fingers untied the cord, and her eyes devoured the loving endearments with which Finn addressed his daughter. No trace of despair—here were only brave, sweet words of assurance, telling her everything would be all right, asking her to come and see him until he could come for her. He spoke of Spain. *Would you like to see Andalusia?* Wistful words to pump up his hope and comfort his daughter, or was he planning to go far away, away from Blackingham, away from Kathryn?

The torchlight above the bed guttered out. Dying light from a late sun barely penetrated the shadowy room. She rolled the letter to Rose inside her own and placed it in her garderobe chest. It would only distress the girl more to know her father was asking for her. She was a strong, willful girl. She might even try to make the twelve-mile journey into Norwich on her own. It would surely cause her to miscarry, and while that might be a blessing, Kathryn could not let anything happen to Finn's daughter, not while she was in her care. She had enough on her conscience already.

Kathryn lay down on her bed in the dusk-filled room, pushed back the throbbing pain in her head. On the morrow, she would tell Rose a messenger had come from her father to say that he was well and sent his love and hoped to see her in the spring. She would not mention a letter.

Closing her eyes, she lay in the dark until Glynis knocked on the door— minutes? hours?—later, bringing her supper.

The maid replaced the rushlight in the burnt-out torch and relit it from the sputtering coals in the grate. "I've a message fer ye, too," she said, taking a piece of folded paper from her pocket.

Kathryn sat up, pushed back her hair, its greasy strands feeling unfamiliar beneath her fingers. "Give me the message. Not the food."

" 'Twas brought by a right comely lad. Said he was from a band of players from Colchester."

"Agnes sent them away, I hope. We've no need for mummers or merry-makers."

She unfolded the paper—it was stained and frayed and smelled of sweat.

"Will there be anything else, milady?"

"Tell Cook to send the dwarf messenger away in the morning. I've no message to send with him."

What was there to say? She knew he had not killed the priest, but she knew, too, that even if she thought he had, she would not have given him over except for her fear for Alfred. Nothing had changed. She would not see her son's red curls on the headsman's block. Not even in the name of justice. Besides, there was not enough evidence to convict Finn. "Above the common prisoner," that's what the dwarf had said. Already Finn had friends. He was smart. He would survive. Alfred might not. He was the heir apparent to a property coveted by both crown and Church.

If only Alfred would come and declare his innocence—but Sir Guy had sent him off with a contingent of his yeomen to train for the bishop's dream of holy war against the French pope. "If the fighting really starts, I can recall him." Guy de Fontaigne had dangled this promise like a plum to ingratiate himself—or to show his power over her. Nothing came free with the sheriff. She would not beg favors of him. Not yet.

Glynis picked up the tray, asking as she backed out the door, "Shall I come back to tend ye before bed?"

"Not tonight."

The girl could not suppress a smile, Kathryn noticed, envying her the energy with which she flounced out of the room, already making plans, no doubt, to spend her free evening in the arms of some snot-nosed groom. Kathryn envied her that anticipation, too.

When Glynis had gone, Kathryn turned her attention to the letter.

Colin's handwriting! She read its contents hungrily, then, letting it fall from her hand, rested her head in her hands. Here was something else to worry about.

She had assumed Colin was safe in the bosom of the Benedictines. But it seemed she was to be denied even this small comfort. Her youngest son was cavorting around the winter landscape with a band of profligate mummers— a sheep frolicking among wolves—while the seed that he had planted in Rose's womb grew into his child. But at least he was safe from bodily harm, though heaven only knew what harm might come to his immortal soul in such company.

A coal shifted among the sluggish embers, emitting a sigh into the chilly air. She turned her face to the wall and gave in to the pain in her head. It was no more than she deserved.

TWENTY

*The mother may suffer her child to fall sometimes, and
to be distressed in different ways, for its own profit . . .
And though, possibly, an earthly mother may suffer
her child to perish, our heavenly Mother Jesus can
never suffer us who are His children to perish.*
—JULIAN OF NORWICH, *DIVINE REVELATIONS*

eeks passed before Kathryn gathered enough courage to make the twelve-mile journey to Castle Prison. She had lain awake each night, rifling the drawers of her mind, searching for words to explain. She'd come up empty. But she owed Finn at least the assurance that she would take care of Rose and an explanation of why his daughter could not come to him. What that explanation was going to be she was not sure. But if she could just see him, if he could look in her eyes, mayhap he would read there the love that she still had for him. Mayhap not. But having tried, mayhap she could sleep again.

Twice, she had bound her hair in its golden snood, put on her fur-trimmed cloak and mounted her palfrey. Twice, she had ridden the three miles into Aylsham. Twice, she had turned back, her groomsman following at a respectful distance.

But today dawned clear and brittle as the ice that would stay on the mill pond until March. No wintry clouds threatened on the horizon. Her mare could easily pick its away among the frozen ridges in the road. Her attention was not required in the brewery, the kitchens, the pantry, or the cellars, and she had settled the crofters' accounts with Simpson yesterday. Her bag of excuses was empty.

When she reached the Aylsham cross, she spurred her heels into the horse's side and headed its nose toward Norwich. Her cloak spread out in a train covering the horse's flank. The furred edge of her hood rippled in the wind, but she welcomed the biting cold of the wind that stung her eyes to tears.

The groomsman reined in his horse at the Aylsham cross in expectation. When his mistress did not turn back, he sighed and tugging his jerkin tighter, spurred his mount to a gallop.

⁓ ⁂ ⁀

Finn stood at the high window and gazed out, resting his eyes from the close work. He should be working on the bishop's panel, instead of Wycliffe's text, because tomorrow was Friday. The bishop always came on Fridays. Finn actually looked forward to these inspections. To a lonely man, even the devil was welcome company. The only other soul he'd seen, except for his jailers and the half-wit who served him, was Half-Tom. He'd seen the dwarf twice since his first visit. Once when he'd returned from Blackingham bringing no message and once when he'd come to pick up the finished Wycliffe text.

The shallow winding river below curved flat and frozen, like a blue-white highway, on the winter-blasted landscape, a highway he could not ride any more than a bird could ride upon a cloud. He could barely see the outside end of the bridge that led across the river and into the prison. The bridge was empty except for a lone rider, a woman, followed close behind by a groomsman. Fresh tracks in the snow marked their progress to the bridge. His painter's eye noted how brightly the blue and silver of the groom's uniform contrasted with the white background. Blue and silver. Blackingham livery! Rose! At last! He moved to the far right edge of the window, trying to see more of the bridge, but the woman had already passed out of sight.

He hurried across the threshold of his chamber, down the crooked stair to the grille at the bottom. Calm down, he told himself. There are many houses with blue livery, and the slash of silver could have been a trick of the light.

He scraped the bars with his pewter tankard. "Send my lackey," he yelled in the direction of the guardroom. "My chamber is cold. My daughter is coming. I need hot coals and some warm cider. Two cups."

The day serjeant came out, buttoning his breeches and mumbling. "Keep yer shirt on. A man can't even take a piss without being harassed. What do you think this is? A bleedin' inn?"

Finn didn't stay to listen to his grumbles but called over his shoulder, "Her name is Rose. Tell the constable I have permission from the bishop to see her."

She would be here any minute, and she would be hungry. It was a long ride. The serving boy would not bring his dinner for at least three more hours, and she would have to leave before then.

He poked at the barely glowing embers in the grate, then scrounged some biscuits from last night's supper and some dried fruit. He sprinkled the stale biscuits with a bit of water and a few precious grains of cane sugar, wrapped them in parchment, then placed them on the hearth to warm. The dried fruit he arranged on a plate and placed on the small table in front of the fire. He sat down to wait, jumped up to find his comb, ran it hurriedly through his hair and beard. Did he have a clean shirt?

❧❧

"I have come to see the prisoner Finn," Kathryn said with as much authority as she could muster. "I am Lady Blackingham."

Handing the reins to her groom, she dismounted in front of the castle keep. The guard stuck his head inside the door, mumbled some words she could not hear. A man wearing a short-sword strapped at his waist appeared. He looked surprised, even a little flustered; he bowed slightly. "My lady, we were not expecting you."

"Well, of course you were not expecting me. Finn the illuminator is here, is he not?"

"Well, yes, but——"

"You do allow visitors?"

"We sometimes allow visitors, even female visitors." He shot the guard a warning look at the sound of a snicker. "But it's a little unusual for a lady——"

"The sheriff was a friend of my husband, the late Lord Blackingham. I was assured I would be able to see the prisoner." Not exactly a lie.

"I will need to check. Perhaps, if you could come back——"

"Can you not see that I am near to frozen? This is no afternoon ride to the hunt. Sir Guy will not be pleased that you have inconvenienced the widow of his friend."

He sighed wearily. "I shall take you to him."

He picked up a large ring of keys and led her across the courtyard, paused at the foot of a sharply curving stairway where another guard lounged in a small anteroom. The door at the foot of the stairs was a network of iron bars. It scraped against the stone floor as the constable unlocked it. Kathryn flinched.

"Is the door at the top unlocked?" the constable asked the guard.

"Aye. His highness was just down here banging on the grille."

The constable motioned for Kathryn to go before him.

"Please," she said, "I prefer to see Master Finn alone."

She smiled, touching him on the sleeve, but she was never any good at playing the coquette. He hesitated. She reached into the velvet reticule hanging at her waist, fished out a silver coin and discreetly pressed it into his hand. Her throat was dry as she said, "I assure you I will be safe enough. I wish to speak to Master Finn about private matters."

The constable shrugged and motioned for her to go up. "It's quite a climb. Just come back down and bang on the grate when you're finished." He started to leave, then turned back, causing her to fear he might have changed his mind. "If you will stop by the castle keep when you leave, I have something that I think might be of interest to you."

He gave her a cursory bow, then she heard the key turning in the lock behind her. Her mind was so distracted at the thought of her encounter that she didn't even pause to wonder what it was the constable might want.

❧

Finn was poking at the fire, trying to stir it with a quill—they would not allow him anything sharper or heavier—when he heard light footsteps behind him. He dropped the quill into the fire. It burst into a bright line of flame. Turning, he saw the cloaked and hooded figure standing in the door, silhouetted against the light. He rushed forward and folded her in his arms.

"My sweet darling," he said. "At last. If you could but know how much your father—" He felt her stiffen. He withdrew, held her out at arm's length, laughing. "I'm sorry if I squeezed the breath from you, it's just—"

She pushed back the furred hood, framing her face.

"Kathryn!"

Not Rose after all. Disappointment first, then elation, but he would not acknowledge any joy the sight of her brought. He pushed it down into the black pit of his heart where it drowned in her treachery. How beautiful she was to him, still, standing there haughty as ever, her back ramrod-straight, her skin rosy and her eyes bright from the cold. He hated himself for noticing.

"I thought you were Rose," he said. It sounded flat, like words spoken into dead air.

"So I concluded from the warmth of your embrace."

"Where is Rose? Why did she not come with you?" Fear ambushed him. He reminded himself to breathe. "Is she ill?"

"Don't worry, Finn. Rose is well. I am taking care of her. May I come in?"

"The highborn lady of Blackingham is not afraid to enter the cell of a thief and a murderer? Left your jewelry at home, I hope. Aren't you afraid I might bash in your skull just as I crushed the skull of that dead priest?"

She stood rigid as a statue, looking at him with unbearable sadness in her face, her upper lip caught in her teeth so tightly he expected drops of blood to ooze from the lips that he, even now, wanted to kiss. How perverse must be his nature that he would find her still alluring.

"I know you to be neither thief nor murderer," she said. "I know you to be a good man." Her face was gaunt and there were shadows beneath her eyes.

"Tell that to your friend the sheriff," he said, turning away, feeling empty. Without her in his direct gaze, the hate—and the desire—drained away.

"May I have permission to enter?" Her words were softly spoken, laden with breath.

"What permission a condemned man can give." He stepped back and she crossed the threshold but stopped abruptly, the color fleeing from her face.

"What do you mean, 'condemned'?"

"Condemned to this." He waved his arms to indicate his surroundings.

She looked around, her eyes lingering on his cot, his worktable. "I imagined worse," she said.

"It was worse," he said. "But I've struck a coward's bargain. I have become the bishop's slave." His hand brushed the air above his worktable with a contemptuous sweep, hovered over the partially painted panel of the Assumption propped beneath the window. "In return for this bauble to decorate his altar, I'm allowed a pale imitation of life."

She touched the painting reverently. "It is no *bauble*. It's beautiful," she said. "As beautiful as all your work."

Odd how gratifying these words were, how important her good opinion was to him. He shrugged. "It keeps the noose from my neck."

She shivered at the word "noose," and that was gratifying too.

"I'm sorry if you find my chamber cold. It often is." Bastard, he thought. Trying to make her pity you more. "My manners appear as lacking as my circumstances. Please, my lady, sit." He indicated the lone chair. "Churlish of me to stand in your elevated presence, but there is only the one chair."

"Finn, don't, please."

He looked away from her, out the window to a patch of brittle sky with its winter-pale sun.

When he looked back at her, she might have been a figure in a painting. He could paint her thus, seated half in shadow, the light from the fire glazing the blue of her robe, her head bowed, her hands folded in her lap, eyes averted, as still and wan as alabaster. Waiting. A woman whose heart was a mystery. Place a baby in her lap and she becomes a Madonna, he thought. Better yet, paint her holding the bloody head of a wounded Christ.

"Why, Kathryn? I just want to know why?"

She raised her head but didn't answer.

"Was it because you hated what we were together, hated that you had bedded with a man who once loved a Jewess?"

"You know why, Finn. I had to choose."

"And you chose to lie."

She closed her eyes, breathed deeply, then opened her eyes, but did not look at him. "Whoever possessed the pearls killed the priest."

"So, when my daughter said Alfred planted the pearls in my room, you assumed his guilt and sacrificed me."

"I would have given my own life, would give my life to save you, don't you know that? But . . ." She appeared to study the fire as if she could find some answer written in the glowing coals. "If you had to choose between me or Rose, Finn, which would you have chosen?"

He'd asked himself that many times over the past weeks. "I could not have let them take you away so easily, Kathryn. I would have tried to find a way to save both you and Rose. I could not have let you go so easily."

"Easily. You think what I did was easy? I am trying. You don't understand. The sheriff—"

He grunted his disgust. "Your friend, the sheriff."

"Friend, enemy, his relationship to me is not what's important. He carries the key. I must need be gracious to him. It's not just you he holds over me. He holds Alfred, too. I have not seen my son since he went to be the sheriff's squire. If I could but talk to him, be sure that he was safe, then maybe I could petition the bishop for a—"

"A pardon? Don't delude yourself. Despenser means to keep me here until he tires of whatever this game is, and Sir Guy Fontaigne will never lift a finger to secure my freedom. Be wary of his promises, Kathryn. Don't give him more power over you. Don't make a devil's bargain on my behalf."

She indicated the table with its plate of biscuits, its two cups of steaming cider. She warmed her hands on one but did not pick it up. "You were expecting Rose."

Her smile, tight-lipped and sad, tugged at his heart. He steeled himself against her pleading face. He did not say he was glad to see her. Did not even invite her to drink.

"I've been expecting her every day since I wrote to her. Did you give her my letter?"

"I—I gave her your message."

Either she was lying or there was something very wrong. Rose would have insisted on coming. He knew it.

"You said she was not ill. Is she still with you? You haven't sent her away." He could feel the panic rising. "I told you, Kathryn, I will pay—"

"I don't want your money, Finn. Is that what you think of me? That I would turn a helpless girl away?"

He laughed at the wounded tone in her voice. "You were quick enough to dispose of your discarded lover. And in such an ingenious way. It could hardly be expected that you would support his Jewish daughter who was left without a farthing to her name."

"Rose will stay with me even if you are hanged, or freed, or die of old age in your bed. Whichever comes first."

Good. She was angry. He would not be moved by her anger, as he was by her sadness. The vehemence in her response reassured him.

"You've no right to think that I would turn your daughter out. Do you know how that wounds me?"

He knew.

She stood up and started to pace back and forth, her cloak swirling around her feet. She punctuated her words with clenched fists. He stared at the floor, her feet pacing in front of him. She was wearing the boots with the silver buckles, the boots he'd bought for her.

"I will treat her like my own daughter, Finn, I swear it. She will want for nothing. She will be clothed and fed and cared for as though she were a daughter of Blackingham. Both Rose and the child. I swear it by the Holy Virgin."

What child? What was she talking about? He sat down heavily in the chair. It was still warm with her body's heat. She had stopped pacing and the edge of her cloak was dangerously close to the grate. He bent over and lifted the edge away from the danger of an errant spark.

He looked up at her towering over him. "Child?" he asked.

"I did not mean to say it so bluntly. It's just that I wanted you to know you can trust me. I know I should have told you before, but things were so strained between us and then the sheriff came . . ." She held her gloved fingers over her mouth as if to hold back the words. Her eyes reddened. She gave a choked little gasp and then a second.

She was crying! He had never seen her cry before and he was unprepared for the strange effect it had on him. He wanted to kiss her; he wanted to scream at her to stop. What right did she have to cry? He leaped to his feet and grabbed her wrist, forcing her to stand still. To look at him. She winced as if in pain but did not complain. He lightened his grip slightly.

"What child are you talking about, Kathryn?"

She removed her hand from her mouth as if to unseal her lips. Her voice was husky with unshed tears. "Rose is with child. She will deliver in May."

His thoughts scattered like birds at the sound of a clapper. He let go her wrist, rubbed his face with his hands. Rose. His Rose. Scarcely more than a babe herself.

"She and Colin were lovers."

"Colin?"

"You were as blind as I. It was as much our fault as theirs. We left them too much on their own while we—"

"You don't have to remind me, Kathryn. I remember well what we did."

Silence as deep as a gulf between them.

"You sound as though you are sorry," she said.

"It's a bad seed, Kathryn, that bears bitter fruit."

Her eyes glittered with tears. "I would not take back one moment. I would not change one of those *bad* seeds for the purest blossoms in paradise."

"My grandchild will not be a bastard. Your son will marry my daughter."

She opened her mouth to speak. He held up his hand to silence her. "Don't say they cannot marry because she is a Jew. Don't say it, Kathryn. If I hear those words from your lips, I'll know you for a liar and a hypocrite whose heart cannot love. Don't say the king will not allow it. The king does not know my true identity. Nobody knows but you."

"They cannot marry," she said dully.

He wanted to strike her. He grabbed his right wrist with his left hand to restrain himself.

She tightened her shoulders in a flinching motion as though she read his mind. "They cannot marry because Colin has run away. I do not know where he's gone."

"When?"

"The same night you were arrested."

"Send your friend the sheriff to find him. Bring him back. Force him to face his responsibility."

"Colin doesn't know about the baby. He probably left to get away from Rose. The temptation to sin—"

"Are you saying that my daughter, who was a virgin when she entered the *protection* of your house, seduced your son?"

"No. I'm just saying that—Finn, you know the power of temptation."

She begged him with her eyes. He turned his back to her.

She reached out and touched the back of his right shoulder. Her voice was hardly above a whisper, but he heard every word. "I promise you, by the blood of the Saviour, I will take care of your daughter. And I will see that her child is cared for as well."

He took a sharp breath, seeking control. His ribs, only half-healed, pained him. The only sound in the room was the sound of Finn's pulse pounding in his head.

"I have to leave," she said. "The road is dangerous after dark."

Not trusting himself to speak, he said nothing. When he turned, she was gone.

The only indication that she'd ever been there was the fading scent of lavender, and the burden of the knowledge she'd brought with her. He listened for her footfalls as they echoed fainter and fainter down the stairs. He picked up the pewter cup and flung it against the wall. The cider splayed against the stone wall, then dripped in sticky, dark drops onto the floor.

⁓ ⁑ ⁓

Kathryn called for the guard to open the door. Her groom, who was warming himself at an open fire in the courtyard, unhitched her horse and brought it forward.

"My lady, just a moment, if you please. I have something that might interest you."

The constable. She'd forgotten about his request. She wanted to get on her horse and ride, put this miserable place behind her, let the wind dry her tears, the cold freeze her skin, until she couldn't feel the ache in her chest. But there was nothing for it. The fellow stood there expectantly. He had done her one favor already, and she knew she would need another soon.

"Quickly, please," she said. "It's a long ride back to Blackingham." She followed him into the keep.

He opened the padlock on a large chest in the center of the round guard tower and withdrew a longish object wrapped in a cloth.

"I thought you might want to redeem this. It belonged to the prisoner. Of course, it cannot be returned to him."

He unwrapped a thin dagger with a delicately engraved knotwork on its hilt. Finn's dagger. They'd been together—new lovers—in the garden the first time she saw the silver dagger. She had tangled her foot in the ivy and tripped and he cut away the offending vine and wove it into a wreath. "A garland of green for my lady's hair." And laughing, he'd kissed the tip of her nose as he'd placed it on her hair.

"How much?"

"Three gold sovereigns?" He looked at her appraisingly. He would bargain, but she was in too big a hurry.

"It seems a fair price. But I have only shillings." He might be in league with robbers. "If you will accept my pledge."

"Of course, my lady. Shall I hold it for you?"

"I would like to take it with me. A swap?" She pulled a small ring from her little finger. "It's worth at least three sovereigns."

The constable took the ring, held it up to the light, bit into its soft gold.

"We've a trade," he said, wrapping the dagger back up.

Kathryn shook her head. "I don't need the wrapper."

She took it from him and tied it to her girdle, beside her rosary. All the way home, each time the horse crossed a rough spot, she felt the handle dig into her waist.

TWENTY-ONE

Item: That no . . . rimers, minstrels, or vagabonds be maintained . . . who by their divinations, lies, and exhortations are partly cause of the insurrections and rebellion.

—DECLARATION OF PARLIAMENT, 1402

Colin sat at the end of the troupe wagon looking out into the empty marketplace through a curtain of rain. The heavy awning was pulled back, and he faced outward, legs folded under him, one already going numb. He tried to ignore the lovers' grunts and moans coming from the back of the carriage.

The Easter Cycle Pageant staged by the Bury Saint Edmunds Mercer's Guild was rained out. The crowds, not willing to stand in the rain for the Resurrection, had gone home to their drowned hearth fires. The guildsmen had covered up their play wagons and followed. Now there was nobody left to applaud—or reward—the antics and songs from the company of gleemen who planned to work the crowds after the risen Christ had taken his bows. Only one of the poor priests who followed the crowds, handing out tracts against the abuses of the clergy, remained. He seemed not to notice that all his hearers had gone away.

The troupers didn't care that their venue had been a washout. They'd entertained at a wedding feast in Milcenhall in March, and its lord had detained them for a fortnight of entertainments. They were well used and well compensated. Even Colin was tired of singing.

Two of his companions had gone off laughing to the nearest tavern, seeking other "spirits" to revive their "doused spirits." The third had sought diversion in the arms of a milkmaid who, with her tambourine, had joined their troupe at Mildenhall. She said their rebellious lyrics emboldened her to run away. But from the way the carriage was swaying, Colin suspected it had more to do with Jack-of-the-Plumed-Hat's fine feathers—or fine something else.

Colin wished he'd gone to the tavern with the others, though he would have felt the intruder there too. He shifted his weight to ease the pressure on his numb leg and tried not to hear the sounds of lusty lovemaking coming from the wagon's deepest interior—even with no one around to see, he felt himself blushing. He longed for Rose, unable to purge her image from behind his eyes. The very thought of her nipped at his heels like a hellhound. The more he repented his sin, the more he longed for the one with whom he'd committed it. Misery puddled around him.

He'd already decided the troupe would never make it to Cromer by summer. Cromer was north of Norwich; Bury Saint Edmunds was south, in the opposite direction. And the roads were flooded. Not that it mattered much anymore. His stint with the players was rapidly rendering him unfit for the company of monks. And he found the whole prospect much less appealing. All he really wanted was to go home.

Could it be that he'd been wrong about the wool house? How did he even know he and Rose had caused the fire, just because they had been together there? Maybe it was John's sin. Maybe he had done it to himself. Colin had seen him drunk often enough. Maybe John got drunk and knocked over a lamp. But one thing he could not reason away. Rose had been a virgin, and now she was not. And that was his fault. All his fault. None of it hers. And it was up to him to make it right.

It was hard to ignore the squeals and moans behind him, even over the pounding rain. If fire were the punishment for lust, then this wagon would long ago have been consumed by a great conflagration. He looked out at a sea of mud, watched it splatter as the rain dripped from the wagon's overhanging roof. The crazy priest—that's how Colin thought of John Ball—was standing in the rain, his arms held heavenward, water streaming down his face, seemingly oblivious to the fact that there was nobody left to listen. "Flee from the wrath to come. He will destroy the world, as in the time of Noah. God will turn his back on the corrupt whore of Babylon."

Colin saw him often, just one of the Lollard priests—though this one was more zealous than most—who collected to spread their unorthodox doctrine wherever there was a crowd. While most of the others remained faceless, John Ball was memorable for both his zeal and his appearance. He was a stocky man in a poor monk's habit, much given to grotesque gestures and inflamed rhetoric as he raged against Church and nobility alike for their greed, their exploitation of the poor. He despised the Divine Order of the classes and preached radical ideas of equality, not so radical as they would once have been to Colin.

The same liberal notions that John Ball preached were in the songs of the other minstrels, tiny word seeds that caused him to question the Divine Order, too. Why would God ordain that some few should drink fine wine from silver goblets and wear rich furs, whilst others wrapped themselves in rough-tanned skins and drank dirty water from a wooden trough? Did God really decide who should serve or be served? Or was the Divine Order just some grand scheme, concocted by kings and bishops, to keep poor men in their place? The Church called it heresy to say that God created each man the same, or that each should earn his own reward.

The crazy priest raised his voice in righteous cadence:

> *When Adam delved and Eve span*
> *Who was then the gentleman?*

Familiar words, words of equality. Radical words that said rich and poor, noble and serf sprang from the same source. Colin had heard these same words sung beneath the great lord's dais, many times. The lord and his guests always applauded, nodding their approval, as though such criticism were not meant for them, but some other nobility, in some other England. But now, on the lips of John Ball, whose eyes burned with fever like a mad prophet's, the words seemed more dangerous. Colin had once seen him hauled off to the stocks for disturbing the peace. He wanted to stay as far away from the man as possible. But John Ball was less than thirty feet from the wagon. And he was in search of an audience. Flee from the wrath to come, indeed! Where?

Not to the back of the wagon. He scrunched into the shadows, but the movement only drew the priest's attention. John Ball stopped in mid-sentence, let his outstretched arms fall to his side, then folded them. They disappeared inside his voluminous monk's sleeves.

Colin tried to look away from the priest, who stared back at him. But each time he looked away, his gaze was jerked back by some invisible chain. The priest's gray hair was plastered in strings around his neck and face. Water ran from his eyes and dripped off his nose like tears. Colin could feel his gaze penetrating the wagon, drawing him.

The priest moved with purpose toward the wagon. It was too late to drop the flap. It'd be like slamming a door in the man's face.

"When Adam delved and Eve span, who was then the gentleman? You would do well, lad, to heed these words."

"I've heard them before." Was it his imagination or was there a cessation of the wagon's creaking motion? Too late to retreat, though; he was already engaged in conversation with the infamous John Ball. "I sang those very words myself, to the accompaniment of my lute." Now that was a lie. He never had. His repertoire contained only love songs. But his fellows had, and it was something to say.

"Ah. But did you sing them from your soul? Do they set your heart on fire?" He beat his chest. "Do you see the starving peasant in his dirt hut when you sing them? Do you smell the stench of pus running from open sores on his rag-wrapped feet? Do you feel the king's burden on his back, the Church's knee upon his neck, the hurt within his heart?"

Colin did not know how to respond to such inflamed—and alliterative— words. Behind him he heard a snicker and a giggle. He coughed to cover up the sound. A gust of wind blew the rain inside the wagon.

"The rain comes in, Father. I must close the flap. I would invite you out of the rain, but the wagon is . . . fully occupied."

The old man's eyes were the color of a stormy sea. "The old order will be destroyed. Are we not all descended from Adam and Eve? There should be neither vassals nor lords. God will not suffer such abuse in His name. Not the flood, this time. We will cast off the yoke of wicked ecclesiastics and evil princes. This time the punishment will come in fire."

"Yes, Father. I will remember." But he was remembering the fire at the wool house. Whose sin? Which sinner?

The preacher drew a damp pamphlet from inside his cassock and handed it to Colin before stalking off, mumbling and shaking his head, oblivious to the rain, no sinners left to heed his warnings but those in his head. Colin glanced at the pamphlet, struggled to make out the strange words in the gloom, *On the Pastoral Office* by John Wycliffe, Oxford. Not French or Latin, but English, but then that made sense if the message was intended for the lower classes. He started to tear it up and throw it into the mud with the other refuse left behind by the players, but instead he looked at it again, then folded the tract and put it inside his shirt. Maybe he should read it. At least the crazy priest had given him something to think about besides Rose.

Behind him he heard the sounds of the tambourine and the high mocking voice of Plumed Hat. "When Adam delved and Eve span, oh, I feel it in my soul."

Answered by a high-pitched giggle. "That's not *yer* soul yer feelin'."

"Your soul, then?"

"A little lower than me soul, I think." Another giggle.

Oh Holy Mother, were they going to start all over? Colin loosened the tent flap, let it drop. It made a slapping noise, and the wagon was enveloped in darkness.

"Hey," the pair shouted in a single protest.

The wagon smelled of mold and musky animal smells. Colin wrapped himself in a blanket, buried his face in his hands, and waited for the rain to end.

❧

The rains came to Blackingham, too, bringing floods to Norwich and to Aylsham and as far south as Cambridge. The shallow Yare and Ouse and Wensum overflowed their banks into the peat-robbed bogs and fens, where the only travelers were eels and water snakes that traversed the broad waters. They crisscrossed the lakes, leaving curving silent wakes behind them. With the floods came misery, and mud, and despair.

Large numbers of pilgrims usually took to the roads in April on their way to Canterbury and Walsingham—fewer trekked to Norwich because it boasted no holy bones of long-dead saints, though some would make the trip to see the holy woman of Saint Julian. But this year, all roads from Cambridge north were abandoned rivers of mud. Only an occasional carter cursed and heaved along the road's bleeding earth as he pried his cart's wooden wheels from the muck.

There was little traffic to and from the prison. Kathryn had not seen Finn since that first painful reunion. Agnes had told her that the dwarf had brought a message to Rose, but he had insisted upon placing it in her hands. The little man had carried no message for Kathryn.

Rose was delighted. "I've had a message from my father," she told Kathryn. "You were right. He says he's happy about the baby, not mad at all. I'm so relieved." Her teeth showed white against her olive-toned skin. "Half-Tom waited for me to write an answer. My father asked for a lock of my hair. See." She indicated a shorter strand of hair that curled around her face. "I thought if I cut it here, each time it falls in my eyes, I'll remember my father and say a Paternoster for him."

Rose glowed with health. She had started to improve the day Kathryn told her that she'd seen Finn, that he was well and asking for his pretty daughter. She'd put the very best light on his circumstances, not telling her about the pain she'd seen in his eyes. She'd lied, saying they had shared a feast of warm cider and sugar biscuits, and she'd promised to take Rose to see her father after the babe was born—yes, she'd told him about the babe—and no, he was not angry with her, though he might be a little bit with Colin. At the mention of Colin's name, Rose bit her bottom lip and squeezed her eyes shut. Kathryn could almost feel the prickle of unshed tears in her own eyes. But her good spirits quickly returned.

After that, Rose found again her former cheerful demeanor. Her appetite even returned. The winter stores were running low, but Kathryn saw that Finn's daughter had more to eat than dried and salted meat and moldy rye. She ordered that two lambs be slaughtered—much to Simpson's chagrin— he'd dared to gainsay her orders, arguing for an old barren ewe. He stormed off grinding his teeth. What business was it of his? She'd also instructed Agnes to prepare Rose's favorite blancmange at least once a week.

Rose's belly was pleasantly round. She carried the baby high. It's going to be a girl, Kathryn thought.

※※

On a day in April, when Kathryn thought the sound of the rain with its incessant drumming would drive her mad, her granddaughter was born.

"She's not breathing," Rose gasped after the midwife cut the cord and laid the tiny babe, still wet and slick, on her breast. The midwife lifted the child by its legs and held it upside down—ignoring Rose's cry—and cleared the mucus from its lungs. Kathryn felt a great relief at the thin but insistent cry.

"Hold 'er close, so she can feel yer heart beat," the midwife said after she had cleaned the babe and wrapped her in a blanket.

"I want to call her Jasmine," Rose said to Kathryn as she cradled her child. "Father said my mother always smelled like jasmine."

"That's a pretty name, Rose, but wouldn't it be better to call her some more common name like Anne or Elizabeth?"

"I could call her Rebekka after my mother."

Rose looked so young, Kathryn thought, hardly more than a child herself, though she'd borne the birth pangs better than some women, screaming out only once when the babe crowned. She'd clutched Kathryn's hand so hard a bruise was already showing on her wrist. Rose's hair was still damp with sweat. One curl, the one she'd cut for her father, had plastered itself to her cheek. Kathryn stroked her forehead, smoothed the curl back in its place, thinking of Finn's high forehead. Thinking, too, about the problems a child with a Jewish name would encounter, about how it would make all their lives harder.

"Jasmine is a prettier name than Rebekka, I think. And it honors your mother's memory. It suits your little girl. She's as small and pretty as a jasmine blossom."

Born four weeks early by Kathryn's clearest counting, the babe was so small she could almost hold it in her cupped hands. After it had sucked, she took it from its mother and swaddled each limb, the tiny fragile torso, even the head, in soft linen bandages to prevent curvature of the soft bones.

"It's a wee mite," the midwife said as Kathryn paid her. "But it shows spirit. Ye needn't worry about its soul. As it was crowning, I baptized the babe in the name of the Father, the Son and the Holy Ghost. I gave it a Christian name. Anna. For the Virgin's mother. I baptize all my newborn girls with that name. It entered this world a Christian child, and will leave it the same way. Though if it lives, of course, ye'll probably want to do it proper in the church."

It *is* a Christian child, Kathryn thought. Colin's child, and she noted with relief how the fuzz on the infant's head was drying to a pale reddish blond. Not a Jew child.

"Your baptism would be sufficient, wouldn't it?" she asked.

"Oh, 'twould for sure." The midwife fished a vial of holy water from her pocket. "Father Benedict blessed it hisself, trained me in the words to say, in cases where the child's life is in danger."

After the midwife left, Kathryn kept watch beside Rose's bed. Had Rose been baptized? Wouldn't Finn have insisted? But then she thought of how much Finn had loved his Rebekka. Maybe she hadn't converted? Would he have married her anyway? She was thinking about the little filigree cross around Rose's neck when she nodded off to sleep, reassured.

The next time the babe needed feeding—it seemed like only minutes with Rose sleeping and Kathryn dozing by her bed—Rose had nothing, not even the pale viscous substance that preceded the milk. Jasmine protested in a thin wail, pushing at the distended nipple of Rose's right breast with her rosebud mouth.

"Try the left one."

But Jasmine only cried harder, screwing her tiny face into a pink rage. Rose, still weak from her long labor, began to cry too. *Two* crying children, Kathryn thought and sighed. She was bone-weary. She felt almost as tired as if she had borne the child.

"You just need to rest now, Rose," Kathryn said, "You'll have more milk. We'll take care of the babe until you're better. We'll give her ewe's milk on a rag in the meantime or get a nursemaid from the village." She was cursing herself for letting the midwife go. She would have known where to get a wet nurse. Kathryn didn't know where to start.

She didn't notice the kitchen wench gathering the soiled linens in the corner until Magda tapped her gently on the elbow. "B-beg pardon, milady, she may be satisfied just to suck the tip of your finger until you can find m-milk. See, like this." And before Kathryn could stop her, she picked up the wailing infant and stuck the tip of her finger in its mouth. She crooned to it softly, "Lulay, lu-lay," as it sucked a few times and fell asleep. The girl laid it gently in its crib.

Kathryn was amazed. "You did that very well, Magda. I think we can use you in the nursery."

The girl flushed with pleasure and dropped a quick curtsy. "Please, milady, if it's a nursemaid you need right away, me mum still has milk. Would you like me to fetch her?"

Would I like you to fetch her! Kathryn could have cried with relief. She knew that some of the peasant women carried toddlers, well past weaning age, still sucking at their sagging breasts, thinking that as long as they nursed they would not become pregnant again. Others, suffering from malnutrition, dried up too soon and their babies died. At least she could prevent this from happening to Finn's grandchild.

"Yes, please, go right away," she said to Magda. "Tell your mother she will be well paid." Then, taking Rose's hand, "See, Rose, we already have a nurse. You just rest," she said. "Everything is going to be fine. I'll keep watch over your babe until Magda gets back."

~ ✵ ~

Magda knew her mother would be pleased. This would mean more food for her hungry brood. Her family had not recovered from the poll tax of last year. They'd not had the eight shillings, one shilling per head, that King Richard demanded, so the collector had taken the pig that was to have seen them through the winter. And Cook said there was talk of another tax to fund the duke's failing Spanish wars. "Taking food from the mouths of babes to fund men's vanities" was how Agnes had put it. Magda's family would be assessed less this time, six shillings instead of eight because Agnes had said she would ask Lady Kathryn to pay for Magda. And her little brother had died—one less mouth to feed, one less head to tax. Nobody had seemed to mourn the little boy but Magda, though she'd since seen her mother, more than once, weeping over three small mounds in the churchyard. Six shillings: it might as well have been a duke's ransom for a family such as hers. And they'd already taken the pig.

The dirt floor of the peasant hut was slick with mud. Her mother sat on a stool at a table made of rough deal boards, the room's only furniture other than the cot where Magda's parents slept. Beside the cot, there was a makeshift willow crib, perpetually occupied. The other three children slept in a low loft above the animals. In winter, the animals were protected from the elements, and the heat their bodies generated helped to warm the children.

All in all, it worked pretty well. Except on a day like today, when the wind and the rain forced the peat smoke back down the smoke hole cut in the thatch roof, and the hut stank of the muck from the chickens and the cow. The smoke stung Magda's eyes. She wondered how her mother could sit, so oblivious to the pandemonium around her, holding her youngest at her breast while she kneaded bread with her free hand. Another child, a four-year-old, clung to her skirts, crying. She thought of the quiet, clean rooms at Blackingham, the feather beds, the cavernous kitchen with its hearth soup always on the boil.

"Where's Father?" She announced her arrival at the low door, shouting to be heard above the din.

"Magda!" Her mother's gaunt face was almost pretty when she smiled, but that was seldom. "I don't know where he's gone." She pushed a stray string of hair back beneath its kerchief binding. "He said he was going that crazy, shut up with us. He stomped out into the rain. Just as well. He fouled the air with his bitterness."

As if the air could be any fouler, Magda thought. "Then I guess he'll have b-bitterness to eat instead of dried apple t-tartlets."

She shook the rain from her mantle and proudly placed a basket of treats on the table. Her little brother stopped crying and started to climb his mother's skirts. The other three, who were engaged in chasing the squawking chickens under the loft, ran over and reached up with grubby hands, grabbing at the basket.

"Careful." Magda snatched it back. "There's enough for all. I brought a sack of fine-milled flour, too, and a side of b-bacon."

Her mother gave a little cry, a sharp intake of breath, and then her eyes glittered with tears. She reached up and touched Magda' s face.

"I thank the Holy Virgin for the day that I took ye up to Blackingham, child, though I'll have to admit I cursed yer father enough times for making me do it. He said ye were simple 'cause ye didn't talk. I reckon ye just didn't have naught to say." Her mother paused, searching her face, as though she was asking forgiveness or confirmation that in giving her daughter away she had done the right thing.

"They're kind to me, Mum. Even milady. Nobody calls me simple. Though I miss the little ones. And as long as I'm at Blackingham, ye'll not starve."

Her mother looked alarmed. "Ye didn't steal?"

"Of course not, Mum. Cook packed the basket herself."

"I wish yer father were here to listen how ye've found yer tongue. He'll not believe how well-spoken ye are."

Cat's got yer tongue, he used to tease, cajole her into talking when she was little. She remembered how she used to sit in his lap and reach for the circle of red light around his head, and how he'd box her ears when she pulled his hair, and later beat her when she would not talk.

"Don't be too hard on yer father, lass. His life's not been easy."

"Nobody's life is easy, Mum." She told her mother why she'd come, how Rose didn't have enough milk to satisfy even the tiny infant. She'd been able to feed the baby only twice and then she'd seemed to weaken.

"I'll go right now," her mother said, "if ye'll tend this one while I'm gone."

"Will there be enough milk for both?" She looked at her littlest brother tugging greedily on his mother's nipple, cutting his big round eyes at her as though he knew something was afoot.

"Billy's big enough to wean. I only kept him at the breast because . . . well, never mind why. There'll be no need now."

In the smoky dim light of the room, her mother seemed backlit by a beautiful violet glow, but Magda had learned not to talk about the colors, not to tell about the souls she read the way other people read faces. Someone would say she was simple.

∼ ✻ ∽

Kathryn kept close watch, dividing her time between Rose and the child. The baby thrived. Rose did not. She continued to bleed steadily. Nothing alarming at first. But then, when it should have lightened, the flow increased. "Flowers," that's the name men gave to this secret property, this monthly purging of women's bodies, a woman's flowers, a pretty term to mark the natural properties of a woman's body. Unnatural now, dark flowers, soaking sheet after sheet of clean white linen.

Candles burned for Saint Margaret, day and night, in the room where Rose bled. Kathryn had moved her into Finn's bed. The small antechamber where she usually slept was now a nursery. Magda's mother made the two-mile trek from her own cottage each day to tend and feed Jasmine. Kathryn had asked what arrangements she had made for her own children and was told that, since the fields were flooded, her husband had naught to do anyway but tend the little ones. Once or twice, Kathryn had seen a small boy in the kitchen with Magda and Agnes, but she said nothing. As long as the woman cared for Jasmine, she would allow her the comfort of having her own child nearby.

Each day, Rose grew paler. The veins in her small round breasts looked like tracings of blue lace beneath transparent skin. She kept trying to feed her child, and when there was no milk, the babe cried. After each futile effort, Kathryn would take Jasmine away and give her to the nurse, and Rose, exhausted, would lie back wearily on her pillow. She would say nothing, but Kathryn learned to watch for the little stream of tears that formed in the crevices between her nose and cheeks.

Kathryn placed a healing stone of jasper beneath Rose's pillow and drowned her in tea of honey and motherwort. She soaked linen rags in an infusion of lady's mantle and packed heavy compresses between her legs. On the fourth day, Rose's skin was hot to the touch, and she no longer tried to feed the baby; once, when she heard it crying in the antechamber, she cried out as though she was frightened, asking, "What's that noise?"

Kathryn moved the nurse and the baby to her own chamber. She had tried once before. She wanted this child close to her, but its mother had protested. She did not protest now.

Rose's fever proved stubborn. She became delirious, singsonging bits of nonsense, love songs—Colin's songs, Kathryn remembered—and calling out—sometimes for Finn, sometimes for Colin, in muttered half-whispers. Kathryn bathed her in cool water, but still the fever climbed.

On the fifth day, Kathryn sent for the priest at Saint Michael's. Rose's soul must not be unshriven.

"Tell the groom I will have him beaten if he does not return with the priest before nightfall," she said when told that he complained that the road was too *slabber'd and sost*. "He'll not melt. I'll have his hide if he tarries."

She sat by Rose's bedside, murmuring prayers and endearments.

By nightfall, the priest arrived, shaking the water drops from his cloak like a shaggy beast.

"Where is the girl?" he asked, obviously not happy to be called out on such a night.

Kathryn took him to Rose's bedside. She lay as still as a corpse, eyes closed, their lids thin and blue-veined, her skin as pale as bleached linen. The last time Kathryn had removed the dressing from between her legs, just two hours ago, it had been as dark and sodden as the rain-soaked earth outside.

"We'd better hurry," the priest said, arranging his vestments, taking out his holy water, his crucifix. He began to recite the *Commendatio animae*.

"*Qui Laȝarum . . .*"

The girl opened her eyes just once during the Office of the Dead and looked wildly around the room. Her eyes were wide with fear and something that looked like surprise—but weren't the young always caught unaware by death? Or was it the priest's presence that alarmed her? Her gaze fastened on Kathryn. "Jasmine," she whispered, clawing at the air as if the babe were being handed to her.

"Jasmine is asleep," Kathryn said in her gentlest voice, though she was fighting her own fear and surprise, and she'd seen death aplenty. I'll take care of your little girl," Kathryn said. "I will guard her with my own life, Rose, I promise you. She will be my daughter."

The girl nodded, lay back down and was very still. Her breath was so slight that once Kathryn held a candle flame to her face to see if it flickered. After a while, Kathryn felt a gentle pressure on her hand. She had not even been aware that she was holding Rose's hand.

"Tell Father"—Kathryn leaned close in to hear—"tell Father I'm sorry."

≈≈

Kathryn sat beside Rose's body for a long time, listening to the hissing of the rain. It came down in torrents, leaked into the flue, making little sizzling noises and filling the room with smoke. Kathryn touched Rose's face. It was already cold. The priest had gone to the kitchen seeking his supper and then his bed. In the morning he would baptize her grandchild properly, in the lady chapel, dipping the baby three times in the font with Kathryn standing as godmother. But there would be no celebration. The child's mother would be lying beneath the baptismal font, below in the family crypt—consecrated ground—beside Roderick. Roderick sleeping for eternity beside a beautiful woman, sleeping beside a Jew. The only fruit he could not despoil.

There would be no father at the christening, either. Had Colin reached the Benedictines now? She'd had word from a tinker who'd been with his troupe at Colchester that he was safe. He might even now be singing his pretty love songs, blissfully unaware his love had died.

When the roads dried out, she'd send a message to the monks at Cromer. Knowledge of his child might bring her child back to her.

She started to pull the bell that would summon Glynis to assist her in preparing Rose's body, and then she remembered. There were those who said that Jews bore some special marking, some deformity on their bodies—Roderick had said he'd heard it on good authority that the women's clefts were horizontal like a mouth. Well, she knew that to be a lie. Rose's womanly parts had been like her own, though she had to admit, she'd had an anxious moment before summoning the midwife. She had finally decided, spurred on by Rose's pain, that if that was true, the midwife's silence could be bought.

She gathered a basin of lavender water left in her own chamber and began to bathe each limb, washing it carefully. There were no marks, no deformities. Everything about Rose was perfectly formed. Kathryn braided the dark hair, winding it in a coronet around her face, weighted the eyelids with two coins, and tied a blue silk band around her head and under her jaw, then dressed her in her father's favorite dress. She looked like a bride in her pale blue dress, as beautiful in death as she had been in life.

Kathryn thought she should remove the little cross on its silken cord. A gift for Jasmine from her mother. Just as Rose's mother had passed it to her daughter. She removed it carefully, examining it really closely for the first time. The intricate filigree was exquisite. It reminded her of the knotwork borders on the carpet pages Finn made for the Gospel of John. Six tiny pearls formed a perfect circle at the apex of the cross. Representing the sun perhaps? But it was not like the Celtic crosses she'd seen in the old Saxon churches in Norwich that mixed the symbol of the sun with the cross. A heresy, some said. This circle was *inside* the intersection of cross arm and stake and looked more like a star, a six-pointed star, but so cleverly worked into the swirling motif that it disappeared if one stared at it. Probably a trick of her imagination.

She wondered if Finn had designed the beautiful ornament for his Rebekka. A small surge of jealousy pricked. What right had she to be jealous? Kathryn looped the silken cord around her rosary—she would not profane it by putting it around her own neck—and wished Finn could see how beautiful his daughter was in death and how tenderly she was cared for. He might find comfort there.

Holy Mother, where was she going to find the strength to tell Finn his daughter was dead?

When the body was scented and dressed, Kathryn thought of pulling the bell. She could leave this last task to others and go to bed. But instead, she fetched the cerecloth from a cupboard and started to sew. It was important she do this final thing herself.

The heavy, wax-soaked cloth resisted the needle and soon the serge was illuminated with little drops of blood from Kathryn's pricked fingers. Rose would take something of Kathryn with her to her grave.

⚶

It was almost dawn when she finished. The rain had ceased. So long had her ears been accustomed to the drumming of the raindrops that the silence seemed threatening. Her crofters would be glad. The rivers would recede. Her pastures would dry out, and the new green would carpet the hillsides. The roads would become passable again. She would have to make the trip to the prison once more. She would have to tell Finn how she had sewn his beautiful Rose into her shroud. She would tell him, too, how she had embroidered it with her tears.

She hoped desperately that he would let her keep the child.

TWENTY-TWO

*Our faith is grounded in God's word; and it belongeth
to our faith to Believe that God's word shall stand in
all points.*
—JULIAN OF NORWICH, *DIVINE REVELATIONS*

athryn lay awake each night, awful words marching through her
mind, heavy-booted soldiers laying waste to sleep. *Naught else could have
been done for her, Finn . . . her suffering was easy . . . a peaceful drifting
away . . . she is safe in the arms of the Holy Virgin . . . I've bought masses for
her soul . . . the child will comfort you. . . .*

Empty words.

Surely he must be preparing himself for the possibility of his daughter's
death. So many women died in childbirth. He'd lost his own wife in just that
way. He may know already, she thought, through some fatherly intuition born
of his closeness to his daughter.

The pain in her head returned again and again as she waited for the broad
floodwaters to recede. Some days she considered the coward's way. She
would send a letter by one of the groomsmen. Once, she went so far as to take
pen in hand, but as she looked at the sharpened quill poised above the parchment, she saw his paint-stained fingers sketching a red-breasted bird in their

September garden, his fingers guiding Rose's to form the graceful capitals their art required. Kathryn's own fingers trembled so, she could not form the strokes. She crushed the blank parchment in her fist and hurled it into the fire.

She rocked the baby for hours, crooning bits of song. Jasmine wrapped her tiny fist around Kathryn's finger.

"You're a pretty babe, just like your mother. She was pretty, too; yes, she was. Pretty babe. Pretty babe," she singsonged. Foolish behavior in a woman her age.

But Jasmine would open her sleepy eyes—blue eyes, Colin's eyes—and fix Kathryn with a wise gaze. Even when Kathryn handed her off to the nurse to feed—though never moving far away, always hovering—the child watched Kathryn's face, twisting away from the nurse's nipple if Kathryn wandered out of her sight. But she seldom did. Those knowing eyes were a lodestone from which Kathryn could not pull away.

It was the middle of May before the road to Norwich dried up enough to make the journey to Castle Prison.

Jasmine was six weeks old.

~ ❧ ~

From his tower window, Finn looked out at the flooded flatlands. The waters were creeping back to their source. For the first time in weeks, he could see the base of the hawthorne hedge lining the river's far bank and the full arch of the stone bridge. In the distance a lone cart lumbered down the mud-tracked road. The light was better today, too—a thin haze veiled a butter sun—and he'd been awakened by a meadow lark. There was a bird's nest on his windowsill. Signs of spring.

But it was winter still for Finn. There had been no word from Blackingham. Rose must be close to term by now. His hands shook when he tried to work.

The bishop had been his only visitor in many weeks. Last week, they had played at chess on Despenser's elaborately carved board and debated the same old argument, but less hotly than was their custom. Finn's mind was at Blackingham.

Frowning, Despenser captured Finn's pawn en passant. "John Wycliffe and renegade clerics like John Ball rant across the country, turning the peasantry against God and king, and would have every dolt, churl, and villein in Christendom acting as his own priest. A damning freedom. Their ignorance would send them all to hell."

Finn countered, "While the bishops keep them slave to the twin devils of ritual and superstition. How can that profit men's souls?"

"They are sheep and must be herded, did not our Lord say as much?" Despenser smiled.

Finn considered a cryptic answer about separating the sheep from the goats but he didn't answer. His heart was not in it. His heart was not in the game either. Despenser held Finn's king in check already. They usually played to a stalemate, or sometimes Finn allowed a checkmate after a struggle. Finn interposed a knight to protect his king. Despenser's pale fingers— as pale as the ivory they fondled—dallied over his bishop, then moved his pawn to take Finn's ebony knight.

"You are not yourself today," Despenser said into the silence. Leaving Finn to consider his next move, he got up from his chair and walked over to Finn's worktable, studied the first panel of the retable. "And your work progresses at a paltry pace." He traced a jeweled forefinger over the uncolored sketch of the Virgin's face.

Rose's eyes, Rose's lips. Finn wanted to slap his hand away. Instead, he pretended to study the chessboard in front of him. "I've been working on the background for this second panel. I lack the proper pigments for the Virgin's robe."

"How can you lack the proper pigments?" Umbrage in his voice. "Did I not provide you with the ultramarine and the Arabic gum you asked for last week? At great expense, I might add, and I had to send all the way to Flanders for it. What's it made from anyway? The Virgin's tears wouldn't fetch a more exorbitant price."

"Lapis lazuli," Finn answered, sacrificing his bishop to screen his king. "It's ground stone. It comes from somewhere in the East. The shades vary from azure to sea-green. It's in the mixing. I need just the right light to mix the pure blue of the Virgin's robe. I've not found the right combination. When the light is better . . ."

The bishop stroked the pectoral cross hanging around his neck, his fingers caressing the pearl-encrusted filigree. "I would remind you, Master

Finn, of our agreement. You enjoy these luxurious accommodations at my pleasure. I hope that you are not putting some profane, lesser task, above your bishop's commission."

Finn watched him from beneath lowered eyes, anxiety growing. He was looking at the chest in the corner, the chest that stored the pigments, the chessboard and its pieces, the chest that stored also the parchment and the quills, and a leather scrip filled with damning papers. "I assure you, Eminence, I have not forgotten the terms. I was led to believe that my stay here would be an extended one, affording me ample time to fulfill—unless of course, some new evidence has come to light which would shorten my stay."

The chest in the corner still held Despenser's attention. "No new evidence. The sheriff remains confident that we have the priest's murderer. Indeed, it is only because you are valuable to me that you have not already been sentenced to hang. But don't toy with me, Illuminator. Nor misjudge my patience."

"I am not a man who plays games, Eminence. I'm well aware of the power you hold. But you must understand it is difficult for an artist to work in this light. That is why I've done only background work." He indicated the gessoed panel the bishop held. "I will return to the Annunciation panel as soon as the light is stronger. I believe it's your move."

"The sketch of the Virgin's face promises to be beautiful. Your daughter is the model, I presume, Master Finn."

Despenser had made his move, and Finn did not mistake the subtle threat in the bishop's thin-lipped scythe of a smile. But at least he appeared to have lost interest in the chest filled with Wycliffe's texts, damning evidence that Half-Tom had not been able to retrieve because of the floods.

"You are a poor opponent today. You may put the game back in its box. You need to get back to work. We will hope the light is stronger tomorrow." The bishop strode over to the window ledge, where a curlew had made its nest. There were three tiny pearl-shaped eggs in the twig basket, eggs that Finn had been watching, just as he'd watched the little curlew building the nest, carrying one twig at a time in her beak. During the cold nights he'd left the shutters open so that she could come and go. One by one, the bishop picked up the bird's eggs and examined them. One by one, he pitched each from the high window. Then he dropped the nest. "So much coming and going might have interfered with your concentration," he said.

After the bishop left, Finn considered burning the papers, even opened the chest and took them out. *For God so loved the world that He gave His only begotten Son* . . . why did churchmen never talk of God's love while waxing eloquent enough on the torments of the damned? The anchoress wrote of God's love. She had felt that love in her own healing. She had seen His passion in her visions. Maybe the others, like the bishop, were closer to an understanding of the devil and his ways. But here in the Gospel of John, flowing from the tip of Finn's own pen, were words of love, words that all men should hear.

But how could those who had never known love understand its meaning? He understood it. He'd felt it. For Rebekka. And for Kathryn. Not just the way of men and women, but deeper, wanting to protect her, wanting his soul to join with hers. But that love had failed him. Rebekka had left him. Kathryn had betrayed him. God's love had to be more than that, as the anchoress said—some greater love, some incorruptible force. And Finn had felt that, too. He could forgive his Rose anything. His love for Rose was like the expensive pigments he used—distilled essence, pure and undiluted.

Yet here was a conundrum. If God's love was like that of a parent for a child—only greater, deeper, wider, more perfect—then how could God have sacrificed His only Child? What loving parent could sacrifice a son to such unimaginable suffering? Certainly not Kathryn. She'd proved that. And neither could he. Did God have second thoughts when he watched His Son hanging there with blood and tears streaming down his face, the crowd taunting him, the dogs circling beneath, the buzzards above? But He hadn't watched, had He? He'd turned his face away, unable to bear it. Finn understood that much at least.

The leather packet hidden beneath the pigments and gums, parchments and quills was full to bursting. Wycliffe would be pleased with the extra copies. And working on them had given Finn a strange comfort these last weeks. It was a way of fighting back. What had begun as a subversive feeding of his rebellious spirit had brought a peace when he could find none elsewhere. If his hands shook too much to work on the bishop's icons, his fingers were calm and sure as he copied the Wycliffe texts. If this Gospel was truth, then shouldn't truth have many copies?

Half-Tom will make it into Norwich soon, he thought. The waters will recede. I'll work on the Virgin's robe tomorrow.

But he had not. He had returned to copying the English translations. And another week had passed. The papers would no longer fit in the chest and now, from his high window—with its empty ledge—though the waters had receded, the only thing he saw crossing the bridge was a horse-drawn cart carrying two women and a girl of about fourteen. One of the women held an infant to her breast. A woman bringing her children to see their father in prison? He hoped, for the sake of the children, the father's offense was a small one.

No sign of Half-Tom. But then, the fens would still be flooded. It might be weeks before he saw his friend again. He would have to find some other way of smuggling out the papers. Tomorrow was Friday.

The bishop was sure to pay his weekly visit.

"Wait here," Kathryn said to Magda and her mother, who, in spite of being on public view in the prison courtyard, was doing that for which she had been hired—nursing the hungry infant. Kathryn found great satisfaction in watching the baby suck, which Jasmine did often and noisily.

"You'll be safe enough here," she promised. "The constable has said he'll keep an eye out for you. I think he can be trusted."

"Never to worry, milady. We'll be fine," Magda said.

But Kathryn noticed a tremble in the girl's voice as she surveyed the castle's forbidding Norman keep. Kathryn had noted, too, her little cry, half-fear, half-awe, when the town walls had first come into view. But the girl was not without fortitude. When they'd gotten stuck in the mud (Kathryn had had the foresight to bring the wagon instead of Roderick's heavy carriage), the girl had been more help than the sniveling groom she'd dispatched to fetch Simpson.

Help had finally come, but not from Blackingham. A couple of passing yeomen had put their backs to the mired wheels. Armed only with her sense of purpose—and Finn's dagger hanging beside her rosary beads—Kathryn had decided to carry on, hoping that Simpson would catch up to them.

He had not. When, once again, they'd mired up to one axle, the two women and the girl freed the wheel. But Kathryn regarded the difficult journey as a dance around the Maypole compared to the task that lay ahead. She touched the babe's cheek, wiping away a drool of breast milk, straightened her spine, and approached the iron grille at the bottom of the prison stairs.

"Door's open at the top," the guard said as the key grated in the lock.

Kathryn set the small hourglass she'd brought with her on the wagon seat. "Give me half an hour, then send the others up." She gave the guard a penny. "The constable says you're to look after them." She indicated the wagon with a tilt of the head. "See that no one approaches."

"Aye, milady," the guard said, pocketing his coin. The iron grille clanged behind her.

TWENTY-THREE

*The great drops of blood fell down from under the
garland like pellets; they seemed to come straight out
of the veins . . . but in their spreading forth they were
bright red.*

—JULIAN OF NORWICH, *DIVINE REVELATIONS*

inn was unable to find the color for the Virgin's robe. He had given it
up and was hunched over his worktable, the Wycliffe papers spread out before him. Maybe he should have tried mixing it with cinnabar, he thought, as
he copied the Gospel of John. A shadow passed behind him, a mere lessening
of the light. He slid the papers beneath the blotter, shielding them from view
with his back, thinking probably not the bishop. He wouldn't approach with
so light a step and without ceremony. Unless, of course, he was trying to
catch his prisoner out.

Finn quickly, but carefully, poured a few drops of the precious luzerite
powder onto his palette, pretended to mix it. Another step behind him. Tentative, uncertain. He arranged his face in a mask calculated to show the
artist absorbed in his work, but when he turned to confront his visitor,
the mask crumpled. He dropped the glass vial containing the ground blue

stone. It shattered. The powder spilled, bleeding bright blue onto the floor.

"Kathryn!" He gaped at her, startled as much by her appearance as her presence. Her cloak was mud-splattered; her disheveled hair escaped in white strands from its netted snood, now slightly askew. Muddy footprints tracked her progress across his threshold. Anxiety etched fine lines around her mouth and eyes, lines he'd not remembered.

"Is it Rose?" he asked, feeling his pulse quicken. "Has her labor begun?"

She looked for a moment as if she didn't know how to answer. His breath snagged on a shard of fear.

"Rose's labor is over, Finn," she said finally.

He exhaled deeply, the fear dissipating.

Her gaze wandered around the room, fixing on the spilled pigment on the floor. Why wouldn't she look at him? So unlike the lady of Blackingham who never shied from confrontation. He could feel the weight of her guilt pressing down on him, and might have reveled in it, but his relief that Rose's ordeal was over was so intense it gave way to grace for the messenger. He restrained himself from wiping the mud from her skirt and straightening her hair.

"What about the child?" he asked.

She didn't answer.

"Kathryn, does the child live?" His heart skittered against his breastbone.

She drew a long breath. "The child thrives. You have a granddaughter. Rose named her . . . Jasmine."

Jasmine. Rebekka's favorite flower. "A granddaughter, Jasmine," he said, liking the graceful sound of it, liking the way it left his mouth formed in a smile as he said it. He touched Kathryn's shoulder. "You've come a hard journey to bring me this news. I'm grateful. No wonder you are tired. Sit down. I'll call for some refreshment. And I'd be very grateful if you would do one other thing for me, though I know you've already done me a great service."

She did not sit. Just kept looking at the broken vial of blue powder on the floor.

He was giddy with relief, his words as frenzied as his pulse. "Your visit is well-timed. I need you to deliver a packet of papers for me. I've been copying for Wycliffe. The bishop would not be pleased. If you could just take the papers to the anchoress who lives by Saint Julian's, she'll see that Half-Tom delivers them to the right place. I certainly can't afford to anger the bishop now, can I? Not when Rose needs me so. Kathryn, I can't tell you how—"

She shrugged his hand off her shoulder and dropped to her knees. "You've spilled the luzerite," she said softly. "Let me help you." She brushed the blue grains into a pile with her gloved hand.

"I was so surprised to see you." He knelt beside her, started to sweep the blue onto a scrap of parchment. "It was too strident for the Virgin's cloak anyway. Tell me about my granddaughter." She said nothing, just answered him with a sniff. Had she caught an ague in the weather? A small drop of moisture wet the back of her glove. Where had that come—"Kathryn? Are you crying?"

He took the reclaimed pigment from her, stretched to lay it on the worktable.

His breath refused to come. "Kathryn, is it Rose?"

The top of her head nodded, barely discernible, except for the stirring of a strand of hair escaping its golden net.

"Kathryn, for God's sake. Look at me. Answer me." He gripped her shoulders and together they rose from a kneeling position. "Is it Rose? Is she not well?"

When she raised her face to him, a smudge shadowed her cheekbone where she'd wiped at her tears with a blue-stained, muddied glove.

"Kathryn, you said . . ."

She wiped her eyes again, spreading the blue stain beneath the other eye. Her face looked bruised. For an instant he saw the face of his weeping Madonna, his Crucifixion Madonna. And he knew what it was she could not bear to tell him.

He choked on the words, his mind refusing to accept what his eyes read in her face. "But you said her labor was over, Kathryn."

"Her labor is over, Finn. She is with the Holy Virgin."

❦

Kathryn sat beside Finn for a long time on the floor, watching helplessly as he held his head in his hands and cried for his daughter. Kathryn cried for them both. She told in a voice hoarse with emotion how tenderly Rose had been cared for, how her last words had been for him, how they'd buried her in the family crypt, in consecrated ground. When he responded to none of this, but still sat with his head in his hands, she sought to move him by telling him how they'd found a nurse for little Jasmine, what a treasure the child was, and how she brought hope to Blackingham, should bring hope to him. She vowed to raise the child until Finn could come for her.

"I will treat her like my own daughter, Finn. No child will be more loved. I swear it, dearest heart." She had called him that the last time they had lain together. The word had just crept in amidst her grief, surprising her. But he took no notice of it. "Finn, I swear it by the Virgin's milk that nurtured our Lord."

But she might as well have been giving her promises to a statue. Finally, she heard footsteps coming up the stairs. The nurse was at the entrance with the baby. Kathryn wordlessly took the baby from her, motioning for her to wait outside. She knelt beside Finn with the baby in her arms.

"I've brought Rose's daughter for you to see."

She touched him lightly on the hand, careful not to startle him. "Finn." She thought he was going to turn away, shrug her off. But he didn't move. With her free hand, she arranged his arms in the shape of a cradle. She placed the sleeping babe there. He looked at the child as though it were some strange, exotic creature, his eyes unblinking, his lips parted. He sat like that for what seemed an eternity to Kathryn. The babe slept soundlessly.

Kathryn urged softly. "Finn, this is Jasmine. This is Rose's gift to you. She was baptized as Anna, but Rose called her Jasmine to honor Rebekka."

"Rose's gift," he repeated dully.

Kathryn stroked the baby's cheek. Jasmine opened dark blue eyes and blinked at him.

"She has Rose's mouth, Finn. And see, she has Rose's high, noble brow."

He held her out in front of him, studying her as though she were one of his half-completed manuscripts. Kathryn had never seen his eyes look so cold. When he spoke, his voice was low and flat. Kathryn had to strain to hear. "She has Colin's fair complexion," he said. "She has Colin's eyes." His tone chilled Kathryn to the hard bone.

He handed the child back to her. "I've lost three women that I loved," he said. "I've not the heart to lose another."

*

Finn didn't know when they left. It was the bells ringing none, mid-afternoon, that roused him. He was alone in the prison cell. Maybe it had all been a dream, he thought, a dream sent by the devil to torment him. The weight in his body began to ease. But the papers were gone—the papers he'd hidden when his visitor approached. And at his feet was the broken vial. A pile of blue powder, mingled with dust, lay on his worktable where the Wycliffe papers should have been.

Grief hit him full-force, sucking his hope. He wanted to break something, anything, to leap from the high window into the river, to hurl his body against the wall until the blood splattered its stones. He cursed and roared at the empty air around him, bringing the constable.

"Bring me opium, I am in pain."

"I don't know—"

"Bring it. Now!" he screamed. He pounded his fists on the table and continued pounding until a guard brought him a goblet of strong wine laced with opium.

He woke later to the sound of vespers bells. He felt feverish. His heart hammered, and his head kept time. He felt like a man in a downhill race who could not stop.

He took up the Annunciation panel. With shaking hands, he mixed the arabic gum and the strident blue powder. A shard of broken glass gleamed up from the blue. He laid it in the palm of his hand to examine the tiny glass dagger. He closed his palm against it and waited, hoping for the sharp prick of pain.

When he opened his palm, a small drop of blood welled up. Stigmata. But self-inflicted. No miracles here. Not for him. Not for his Rose.

The drop of blood mingled with the blue powder in the crease of his palm. With the index finger of his left hand he scooped the sticky mixture onto his palette and began to stir it. His hands no longer shook. Carefully, methodically—he might have been merely mixing cinnabar to tone the blue—he stabbed his index finger.

He squeezed a drop. Stirred the mixture.

Stab. Drop.

"*Aurea testatur.*" It is witnessed in gold.

Stab. Drop. *Sanguine testatur*. It is witnessed in blood.

Stab. Drop.

Now he had it. The perfect shade of blue for the Virgin's robe. A deep blue-stained royal.

It was the color of his granddaughter's eyes.

TWENTY-FOUR

*Yet in all things I believe as Holy Church preacheth
and teacheth . . . It was my will and meaning never to
accept anything that could be contrary thereto.*
—JULIAN OF NORWICH, *DIVINE REVELATIONS*

The anchoress awoke from her nightmare to the sound of a light tapping at her supplicant's window. She'd dreamed the devil was choking her—a devil who bore a remarkable resemblance to the bishop—and at first found herself disoriented, so real had the dream been. She was drenched in sweat in spite of the chill she had felt during the prayers of mid-afternoon. Had she fallen asleep reciting the none office? No wonder the devil approached her. How long had she slept? From her communion window, she could see afternoon light picking out the colors on the windows deep inside Saint Julian's shadowy interior.

Tap, tap, tapping again. More urgent this time. Unmistakably, voices coming from outside, women's voices. She'd not had many visitors since the rains began. She missed her visitors. But she dreaded them sometimes, like now. Who was she to offer holy comfort? The Paraclete had departed from her, leaving a paucity of comfort.

She got up heavily, feeling older than her thirty-seven years, and pulled back the curtain. The company of women and children. How welcome, she thought, and said as much to her visitors, though she could see little through the narrow window but three pairs of eyes peering into her cell.

"I'm Lady Kathryn of Blackingham," the first pair of eyes said, indicating two others behind her. "These are my servants." She held a bundle in front of the window. "This is my ward and goddaughter."

"This window is too small for all of you. Please, go around to the back and come into my servant's room. We can talk better through the window where she serves me. It is much larger. Alice has gone out but she left her door open so I could have the benefit of the afternoon light."

A few minutes later three pairs of eyes appeared at Alice's larger window, but this time they were attached to faces, and the faces were attached to three travel-stained female figures. The one holding the child was dressed like a noblewoman.

"Hand the babe to me," Julian said, "so that I may bless her. What is her name?"

After the slightest hesitation, the sleeping child was passed through the window. "Her mother called her Jasmine, but she was baptized as Anna."

"She is as beautiful as a jasmine blossom."

After Julian made the sign of the cross over the child and murmured a prayer, the lady lifted something else onto the wide windowsill.

"I've come as a messenger from Finn the illuminator," the visitor said, pushing a wide roll of papers forward.

"Finn. I hope he's well. He is a good man and a friend." Thank the Virgin he's still alive, she thought. She'd meant to intervene in his behalf with the bishop, but that was before she had incurred the bishop's ill will. After ordering her to write a statement affirming her faith, he'd not returned, leaving her to stew in the elixir of his disfavor. It had been a trying time. No news from the prison all during the bleak rainy season. Just she and her fear alone in her cell. Repeatedly she'd struggled with the apologia, only to crumple the parchment in frustration. Then she would have to pray for forgiveness for her fits of pique and the process would start all over again, until the inner light that guided her was as dim as the dreary daylight outside her cell. When she prayed, He no longer listened and the wounds of contrition, the precious revelations, might have been the mad imaginings of a fevered brain. Today, she'd fallen asleep saying the Divine Office.

With one hand—the other cradled the sleeping infant—she untied the string securing the thick stack of papers. *In the beginning was the Word*. And the Word was in English!

"Finn asked that you pass these papers to the dwarf, Half-Tom, the next time he visits you," Lady Kathryn said. "But if you think they will place you in danger, I will take them away and burn them."

"Burn them! Burn the precious words of our Saviour, Saint John's record of the acts of our Lord. Could you really do that?"

The woman's gaze was as direct and forthright as what she said. "They are only words."

"But holy words. *The* Word!"

"I am a practical woman, anchoress. Holy words, yes. But life is sacred, too. Do we not have a duty to the Creator to preserve the creation, or should we just all march merrily to our graves, holy martyrs for some words scribbled on a piece of paper that can be reproduced? If we are alive to do it. Besides, it is the role of the Church, is it not, to spread the Word? You should know that better than anyone, having withdrawn into it."

"I have not withdrawn into the Church. I am not like the nuns and the monks. This is no cloister. I am anchored in the world. Though I am, of course, loyal and obedient to the Church." A hasty disclaimer. What did she really know of this woman anyway? The bishop was reputed to have spies.

"My purpose is to seek to know Him better, to contemplate His passion, and to reveal His passion to those who seek me out. Besides," Julian continued, "the Church has made no edict saying we cannot translate Scripture. I write my own Revelations in English." She did not add, "at Finn's urging." Finn who was in prison.

Lady Kathryn's skepticism showed in her face. "The king's law is one thing. I've heard some of the king's law is being written in English. But there is also the goodwill of the Roman Church. I do not intend to stub my toe against either."

The baby stirred and whimpered. Julian put down the text she was examining and held the infant over her shoulder, rocking gently back and forth. It felt good to have the child in her arms. "How do you know Finn?" she asked her plain-speaking visitor.

"We were lovers," Lady Kathryn said bluntly.

"It must be hard for you, loving him, knowing he is in prison."

"Made harder because I gave false testimony against him in the matter of the priest's murder, to save my son who may be guilty."

It was such a bald confession, such an unvarnished statement of priorities in conflict, that the anchoress for a moment didn't know how to respond. Rarely did she encounter persons of such honesty. The woman appeared so cold, sitting ramrod-straight as she delivered this assessment, but Julian noticed her restless fingers, straightening the stack of papers, smoothing the top pages, as though she were trying to smooth the wrinkles of her conscience, straighten the mess she now found herself in. Here, at least, was one sinner who knew what she was. Julian found this lack of hypocrisy redeeming.

The child started to cry.

"Better give her to the nurse. She's a greedy little sprite."

Julian noticed how the rigid line of Lady Kathryn's mouth softened with these words.

"This is Finn's child?" she asked, handing her over to the woman, who held out her hands.

"No. This is Finn's grandchild. The lust in our houses apparently runs to the second generation," she said wryly. Her restless fingers stilled, then she looked down and breathed deeply. When she lifted her head to meet the anchoress's gaze, her eyes glistened. "May I make confession?"

"I am no confessor, my lady. But I will listen to whatever you have to say gladly, if it will lighten your burden. I can see you are greatly troubled."

Lady Kathryn told her about Colin and Rose, how she'd just left Finn, how he'd refused the child.

"He'll change his mind when his grief has seasoned," the anchoress offered.

"It doesn't matter to me. Except for him. This child will be my daughter. But she could comfort him as she comforts me."

The anchoress placed her hand over Lady Kathryn's gloved hand that rested on the window ledge. She noticed blue smudges on the fingers and wondered idly how they came to be there. "You understand," she said.

"Understand what?" Lady Kathryn looked puzzled.

"The kind of love that makes a mother sacrifice everything for the love of a child." She felt the other woman's fingers withdraw into a fist beneath her sheltering palm. "That's the kind of love the Saviour has for each of us. The kind of love He has for you."

The fist tightened. "If He loves me so much, why does He put me, why does He put all of us, through this?" She withdrew her hand. The long fingers fluttered in the air. "Never mind. I know what you're going to say. 'Sin.' It is for our sins that we are punished."

"Does a loving mother take pleasure in punishment? She only punishes to teach. To make the child stronger. Suffering strengthens us. Nothing happens by chance. God doeth it all."

"What about Finn? Why would a loving God allow a good man to be persecuted?"

"Through suffering He redeems us, perfects us."

"Did you know that Finn's wife was a Jew? It must be for that he is being punished. And his daughter. The sins of the fathers. He fornicated with me. Yes. But that cannot be so bad a sin. Anchoress, I know you are a holy woman and know little of the venial sins. But surely such a sin as lust deserves not such a heavy price. If so, the prisons would be so full of priests and bishops, there'd be no room for the rest of us. Why take away Rose, the creature Finn loved most in the world, except for some weighty sin?"

"For the profit of his soul a man is sometimes left to himself, without his sin always being the cause. Finn is not necessarily being punished. God loves Jews and Gentiles alike. He is Father to all. Be assured, my lady, that in taking in this child of Jewish descent, you do not harm but good for your soul. Though I suspect you would do it even on peril of your soul. And that's why I know you understand that kind of love. *All will be well.* Your suffering only binds you closer to God."

"Then why can I not pray? I recite the offices, I count the beads. Empty words falling in a void. Anchoress, don't you ever think that it might just all be some grand charade, or some great lie perpetrated by powerful men for personal gain?"

A brave question. It deserved an honest answer.

"I suppose about twenty times, in the times of joy, I could have said with Saint Paul, 'Nothing shall part me from the love of Christ.' And in pain, I could have said with Saint Peter, 'Lord, save me. I perish.' It is not God's will that we keep step with our pain, by sorrowing and mourning for it. Pass over it. I promise—I know because He told me—the pain will come to nothing in the fullness of His love."

These are words meant for me, Julian thought. Physician, heal thyself.

God has sent me this woman so that in ministering to her I can lay new hold on my own faith. Stop worrying about the bishop's anger. He is either a tool of the devil or an instrument of God. Either way, *all will be well.*

"I have not your faith, anchoress, though I find some comfort in your words. But I've lingered longer than I intended. It's too late for the journey back to Blackingham. Have you knowledge of an inn nearby?" She looked nervously at the baby who, having drunk her fill, had fastened her blue-eyed gaze on Julian.

"An inn might not be the best choice for a company of women. Just five miles north on your way home is Saint Faith Priory. Their tradition of hospitality is well known."

"Aye. I know it. In the village of Horsham. I stopped there once as a girl with my father. The sisters there are very kind."

The women rose and prepared to leave. The little coterie of females looked suddenly vulnerable. The younger woman, who now held the baby, was really hardly more than a child, fourteen or fifteen. She had a rapt expression on her face. She stared as though she was seeing some strange apparition deep inside the cell.

"Is there something you'd like to say, child?" The anchoress asked.

The girl leaned forward, spoke, her voice scarcely above a whisper. "The light around you sh-shimmers. L-like hope. It b-beats like a heart."

"But there is no light—"

The nurse interrupted. "She has a gift, milady." And then added quickly, "From God."

These women are special, the anchoress thought: not just the strong-willed noblewoman who loves so intensely; but this infant, too, with her blue eyes and Jewish blood, a symbol of God's love, of his Oneness; even the nurse— who now that she looked more closely, resembled the girl with the spiritual gift. Some nurturing quality bound them all together.

Kathryn gathered her cloak about her. "I thank you for your counsel. You've given me somewhat to think on." Then, as an afterthought: "Do you wish to keep the papers? Or shall I take them?"

"I will see that Tom gets them. I am not afraid of the bishop."

Lady Kathryn merely shrugged and turned to leave.

"The Lord go with you," the anchoress shouted as she waved good-bye to her visitors' backs.

Only the young maid turned and smiled a grateful acceptance of the benediction.

After her visitors departed, Julian's spirit was so renewed that she wondered if they had been real or some angel visitation, another of her visions. One thing was sure: real or not, they had been sent to her from He who was her source. In ministering to them, she had watered her own soul. She would write her apologia, and she would write it in English.

But whatever happens, *all will be well.*

"Come on, Ahab," she said to the fat feline, who leaped onto her windowsill. She picked up the Wycliffe papers and hid them under a stack of linen. "We will look forward to Tom's visit, you and I. He will bring us news of Finn and perhaps a gift from the marshes."

Ahab purred his anticipation.

TWENTY-FIVE

Grant harvest lord, more, by a penny or two, to call on
his fellows the better to do; Give gloves to thy reapers,
a largess to cry, and daily to loiterers have a good eye.
—THOMAS TUSSER, *GOOD POINTS OF HUSBANDRY*

During the late spring, Kathryn did not return to Castle Prison.
Half-Tom appeared at Blackingham Manor frequently, a circumstance of
which Agnes did not approve. "I'll not have him sniffin' around my girl."
But Kathryn encouraged the dwarf's visits, finding errands for him to do in
her service, sending him as a messenger to the abbeys around Norwich with
inquiries about Colin. Was her younger son a vagabond, sleeping in ditches,
hungry, dirty, alone? Or was he even now, as she thought about him, thread-
ing the stone corridors of some faraway cloister, drugged by plainsong, lost
to her forever? But Kathryn would have found something for Half-Tom to
do even had she not been desperate for news of Colin. Half-Tom was
Kathryn's only link to Finn.

"Ask him if he wants to see the child," she asked often.

The answer was always the same. "My lady, with regret I must say, he
says he has no time. His work for the bishop keeps him busy."

So there was no pilgrimage to Castle Prison during these warm sunlit days. Summer came. Jasmine learned to coo and laugh and play patty-cake to Kathryn's singsong. Plans for the harvest began with its pressures to find workers to beat the blight, to beat the rains—all made more burdensome by the absence of Kathryn's sons.

It was the second harvest since Roderick's death. Simpson would be lord of the harvest again this year, and there would be no lord of the manor to temper the steward's growing arrogance. And just where was she to find the extra pennies to pay the day laborers who demanded more each year, not to mention the largesse that her own villeins expected at harvest time? The blind loyalty with which the serfs and peasants had served her father had vanished, wiped out by labor shortages and notions of equality fostered by mumbling lay priests. The old order was threatened, might even disappear, and that was the order in which she knew her place. Roderick had bound the serfs to him by power and tradition. Where was her power? Where was her tradition?

Some days she felt she simply could not go on. Except for Jasmine.

It was Magda's fourth trip of the day in the noon heat, carrying the leather bottles of ale, the baskets of bread and cheese, oatcake and onions to the reapers in the fields. Her load was heavy but well-balanced on a long pole across her shoulders. She didn't mind, because though she was small-boned, she was strong and sturdy, and she welcomed the chance to escape the stifling kitchen. Cook had lately been in very bad temper. And Magda enjoyed watching the long scythes swishing through the rye like Morris dancers. Her father was the best of the lot. She watched proudly as he brought his body low, right leg bent under his body, left arm stretched out for balance, right arm swinging through the grain, the scythe cutting parallel to the ground, his body shifting rhythmically with each swipe.

Small wonder the reapers ate so much at their midday meal. Small wonder, too, that Agnes was so ill-tempered withal. Last week she'd chased Half-Tom away with a broom, accusing him of stealing an egg! Agnes! Who always kept her stockpot on the boil for hungry beggars. She was cross, always finding fault when she had heretofore been so easily pleased.

Out here was sunshine and fresh air, and mare's-tail clouds floating free in blue sky (not to mention a fair amount of goodwill for the kitchen maid who brought the meal). The fellowship among the yeomen and the serfs reached out and gathered her in. She felt herself a member of some happy family, happy because, though the work was hard and the hours long, for this one month out of the year, they would be well-fed. If the harvest lord was tight-fisted, he would find himself short-handed. The villeins had no choice, but the yeomen were free to move on to more generous fields. All expected largesse. Though, this year, Magda wasn't so sure. She had measured the steward's soul-light—if light it could be called. It was more an absence of light, and she'd never seen that before. Could it be that he had no light because he had no soul? A devil in the guise of a man? She shivered as she saw him coming toward the hedge in whose shade she'd laid the board cloth. She looked away to avoid his gaze lest it put an evil spell on her.

She watched the soft lights of the children, blending and merging like a rainbow as they played tag beneath a large oak tree at the edge of the grain-fields. She'd played under this same tree at harvest time—and not so long ago—while her father danced with his scythe and her mother bound the sheaves. She would ask Lady Kathryn if her mother could bring Jasmine to the field tomorrow. Her mother would like it, too. She only ever smiled at harvest time. Even if her belly was too swollen to work, she'd watch the other women's children. Happy memories. Except for the bad times: when the harvest had rotted in the fields, when the devil brought the blight or the plague or the rain. Many died of hunger in the bad times. Her little brothers had been two such.

But she would not remember that today. Today, the sun was shining and the grain was ripe, and Blackingham kitchens had provided a groaning board for the harvest workers. And in the distance she saw a familiar light. She waved and shouted welcome to the squat little man who lurched toward the kitchen. She was glad that Half-Tom had not been scared away by Cook's broom and scowls. He was her friend, and he'd come back, bringing his beautiful soul-light with him.

But it was the man with no light who approached her.

The steward came up beside her and grabbed the leather bottle of ale. The pole balanced on her shoulders tipped. To keep from dropping it, she set it down clumsily on the ground. He swigged at the bottle, letting the ale dribble down his chin, as he watched her. She pointed to the water bucket on the ground. The water was cool; she'd fetched it from the stream herself. When

Simpson ignored her, she made an effort to loose her tongue, even though he frightened her with his leering eyes.

"S-sir—"

He laughed, moved closer to her. His breath stank of onion and rotting teeth. He took another swig from the bottle. What was she to do? He was the harvest lord, but there would not be enough ale for the workers. Already there was a slackness in the neck of the bottle. Maybe if she brought the water to him . . . She backed away, crossed the few paces to the bucket and brought him a gourdful.

He took the gourd from her, staring at her all the while, and poured the water over his head. Then he shook his greasy hair like a shaggy dog.

"Sir . . ." hard to wrap her tongue around the sounds. "S-sir, the wa-ter is for drink-ing, and C-cook says—"

"'Cook says,'" he mocked in a slow, dragging whine. "I don't care what Cook says. I am harvest lord, not Cook. Do you know what that makes me? That makes me your lord, and I can have the ale or the water"—he flung the gourd and a string of spittle at her feet—"or anything else having to do with the harvest. And that includes the simple-minded kitchen maid who lays the board."

He grabbed at her bodice. "Let's see if you've got any tight little buds in there ready to bloom."

She recoiled, wrenching free, and the oft-washed linen tore away. Her face grew hot with shame as she frantically tried to cover her breasts with the torn fabric.

"You might be ripe for plucking after all."

His laughter was lewd and harsh. It made her feel dirty.

Quick as lightning, he moved around behind her, trapping her in his dust-coated arms. His breath was hot on her neck. His hands fumbled at her breasts. Something hard poked her from behind. She could feel it through her petticoat. She knew what it was, and she knew what he wanted, but her lips were too rigid to form the protest, and her tongue tripped on the words.

"P-please—"

The pressure behind her increased.

"Get on your hands and knees and lift your skirts." His words were hardly more than grunts.

Not here, her mind cried, not in the fields like an animal. Not with one who has no soul-light. But, Holy Mother, what was she to do? He was the harvest lord. And she was a vassal.

"P-please, sir, please." Hardly more than a whimper.

"Now you find your tongue."

"My f-father is—"

"I'll pay him an extra penny. If you please me. Now, hold up your skirt and get down."

Whimpers and tiny dry sobs escaped, but she tried to hold them back. The more fuss she made, the more the others would see, and they could do nothing. He was harvest lord. She clutched at her skirt, holding it just above her ankles. Her trembling hands would not raise it higher. He jerked at her skirt and gave her a push from behind. She landed on all fours like a dog. He wrapped one arm beneath her waist, pinning her in that position. The rough field stubble scraped her bare knees and hands. She dug her fingernails into the dirt, clutching at the earth. His rough hands lifted her skirts over her head. She cringed beneath the touch of his hands on her skin, the pinch of his fingernails. He grunted like an animal as he bumped against her. It hurt. But it hurt more to think the others witnessed her shame. Vomit welled up inside her mouth. She could not cry. She could not even breathe.

⁓⋇⸜

"Get back to the field, Simpson."

At the sound of Lady Kathryn's voice, the steward let go of the girl and straggled to his feet, pulling on his braies. Kathryn could have laughed at the startled expression on his face had she been less angry. Not for the first time in her life she wished that, just for a few minutes, she could be a man. Simpson would be feeling the sting of a whip across his backside instead of struggling to cover his bare arse with his breeches.

Magda scrambled from beneath him, smoothing her skirt with one hand, holding on to her torn bodice with the other. The girl's face was as white as marble. Kathryn resisted an urge to take her in her arms and comfort her. She knew such a display might be the girl's undoing. Kathryn could see that she was struggling to hold herself together, to preserve some vestige of dignity, even though tears were running in tracks down her dusty cheeks.

"Magda, go back to the house."

By this time, Simpson had gained his feet but had turned his back to her and was fumbling with his breeches.

"Tell Cook you've fallen in a pile of horse dung." These last words Kathryn spat in the direction of the overseer.

He turned, shrugged, brushing straw from his tunic. "The girl was willing enough. No harm done. I'm always careful of your property, milady."

"We are all somebody's property, Simpson. You'd do well to remember that. You touch the girl again, and I'll deny your wages and ban you from my land."

His smirk widened. She knew what he was thinking, even wondering if he dared say it. Where would she get another harvest lord? How it galled, that she must suffer this evil presence among her servants because she had no other to depend on.

"Call the workers for their meal break. I will serve the food myself," Kathryn said as she watched the girl to see that she was able to walk unaided.

When Magda gained the edge of the field, she broke into a run, half-stumbling in the direction of the main house. Kathryn was relieved to see that there was no blood on her skirts. As soon as the meal was served, Kathryn would see that Agnes treated the maid with extra care. Some special kindness.

"With milady's indulgence, I would point out that Sir Roderick—"

"What Sir Roderick would have said is that the maidenhead of a servant has no value. But it is valuable to the maid who owns it. And it should be hers to give away. Or not. You work for Blackingham, Simpson. You work for me."

"Certainly, milady." But beneath the lowered lids, she saw a flash of hatred as strong as lightning and just as dangerous. She would be rid of him. As soon as the harvest was done.

"And Simpson, one more thing. The girl will be paid a shilling out of your wage to compensate her."

"For what? She's still intact."

"A shilling, then, for her humiliation. And to remind you of who is master here."

"As you wish, milady." His eyes were like bright little pieces of burning coal. "But I'd have got my money's worth if your ladyship had arrived a minute later."

Then he turned his back to her and stalked off across the fields, with only an abrupt wave at the staring laborers to indicate it was time for dinner.

⊰⊱

The harvest finished late, but by September the last haywain had been stacked and the rye and the barley stored safely in the barns for winter threshing. The Michaelmas geese, grown fat from gleaning the fallen grains among the stubble, were roasting on the kitchen spits for the harvest-home feast. Kathryn anxiously counted her casks of mead and cider and ale, all home-brewed, along with the twenty gallons of beer she'd purchased for fifty shillings to supplement her store. She dreaded the evening's feast. It would be a night of drunken revelry, and though Kathryn did not begrudge the laborers—she knew they deserved the feast—her purse was as thin as a hermit's. Twice during the two weeks of harvest, Simpson had come back to her demanding largesse for the yeomen. Thank God the quarter-day rents were due. He was collecting them today and would give his accounting at the feast.

Kathryn lifted her veil to wipe the sweat and called for Glynis to lay the board in the great hall. Where was the lazy girl, anyway? Agnes and the little kitchen maid were working themselves into the ground. Magda's hands were as busy as her tongue was still. She had retreated back into her silence since the episode with Simpson. Unfortunate happenstance, but fortunate that the dwarf had come to Kathryn for help. She supposed there were others, both willing and unwilling, upon whom Simpson had heaped such abuse, but there was little she could do about it. She shouldn't worry about them. Hadn't God ordained their lot in life?

She surveyed the long boards laid out on trestles in the great hall. There would have to be a dais. Not fitting that she should sit below. But who would sit there with her, a widow, mistress of the manor, with no sons to attend her? Simpson? She shuddered. Anyway, he was not noble born. He would sit at the long table. The priest at Saint Michael's would sit on the dais with her to bless the feast, but below the salt.

She had sent Half-Tom to Norwich to find some entertainment. The harvest workers were entitled to a little mirth. It was her duty to provide it. "Not too many," she'd instructed. "A juggler or two, a pretty sound upon the lute is all Blackingham can afford."

Garbed in her second-best brocade gown and braided coronet, Lady Kathryn sat alone. The hall was aromatic with newly strewn herbs among the rushes, and the smoky smell of roast geese found its way from the kitchen into the hall. The board appeared abundantly laid under the weight of harvest fruits. Agnes was an alchemist. She might not be able to turn base metals into gold, but she could always turn yesterday's broken meats into wonderful suet puddings flavored with spices and colored with saffron (at least the color of alchemist's gold) to disguise their age.

Kathryn watched from her elevated carved chair as the entertainers slipped in at the other end of the great hall. One wore the skeletal costume of the grim reaper to parody the harvest of souls; another wore a hooded cape—in this hot weather—and carried a lute slung over his shoulder; a third one wore only breeches knotted around his loins. The muscles of this one's body rippled beneath well-oiled skin. He entered first, turning cartwheels down the long hall, coming to rest finally in front of my lady's chair, where he did a handstand and juggled three colored balls with his feet. Lady Kathryn applauded and the crowd echoed her approval.

Half-Tom augmented the small company of minstrels by playing at hide-and-seek with the grim reaper, making rude gestures and taunts to the macabre figure, who chased him around the hall with his scythe. The peasants hooted with laughter. Here was a chance to make death the butt of their jokes for a change. At the other end of the hall, the lute player strolled along the long table and strummed. Kathryn could not hear his song above the raucous laughter and applause for the contortionist and the reaper. And just as well, the music of the lute only made her think of Colin and she didn't have time for that now.

Simpson came late to the feast, entering well after the banquet had begun. An insult to the workers. An insult to her. He sat down, silent, sulking, nursing his cup. As steward he was entitled to wine, but Kathryn had watered it well, both for economy and for prudence. From the way he swaggered into the hall, she judged that this was not his first cup of the day. After the last course, the *raffyolys,* patties of chopped pork and spices, had been served, he progressed on unsteady legs to the dais, and laying the bag of coins, the quarter-day rents, in front of her, mumbled with slurred speech that the accounting was inside the bag.

"It's short," he muttered. "The villeins plead the king's poll tax."

She weighed it in her hands and sighed. It felt light, and she was sure if she read the accounting she would find more promises than coin. She would have to take her rent in chickens and eggs and vegetables from the small garden the crofters scratched out in the dust beside their huts.

She laid the bag beside her trencher and stood and gave the required toast to the harvest and its lord. But at the conclusion of the salute, the hall remained silent. The yeomen did not lift their voices in hurrahs.

A few men at the other end began to beat the table with their fists in a steady rhythm. The pounding rippled down the board until the sound filled the hall and echoed in her head.

"Largesse, largesse. We demand largesse." The cadence began low and rose to a crescendo.

Hardly the response she'd expected. They were a greedy lot. Did they think to rob a poor widow? She would not stand for such insolence. She stiffened her back, raised her hand.

The chanting stopped.

"Where's the gratitude you owe for the largesse already given? Twice I gave Harvest Lord extra pence to augment your wages."

One, emboldened by drink, stood up and shouted back at her, "Harvest Lord gave us nothing. He promised largesse at harvest home."

A chorus of agreement and the chanting and the pounding began again. *Largesse. Largesse.*

Kathryn glared down at Simpson who, still seated, stared into his cup. "What's the meaning of this, Simpson? What did you do with the extra coin?"

The pounding was deafening. *Largesse. Largesse.*

He looked up, not at her but past her, and shrugged. "I had to use it to hire extra hands."

"The harvest was late. And there are no more than the usual number here."

"Some quit and moved on."

They were shouting above the din when, abruptly, the pounding stopped. A hush fell over the hall. No one moved except the hooded lute player, who had stopped strumming and was walking toward the dais. Was he about to ask for more money, too? The room suddenly felt very close. She clutched the edge of the table for support. This was the last straw. The steward's perfidy knew no bounds.

"You are a thief and a liar, Simpson." She said it loudly enough for all in the hall to hear.

He just sneered at her.

"I'll suffer your insolence and your calumny no longer. The meanest serf of Blackingham is worth more than you. And I'll not have you on Blackingham land any longer. If you are still on manor property tomorrow, I'll have you whipped."

There was absolute silence. At the other end of the dais the priest coughed discreetly. The only other sound in the room was the endless chorus of the summer crickets from outside.

Simpson's drunken laugh rose high and shrill, hanging in the pregnant silence. "And where, your ladyship, will you find a man to do the whipping?"

She swept her arm out in a gesture meant to gather the workers to her, an encompassing gesture, allowing her gaze to sweep across the tables, willing them to take her side. "These men from whom you've stolen will show their loyalty to their lady."

But there was no chorus of support. The peasants looked from one to the other as if not knowing whom to believe, trusting neither.

"Good men." Kathryn stood as she addressed them. The smoke and heat in the hall made her dizzy, but she steeled herself for what she had to do. "You have worked hard for Blackingham Manor. I value your service. I hold your loyalty in greatest esteem, and I'll see that you receive the largesse this greedy steward has stolen from you. Come to the gate tomorrow at prime. For tonight—"

"More promises," a few muttered, but there was a scattering of applause and a cry of "Let her finish."

Encouraged, she held up her hand for silence and continued. "For tonight, enjoy the feast our kitchens have prepared for you." And she motioned for the cellarer to pour another round of cider. "Enjoy the entertainment that you have earned."

Half-Tom and the reaper began again to mime their macabre antics. One or two in the hall still muttered complaints, but the solidarity was broken, the gathering temporarily appeased.

As Kathryn was wondering where the extra coin was to come from—she would demand it of Simpson; she'd just proved she still had some authority—the lute player approached the dais.

"My lady."

That voice. A trick of memory?

The lute player bowed before her as he threw back his hood. The pale skin of his bald head was startling in its whiteness. She had a flash of memory: a mother's hand, her hand, washing such a hairless pate, caressing the shape of each skull bone. But before she could even draw out that vision full-blown, the young lute player looked up at her. Jasmine's eyes stared back at her.

She stumbled down from the dais and crushed him to her.

He returned her embrace, but it felt different somehow, more restrained. He had grown. It was the muscled shoulders of a man that she embraced.

"Colin! Oh, well come, my son, well come." She wiped tears from her eyes when she held him out at arm's length to drink in his face.

"You've grown. More a man. Less a boy," she said. "What have you done to your beautiful hair?"

"An act of propitiation," he said, not smiling. His voice was deeper, too.

She waited for him to say more, but he did not explain.

"Why are you on the dais alone?" he asked. "Where's Alfred? And the illuminator?"

A familiar grief threatened her joy.

"You do not ask about the illuminator's daughter. Why do you not ask about Rose?" Just a touch of condemnation, a hint of bitterness crept in.

"Has something happened? Have they left?"

She sighed. "Much has happened, Colin. Your leaving was only the beginning." She instantly regretted the sound of recrimination in her voice. The fault had been hers alone. She must not chase him away again. She patted his hand. "I've much to tell you, but it must wait until after this business with Simpson is complete. It is good that you've come. He will be less truculent when he sees I'm not a woman alone."

She turned to continue her confrontation with the steward, but his seat was empty. The bag of receipts was gone too.

⁓ ✢ ✲⁓

After the feast of harvest home ended and the revelers had all staggered to their beds—the hovels, cots, stable, even the occasional ditch where they slept—Kathryn instructed Colin to come to her chamber. The trials of the evening had worn her down, but she knew what she had to tell Colin would not wait for daybreak.

They sat at a small table in the corner of the room where she had sometimes supped with Finn, the two of them alone in her chamber, enjoying the intimacy of a shared meal. But she could not think about that now. It was her son who sat with her, and she had to think carefully about what words she would say.

"It was foolishness, you know, your leaving. You've come home to stay, I hope."

"Aye, Mother, I've come home to stay. I found I am not suited for the life of a monk, after all."

He had changed. The shaved head was unnerving—she mourned the loss of his beautiful hair, and the blue eyes had lost some of their innocence, replaced by a burning, restless brilliance.

"You've been traveling with the players since you left?"

"Most of the time. Did you get my letters?"

"Letters? Only one. And I had no way to answer, or I would have told you already what I have to tell you now." How to begin? She offered him a glass of wine. He declined. She took a drink. "Fortune has not been kind to Blackingham since you left, Colin. As I told you, your leaving was the beginning."

Then she told him about Alfred leaving, about Finn's arrest, about the baby, and finally, about Rose's death. He listened to all in silence. He did not interrupt her with questions or laments, even when she paused in expectation, and when, at the last, she reached across the table to clasp his hand, he withdrew it.

"Rose is dead, then." He said it flatly. His eyes clouded, and his Adam's apple worked as he swallowed hard. She longed to fold him in her arms, but knew he would not welcome it. This was not her gentle Colin who, as a child, had once enraged his father because he cried over a nest of dead hatchlings a fox had robbed.

"I am sorry" was all he said, dry-eyed. He stared past her into the middle distance, but she knew he was not studying the tapestries hanging on her chamber walls. Neither did she see the pain she'd expected—no tears, just a hard, unwavering gaze. "I will pray for her soul," he said. His voice held no quiver of emotion. "I've met a man named John Ball, Mother. He opened my eyes to many things."

Surely, to hide his grief so easily, this was not her Colin but some changeling child.

"What kind of things?" she said, thinking that he was shutting her out, did not want her to know how much he had loved Rose, would not let her see his pain or his guilt. A silly child, hiding his guilt from his mother.

"About the Church," he said.

"About the Church?"

He nodded eagerly, his voice no longer flat. "About the way the priests and bishops have enslaved the poor in ignorance, how they abuse them, how they steal from them to fill their abbeys with gold and their coffers with silver."

He was animated, now, his eyes bright, almost fevered. He's overcome with grief, she thought, just talking to keep it away.

"I've learned other things, too, in my travels." He stood up and began to pace the chamber. "The troubadours have a song they sing about Adam and Eve. How there was no servant, no *gentleman* in the Garden of Eden. John Ball says God did not ordain this social order. God loves us all equally. The nobleman is no greater than the gentleman, the gentleman no greater than the peasant. Don't you see, Mother? This notion of a Divine Order that puts one man over another is all wrong. In the sight of God we are all the same!"

Her son was turning into a heretic before her eyes. He was raving, like the Lollard preachers who roamed the countryside.

"Colin, you have a daughter. Don't you want to see her?"

He dropped his head into his hands, rubbed his face impatiently, almost angrily, as if to scrub the skin away. He made a little sucking noise with his breath. Here it comes, she thought. Now he will cry, and he can start to mend his sorrows. But when he looked up at her, his eyes were dry and his mouth was set firm and determined. "There will be time for that later," he said. "Tonight, I must prepare. Tomorrow, I'm going out to preach at the Aylsham crossroads. The harvest is ripe, Mother, don't you see? There's so little time."

And so one of Kathryn sons had come home. But not really.

TWENTY-SIX

Colin had been home for two months when the invitation came bearing the ducal crest and promising a fortnight of feasting at Framlingham Castle. Kathryn's first thought was to decline the Yuletide celebration from the duke of Norwich "honoring Sir Guy de Fontaigne upon receiving the Noble Order of the Garter." She had neither the finery nor the spirit for such a protracted festival, and wondered how came the widow of a lesser knight to be on the guest list. The castle was in Suffolk, at least a two-, maybe a three-day journey in the heart of winter. She had no gentlewoman to attend her and no armored soldiers to protect her, and she could hardly take Colin with her the way he was behaving.

He spent his days preaching in the crossroads and marketplaces, anyplace a crowd gathered. He showed no interest in his daughter. Even his lute gathered dust on a peg in the great hall. He has replaced melody with rant and love with obsession, she thought, as she half-listened to his harangues on the evils of the Divine Order, the cruelty of the nobility, the abuses of the clergy. The names of John Ball and Wycliffe were so often on his lips, they might have been the words to the rosary. No, she could not bring her youngest son into noble company. To do so would only place him and Blackingham in peril. Not that he cared aught for Blackingham, either. Some nights he didn't come home at all. On those nights Kathryn, driven from her bed by wakefulness, found comfort in rocking Jasmine into the night, long after the child slumbered. "What will happen to you, little one? What will happen to us all?" In those long, sleepless nights, she would think of the anchoress and her promise that *all will be well*. "I don't see how, sweeting. I don't see how," she would whisper to the sleeping child.

How did one in her precarious position dare refuse the invitation of a duke? She could plead some womanly illness to avoid a difficult journey— which, if truth be told, she dreaded less than the pretense of honoring a man whom she loathed. When her mind pictured Sir Guy de Fontaigne, what she saw first was the cruel curve of his mouth. There had been no misreading the gloating in his predator's smile the night he'd arrested Finn. So the question was not how to refuse but *if* she dared refuse. Sighing, she laid the invitation aside. But there was a chance she might see Alfred. After all, he was squire to Sir Guy. One of many, but still . . .

She opened her clothing chest and rummaged through it, shaking out her newest gown.

Two days later, the sheriff's messenger came. Sir Guy would be honored if Lady Kathryn would travel under his banner of protection. He would send a carriage and an escort for her on Christmas Eve. The message was left in the great hall. The messenger had not even waited for a reply.

❧

Kathryn traveled with the sheriff's retinue, but in a private carriage provided for her and her attendant. She'd had no choice but to bring Glynis, though the silly goose of a girl spent all of her time peeking between the curtains, hoping for some attention from man or boy. At least, she had nimble fingers when it came to dressing Kathryn's hair, though her styles tended toward elaborate braids, not something a widow who did not want to call attention to herself should wear.

"My lady, it's all so exciting. Such pretty banners. And grand steeds. All trotting three abreast behind us."

And a man mounted on every one of them, Kathryn thought. "Close the curtain, Glynis," she said. "You're letting in the chill. My hands are blue with cold already."

At night they camped. Kathryn hardly slept at all the first night. She lay awake listening to night sounds: the creaking of the carriage on its wooden wheels, night-calling birds, and once she thought she heard a pack of wolves howling. Tonight, she hoped, would be better, but her head had already begun to ache from breathing the smoke from the campfires.

The soldier who delivered supper to her carriage lingered, flirting with Glynis. But to Kathryn's relief, Sir Guy did not impose his company. The joint of meat held little interest for her, but she chewed a heel of bread and welcomed the short purple twilight, welcomed the cessation of the carriage's bumping and groaning across the frozen ruts. As on the night before, she slept badly, waking several times to worry about Jasmine. She heard Glynis sneak out—an urgent call of nature or some amorous assignation with a soldier?—and she heard her sneak in minutes, hours, eons, later.

In the morning, they broke camp in a pearly dawn mist. When Glynis came back from emptying the slops, she told Kathryn she thought she'd seen "Master Alfred" among the men.

"Are you sure, Glynis?" Kathryn had searched and asked among the sheriff's squires and soldiers when they first set out.

"Aye, milady. He was not close up, but I'd know that noble head anywhere."

Kathryn, drawing her hooded cape tighter, grateful for its squirrel-lined warmth, lifted the tapestry curtain. "Show me," she said.

Glynis pointed through the mist to a clump of men huddled around a fire. They broke their fast with hunks of hard cheese and passed around a skin of ale. There was no redheaded Dane among them.

~ ※ ~

They arrived at Framlingham just as the watery sun reached its apex. The keep was imposing with its concentric curtain wall of stone, its ramparts and gatehouse. It was a military fortress. All of Blackingham Hall could fit in the bailey, Kathryn thought, as they passed through the portcullis. Large as it was, though, the yard was still crowded with bright tents and pavilions, their colorful banners curling in a brisk wind. Liveried servants in bright silks of red and blue and green bustled about, shouting to be heard over the creaking wheels and yapping dogs and clopping horses. Curtained wagons, like the conveyance that carried Kathryn, were pulled into corners before campfires. Each had its own cord of wood stacked high beside it. The wood to stoke the fires over a fortnight would denude a sizable forest.

"Are we to camp in the yard, milady?" Glynis asked, excitement spiking her voice.

"We shall wait and see," Kathryn said. "It looks to be a large gathering. The house may be reserved for guests of higher rank."

"I like it here. It's more festive and friendly-like. And this carriage is fine enough for a duchess. Sir Guy must be very rich. And very fond of you, mi-lady."

Kathryn ignored the girl's impertinent wink. She was thinking that the sheriff had forgotten her. Even though she didn't desire his company, simple courtesy should have made him greet her by now. If they were to encamp in the yard, surely she would not be left on her own. Glynis might like the idea of lodging in the company of knights and their soldiers; Kathryn did not. At a sharp tap on the side of her carriage. Kathryn pulled back the tapestry. Not Sir Guy, but a servant wearing the crimson shirt and cap of his house.

"If my lady and her gentlewomen will follow me," he said with a perfunctory bow, "I'm to escort your ladyship to chambers. You are to lodge within."

Thank the Virgin, she thought, blowing on her hands for warmth. What had that girl done with her gloves?

As Kathryn alighted from the carriage, she counted the towers at each juncture of keep and courtyard—thirteen in all. It was to one of these tall, multi-storied towers that the servant led them.

"I had not expected such an imposing castle," Kathryn said as she followed the servant carrying her trunk up several flights of curving stone steps. "The duke of Norfolk must be very powerful."

"Powerful enough," the usher said. "But Framlingham belongs to the king."

"Will the king be in attendance then?" Kathryn hoped she sounded more curious than distressed, but the truth was she had neither the clothes nor the heart for court intrigue, and she certainly had no desire for the king, or his regent, to be reminded of her existence.

"Don't know." The servant was breathing hard.

The tower steps curved yet again, and they climbed higher. She thought of Finn in his high square Norman tower. Still higher. Another curve, and suddenly, when it seemed the spiral would go even more heavenward, the stairway opened onto a landing. She followed the usher across the threshold of a small but pretty chamber. The walls were washed with a plain ocher color, not painted with bright murals, like those she had glimpsed in passing. But the simple room had been enhanced with a rich tapestry hanging above the fireplace. A sitting bench graced the hearth. It, too, was draped with a pretty scarf and scattered with tasseled pillows, all slightly askew as though they had been hurriedly and recently placed.

"Will that be all then?" the servant asked, his chest heaving, as he put down her trunk.

"Is there a message for me from Sir Guy?"

"Message?"

"Further instructions? The custom of the house? Schedule of festivities?"

"No message. You should mayhap send your maid to the gallery to inquire."

"Are there many other women in attendance?"

"I've seen no other. Though I suppose the duchess and her gentlewomen to be in residence." He cast a sidelong glance at the door.

"You may go."

Kathryn put down her jewel casket and surveyed her quarters more carefully. A garderobe was attached to the chamber—at least she didn't have to seek out a common privy. There was a welcoming fire in the grate, clean-burning English oak, not peat. Beeswax candles, not tallow dips, dressed the wall sconces, and a bed warmer lay on the hearth, with a pallet for her personal maid rolled beside it. A small but curtained bed, a chair, and a chest comprised the room's other furnishings. A basin and a ewer of water waited in the garderobe; a bundle of herbs hung above the privy, and fresh herbs were strewn across the floor. Certainly better than camping in the courtyard. It was blissfully quiet here, only a faint echo of slow steps—were they ascending?—then a diffident knock.

At Kathryn's nod, Glynis opened the door to a girl about Magda's age.

"I've been sent to see to my lady's comfort. Does my lady require anything?"

At the sight of the girl's skinny limbs, Kathryn knew she would not have the heart to ask for hot water or more than a few small sticks of wood. The servant was hardly more than a child. Her arms were pocked with chilblains—probably a scullery maid pressed into extra service for the festivities.

"I have my own maid. If you would just show her the kitchens and the laundry, she can assist me."

The child, looking relieved, muttered a "Yes, milady," accompanied by an uncertain curtsy.

"Go with her, Glynis. Drop off this roll of laundry. Find out from the other servants the household routine. And when you come back, bring a small ewer of hot water."

"The Christmas Feast is in the great hall at three bells, milady," the child offered.

"Mark the time, Glynis." Kathryn fixed her with what she hoped was a meaningful gaze. "And don't dally."

When the girls had gone, Kathryn stooped to her trunk and rummaged through her finery. Her newest gown was a velvet brocade of deep claret, embroidered and banded with silver threads. It had been an extravagance, but her heart had been much lighter then, her future more hopeful. It was Finn's favorite color, but he'd been arrested before she could wear it for him.

It was time, now, for the dress to earn its coin; nothing to save it for, she'd said to herself as she'd packed it to bring with her. Perhaps it would be better to reserve it for the Feast of the Epiphany on Twelfth Night. No. That was merely to put off the pain of wearing it. She'd wear the velvet brocade now and again on Twelfth Night. And when she got home she would wear it again and again and again, like a pilgrim's hair shirt.

She'd gone so thin, the skirt would hang loosely from its high waist. Would there be time for Glynis to tuck it in? There was a velvet cap with a silver snood to match her hair. The cap would have to be brushed, but she could do that herself while Glynis tucked the dress. Kathryn shivered, dreading the moment when she would have to strip down to her shift. Would the guests be expected to attend prayers? She lay across the bed and, covering herself with her cloak, curled into a ball.

Christmas Day. Finn was alone in his tower, and she in hers. And heaven and hell lay between them.

⚬

"Sir Guy has sent me to escort my lady to the Christmas Feast."

It was the same servant who had carried her trunk. He looked at her admiringly but said nothing. Though he was little older than Colin and Alfred, she appreciated the look. It shored up her sagging confidence. There was no pier glass in her room, only a small mirror that showed her a thin, pale face. Too much white hair and white skin against the deep red velvet.

As they entered the great hall she felt a moment of panic—so many people, at least two hundred or more, and so much noise. She recognized no one, and there were not many women scattered among the trestle boards.

She was wondering where she would be seated when the servant led her toward the front of the hall. Probably above the salt, for Roderick and her father had both been knights. She surveyed the knights' boards, hoping to see the face of a congenial wife. She saw with relief that a few of the lords were accompanied by their wives, but there were no vacant seats, and the servant led her past the knights' board. Mayhap, then, she was to be seated with the gentlewomen of the duchess. An unusual, but unwelcome, honor, to be sure. She blessed her choice in choosing the elegance of the fabric, if not the color. At least she would not suffer the embarrassment of looking like a common robin roosting among royal birds of paradise.

But they passed the ladies' board and approached the dais where the duke and duchess perched amid a horizontal string of noble dignitaries.

"There must be some mistake," she said. But the servant, several paces ahead of her, either didn't hear her or chose to ignore her.

Sir Guy stood up. Of course, as guest of honor he would be on the dais, and since she was his guest, he would escort her to her seat. But, instead of coming down from the dais and leading her to one of the boards below, he merely held out his hand, indicating the empty seat beside him. He smiled that crooked smile she detested. "A rare delight, my lady, to be your mess mate for a fortnight. An auspicious foreshadowing."

Her heart sank. Holy Mother, she had been invited by the duke of Norfolk as the lady designee of Sir Guy de Montaigne. She did not even want to think about what that might portend.

"An honor made more delightful by its singleness, my lord," she said as she took her place beside him.

✣

By Twelfth Night Kathryn was weary of the nightly feasts and longing for home. Her smile felt as frozen as the hoarfrosts that greeted her each morning. She was weary, too, of Sir Guy's company, though she had to admit that his demeanor had been courteous, and in this alien courtly society, she was grateful for even his companionship. At least he was a familiar face. But thank the Holy Virgin, this was the last time she would have to sit at this high table.

It was the Feast of the Epiphany, but like the feasts that had preceded it, there was more of sacrilege than sanctity about it. From her seat at the far end of the dais, Kathryn could not see the bishop of Norwich seated between the duke of Norfolk and the archbishop of Canterbury, but she recognized his drunken laughter. She had heard it enough these last few nights; the bishop was often in his cups. She had only seen him from a distance, having no occasion to be presented to him, and had been surprised that he seemed so young, both in appearance and deportment. Poor Finn. A double indignity to be prisoner to such a green and arrogant upstart. Kathryn winced as she heard his snorting approval of the ribald antics presented for their amusement.

On an opposing dais at the rear of the hall, an urchin dressed in the robes of a bishop entertained the revelers. He wore his Cistercian vestments wrong side out, his oversized miter cock-eyed, and carried a monkey on his shoulder. As he swung his censer wildly, an old shoe hanging from a stick—the stinking smoke of incense—he traded obscene gestures with another, older youth, the designated lord of misrule, who mocked him by making lewd gyrating motions with his hips. The crowd grew rowdier with each pantomimed insult until finally the lord of misrule emptied the contents of the Eucharist chalice on the "bishop's" head. The monkey chattered, and scurrying from the "bishop's" shoulder to his partner's, snatched the gaudy coronet from this "lord's" head and then thrust his bare little backside at both of them. The occupants in the hall roared with laughter.

Kathryn did not find the profaning of the Sacrament, or the raucous charade, amusing and wondered how the other nobles could. Were they too blind to see that beneath this traditional Yule amusement boiled disdain, even hatred? And not just for Church ritual but for them as well?

Beside her, the sheriff inclined his head and shouted above the laughter. "My lady is not offended, I hope. It is but harmless playing."

"No, Sir Guy." She must not draw attention to herself by protesting. "Not offended. Just overwhelmed. I had not expected such excess."

A trumpeter appeared in the center arch of three doors leading to the pantry and the kitchens. The "bishop" and the lord of misrule took their places with exaggerated pomp on the alternate dais. The latter made a loud farting noise, and the monkey held his nose and scolded. The crowd howled their appreciation. Then the herald blared his trumpet, and the procession of servants bearing food began, as it had each night, with the marshal of the hall carrying his white staff. The yeomen of the buttery, pantry, ewery, and cellar; the carver and the duke's cup bearer followed behind, each carrying his respective offering high above his head. But unlike the other feasts, this time the courses were paraded first before the lord of misrule and the boy bishop, who pounded the dais in feigned rage, screaming, " 'Tis not fit food for lords. Let the almoner take it to the almsgate."

The procession then paraded to the real dais, and the food was set before the duke. Kathryn wondered what Agnes would have said had she seen the two roast swans, redressed in their plumage, elegant in their nest of gilded reeds. Roast peacock (also in full dress), souse, and a mince pie, artfully contrived in the shape of a manger, completed the meal. The riot in the hall lessened to a murmur as other, more plebeian fare passed down the boards. The swans were reserved for the dais, the peacock for the knights' board, but there were pies and blood puddings and custards in abundance down to the farthest trestle, where the guildsmen and the merchants sat.

"Look, the duchess is leaving," Sir Guy said as they waited for their trencher to be placed on the silver plate they shared.

The woman rushing from the table was two, maybe three, years older than Kathryn, but the parting of her mantle showed her belly round and full beneath its silk covering. The veil on her horned headdress swayed dangerously as she rushed through the archway, holding her hand to her mouth. Two of her gentlewomen followed behind at a more leisurely pace.

"It must be hard for her to be with child at her age," Kathryn murmured more to herself than to her companion.

"It's but her duty. She's lost six already. Were I the duke, I would be looking elsewhere to get an heir."

Six dead babies. Kathryn felt a quick stinging behind her eyelids. "Miscarriages?" she asked.

"Two were stillborn. Two lived a few months, I think."

No wonder the duchess appeared so sad. Kathryn had spoken with her only once during the whole fortnight, and that had been an abbreviated, obligatory conversation between hostess and guest. Though Kathryn had spent many tedious hours doing needlework in the solar with the duchess's three attendants, most days the duchess pleaded fatigue and absented herself. Kathryn sometimes also feigned exhaustion, but how else was she to fill the long hours between feasts? Sir Guy had invited her to the hunt once, but Kathryn had no peregrine, and hawking was not a sport she enjoyed, identifying more with prey than with predator. She eyed the stuffed carcass the carver placed on the trencher in front of her—yesterday's prey?—and wondered how much courtly manners required her to eat. The trumpet blew again.

"My lords, the meat is on the board."

The great hall filled with noise again as the guests sounded their approval.

"Your appetite is small, Kathryn. I hope it is not because you weary of your companion."

"Weary of you, Sir Guy?" An effort to keep the sarcasm from her voice. Just one more night, she told herself. "Of course not. Indeed, your company is congenial, and I'm honored. But I'm a little surprised that you chose me to be by your side at such an important celebration. I'm sure there are others more worthy—"

"Come, Kathryn. Don't play the coy maiden. By now it must be plain to you that I seek an alliance between us."

Such bluntness. For a moment she almost lost her breath. Well, she could be blunt, too.

"Is that meant to be a proposal of marriage, my lord? If so, it is an untimely one. In this age of chivalry, is it not custom for the wooing to precede the proposal? Truly you have been an attentive companion, but I hear no declaration of love."

"But you hear a declaration of intent. Isn't that worth more to a well-seasoned woman than pretty vows of courtly love? But I can assure you, madam, there is much about you I admire. And I can offer you protection."

Well seasoned! She pierced the meat in front of her, then dropped her knife. It clattered against the silver plate. "So it is a practical arrangement that you propose. Tell me, sir, is it me you admire, or my land?"

He merely shrugged.

At least there was no deceit in him. "As for your offer of protection, I have my sons to protect me. Colin has come home."

"I know." His nose appeared even more beaklike when he smiled, and his eyes narrowed as though he were about to release an arrow. "I saw him preaching at the crossroads in Aylsham." He shouted to be heard above the noise.

The marshal of the hall waved his white cane at the trestles below the dais. "Speak softly, my masters."

The noise level subsided a little at this admonition. Kathryn answered softly as she picked up her knife to separate a sooty feather from the swan's breast. "Don't forget about Alfred. He is Roderick's heir, too."

"I haven't forgotten about Alfred." Sir Guy offered the shared wine cup. She shook her head.

"I hoped to see him among your retinue. All my attempts to correspond with him have been"—she could not say rebuffed—"futile."

"There was a small uprising in November. Rebels incited by the Lollards. The king called for men bearing arms. I sent what men I could spare."

Of course, she knew it would come to this. Alfred was, after all, in training to be a retainer of the king. She had tried to avoid that thought even at the jousting tournament the duke had sponsored for their entertainment—the tournament where Sir Guy had unhorsed his opponent and then kneeled half-mockingly before her to beg a token. She'd winced at the clanging sound of lance against hauberk and helmet and told herself she was glad that such sport was for men; told herself that Alfred was yet a boy.

"I suppose it is to be expected that a boy king would send boys to do his battle," she said.

"Please, Kathryn, make your tone less strident or you may be even beyond my protection. It wasn't Richard, of course, it was John of Gaunt put out the call to arms. An irony. It was he who fostered Wycliffe in his heresies in the first place. Seems Lancaster prodded a cub and baited a bear."

And what of my cubs? Kathryn thought. What's to become of them? One who dances with the bear and one who will be sent to kill the bear?

Sir Guy drained the cup and motioned behind him for his cup bearer. "Alfred is no longer a boy," he said.

The cup bearer served Sir Guy from behind his shoulder but on bended knees, with downcast eyes, as he had each night. Kathryn had paid scant attention to the arm that reached for Sir Guy's empty cup.

Until she noticed this one was different.

This one had fine red hairs that covered it, and squarish moons on his nails, like Roderick. Like his father. Alfred's arm. Alfred's hand. She turned around, greedy for a sight of the face that matched the arm.

"Alfred." She dared not touch his cheek for fear he would shame her by pulling away.

But his face was a mask of courtesy, none of the insolence she'd seen at their last meeting. "My lady mother," he said, acknowledging the greeting politely.

He bowed to Sir Guy and retreated to wait beside the cup board with his fellows, according to custom.

"He is much changed. More subdued. I trust you have not broken his spirit. His father would not have liked that."

Sir Guy laughed. "A squire's training involves more than battle skills. He serves me well. He will be a fine knight one day. Already he sleeps in the knights' hall."

"Thank you for that," Kathryn said sincerely. She knew this was a sign of favor. Most squires slept wherever they could find a corner to make a berth. In winter this was especially a hardship—she could not bear to think of him sleeping on the cold ground.

"I show him favor because I was a friend of his father." He took another drink from the silver cup they shared. "And because I desire marriage with his mother. But we will speak of that later."

Something else to avoid. The duchess had not returned. Kathryn should have used her hostess's indisposition as an excuse to escape. But then she would not have seen Alfred.

"In the meantime," the sheriff said, "would you like me to summon your son so that you may speak privately with him? After the banquet, of course?"

"Oh yes, please."

He speared a sliver of swan's breast with his knife and held it to her lips. "Now, we must not offend the duke, must we?"

She opened her mouth and slipped the bite from the blade of the knife with her teeth. He smiled his predator's smile.

TWENTY-SEVEN

. . . rivers and fountains that were clear and clean
they poisoned in many places.
—GUILLAUME DE MACHAUT
(14TH-CENTURY FRENCH COURT POET)

ight bells. Mayhap now she could excuse herself from the feast without being rude, Kathryn thought. The table linens had been drawn and the mead and ale and cider replenished until the noise level in the hall rendered polite discourse impossible. A few of the revelers, deep in their cups, lay in snoring heaps between the trestles. The duchess had not returned, and the remainder of her gentlewomen had retired—all but one who flirted outrageously with the knights around her, apparently delighted that her sisters had left the field to her.

"Will you have need of Alfred much longer?" Kathryn shouted in the ear of her mess mate. Sir Guy held his liquor well, but she didn't want him to forget his promise. This might be her only chance to speak with her son.

He sloshed the liquid in his half-filled cup, appraising further need for his cup bearer. "I'll send him to you later," he said.

"I'll be waiting." She removed a silver ribbon from her sleeve and laid it in front of his trencher. A shiver crawled up her spine. "To remind you," she said.

As Kathryn passed the duchess's quarters, she paused. Since she was leaving at first light, she should thank the duchess for her hospitality. But as she suspected, her ladyship was still indisposed. Kathryn made the obligatory inquiries, thanked the women and asked that they convey her thanks to her hostess. "Tell the duchess I will pray to Saint Margaret for her lying-in." This sentiment she sincerely felt. Kathryn doubted the woman could survive a difficult birth.

As she climbed the last of the steps, she saw that her door was ajar. Good. Sir Guy had not been too drunk to remember. She paused just outside the half-open door. Alfred's back was to her. Her pulse quickened; her palms began to sweat. He was talking to Glynis, and the flush on the girl's cheek and her high-pitched laughter revealed her delight in finding Master Alfred at last. The laugh died when she looked up to see Kathryn framed in the doorway. She bobbed her usual attenuated curtsy.

"Glynis, you may leave us."

"But, milady, I'm not done with the packing, and it's cold in the hall—"

"You can go to the kitchens and gossip with the others. You'll be welcome there to sit by the fire. When you come back, we'll do the packing together."

Blushing, Kathryn suspected, now more with anger than pleasure, the girl dropped a hurried half-curtsy and retreated, flinging a last flirtatious glance in Alfred's direction. Her son looked embarrassed.

"I can't blame her," she said when the girl had gone. "I would be reluctant to leave such a handsome young man were I still a maid." She held him out from her extended arms, like a length of fine silk. His hair and the faint stubble of a fledgling beard glowed rust-colored in the candlelight. She stroked his jaw lightly, a tentative touch, lest he draw back. "You've your father's beard." A slight inversion of his head? Her imagination? Or a signal that his mother's touch was unwelcome? "Sir Guy's livery becomes you."

He said nothing. How to fill the awkward silence? If she embraced him, would he draw back? She had never understood that last meeting, the hard flint of his eyes the day he'd asked her permission to go to Sir Guy. Had his eyes softened? Or were his courtly new manners merely a mask?

"Have you no kiss of greeting for the mother you've not seen in months?"

He reached for her hand, lifted it to his lips. She jerked it back. "I want to hold you in my arms," she said, pulling him to her. He didn't hug her back, but neither did he pull away, and when she released him she thought she saw a glittering wetness in his eyes.

She sat on the bench in front of the fire, parted the pillow beside her. His maroon-stockinged legs scissored beneath him gracefully, and he sat, not beside her but at her feet, facing away from her. His back rested against the bench.

"I've missed you, Alfred," she said to the back of his head as she picked at the gold embroidery on his shoulder. It was hard to keep her hands off him. She wanted to stroke his hair. At least *he* still had hair.

"You had Colin . . . and the illuminator to comfort you."

The illuminator. So that was the source of his anger. How long had he known?

"I had neither to comfort me," she said, still speaking to the back of his head. Then she told him about Colin leaving. About Rose and the baby. Suddenly, she had his full attention. He turned to face her.

"Colin! Sweet, innocent little brother deflowered a virgin!"

There was a bitterness in his laugh that Kathryn didn't like. She would never be able to tell him that Rose was a Jewess.

"It's too bad about Rose. She was very beautiful," he said wistfully. "It's funny, isn't it, Mother? You were so afraid that I would make trouble, when all along it was Colin you should have sent away, sweet, honey-voiced Colin, instead of me."

He hugged his knees up to his chin and said nothing for a long moment, apparently rolling this new knowledge around in his head. "So, I'm uncle, then. Uncle Alfred. Jasmine. A funny name. But I like it. The world is peopled with too many saints already."

He flashed a grin, reminding her of the merry, irascible Alfred who had always made her laugh even when he needed whipping for his misdeeds. Was that little boy somewhere in this austere young man with his courtly manners?

He frowned and the bitterness was back. "I don't understand why Colin ran away. I should have thought Saint Colin would have stayed to pay the piper. Rose was comely enough to be his wife, that's for sure. He could not likely do better."

"No. He would not likely have done better. Rose was as good as she was beautiful for all her youthful indiscretion." *Goodness in a Jew?* Kathryn shook off the voice in her head as she explained. "Colin didn't know about the babe when he left. He left because he felt guilty about the shepherd's death. He and Rose had used the wool house as their trysting place. He thought it was his fault, all of it, and he would go away and—I don't know—atone by shutting himself up in some dark monastery."

"What a damn-fool way to think! How like him. Glynis and I were—" He squirmed and turned away. "*If* I had been in the wool house, I wouldn't think that the fire was my fault. John was probably drunk, started it himself, or maybe it was Simpson, covering up his thieving."

He leaned forward and poked at the fire, then half-turned so she could see his profile. His shoulder touched her knee. He did not look at her. "You were right about him, Mother, that's what I was coming to tell you, the night I saw—the night I found your pearls."

"You found my pearls?" Kathryn's throat tightened. *It was Alfred. It was the young master of Blackingham who placed them there,* Rose had said. "Then why didn't you bring the necklace to me, Alfred?"

A log split apart with a crack, sending sparks up the chimney.

"Alfred, what did you do with the pearls?"

A hesitation, and then he said, "I'm surprised you haven't already found them. You've only to look in the illuminator's quarters." His full mouth contorted his face. He had his father's full mouth. His father's sarcasm.

"Why would my pearls be among the illuminator's possessions?" she asked evenly.

"I went to your room after the shepherd's burial." He turned away, stared into the fire intently as though he were divining pictures in the dancing flames. "I saw you with him. I planted the pearls in his room. It was a foolish, childish thing to do, of course, the girl was in her room. She could have told you I did it. It was stupid."

"Then why did you do it?" she said to the back of his head.

"I guess I was hoping you'd think he stole them. Maybe even be angry enough to send him away, instead of me."

So he had planted the pearls, just as Rose had said, just as she had feared. But not because he'd killed the priest. She wanted to laugh and cry all at the same time. So much pain for all of them. And all for a child's prank. But it could be fixed, Holy Mother of God. It could all be fixed! It was not too late.

But first, she had to fix this.

She wanted to shake him in her frustration. She wanted to hug him to remove the pain she'd caused him. Her voice trembled slightly when she said, "Alfred, what were you thinking to commit such folly?"

"I'll tell you what I was thinking, Mother. I was thinking that you betrayed my father."

He worried the crimson cloth of his tunic, winding it with his fingers, still not looking at her. She disentangled his hand, clasped it between her own.

"Your father is dead, Alfred. Did you think harming an innocent man would ease your hurt?"

His lips were pressed into a hard line that quivered slightly. He didn't look like a man now. He looked like her little boy trying to put on the face of a man, a boy mimicking a father's rough ways.

"Did you think I was betraying Roderick?" Her voice was low, her tones somber but gentle. She stroked the back of his head. "Or did you think I was betraying you?"

She might as well have shouted at him. He jerked his head away as though her touch burned, and turned to face her, waving his hand in the air like an actor in a mad mystery play.

"You despised my father! Don't deny it."

She kept her voice low, her movements slow, so as not to startle him.

"I don't deny that there was no love between us, had never been. But how could I say I despised the man who gave me the two things I treasure most? You and your brother."

"You hated him. And you said I was his image."

"But I never—"

"You said it many, many times." His voice had grown deeper as he'd grown taller. He even sounded like his father. "I reminded you of Father too much. Is that why you sent me away? So you could be alone with your paramour?" His voice cracked and the last word came out shrill and brittle.

How to answer him best? Which charge did she take on first? But he didn't wait for her to decide.

"Nothing to say, Mother?"

"Alfred, Alfred, you must know how much I—"

"Now they say you're here as the sheriff's lacy. I've watched you on the dais, flirting, smiling up at him, night after night. It makes me sick. My lady mother twice a whore."

The slap echoed in the air. The imprint of her hand glowed white against his cheek. Tears pooled in his eyes, she could feel them welling in her own. Her palm still stinging from the slap, she reached up to touch his face, longing to kiss the hurt away, but he flinched and she withdrew her hand.

"The sheriff hasn't told you, then?"

His rage had chased away all courtly courtesy; resentment contorted his features. He mumbled, "The sheriff tells me nothing except how to walk, how to stand, how to ride, how to fight, how to talk—and how to polish his armor."

"The illuminator is in Castle Prison for the priest's murder. I refused to give my *paramour*, as you called him, an alibi in order to protect you. I loved you enough to sacrifice my own happiness for you. And the happiness of a good man. If you can't feel that love, Alfred, I know not how else to prove it."

The tears that had pooled in his eyes now poured down his cheeks. She touched his face, the fading imprint of her hand.

"I'm sorry if I've hurt you," she said, sighing deeply. "The devil makes pawns of us all."

⊸✺⊶

"Was your reunion with your son satisfactory?" the sheriff asked from the hall outside her chamber. Kathryn was in her shift and had hastily thrown her cloak around her to answer his knock.

"Quite, my lord," she said through a crack in the door. His breath was sour, but his speech was not slurred and he'd been sober enough to climb the stairs. "Thank you for arranging it."

His shadow lengthened and flickered against the wall in the guttering rushlight. "I would train my own son no differently," he said. "Which brings me to another subject."

Kathryn pulled her cloak tighter. "By your leave, my lord, may we speak of it another time? The hour is late to be visiting a lady in her boudoir. As you can see, I was preparing for bed and tomorrow's journey home—"

But he leaned his weight against the heavy oak door and pushed past her. "God's Blood, Kathryn, it's a long climb up these tower steps, and I didn't undertake it for my health."

He was still wearing the costume to which his new honor entitled him. It was a woolen mantle lined with scarlet. Blue garter symbols, each one embroidered with the motto *Honi soit qui mal y pense*—"Shame on him who thinks ill of it"—stitched in gold thread, decorated a lighter background. Over this he wore a surcoat of crimson wool.

"We will speak of it now," he said. "Tomorrow, we leave at dawn and there will be no time. I have to go on ahead. My men will accompany you, of course."

She turned her back on him and bent to stoke the paltry fire with the last piece of wood. She'd hoped to save it for the morning to warm her departure preparations.

When she turned around, he was sitting on the bed, leaning back against his arms for support, one blue-stockinged leg crossed over the other, watching her.

"Do not look at me with that calculating eye, sir. I am not a mare that you are appraising in the horse market."

She hugged herself, rubbing her arms for warmth. He shifted his weight, crossed his legs at the ankles. The toes of his leather slippers pointed at her like poised darts.

"Say what you have to say, please," she said. "I am bone-weary."

He nodded. "As you know, Kathryn, I have no heirs, and—"

"I thought you had a son in France." She knew he'd lost his firstborn to the plague, and that his second wife, Mathilde, had died in childbirth three years ago. The child had been stillborn.

"Gilbert died in the same battle as your husband."

"I'm sorry. I did not know. You never spoke—"

"Are you still fertile?" He drummed his ringed signet finger against the counterpane.

"I beg your pardon." She felt her skin flush. 'Did you say—"

"A simple question. Is your womb still viable?"

"If you mean—well, yes, but that circumstance is more burden to me than boon. My sons are sufficient, and I have a ward."

"You have a ward!" His eyebrow arched.

"I'm godmother to—to the granddaughter of Finn the illuminator. His daughter was defiled and found herself with child. She died giving birth to it."

"Was the miscreant who took her hymen brought to justice?"

Her face felt like a burning brand. "The perpetrator was a wandering minstrel." She turned her gaze to the fire. "We never knew his name."

"And you care for the child out of fondness for the illuminator." The steel of his sidearm glinted cold, like his eyes.

"I care for the child out of Christian charity until such a time as her mother's father will be set free and can come for her."

He grunted and grinned the lopsided, crooked smile that she detested. "You will likely see the child's troth plighted and stand godmother to her children ere that happens."

The room was warmer now. She would like to have removed her cloak, but as she wore only her shift beneath it, she merely moved away from the fire and sat in the chamber's lone chair.

"How so, my lord sheriff? When the illuminator is innocent?"

He appeared to be examining his cuticles. "You were not so sure on the occasion of his arrest."

"Alfred has told me the truth. He planted the pearls in Finn's—in the illuminator's—chamber because he was angry over some perceived slight. It was a childish thing to do. He had no knowledge of the consequences. When I told him, he repented that childish action. He will testify before the bishop that it was all a mistake."

"Ah. But how came Alfred to be in possession of the pearls? That's the question, isn't it? Is he prepared to explain that to the bishop as well?"

"I like not that insinuation, sir. He found the necklace among the overseer's belongings. My steward was a thief. If he stole from the living, he would suffer fewer pangs to steal from the dead. He has since been turned off Blackingham land. I'm sure when the bishop hears the truth, he will release the illuminator."

"I wouldn't set my heart on it, Kathryn. The bishop likes having an artisan of the man's particular talent under his thumb. He will be loath to let him go without explicit proof of innocence—or strong influence. And then there's the matter of the heretical papers found in his possession. Anyway, if the illuminator is exonerated, the matter of the priest's murder goes unresolved. The archbishop pressures the bishop, and the bishop pressures me, and we have to begin the search all over again. You see how complicated it all is?" He heaved an exaggerated sigh. "Of course, if as my wife you found the circumstances revolving around the illuminator distressing, I would feel obliged to speak to the king's regent. The king has already given permission for an alliance between our houses. As wife of a knight of the Garter, your testimony would carry considerable weight."

Kathryn reminded herself to breathe slowly. "You overstep your bounds, sir, to speak to the king without my permission. And even if I agreed to such a scheme, would you not still have the problem of solving the priest's murder?"

"Kathryn, Kathryn." He shook his head and made sucking sounds with his tongue. "You surely know that as a widow, the king can place you under his protection and seize your lands at any time; then your sons would be disinherited. An alliance with me will prevent that. Your sons retain their heritage; you gain a greater status and can use that influence on behalf of your *friend*. As for the murder? Easy enough. Blame it on some Jew." His mouth curved at her quick intake of breath. "Yes, I quite like that. The archbishop will like it, too. It is quite a politic solution."

"You would blame an innocent man!?"

"Why such surprise and indignation?" He examined his fingernails, his ringed fingers, slender and effeminate. "If the particularity of it bothers your sensibilities, I can uncover a general plot." He brushed a sooty flake from his new mantle. "One emanating from the Jews in Spain, exact perpetrator unknown."

"No less scurrilous, sir, to charge a whole people wrongfully."

"Wrongfully? Jews? Not possible, I should think. Surely, Kathryn, you are not a Jew lover! That would be a dangerous affinity indeed." He scowled a warning against further protests. "What does it matter if they're blamed for one more crime? They are known to spread plague; they poison our wells; they steal the king's wealth; they even sacrifice our youth at Eastertide in mock Crucifixion."

He was referring to the nefarious charge of blood libel, never proved, often cited. And now there would be added to their burden of allegations the brutal murder of priests.

"The addition of the priest's murder would be a mere fly riding on a cart of dung. Think about it, Kathryn." He smoothed a gold thread on his surcoat. "What choice do you have?"

What choice, indeed? She had known it would come to this, but had not thought that he would mount such a frontal assault or that he would catch her when her defenses were so down. She was too tired to think. Her meeting with Alfred had offered such hope, and now that was dashed, too.

He stood up, and reaching for her hand, brought it to his mouth. His lips scarcely touched her, but her skin crawled.

She stood up too, and drew herself up to her full height. She was almost at eye level with him. "And you, sir, what do you gain from such an alliance?" she asked.

"You named it already. I admire your lands. There is only one fiefdom between your holding and mine."

She was surprised. She had not known his lands were as vast as that, though Roderick had spoken more than once and warily of the sheriff's ambition.

"What assurances do I have that you will intercede for Finn after such a marriage?"

"My word as a knight of the Garter. I hope that you do not question my honor. Think about it, Kathryn. I will be in Suffolk mopping up this little rebellion. When I return, I will call upon you and we will draw up the terms of our betrothal. I repeat, *what choice do you have?*"

"Has it not occurred to you that I could go to a nunnery? The abbess at Saint Faith Priory will gladly receive both me and my lands into their keeping."

His eyes narrowed. "Yes, you could do that. But think about the consequences to your sons. To your ward. And if you do that, I warrant on my honor as a knight of the Garter that your lover will never place his feet on terra firma again."

He opened the door, and the cold air from the hall rushed in. Sleet had started to fall, pinging against the narrow window at the end of the hall.

"Choose well, Kathryn." He bowed mockingly and backed away.

She shivered in the hall, listening to the sound of his descending footfalls. Where was Glynis? Probably warming herself in the arms of some soldier. Her serving girl, a serf, had more freedom than she did. She turned back to finish her packing, foraging in her mind for some tactic to answer this new threat. The sheriff had left his impression in the feather ticking. Angrily she beat at it until it was obliterated.

TWENTY-EIGHT

*By contrition we are made clean, by compassion we are
made ready. And by true longing we are made worthy.
By these three medicines it behooveth that every soul
should be healed.*

—JULIAN OF NORWICH, *HEIRLOOMS*

inn played his queen of hearts. The bishop trumped it with the king
Finn knew he held.

"You have lost your queen of hearts. A tragedy to lose such a lovely
queen."

"It was inevitable, Eminence."

The challenge of the game was to let Despenser win and yet play well
enough to keep him interested. Finn was hungry for company, even dangerous company, and each time the bishop came he brought some small amenity.
The brazier fire was now well stocked, and there would be sweetmeats to enjoy until the next visit—if he rationed them carefully. Best, of course, was
the ready supply of paints and papyrus and quills and ink.

"You have a weighty burden of correspondence, Illuminator," the bishop
had complained as his attendant piled the bundles of supplies beside the
worktable.

"I'm writing my philosophy to pass the time."

"I thought that you were painting my altarpiece to pass the time," the bishop said.

"On these winter days the light is too poor to paint, Eminence. And confinement is a stingy muse."

The bishop's eyes narrowed to slits as he said, "I should like to read this philosophy of yours."

"You would not enjoy my philosophy. I write in English."

"It's well enough for the common sort. Good enough for lists and ciphers, mayhap even good enough for your philosophy." The bishop pointed to the captured queen. "I saw her at the duke's Christmas revels."

"You saw the queen of hearts?" Finn asked casually. The bishop often bragged about his amorous conquests.

"*Your* queen of hearts." He stroked the card as though it were a woman's breast.

"My queen?"

"The lady of Blackingham. I don't wonder you took her for your model. A bit overripe for my taste, but quite striking." He shuffled the cards, peered at Finn from beneath lowered eyelids. "She was companion to Sir Guy de Fontaigne. He's the sheriff, you may remember." His eyelids fluttered like a girl's, setting Finn's teeth on edge. "But of course you remember."

Finn said nothing. He got up from his seat to stoke the fire, turning his face away to hide his distaste and the unease this information stirred in him. What did he care whom she supped with—whom she bedded, for that matter? Whatever he'd felt for her was long dead, killed by her betrayal.

He told himself that each time he woke from dreams of her.

"They made a striking couple."

"Did they?" Feigning unconcern, Finn poured himself a glass of the bishop's wine.

Despenser held up his goblet to be refilled. "She wore crimson velvet. It clung to her bosom and was girdled about the waist with a silver cord draped in a V-shape"—he demonstrated with his free hand—"to show off the curve of her hips."

A drop of wine splashed onto the floor, just missing the pointed end of Despenser's velvet shoe. "You are trembly today, Master Finn. Not a touch of the palsy, I hope."

Finn returned to his seat, picked up his cards, fingered them restlessly, laid them down. The queen of hearts stared up at him. "I feel a touch of the ague, Eminence. I fear I am a less worthy opponent than usual. Perhaps another day."

His face grew hot beneath Despenser's knowing look.

"You will forfeit, then?"

Finn sighed, obsequiousness dripping in his voice. "You would have beaten me anyway, Eminence. I fear you are the better player."

"Don't patronize me, Illuminator. My goodwill is not boundless. I'm not altogether pleased with your progress on the reredos. You should have completed more than three panels by now."

He rose, motioned for his attendants, who draped his ermine robe about him. His furred mantle made angry swishing noises against the stone flags as he paused at the door for a parting shot. "I suggest that before we meet next you devote yourself more to the work of your Church and less to your *philosophy*."

※※

"Tell Lady Kathryn I need to see her," Finn said to Half-Tom two days later. "And tell her I want to see the child as well."

What would happen to Rose's daughter? That had been only one of several thoughts that had disturbed Finn's sleep for the last two nights. He'd always known the sheriff had designs on Blackingham and its lady. He'd figured that out long ago, though he'd thought Kathryn honorable and strong enough to resist the advances of a man she professed to despise. Unless, of course, her disdain for the sheriff was as inconstant as the love she had declared to him. What of her promise to care for the child? Was that as mutable as her affections? That he could not chance. He would have to see Kathryn one more time. Even though the thought of facing her, the exquisite pain of it, made him weak in the knees.

Half-Tom said, "If I take her ladyship such a message, she'll light out straight away, and the snow is drifting high."

"Kathryn's tall. The snow will scarce be past her ankle."

"Comes up to my waist. Would be a hard journey for a gentlewoman and a child."

"Then tell her to come as soon as the weather clears," he said.

The weather did not clear. The snow drifted so high that Half-Tom could not even leave the city walls lest he be buried up to his eyeballs. At night, he camped out around the prison yard, earning his bread by running errands for the guards—all but Sykes, whom he avoided as he would plague. In the day, he struggled the two furlongs down King's Road to visit the holy woman of Saint Julian, gathering fuel along the way for her tiny brazier. He noticed the chilblains on her hands, and when he asked why her fire was so puny, what happened to the coals he'd brought her the day before, she just smiled and said others had greater needs. Easy pickings were all gone. Sometimes he had to struggle in the snow drifts outside the city walls just to gather her fuel. He was feeding the fires of the city's poor when all he'd really wanted to do was to keep one holy woman from freezing.

At night he shared the beggars' fires. It was there he learned that the city was threatened by more than winter. There was a stirring among the peasant classes. A restless, angry spirit waited for the rising of the sap, hovered around the poor men's smoky fires.

" 'Twixt the king's poll tax and the bishop's tithe, don't do no gain for an honest man to work."

" 'Tis naught to me. I've nothing to tithe. And the excise man took my last pig for Lancaster's war with the Frenchies."

"Then the bishop'll take the shirt off'n yer back."

"Aye, and the wee king's uncle will have yer pants."

Mirthless laughter all around. The dirty men with their rag-wrapped feet, filthy tunics and scraggly beards huddled under a haphazard tent they'd constructed to shield them from the elements. The twin tent poles wobbled from the weight of the snow and the patched awning sagged. Half-Tom stamped his feet and blew on his hands, edging between the last speaker's legs to get closer to the fire. He thought of Blackingham and the little kitchen maid. He hoped she was warm. He had more than the illuminator's message to spur him to trek the twelve miles to Aylsham. But the snow was still falling in big feathery flakes, covering Castle Prison, decorating the eaves of the great cathedral and painting the beards and slumped shoulders of his companion white in the firelight.

"Nobility don't care if ye starve. Last Boxing Day 'twas sure meager pickings."

"Aye. All them great lords and fancy ladies in their palaces pleadin' poor." The speaker ate a handful of snow, then coughed a wet, phlegmatic wad and spat it into the fire. "All the while they're gorging on fine vittles and sendin' picked-over bones and moldy bread to the alms gate. They don't know what poor is."

"Maybe 'tis time they learned."

"Aye, burn one of them fine homes to the ground, that'd be a start."

Half-Tom held his hands out to the flame. From behind, he heard the growling of a hungry stomach.

The fire spewed a shower of sparks against a black sky. Half-Tom rolled himself in his blanket and lay down close to the beggars' fire. Footprints, frozen ridges in the mud, dug into his back. He envied the old man who snored beside him, escaping the misery. At last, Half-Tom closed his eyes and slept too.

And he dreamed of going home.

He is in his hut at the edge of the fens. There, his clay hearth is warm, and his kettle bubbles with a rich eel broth. There, his nest of piled beaver skins makes a bed soft enough for young King Richard. There, he wakes to birdsong in a pearl dawn as fresh as a new-cracked egg. It is a welcome and familiar dream.

But on this mid-winter night, in this particular dream of homecoming, there is a difference. In this dream he is not alone in his velvet marsh. Magda is beside him. It is summer. He shows her how to strip the willow bark and weave the baskets, how to set the traps, how to dip the oar into the water soundlessly as they glide among the rushes.

In this dream he is tall.

When Half-Tom woke from his dream of home, the beggars' fire had puddled to charred ash in a creeping, dirty dawn. And he was once again alone, except for the snow-covered corpse of the old man who no longer dreamed beside him.

❧

Kathryn prayed that the snow would linger, that the harsh winter would keep the sheriff away. His proposal of marriage hung over her head like the ice daggers suspended from Blackingham's eaves. She knew Guy de Fontaigne was not a patient man. But maybe she could put him off a year. *Yes, Kathryn. And maybe the time is out of joint and the snow will never melt and the trees will never bud and the spring will never come.*

And indeed, some days it did seem as though the bleak winter—at any other time a circumstance to be complained against—could hold him at bay forever. But on a raw day in March when the roads were scarcely passable, Guy de Fontaigne sent a message saying he would call on her at Eastertide. The next day, Half-Tom came with the message from Finn.

✄

The day had finally come that Kathryn had longed for and dreaded for a year. It was early morning and Kathryn, her son, and granddaughter were in the warm, cavernous kitchen. Prying a poppyseed cake from Jasmine's fist, Kathryn answered her wail of protest. "We're going bye-bye, you want to go bye-bye, don't you?"

The child's eyes brightened, and she chattered "Bye-bye." Cake crumbs spilled out along with the words. Kathryn hastily wiped Jasmine's bulging cheeks.

"You look so pretty, my little sweeting. Doesn't she, Colin?" Kathryn asked her son.

Colin only nodded, patting the child absently on the head as Kathryn dressed his daughter for the journey into Norwich. He was pulling on his own homespun garment, making ready for his daily trek down the highway. A cloak worthier of a rag picker than a young nobleman—where did he get such a piece of trash? At least nobody would recognize him. If he was going to shave his head and stand on the street corners preaching, thank the Holy Virgin he had the good sense not to dress in Blackingham blue.

Jasmine squirmed as Kathryn tried to stuff her into the little rabbit cloak and mittens.

"Do be still, darling, you're mussing your pretty curls. We're going to see your *grandpère* today. You will sing for him, won't you? Like you do for Magda and me?"

Kathryn tried to distract the wriggling child, singing "La, la, la, la" up the scale. Jasmine blinked her blue eyes, stopped squirming, and jabbered to the melody.

"My little songbird," Kathryn said, kissing away an errant poppy seed that rested like a beauty mark on the child's cheek. "Your father was a songbird too," she said pointedly.

Colin didn't hear her; he'd already left. But Kathryn was not going to let her obsessed son ruin this day. Finn had asked to see her. "Tell me his exact words," she said to the messenger. "Tell Lady Kathryn I need to see her," the dwarf had repeated. *Need.*

It might be the last time she would ever see him. She would store up the memory of his eyes, the curve of his jaw, the way he wrinkled his brow, his beautiful hands: store all the memory of him so that when she thought she could not bear it all, she could take it out and remember.

It was a good sign that he'd asked to see the child. A sign that his heart had not turned to stone after all.

Should she tell him of her plans?

"We're ready," Kathryn said to the dwarf, who opened the door.

᛫᛫᛫

Finn sat on a blanket on the floor with his granddaughter. Kathryn sat in a chair positioned between the child and the hearth. Each avoided looking directly at the other.

"She's beautiful."

"How could she be anything else? Born of your daughter and my son?" He stroked the child's red-blond curls.

"You have taken good care of her. She looks happy."

"I promised you that I would."

"Yes."

There was no sound in the room except a gentle thudding. The little girl amused herself by pounding on the floor with one of the empty oyster shells Finn used as paint pots. He felt a sudden stab of pain, remembering another blond child with bright blue eyes. The child he'd carried to the anchoress, the child who had not lived. A sudden burst of fear, just when he'd thought himself numb to such. It had been a mistake to send for her. To lay himself open again.

"Is she walking yet?"

"A few tentative steps. I fear I hover too much." Kathryn's laugh was low and musical, as he remembered. "I'm afraid to let her fall."

"She is not too much of a burden, then?"

"She is no burden." Her gaze appeared to be directed at the window, at the hard sunlight striping the shutters. "She gives me reason to live."

Neither said anything for a minute. Such awkwardness between them. A shyness as though they were strangers. He wanted to say he heard from the bishop that she had other interests to fill her lonely hours. He bit back the words.

"She wears her mother's cross," he said. It was on a small but sturdy silver chain around her neck. He quickly turned his gaze away. The sight of it pierced deep.

"It is a family heirloom. It should be passed from mother to daughter. Rose would have wanted Jasmine to have the necklace that her mother wore."

"Rebekka never wore it," Finn said, grimacing with the pain of the memory. "She was a *converso*. She hated it. It was a symbol of oppression for her."

"Converso?"

"A forced conversion to Christianity." It was like a fresh wound to the heart, even after all these years. He watched the child playing on the floor as he explained. "There was a purging in the Jewish quarter. Her father's stationer's shop was burned to the ground. Her parents perished in the flames. Rebekka recited the confession of faith to save her life."

"Did they . . . did they torture her?"

"No. But I think she would have resisted except for me. I begged her." He reached out and stroked the child's hair. Rebekka's grandchild—blond and fair, no hint that she had any Jewish blood running in her veins. "They would have killed her. Or at the least taken her away from me. We were already lovers by then. She did it for me."

"Where did you meet her?"

"In Flanders. I'd gone there to return my grandmother's body for burial in her homeland. Even then, I was a fair scribe, and I liked to paint. It was a gift passed down through my grandmother and my mother. Rebekka's father was a seller of fine parchments. I was going to make a book in my grandmother's memory. My parents had already died. I was the only heir. I had grand visions of a book collection copied from borrowed books. I still remember the name above the door. 'Foa's Fine Papers'—Foa was her family name. Rebekka was minding her father's shop that day."

"I'm sure she was very beautiful," Kathryn said, "like her daughter. You went to find supplies and found the love of your life." The softness of her voice made Jasmine drop her oyster shells on the floor and turn to look at her as though her name had been called.

One of the loves of my life, he thought. But he could not say it. Not now. Not with all that had passed between them.

"I've never seen another cross quite like Rose's," Kathryn said. "Instead of a crucifix, it has a circle of pearls. If you look at it just right, the circle looks almost like the points of a star. Except there are six."

He smiled. His face felt tight with the effort from muscles grown taut with misuse. "You've a good eye, Kathryn. It is a star. Magen David. I thought it too cleverly contrived to be discernible."

"Magen David?"

"It means 'shield of David.' A six-pointed star. A hexagram. Some among the Jews thought it warded off demons, a sort of charm. Some alchemists used it. The House of Foa adopted it as a family symbol."

"But why did you——?"

"*Conversos* were constantly watched for signs that their conversions were false. I thought if she wore the cross . . . I thought the symbol of her family, her heritage would make it not such a hateful thing to her."

"But you gave it to your daughter, even though Rebekka hated it?"

"It was to protect her. As it was meant to protect her mother. Though Rebekka never wore it."

"Did Rose know about the star?"

"No. I would have told her if she asked. She never did. She never knew her mother was a Jew." He felt shame at this, as though he'd failed his daughter, and worse, been disloyal to Rebekka. And now there was no chance to tell her. "I just wanted to protect her," he said.

Kathryn scooped up the child and walked across the room to his worktable, on which lay a large painted wooden panel. He scrambled to his feet and followed.

"I see how you fill your hours," she said, still not looking at him. "The painting is beautiful. The bishop must be pleased."

"The bishop thinks me slow. There are to be five such panels: the scourging of Christ, Christ carrying the cross, Crucifixion, Resurrection, and Ascension."

"And you are only on the third one?"

"I seem to be fixated on the Madonna standing at the foot of the cross."

She touched the face of the Madonna with a fingertip. "She is beautiful. She favors Rose and yet not Rose. Is she Rebekka?"

"I have been fortunate in my models." *I saw your queen of hearts.*

Kathryn shifted the fidgeting child in her arms, to prevent her reaching for a nearby inkpot. Finn broke off the sharp end of a quill and tickled Jasmine with its feathered end. She giggled and grabbed for the feather. He let her have it and ducked as she tried to comb his hair.

"More quills than sable brushes? Why? When you have no manuscript to—" A sudden intake of breath. "You're still translating the Wycliffe papers! Right under the bishop's nose."

He shrugged. "What have I left to lose?"

"You have this child."

Kathryn returned Jasmine to the blanket and sat down beside her. Finn sat with them. He was so close to Kathryn he could see the tiny laugh lines around her eyes, smell her hair. It made him dizzy with desire. He stood up and went to the window, opened the shutter. The chilly breeze cooled his hot skin. The sun was bright. It laid its light pattern across his worktable, highlighting the scene of the Crucifixion, the blue of the Madonna's cloak. He looked back at Kathryn from this safer distance. When he spoke, his voice was tight.

"I sent for you, Kathryn, because I want to talk to you about my granddaughter."

She did not say it was late enough coming, but her expression said it for her. He could always read her thoughts.

"I hear from the bishop that you are . . . that you attended the duke's revels with Guy de Fontaigne."

She said nothing, just rubbed her arms as if she felt a sudden chill, though the room was well heated with extra coals for the child's sake.

"I am naturally concerned that if there should be . . . an alliance between you . . . I'm concerned about what would happen to Rose's child."

"I see rumors are fleet of foot." She tossed her head in a gesture he recognized as a flash of anger. "Is that all that concerns you, Finn? Well, you need not worry on that cause. He knows about Jasmine. I intend to make it a term of my—of any—contract with him that she shall remain as my ward."

So it was true, then. He realized how much he had hoped otherwise. Some demon had sucked all the air out of the room. He looked anxiously at the child. She was busy trying to paint the oyster shell with her feather, dipping it into a patch of light as though it were a paint pot. A gift passed from father to daughter to granddaughter. The light around him swam with color, vibrant, swirling, all the bright hues of his life swirling into a single cord—and that cord girdled his neck, cutting off his wind. He suddenly hated the colors. There should be no color left in such a drab universe. Only shades of safe, muted gray.

"You would trust him in such an important matter?" Hardly enough breath left to say it.

"Why not, if I trust him enough to marry with him!"

She was clearly angry with him for some reason that he could not understand. But he fastened to her anger, and it gave him breath.

"And why would you marry with a man like that, Kathryn, a man whom you professed to despise?"

For the first time since she entered the room, she looked at him levelly. Her words were slow and deliberate.

"I am marrying him, Finn, to gain your freedom."

The colors in the light, in the air would surely smother him. The reds, the blues, all mixing into dark purple, then to black. He fought to hold the light. *Inhale deeply, inhale the light*. It took an eternity to find his voice. When it came, he was surprised to hear it boom across the room, splitting the colors with a groan. Jasmine looked from one to the other of them, her eyes widening.

"Don't be a fool, Kathryn."

Jasmine's mouth turned down, and her chin started to quiver. He was frightening her, but he couldn't stop himself. He slapped his hand hard against the wall.

"It's a trick. Don't you see? He's not going to let me go. The bishop likes having his own personal artist slave. And they still have not found who killed the priest. It's a crime that must be answered for, and I'm the answer. They will look no further. That's the way scapegoating works. Don't you understand?"

"What I don't understand is why you seem reluctant to leave. Is it that you want to stay holed up here forever, buried alive like an anchorite, with your holy paintings? Where you can nurse your grudge against me and spend what's left of your life grieving over Rose? Finn the martyr. Is that it?

Has this cell become more sanctuary than prison? Well, I'll not let you be buried alive, even if you are willing. Alfred will testify to planting the pearls in your room. Then they have no case against you. And Sir Guy has concocted a scheme whereby the archbishop's justice will be satisfied."

"No. No! I will not consent to it." He crossed the room and seized her by the shoulders. He shook her harder than he wanted to. "Don't you realize he is not to be trusted?"

Kathryn's eyes glistened. "I have no choice, Finn. He will see that you or Alfred or both answer for the crime and that my lands are forfeit to the crown. I have no choice. It's either go into a convent or marry Guy de Fontaigne." She started to pace. "Don't you see? I either sacrifice you and disinherit my sons, or sacrifice myself."

Kathryn in the arms of the hawk-nosed sheriff. Finn shook his head violently as if shaking off the image. The image held on stubbornly, writing itself on his eyelids, searing into his brain. He wished that Guy de Fontaigne were here now. Finn would rip off his head with his bare hands.

Instead, he grabbed Kathryn by her shoulders. "Then, my lady, remember this on your wedding night." And he kissed her hard, harder than he meant to, a kiss that held all the passion and regret and anger that lived in his nightly dreams.

When he pushed her away abruptly, she swayed for a moment, limp as a child's cloth poppet, as though she might crumple at his feet.

Jasmine started to wail and tried to climb Kathryn's skirts. Finn picked her up, but she held out her arms to Kathryn. The hexagram in the star around her neck peeped out at him from its tangle of filigree.

"Remember this, too. If I am released, I will come for my granddaughter and take her away. I'll not have her in his clutches."

TWENTY-NINE

athryn heard the door to her chamber open and cringed in pain as a shaft of light pierced the semidarkness.

"Mother, is it one of your headaches?" Colin asked.

His shorn head moved like an elliptical moon toward her bed, then hovered just above her. His hand felt cool on her cheek.

"You're burning with fever! I'll go get Agnes. She'll know what to do for you."

"No." The bed beneath her rolled as he sat beside her. She fought back a wave of nausea. "Tell them not to come up here. And tell them to keep Jasmine away. Don't even bring her to the threshold."

"Then what should I get for you?"

She covered her mouth with her hand, lest her breath cast some foul spell on him.

"Nothing. It will pass. You've come too close already. Just go away and let me sleep."

"I'm not going to leave you sick and alone! God will protect me."

If he didn't protect His own Son, why would He protect mine? "Then call Glynis," she said.

"You're not Glynis's mother." He raised her arm and probed tenderly at her armpit. She knew he was looking for the telltale bubo.

"There's been a report of plague at Pudding Norton in Fakenham," he said. Worry abraded the melody in his voice.

She coughed, a wet, strangling cough, and he raised her shoulders and held her until the seizure passed. When she could talk again, she reassured him. "I've already looked, Colin. There's no swelling in my groin, either."

"But your skin is so hot."

"It's just an ague. Tell Agnes to make me a syrup of angelica root and leave it outside the door." Another seizure of coughing. "Then you go away and stay away."

He slipped soundlessly out, and she turned her head to the wall and went to sleep.

⸙

When she opened her eyes, it was morning and the bright light slicing through the window cut across her eyes like the sting of a lash. Someone—an angel?—separated itself from the light and bathed her face with cool water.

"Drink this."

The cup's lip was cold against her mouth. She shivered. Two sips were all she could swallow. The smell of sickness was in the room. Hadn't she sent Colin away? Yet it was Colin's voice, Colin's face, but framed with a stubble of blond hair. Not Colin, who shaved his head each morn before he went out. Colin was on the highway preaching Lollard heresies. She closed her eyes against the throbbing light, but the darkness threatened to smother her.

"Keep the babe away," she said to the angel who tended her so lovingly.

But instead of her voice, a piercing gibberish rode the air. Its shrillness ebbed and flowed like ocean waves. Demons arguing for her soul. Coming to claim her for her sins. She wanted to cry out to God, to plead for mercy, but there was no priest to plead for her soul. No priest. But the anchoress came. Smiling, gentle, telling her that all would be well. If only she could believe.

I will try. I will try to believe. Her mind clawed at memory, prowling for the words to the *migratio ad Dominum.* But she could not remember the words her tutor priest had taught her as a child. *Receive my soul, Lord Jesus Christ,* her mind cried out. But she pleaded in her father's Norman French, and God answered only Latin prayers. He would judge her prayer profane, the words unworthy. Like Cain's offering.

The voices stopped, and she slept.

Once she thought it was Finn who tended her so gently. He had forgiven her, then. But it was too late. Her body was as dry as a husk of threshed wheat, and the tongue she would have used to thank him cleaved to the roof of her mouth. She was a moth and her wings would soon be dust. Dust everywhere, sealing her eyes, filling her ears, muffling all sound. So this was dying. This pressing heaviness that drove one's soul deep inside. Once she thought she heard Jasmine crying, and wanted her. But Jasmine could not come. She would never come again.

❦

The anchoress lay awake in her cell, listening to the cathedral bells toll matins. The midnight silence swallowed the muffled peals, and quiet settled again, eerie and thick. As she recited the Hours of the Cross, *Domine labia mea aperie,* she thought, Lord, You will have to open my lips. I cannot. They're too stiff and cold. Then she repented the unworthy thought and muttered the response, *Et os meum annuntiabit laudem tuam.*

As she often did, she departed slightly from the scripted response of the Matins Hours, the *Deus in adiutorium meum intende,* asking not for help for herself but for the souls who crowded into her mind: the poor, the sick, the hungry, the many supplicants who, even in winter, found their way to her window. From outside, she could hear water drops plopping from the long icicles that hung from the church eaves, dripping onto the winter-hardened ground like Christ's tears. Soon the world outside her tomb would be the green of some long-ago-remembered spring.

And she would be warm again.

It was a sin to think of her creature comforts when so many had died in the harsh winter. A sin too, perhaps, to say her prayers from her bed, where she shivered beneath the single thin blanket she had not given away. The stone floor was so cold her chilblained wrists, wet with the tears of her passion, stuck to it when she prostrated herself before her altar. Holy Church taught mortification of the flesh, especially during Lent, but what mother would willingly see her child's flesh so punished? And was not Christ her nurturing, loving, gentle Mother?

It was a sin, too, to worry about her security, when she should trust Him in Whom her true security lay. But she'd had no word from the bishop. It had been weeks since she sent him her *apologia*, her confession of faith, written in English. She supposed his silence to mean he accepted it, or that he thought her beneath further notice, or that he was too preoccupied with the Lollard rumblings to bother with her. She prayed to have enough faith to stop worrying about it. Prayed to feel the warmth of His Love.

Her hands, resting outside the coarse wool of the blanket, held the rosary. Except for the fluttering lips and the slight movement of blue fingers against the beads, she lay as still as a stone effigy carved onto a sarcophagus. Though she still recited the Latin Hours, in recent weeks she had begun to say her personal prayers in the Midland English dialect in which she wrote her Revelations.

Her lips moved only slightly now, murmuring these whispered English prayers, needs from her own heart. Prayers for Half-Tom, who braved the snows to bring her wood—*bless him, Lord, for the kindness of his heart;* and Finn the artist illuminator held by the bishop—*protect his body and his soul from evil;* and the mother of the dying child Finn had brought to her so long ago—*comfort her mother's grieving heart,* the dripping from the eaves accented her unlovely guttural English words; and Father Andrew, so unhappy in his parish and ill-suited for his curate's job; and her servant, Alice, who tended her devotedly.

Lastly, she prayed for Lady Kathryn of Blackingham and the two beautiful children she'd brought with her on that night when she'd come, distraught and angry, from Finn's prison. She had a sense the lady was as deeply troubled now as then, and in need of intercession. *Give her strength to face her trials; and faith; Lord, give her faith.*

Outside, an icicle broke away, splitting the silence with a crack, and crashed to the ground. She placed her hands, still clutching the rosary, beneath the blanket and sank into a deep sleep filled with visions of her weeping Christ. As she slept, the blood oozed from her chilblained wrists, forming a crusty bracelet.

Agnes was worried. She'd never known Kathryn to be sick so long. Even as a girl she'd never been sick for more than a day or two. It had been a week. And young Colin would not even let Agnes in the room, but made her leave the healing potion she brewed for her mistress outside the door.

"Just see that Jasmine is taken care of," he said.

He looked sick himself. She wondered how long he could keep vigil. "Aye, young master, don't worry on that cause. Magda watches the babe well. Let me tend milady awhile."

But he refused.

When Glynis returned with the tray, the maid just shook her head in answer to her unasked question. Agnes emptied Kathryn's still-full bowl into the slops for the swineherd.

"The sheriff's in the hall demanding to see Lady Kathryn," Glynis said. "What'll I tell him?"

"Tell him she's too sick to see anybody."

Agnes knew what he wanted. The thought of it filled her with dread. And not just for Kathryn. Agnes had no desire to be a serf of Guy de Montaigne. There was talk in the village of rebellion. And of safe places for runaways. All those times that John had talked of freedom and she had refused. How could she be thinking of such now that she was so old and tired and John in his grave? Though times were different. Even some churchmen preached against the old order. But it was too late for her. In Sir Guy's household her mistress would need her protection more than ever—poison was a too-easy way for a man to shed himself of a wife who'd outgrown her usefulness. Then there was the little one. And Magda. They needed her protection too. Whether Lady Kathryn lived or died.

"Tell the sheriff it might be plague," she said

When Kathryn woke, the light had shifted. It no longer hurt her eyes. She was thirsty. She tried to sit up and knocked a goblet from the chest beside her bed. The slumped figure, sleeping in a chair at the foot of her bed, jerked to its feet. No angel, then. Angels did not sleep.

"Mother, you're awake. You're back with us," Colin said, stooping to gather up the goblet and refill it. He held it to her mouth. She gulped as though she had not drunk in days. Where had this terrible thirst come from? When she brushed the water from her mouth with the back of her hand, the skin on her lips felt as rough as bark.

"Back? Where have I been?" The words came out heavy with breath.

"You've been very ill. I thought once you might leave us, but your fever broke last night."

"Did you send for a priest? I dreamed—"

"I sent for a priest. But none came. I prayed for you myself. I wrestled with God for your soul, like Jacob wrestled with the angel." He was smiling, half teasing her.

"I'm glad you won. Hand me that ointment on my dressing table. My lips are so cracked they're bleeding."

"Let me," he said as he dabbed the lanolin on her lips.

She did not protest. Her hand trembled when she tried to do it.

"You stayed with me the whole time, then?" she said, lying back on her pillow. "It must have been a while. Your hair has grown out."

"Two weeks."

"If I had tarried at death's portal a little longer, you would almost look like my son again." She smiled, and winced when her lips cracked. "Is the baby . . ."

"Jasmine is well. Magda and Agnes looked after her." He pulled the bell beside her bed. "I'm going to get you something to eat."

Glynis came and Kathryn was able to take a little broth with Colin's help. Afterward, she lay back, exhausted.

"You had a visitor while you were ill, milady," Glynis said.

"A visitor?" She had not dreamed it then—Finn and the anchoress.

"The sheriff," Colin said. "He was rude, insisted on seeing you when I told him you were indisposed."

Her disappointment was a physical hurt. But, of course. This was no fevered dream. This was the real world, and in the real world Finn and the anchoress were alone in their solitary prisons, their solitary hermitages.

Glynis collected the broth cup and dropped her little curtsy, then added, on her way out the door, "His legs couldn't carry him away fast enough when I said plague."

"I suspect that's why the priest never came." Colin frowned.

And they had Latin prayers to protect them, Kathryn thought wearily. But at least, her illness had bought her a little time with the sheriff.

"I'd like to sleep now, Colin," she said. "You look tired. You do the same."

When she woke, a little after three in the afternoon by the sundial scratched on the wall, Colin was still there. But he had changed his clothes. A clean shirt and leggings. No friar's cloak? "I thought you'd be gone now that I'm better. You're a good son, Colin, and I am grateful, but you don't have to stay with me every minute. I feel stronger. I know you're anxious to get back to your preaching." She tried to keep the disapproval from her voice. She at least owed him that.

"Not so anxious as I was. I needed a respite. Time to think."

"You're rethinking it, then? The whole Wycliffe notion?"

"Not rethinking, exactly. Wycliffe's ideas of dominion founded on grace, I agree with that. Even the right for every man to own property, a right given by God, I agree with that, too. But some have taken his ideas too far. I heard John Ball telling a bunch of yeomen and villeins assembled on Mousehold Heath that they should kill all the apostate priests to purge the Church from sin!"

"Kill the priests!" It came out in a hoarse croak. "He said that aloud at a public gathering? Surely, even he would not be so bold. You must have misunderstood." Kathryn lay back, grateful for the pillow. The room still had a tendency to spin if she moved too quickly.

Colin shook his head. "No, I heard the words myself. He said that poor men should plunder the wealth of the Church and the nobility. He's spreading poison among the people, inciting them to abominations. That's not what Jesus taught. When I said so, John Ball railed at me and called me a tool of Satan."

"He's a madman, Colin. I'm glad you're giving it up."

"I'm not giving up the preaching. It's right. But I'll not be connected with rabble-rousing. I'll keep preaching. Like Saint Francis, I'll preach the Peace of our Lord. I'll not preach hate."

"Then you'll be aligned with neither faction. For they both teach hate. And you will make enemies of both camps."

"But don't you see, Mother, that I must be about spreading the truth as I see it? We are all held bondage by a Church that has abandoned us. Greed is now her master, not God. She is the Great Whore of Babylon. Look at Henry

Despenser, building his grand new palace. Where do you think he gets the money for the gold and alabaster they say he's lining the wall with? Or for all the stonemasons it takes to build the largest cloister in all of Christendom? He takes the bread out of the mouths of the poor."

And robs widows of their jewelry, she thought. She was too tired for this discussion, but a mother had to take her moments when they came. She saw a hanging thread in the garment of his devotion and she must unravel it if she could.

"But, Colin, you admit John Ball, who preaches sedition and murder, is not the way. And John of Gaunt—doesn't he just want an excuse to raid the Church's treasure to enrich the royal exchequer?"

"But not Wycliffe, Mother. He seeks nothing but to spread the truth about the abuses of the priests and the need for every man to be able to read the Holy Book in his own language."

She would not argue the gist of what he said. She had prayed in her father's language, in her language. Had God heard? Did He even need a language? Could He read hearts as others read words?

"But what if this truth, if truth it be, is being twisted by evil men for their own desires?"

"That is not my concern. I must tell the truth as I see it and not worry about the costs."

Her head hurt with so much talk; still, she persisted. "Colin, you are just a boy. I know another, and he a man, a good man, who did not concern himself enough with cost. If he was no match for such enemies, how do you think you can be? If you will not consider your mother, then have a thought for your daughter." She started to cough.

"It's of my daughter I'm thinking. And others like her. But let's not argue, Mother. You need to rest." He kissed her on the cheek, then retrieved his tattered friar's robe from a peg behind the door. "I'm just going out for a little while."

The cough had left her too weak to answer. After he was gone, she groped beside her bed for her rosary and spied it hanging on a peg across the room, but she was too weak to get it. She murmured the Our Father in her native tongue. And wondered aloud to God why His mercy was meted out by the dropper and not the bucket.

THIRTY

And so the gospel pearl is cast abroad, to be trodden underfoot of swine; and what was dear to clergy and laity is now rendered as it were, the common jest of both; so that the gem of the church becomes the derision of laymen, and that is now theirs forever.

—HENRY KNIGHTON,
CANON OF LEICESTER (14TH CENTURY)

Sir Guy was not surprised when the call came from Essex for help. It was May, and the bailiffs were making their rounds in the warm spring weather, collecting the king's taxes. Some resistance was to be expected in small pockets, among the poorest classes. And then a gang of peasants took a pitchfork to two of the king's excisemen and set fire to some abbey hayricks. Such blatant insurrection must be met with unwavering force. Must be stopped before it spread to his shire. He had his own troublemakers to deal with, but he'd send what he could spare. So he dispatched a coterie of young squires, green like Alfred—who was among them—green but sufficient to put down a few ragtag rebels armed with scythes and pitchforks. The experience would be good for them.

The word came two weeks later. The rebellion was spreading like pestilence, and a peasant army of Kentish and Essex men was marching toward

London under a rabble-rouser named Wat Tyler. The sheriff gathered more retainers—battle-hardened men this time. Guy de Fontaigne knew what was needed. Torture a few of the miscreants, cut out their tongues, crush a few knackers, and the rest of the rabble would get back to their fields and guilds soon enough. Find the head of the snake and cut it off. He couldn't get his hands on the cleric Wycliffe, not as long as he was under the protection of the duke of Lancaster. But he could find John Ball. And that was a notch he'd enjoy putting on his girdle.

Still, the timing was a nuisance. There were other gates he'd planned to storm. No black flag flew at Blackingham Hall, though his spies told him its lady had indeed been at the point of death. She was still frail, but it didn't take much strength to plight a troth. Nor to consummate one. At least on her part. All she had to do was lie on her back with her legs apart.

He shouted for his horse and battle gear whilst he penned a hasty but polite note in which he claimed he'd prayed day and night for her recovery. Being overjoyed that his prayers had been answered, he was now prepared to publish the banns for their marriage. Upon his return, he would wait upon her for the purpose of settling upon a nuptial contract.

On his way south to Essex, the sheriff detoured into Norwich and stopped in Colgate Street to order a gown for Kathryn and a wedding surcoat for himself. "Don't forget to embroider upon mine the Order of the Garter," he told the fawning clothier. For Kathryn he chose a plum-colored brocade shot with silver. The little Flemish merchant bobbed his approval. It was an expensive gown, but it would help him to press his suit. And if she did not recover, she'd wear it in her crypt. In any case he'd get the land he wanted. He already owned her oldest son.

ン⁓

Colin was on his way back home. He needed to get back to his mother. She had recovered, but she still was not strong. He had kept his promise to her; he had made the rounds of the crofters to see that all had sufficient means to pay the poll tax. She was determined to pay the taxes herself, she said, rather than have them deprived of their last farthing. "I'll consider it my tithe," she said. "It is as well to give it to them to buy off a warring king than to let a warring bishop get his jeweled fingers on it."

It was not a sentiment with which he could argue, but it made him uncomfortable. It was one thing for him to harangue against the corruption of the Church from the relative safety of his poor friar's garb, quite another for a noble widow to withhold her tithe in protest. But he'd agreed to survey the crofters for her and assured her he would see that none of their children went hungry to pay the king's tax. He was approaching the Aylsham cross when he heard the loud angry voices.

His first inclination was to make a wide path around the bunch of ruffians and whatever poor soul they were tormenting, but he remembered the good Samaritan. What kind of Christian would he be not to intervene? So he approached the knot of men, burly laborers, by the look of them, seven or eight in number, and, from the sound of them, fortified with much ale. They held one of the cathedral brothers, arms pinned behind his back, in the middle of a tight circle. One of them, the tanner, Colin recognized. He'd bought parchment hides off him once for the illuminator. But even if Colin hadn't recognized him, the reek of him announced his trade. He smelled of the excrement used in the curing process, which apparently he'd been collecting in the large sack at his feet. The tanner had hold of the monk's cowl with one hand and was rubbing a dark, redolent substance on the poor monk's tonsure with his other hand. Colin wrinkled his nose in disgust. The monk squirmed in outraged protest. The other men laughed. A look of disbelief crossed the monk's face and then veered into pain as the men tightened their grip.

Colin stepped into the circle. "Let him go."

The tanner looked up in surprise. "You want some of the same, lad? Just a little unholy anointing for the *brother* here. If you're thinkin' that priest's garb is going to protect you, well . . ."

A stocky fellow grabbed Colin and pulled his hood back. The tanner stopped short, waved his hand. "Wait. I know who you are. You're one of the sons from Blackingham."

"From Blackingham! Nobility. You hear that, lads?"

"No. Wait," the tanner said. "He's one of them Lollards. He's a poor priest."

"No such thing as a poor priest. You said he was nobility." But he let go of Colin, though he was still so close, Colin could feel his scruffy beard on his neck and smell his rotting teeth.

"He preaches against the Church. Like John Ball and Wycliffe. He's one of us."

"If he ate today, he ain't one of us." The man growled, but he backed off sufficiently for Colin to see the hard ridges of the squint lines around his eyes.

Colin squared his shoulders, tried to marshal his dignity. "What is the monk's offense, Master Tanner, that he should be so ill-treated? Our Lord said—"

"Our Lord said something about stealing. If he didn't, the Commandments did. This *brother* is a thief. He took hides for the scriptorium to use for parchment and now he says the bishop will not pay. Says it can be my tithe. Well, I'm going to tithe this, too." And he indicated the sack of animal dung at his feet.

"It's not his fault." What was the tanner's name—Tim, Tom? "It's his bishop's."

"Well, the bishop ain't here, is he?" the stocky one said.

Colin had him marked for the ringleader. But he spoke to the wronged tanner. "Exactly. So let the monk go, Tom, before this all goes too far. As good as your revenge feels, it'll not get you payment for your hides. It might get you a whipping, though." He gestured toward a band of armed riders bearing down on the crossroad. On the front rider's shield Colin could make out the crest of Henry Despenser. "It might even get you worse than whipping."

The stout one with the scruffy beard saw the approaching riders at about the same time. "It's the bishop's men. Run."

The men scattered, like rats in a grain bin, toward a nearby hedgerow.

The monk ran, too, but in the other direction, toward the horsemen. He gained their attention. They reined in their horses. From where he stood, Colin could not hear his words, but the monk began gesticulating wildly.

Three of the riders dismounted and headed into the thicket. Two got off and strode toward him. He started toward them, closing the gap between in a gesture of friendliness.

One of the soldiers drew his long-sword as he strode forward, his boots stirring up little swirls of dust. Colin recognized the menace in his face, recognized it but didn't understand it. He was on the monk's side. He opened his mouth to explain. "No harm has come to the—"

The cold blade entered his belly before he could finish his sentence. It went in clean. With one hard upward thrust, it cleaved his heart. The words forming on his lips died in a hiss and froth of blood.

Colin's last thought was that he could not keep his promise to his mother.

"But he wasn't one of them," the brother protested. "You killed an innocent man."

"No matter. Just one more rabble-rousing priest for His Eminence," the swordsman said.

He kicked the body into the ditch at the side of the road.

The bishop had just come from celebrating the mass. It was June 11, the Feast of Saint Barnabas, and there had been precious few in attendance. He thought he knew why. Attendance at the obligatory feast days was slipping. No respect for the holiest days. That's what all this talk of equality and English Scriptures was leading to. Some even talked openly—not to him; they'd not dare, but he'd heard reports—that there'd be no need to come to mass if they could go directly to God. Every man his own priest! Every cowherd, dung collector, scullery maid, general dogsbody handling the Holy Word. The very idea of it made the bile back up in his throat.

As he strode into his chamber, he flung the sacred vestments and robe at the chamberlain, Old Seth, who stood dozing in the corner, hitting him in the face and almost toppling his frail frame. Fresh from his Latin homily, Despenser swore at the old man in the same language, *"Fimus, fimus, fimus,"* and then, realizing that his servant understood his condemning tone but not the words—though he wouldn't stoop to *shite* in the peasant Saxon tongue—continued his harangue in Norman French so that Old Seth might receive the full benefit. "You piece of dog dung, I don't know why I put up with your slovenly ways. Sloth's a sin, you know." He stabbed his finger at the air beneath his servant's nose. "That kind of sin can send you straight to hell." The old man's French was good enough for him to understand. Despenser noted with satisfaction how he cringed as he shuffled off in agitation. "Fetch my riding tunic and side arm."

The idea had come to him as he stalked across the cathedral close from the ill-attended mass. There were other tasks he could perform for his Church that required more than holy words and pectoral crosses. But he removed the cross reluctantly, his fingers lingering on its gem-encrusted crossarm. It was too heavy for a mission such as this. Better suited for a cleric's silk robe than the chain mail he slipped over his lawn shirt.

"Now my rapier. And hurry, if you don't want the back of my hand." His hand flexed with wanting to act out what his words threatened. Save it for the rebels, his reason cautioned. This was the life he was suited for, and this rebellion against Holy Church was all the reason he needed. The word had come that a rebel army led by a miscreant named Wat Tyler had actually entered London and set fire to John of Gaunt's palace. Like a dog biting its own tail. He'd have to say the duke got what he deserved, no love lost there. Lancaster should've known better than to encourage Wycliffe. Lie down with pigs, you'll get up smelling like one. The Church would be next. They'd go after the bishop's palace and the abbeys. No good to rely on that incompetent sheriff and his green squires. Despenser had already sent out a cadre of soldiers, but he'd get more and this time he'd ride with them.

He clamped his rapier on with its new buckle, tested the fastener, satisfying himself that it would hold in a fight. Interesting invention. Wonder why somebody hadn't thought of it sooner. He'd purchased it months ago, but now was his first chance to use it. He could feel his blood coursing. He hadn't felt this alive in weeks. He'd show the king's soldiers how to put down this rabble skirmish. Good practice for taking on the French pope.

He knelt briefly, genuflecting perfunctorily before the cross. Then, for good luck, he kissed the crucifix hanging above his chamber altar. His sword clanged against the stone floor. He liked the sound of it. They called him the warring bishop, complained that his men had already killed a handful of rebels and a Lollard priest. Well, he'd show them a warring bishop.

When he was done, there'd be no rebel man, woman, or child left standing in East Anglia. *Expugno, exsequor, eradico:* capture, execute, destroy.

☙ ✾ ❧

When Magda returned to the Blackingham kitchen from her weekly visit to her family, she was troubled. Her mum had whispered to her as she kissed her good-bye, "Tell milady to look to the safety of her house." Magda hadn't really needed the warning. She felt danger all around her, tasted it on her tongue, and if she needed real evidence, she had heard it with her own ears. People were careless around her because she was simple.

Once, when she was serving ale to her father's visitors, she'd overheard him talking with some rough men she'd never seen before. In a fit of rare hospitality her father had offered them drink. A man named Geoffrey Litster was telling them to arm themselves. telling them they should burn the monks' houses, and the royal palaces, even the manor houses. Magda had never seen a royal palace or a monk's house. Maybe they were homes for evildoers like the Litster man said. But manor houses? Wasn't Lady Kathryn's house called Blackingham Manor? Maybe they only meant the manor houses of evil people. But still she shivered when she thought of burning. She remembered the wool house, and the shepherd with his flesh melted into black soot.

She told Agnes what her mother had said as she washed her hands the way Agnes had taught her in preparation for kneading dough for the bread oven.

"Aye, child, I know. I've heard some talk myself. But Blackingham is not a great house. And milady has been good to her tenants. It's just rebel talk. They're mad about the tax. They'll not like to bother with small-fry like us. Never you mind. And tell your mum not to worry."

"Should we warn the mistress?"

Agnes pounded the dough she was kneading in silence, then frowned and shook her head. "Nay, child, it would only add to her burden. Young Master Colin has not been home for three nights and milady is that distraught with worry. She can speak of nothing else but how he may be hurt or sick, lying somewhere in a ditch. 'He's just run away again,' I told her. 'Just weary of women's company. Maybe he met up with some of his road companions. Not to worry. He'll be back,' I said, but she just shook her head and said, 'Not this time, Agnes, I can feel it. Something's happened. A mother knows these things.' Like how could I know, since I've never been a mother, I wanted to say. But she'd worry enough, so I let the gibe pass. We'll be safe enough. Nobody will bother us. My lady has powerful friends."

Agnes passed the dough off to Magda, whose small palm pummeled it with lighter hands. She took some comfort in Cook's words, because she trusted her. But she noticed how Agnes rubbed her shoulder. She always had shoulder pain when she was worried.

※

Another warning came two days later. It was the middle of June. Magda knew the date because that was the month the sheep washing and shearing began and the kitchens were busier than usual with food for the extra laborers. Her little brother brought the second warning. "Tell Lady Kathryn to be wary. Trouble coming closer."

Magda went straight to Agnes. Together, they went to Lady Kathryn. They found her in the solar with her accounts book and baby Jasmine playing at her feet. Magda told her of the message, but not of the overheard conversation between her father and the men. How could she, without making her father look like a bad man? Lady Kathryn might have him locked up in Castle Prison, like the illuminator, and then there would be no one to help her mum and the little ones. Milady looked so frail that at first Magda feared such a worry on top of all she'd had might be too much for her. But when Magda looked closer, she saw that Lady Kathryn's soul-light was stronger than ever, like a clear stream reflecting a blue sky.

When Lady Kathryn spoke, her voice was weary. "I have sent every reliable male servant I can find to search for Colin," she said. "We are a household of women, undefended. We must pray that our Lord will come to our defense," she said. Then she looked up and Magda saw the determination in her eyes. "And then we must make a plan."

"What about the sheriff?" Agnes asked.

"The sheriff has gone south to put down rebellion in Essex."

Sunlight from a high window painted stripes on the floor where Jasmine played. Magda watched with fascination as the little girl's light merged with the stripes whenever she toddled across them. It was hard to tell if she was drawing the light or if it was coming from her. She too seemed fascinated with it as she grabbed for the dust motes that floated in its beam.

We are all like that, Magda thought. Dust motes floating in the light.

"We must have a plan so we will not panic if the rebels attack us," her mistress was saying. "I have sent a message to the sheriff's house, asking that my son be sent back with whatever men he can spare to protect a company of innocent women. If an attack comes, we will gather in the kitchen. There is safety in numbers and the kitchen will be the safest place."

At the word "kitchen," Jasmine gave up chasing sunbeams and went to Agnes, holding out her arms, making grabbing motions with her chubby hands. "Cake," she demanded.

Lady Kathryn smiled. "In a minute, poppet, Magda will get you cake." She looked hard at Magda. "Magda, listen carefully. This is very important."

"Aye, milady."

"This is the most important part of the plan. If trouble comes, you will take Jasmine to your mother's hut. She will be safe there."

But Magda knew that was not true. Should she tell? Her mind searched desperately for a solution. She could not go to her mother's, but she could not tell Lady Kathryn.

Lady Kathryn was waiting for an answer. "Do you understand what I have said, Magda?"

"Aye, milady. I understand."

Then she gathered up the child and took her to get some cake, leaving Agnes and her mistress to their plans. But for two days, she worried and wondered what she should do. And then she hit upon a solution. She had a place where she could hide the child in safety. A place where nobody would ever think to look.

❧

Alfred was back in Norfolk, in the sheriff's stable yard, when Lady Kathryn's message came. The sheriff was still in Essex. Sir Guy's mount had been killed just outside of Ipswich, and though he quickly conscripted another, it was not to his liking. So he'd dispatched his armor bearer to retrieve more arms and his second-favorite charger. Alfred was glad enough to go. It wasn't that he minded a good fight. But he'd seen enough of dead men. Enough hacked limbs, and frozen death masks, and bloated, flyblown bodies.

For the past two weeks, they had encountered fierce fighting with rogue bands of rebels, remnants of a mob from Kent and Essex who'd been betrayed by the king's men in London. Alfred didn't know all the details of the London rebellion, but he'd heard enough to piece together what happened. On the thirteenth of May the rebels had entered London and razed the palace of the duke of Lancaster. They also killed some Flemish merchants as they burned and pillaged and created general mayhem in the streets of the city. The next day the young King Richard met the rebels at Mile End outside London to negotiate a peace.

Alfred wished he'd been in London to see the boy king face down that angry mob. The king was not even as old as Alfred, yet he'd made an impression on the peasants. Maybe they identified with his youth; maybe they admired his courage—anyway, they'd listened as he'd promised redress of grievance: cheap land, free trade, and the abolition of serfdom. But apparently, at the same time the king was negotiating peace, some of the rebels were still in London. They captured and beheaded the king's treasurer and the archbishop of Sudbury.

On the third day of the uprising, when the king again met the rebels—this time at a place called Smithfield—the enraged mayor of London murdered the peasant leader Wat Tyler in the presence of the king and the peasant mob. The rebels didn't stay to see their leader's head on a pole—Alfred could understand the logic of that; his father had taught him the concept of strategic retreat—but instead dispersed at the king's urging. He promised them amnesty if they'd go home. But they'd already been betrayed once. They did not return to their homes, where they feared the king's soldiers would hunt them down. Instead, they fled to the northern shires, more enraged than ever, desperate men with nothing to lose.

Sir Guy and his men had encountered them in Ipswich.

Now, fresh from the fighting, Alfred was exhausted by his hard ride north. And hungry. He'd ridden for three days, hardly stopping to eat or sleep. Sweat ran down his face and he swore loudly as he tried to put a bridle and a lead on the roan stallion—he would never attempt to ride the ill-tempered beast—when the horse reared up, threatening Alfred with a pounding from his forelegs. One of the grooms, hearing the ruckus, rushed to his aid.

When they got the horse harnessed and somewhat settled, though still snorting his considerable displeasure, the groom reached inside his shirt and handed Alfred two sealed parchments. "Steward said to give you these to take back to Sir Guy. He said they looked important."

One of the letters, Alfred noticed, bore the seal of the Church. Probably the bishop's crest. The other impression he also recognized, a twelve-point stag with raised foreleg against a background of three bars. That was the Blackingham crest. A flash of resentment stirred in him.

A billet-doux from his mother to her lover?

The letter had obviously been sealed in haste, the wax scarcely melted on one side. He fingered it lightly, teasing the edge. It would be easy enough to reseal, and besides, it was *his* family crest. He had a right. He slid his thumb under it carefully. The seal slipped and the parchment unfurled with a whisper. He recognized his mother's spiky, graceful hand.

*Sir, since I am an unprotected widow in your shire, I must apply to you
for protection during the current crisis. If it pleases you, send my son to
me, along with any other archers that you might spare. I received the gift*

you sent as a token of your protection and goodwill, but I cannot take delight in its elegance when I fear my very household may at any moment come under siege.

The letter was signed by his mother but in a shakier hand than he remembered, for all its bold words. It was dated June 1. Two days ago. He'd never thought—but he should have—hadn't he seen for himself the rage vented by the peasants against some of the nobility? Still, to think of his strong, competent mother in need of protection was a strange concept. And she had Colin.

The horse stomped and pulled against the lead the groom held, pawing against the ground. A cloud of dust whirled up then settled on the tortured verge of grass bordering the stable yard. Alfred could taste the grit of it between his teeth, feel it seeping into his pores with his sweat.

What was he to do? He had a direct command from Sir Guy, yet his mother needed him. She'd asked for him. Him. When she had Colin. It would take three, maybe four days, leading the horse, to get back to the fighting. Then he would have to gain permission, and it would be two days back even if he rode all night.

"Leave the horse. Bring me pen and paper," he said to the groom in as authoritative a voice as he could muster. After all, he was squire to Sir Guy. The groom would have to obey him in the absence of a higher authority.

When the groom returned, Alfred hastily wrote a note explaining that his lady mother was in distress and had sent for him. Because Sir Guy had taught him the true meaning of chivalry and because of the friendship between the two houses, he was sure Sir Guy would want him to go to her. He was sending the horse and arms, and would join the battle as soon as he'd seen to his mother's safety.

"Deliver this missive, and the other one, along with the horse, to Sir Guy," he said, flinging a few grains of sand across the page to soak up the excess ink.

The groom's eyes widened in alarm. He'd probably never been off the feudal holding, let alone out of the shire. "But Master Alfred, I don't know—"

"I'll draw you a map," he said. "You'll have no trouble finding it." He was already hastily sketching a circle beside which he wrote "Norwich," then a strong black line ending in another, smaller, circle, marked "Colchester," and then another horizontal line leading off, ending in a still smaller circle, which he labeled "Ipswich." Beside the smaller circle he drew a rough sketch of a door with a header pole and a swinging sign.

"This is Colchester," he said, pointing to the second circle. "You take the old Roman Road south out of Norwich through Bury Saint Edmunds and then on to Colchester. Turn east toward Ipswich. Tell the keeper at the tavern at the crossroads that you are a serf with a message for the sheriff of Norfolk." He considered the groom's youth and his inexperience. He was only a year or so younger than Alfred. He had proved his competence with the horse, but he'd be ripe for harassment because of his age. "You can handle the horse well enough. Ride him instead of leading him."

"Aye, I'd have no problem with the horse."

Alfred thought he said this with a little too much smugness. "But don't wear the livery of the house. Dress like a peasant, and if you encounter any rogues, say you're a runaway serf and you're carrying a message for John Ball or Wat Tyler. Say the horse is stolen. They won't bother you then."

Alfred was rewarded as the look of smugness evaporated. The groom looked at the paper, puzzlement and chagrin playing across his face. "But Master Alfred, I can't read."

"You've been to Norwich?"

The boy nodded, said with some pride in his voice, "Twice."

"That line is the main road south out of Norwich. If you get lost, just ask for the road to Colchester, then to Ipswich."

"But—"

"Don't worry. You'll be fine. You're a brave lad." And Alfred climbed onto his own mount, whose muscles still trembled with fatigue, and spurred it toward Blackingham, leaving the groom scratching his head as he stared at the undecipherable lines and squiggles.

~ ⚜ ~

Alfred noticed the stench as he approached the Aylsham cross. His own sweat-stained body? Disgusting. Or maybe that of his horse ridden so hard, his neck and shoulders were flecked with white foam? No. It was growing stronger and all too familiar by now. It was a smell he thought he'd left behind him in an Ipswich field. It was the smell of dead men, rotting in the sun.

A buzzard roosted in an oak tree that anchored the hedge about a hundred feet from the road. *No need to investigate; just hold your nose and ride on by as fast as you can. Too late for the poor sods there.*

But as the buzzard receded from his peripheral vision, the smell grew stronger. His tired horse smelled it, too, and whinnied its disgust, but did not answer when Alfred dug in his heels. He should have remembered to feed the horse. "Just a little further, old boy, there'll be a bucket of oats for you when we reach home." He'd been thinking himself of something good from Agnes's kitchen. But that no longer seemed appealing.

"Come on. Pick it up." The horse clopped a little faster, then jerked sideways, startled by a buzzard suddenly flying up from the ditch along the road, where he'd been feasting on carrion. So. That was the source of the smell. This one didn't even make it as far as the false cover of the hedgerow where his fellows had been cut down, where the startled buzzard was now perched in the oak tree beside its mate, waiting for the interlopers to pass on by. His gaze lingered long enough to see the corpse was dressed in poor priest's garb, or what was left of it after the buzzard's feast. Probably a Lollard priest dispatched by the bishop's guards, not by the peasants. The rebels would have considered him one of their own.

His horse had stopped beside the body and stood with its head hanging down as though the last bit of energy had drained from it, yet Alfred did not spur it on. He was unable to draw his gaze away from the gruesome sight. The birds had picked the face clean. Empty eye sockets stared up at a hard sun in a cloudless sky. Some flies swarmed around the corpse's lower extremities where the birds had not stripped the bones. There was something achingly familiar in the shape of the skull. The stench was overpowering. He pinched his nostrils shut. But he got down from his horse and walked over to the ditch. Gently nudged the corpse with his foot, turning it over. Maggots crawled in the place were the head had lain.

Alfred turned his face away to retch.

It was then he saw the golden hair, gleaming in the brittle sun like some lost treasure, and the skull—he knew that skull—picked clean as a chicken bone, the flyblown flesh oozing putrefaction in the heat. It all belonged to the brother with whom he had shared his mother's womb. It belonged to Colin. Sunlight snagged on a patch of blond hair in the dust. Hair the color of light. Hair like the angels, he'd heard his mother say as he'd watched her stroke it when they were little. Stroked it in the way she never stroked his coarse red curls.

"You're one of Sir Guy de Fontaigne's squires," a soldier said as he reined in his horse, motioning for his two fellows to pull up as well.

Alfred was still on his knees, picking up strands of Colin's hairs, winding them around his fingers as though they were threads of gold. Something at least to take to his mother, some keepsake that she could inter in a velvet-lined reliquary along with his bones.

"Why are you sniveling over this piece of buzzard meat?"

He looked up at the sound of the soldier's voice, recognized the crest embossed in gilt on the leather harnesses of the horsemen. The same crest on the letter he'd presumed to be from the bishop.

"He was no—"

"I know who he was." The soldier laughed, leaning forward, the reins dangling loosely from his hands. "One of those *poor priests* with shite for brains. You should have seen the look of surprise on his face when my blade split his Lollard belly."

A great surge of rage started somewhere in Alfred's gut and bubbled like bile into his throat, pushing out a roar like a young lion. He leaped to his feet, drew his sword and lunged at the speaker in a whirl of motion.

Three flashing swords hewed him down before his blade drew blood. The soldiers never even dismounted.

Alfred's body teetered for an instant before falling backward, and then, as if pushed by an unseen hand, it arced sideways so that it landed, not in the road, but in the ditch. It nestled spoon fashion against his brother's smaller body, with one arm hugging his brother's chest. The other hand still held the three strands of pale blond hair in his clenched fist.

"He was one of the sheriff's men," one of the riders said. "Shouldn't we bury him or at least strip his livery?"

"Nay. Just leave him be. Whoever finds him will think they died killing each other." Clicking his reins, he nodded at the pair of buzzards who had watched the whole affair from the oak tree. "They'll do the work for us. One man's skull looks much like another's."

THIRTY-ONE

*For He will be seen, and He will be sought. He will be
waited on and He will be trusted.*
—JULIAN OF NORWICH, *DIVINE REVELATIONS*

agda was playing with Jasmine in the little anteroom off
the illuminator's old quarters. The room that had been Rose's now was her
daughter's nursery. "Her mother's spirit will watch over her," milady had
said. But Rose's spirit was not there. Magda knew such things. Besides, Cook
said Rose's spirit was with Jesus. There was no one to watch over the babe
but Magda.

Lady Kathryn was weak and listless since her illness, and heartsick with
Master Colin gone, so Magda took Jasmine in the afternoons while milady
rested in her great four-post bed. Today, when Magda had gone to Lady
Kathryn's chamber after her kitchen duties, milady had looked longingly at
the bed with her shadowy eyes and motioned for her to take the child away.
She could see Lady Kathryn now, in her mind, lying in a heap behind the
damask drapery that would be drawn against the light despite the summer
heat. She could hear, too, in her mind, weak sobbing sounds, like little
wounded animal whimpers. She could even feel the ache of milady's pain
pulsing in her own temples.

As Jasmine sang her child's gibberish and rattled the oyster shells—the illuminator's empty paint pots with dried residue of color clinging to their edges—Magda looked out the second-story window, keeping watch. She could see across the courtyard, past the gate and into the pasture beyond where the Norfolk sheep grazed. They looked like woolly pillows scattered on a green silk counterpane. Above them, more woolly pillows floated in a clear blue sky. If not for the danger, it would be a fine June day, a day to take Jasmine out to play in the sunshine. They could play hide-and-seek among the hedges and chase the butterflies that sucked the nectar from the honeysuckle. But not today. And maybe not tomorrow. Milady had said to keep close and keep watch.

She was keeping watch, looking out the high glazed window as she did every day, when she saw him, the evil one, the one who had tried to take her in the fields like an animal. She thought milady had sent him away. But now he was back, stomping across the fields with a ragtag band of workers armed with scythes and pitchforks. Some of them carried torches—in broadest daylight—and buckets. The sheep stopped nibbling the sweet summer grass and watched them with wary eyes. Magda couldn't see their faces clearly from so far away. But she didn't need to. The tall one in front, he had no soul-light. The sight of him made her sick to her stomach with fear.

Cook had said the rabble mob might come at night and murder them in their beds. Cook and Lady Kathryn slept in the day and held vigil at night. She should wake Cook. She could hear the men now, their coarse laughter in response to what the tall one said, their voices loud and shrill like her father's when he drank too much. She wished she could say how many. There were more than the fingers of one hand but less than two.

She glanced nervously at the child playing at her feet. When she returned to the window, the tight knot of men had begun to unwind. Some of them were drifting off among the sheep. Maybe they had only come to steal the livestock and they would leave.

Milady had made a plan. What had Lady Kathryn said her part was to be? The one with the darkness hovering around him, the evil one, came on toward the house, bringing a little bunch of men with him. She could only see the tops of their heads and the sunlight glinting off the scythes they carried and their soul-lights blending into a dark cloud. She was glad her father was not among them. She would have recognized his flat, rolled cap with its ragged crown.

What was the plan? She had said her part over and over to herself as she lay awake on her straw pallet in Cook's room. Now, the devil had stolen it from her mind. *What was she supposed to do if they came?*

She heard Cook's voice, loud and strident, belowstairs. "What are you doing back here? Lady Kathryn will set the dogs on you. You'd best be gone if you know what's good for you. And take that sorry lot with you." Cook was awake then. Cook would send them packing, and then she would warn milady.

The bleating of the sheep drew her gaze to the pastures. The white woolly pillows wore scarlet ribbons around their necks. They bleated louder now, thin, helpless sounds that made Magda want to cry. The men weren't stealing the sheep! They were slashing at them, slaughtering them in the field! Then leaving them to bleed to death as the men marched toward the house. One stuck his torch to the grass, and little yellow teeth began to chew the pasture. The acrid smell of the smoke made her nose wrinkle.

What was the plan? What was her part?

Take the baby, Magda. Take the baby to your mother's cottage.

No, that was Lady Kathryn's voice in her head. But that was not the plan.

A honeybee lit on the windowsill and buzzed away.

Magda remembered.

She scooped Jasmine up in her arms.

"Hide-and-seek with Magda? D-does Jasmine w-want to hide from milady and let her find us?" she whispered.

Jasmine bobbed her blond curls, giggled something that translated, "Jasmine hide."

"Shh. She's c-coming."

Magda could feel the baby's breath, feel her small body shiver with the stifled giggle she held back with a pudgy hand as they fled down the stairs to the kitchen, then out the back door to the old dead tree standing sentinel on what passed for a hill in flat country.

"We will hide with the honeybees. The bees are our friends," she said, her voice so low it melted into the summer breeze. "But you must be very still and very quiet. Still as a mouse. So m-milady can't f-find us." They crawled in between the gnarly roots to the womblike space just big enough for the two of them.

"Me mouse." The blond head bobbed a promise in an answering whisper.

"Suck on t-this," Magda whispered, breaking off a bit of honeycomb and giving it to her as she covered the child's head with her apron to protect her from a curious bee. But she knew the bees would not harm them. They would remember her gifts during the long winter, her gifts of sticks soaked in honey-and-rosemary water that kept them alive.

Magda could feel the child sucking on the honeycomb, feel its stickiness as it dribbled between her own budding breasts, where her heart beat the rhythm of a warrior's drum. It was cool inside the tree and dark and smelled of honey and tree mold and earth, and the drone of the bees made a sweet lullaby. They settled on her arms in soft brown patches and lit on the apron that covered the sleeping child. But they didn't sting. Not one.

Soon the sucking stopped, and the baby's breath rose and fell moist and rhythmic against her skin.

But Magda did not sleep. Her bladder was full and she could not relieve herself. She would not sully the purity of the bees' home. She tried to think of something else. She thought of Half-Tom and how funny he'd been when he heard her singing in the bee tree. How his kind eyes smiled at her. She wished he were with them. She felt safe with him. And he thought she was smart. She almost felt smart when she was with him. Her foot was asleep. She shifted her weight gently, so as not to wake the sleeping child.

The smell of smoke was strong now. From inside the house she thought she heard a woman scream. But she had to stay here. She must protect the child. That was her part. She prayed to the Virgin and to the god of the tree to keep them safe.

~≈≈~

Finn heard the commotion before he saw it, but he paid scant attention. He was on the fifth panel of the bishop's retable. He'd been working in a fever to finish it since Kathryn told him of her plans to marry the sheriff, her plans to take Rose's child. It had become all there was of his life. He no longer feared that if he finished, the bishop would have no further reason to keep him alive. It was a last gamble. Please the bishop. Promise more. Use it as a bargaining tool for a pardon. So he ignored the shouts and curses coming from below, ignored even the constable's voice rising loud and threatening above the rest. "Halt, I say. Disperse in the name of the king."

Finn didn't even look up. Whatever happened outside his chamber did not matter to him. He worked with the force of a whirlwind, his sable brushes scattered higgledy-piggledy, his paint pots no longer lined up neatly on his worktable. Patches of gold and crimson stained his shirt, and large brown circles spread beneath his armpits. For this last panel, the Ascension, he was unable to see the face of Christ. The Saviour's triumph over suffering when Finn was so locked into his own torment was not something his muse could conjure. Frustrated with repeated efforts, he blotted out the figure's upper body and in a fury of ocher blended it into the background so that Christ ascended into an opaque cloud. All but his legs, which dangled above the gathered apostles, was obscure. A suffering Christ he understood. A triumphant Christ eluded him.

Finn spread the last of the azure onto the Virgin's cloak. The figures of the last two panels were clumsy, lacking the grace and detail of the earlier panels, but haste drove him with an overseer's whip. He daubed the finishing touches on the apostles' rapt faces—more fearful than triumphant; rapture, like triumph, was becoming a distant memory. He surveyed the whole. He took an artist's pride in the five panels—not painted with the intricacy, the fine detail of his initial letters, lacking the imagination of his marginalia and the sensuous, convoluted swirls and knots of his carpet pages that so delighted the workings of his mind—but beautiful in their mass of color, color so vibrant it almost overwhelmed the senses. Even the hurried work at the last showed passion. On the whole it would do.

Send for the bishop to negotiate a furlough: that was his next task. Gain his release at least long enough to get his granddaughter away from the sheriff's clutches. That was all that mattered. No use to reason with Kathryn. She'd made up her mind. He would take Rose's child to the anchoress to be cloistered with her, just as Saint Hildegard of Bingein was given to the sainted Jutta.

A little bit of azure was left in the pot. He cut it with a glaze of white and applied it to the horseman's cloak in the second panel, then stepped back to survey it. The mounted figure following Christ as He carried His cross looked more like a fourteenth-century courtier than a first-century Jew. It was no accident that the youthful figure bore a remarkable resemblance to the bishop, but without the arrogant expression. A flattering portrait by design.

Finn was applying the last stroke of blue, emptying his brush of its expensive pigment, when he heard the shouts from the yard, the clash of metal, this time too loud to be ignored. He went to the window and looked out. In the courtyard a melee had broken out. A couple of prison guards grappled with a score of rebels, who looked like burly farm laborers and seemed to be getting the best of the slack-bellied guards. The door at the bottom of the steps scraped—the unmistakable sound of metal against stone. More shouting, closer now. On the stairs. A rush of stamping feet, then a gruff, familiar growl behind him.

Finn turned to see Sykes crossing the threshold to his cell. Another quick glance out the window showed the constable on the ground, wounded or dead.

"So this is where ye've been keeping. Better quarters than the dungeon, I'd say." Sykes waved a short-sword—Finn recognized it as one the constable sometimes wore—around the room, then picked up a half-eaten joint of meat from the remains of Finn's meal and proceeded to take a bite of it. His mean little jet eyes bored into Finn as his broken teeth stripped the meat from the bone before flinging it into the air. Finn ducked to keep it from hitting him. Sykes laughed as he wiped the grease from his left hand onto his sleeve. His right hand still held the sword pointed at Finn. "Where's yer little midget friend, Illuminator?"

Finn tried to keep his voice calm, though his quick assessment of the situation made him feel anything but. "You wouldn't be taking advantage of a little rebellion to settle an old score, would you, Sykes? Before you do something you'll regret, you might consider that I'm under the special protection of the bishop. You've already committed an offense against the crown. Will you offend the Church as well?"

Sykes laughed, showing a jagged canine among his long yellow teeth. "Listen to them fine words. 'Offend the Church, offend the Church'! What did the Church ever do for the likes of Sykes?"

He staggered a little. Drunk on ale or power? Finn wondered, half hoping it was the former. He would be easier to handle.

"The Church's day is over. We're giving them high-flying bishops and nobles a taste of their own." He sniffed the air. "Smell that? That's probably some nobleman's fields, maybe even his castle aburnin'."

Finn had noticed the acrid smell earlier and thought it was just some steward burning off his lord's pasture to sow it fresh. But it was stronger now.

"And it's not just here, neither. It's all the way to Londontown. Won't be none of them rich palaces or abbeys left standin' when we're done."

So it was a mob, not just a prison riot. And they were burning and pillaging nobility in all of East Anglia. Blackingham would be undefended except for Colin. That meant the child was in danger. And Kathryn.

"Listen, Sykes, whatever it is you want, I'll—"

More steps on the stairs. A motley crew, mostly peasants, one or two disgruntled guards, gathered behind Sykes. One of them warned, "Someone's coming. The constable is dead. We've turned all the poor sods loose. Now we'd best git while gittin's good."

"Well, this here's one bird's not going to fly." And Sykes lunged at Finn. But Finn had anticipated his move and ducked under, came up behind him, and twisted the sword from him. He shoved Sykes hard with his body, then bolted toward the stairs.

"Stop him! Kill the bloody swine!"

The lone man standing beside the door shrugged. "He's done naught to me. We let the rest go. Do your own killin', Sykes."

Only loud angry curses dogged his heels.

When he got to the yard, Finn looked frantically around for a horse.

A young blond boy was mounted on the constable's horse, looking pleased with himself and his new mount. A shock of recognition sparked in his blue eyes. When he spied Finn, he jumped down, flinging the reins at him. "Here. You've more need of it than me."

Finn looked at him in surprise. "Thanks," Finn said as he mounted. "Where can I send it back to you?"

"No need."

Where had he seen that cocky grin before?

"Just call it even." The boy gave a cheeky salute.

It was the lad who'd held his horse for him outside the tavern on the day he'd first encountered Sykes. The boy he'd given the blanket to.

"But I wouldn't be seen with that horse around here, if I was you."

Finn didn't hear him. He was already halfway across the bridge and headed toward Aylsham and Blackingham Manor.

⹑⹐

Kathryn was dreaming. Smoke. Smoke everywhere, pinching her nostrils, stinging her eyes. The wool house was burning. Her throat constricted. She couldn't cough. Couldn't breathe. *Jasmine! Where was Jasmine?* She struggled to call out for Magda. For Agnes. But her mouth wouldn't open. She couldn't move. Her limbs were heavy, her bones turned to lead. The wool that she was saving for her sons' celebration. Up in smoke. Agnes was crying. Poor Agnes. Crying for her shepherd with his melted flesh. No. Not crying for her John. Screaming Kathryn's name. Shrieks from far away.

"Milady. Wake up, milady. They've come. They've come!"

Kathryn woke with a start. The smoke was real. And Agnes was real, too, leaning over her, coughing through her shouts, the irises of her eyes bright with fear, the whites red and tearing.

Kathryn sat upright. "Jasmine! Agnes, where's the babe?"

"She's not in her cot, milady. I went there first. Magda must have taken her. Don't ye worry none, milady. The babe will be safe with Magda."

Kathryn tore open the bed curtains. No smoke was visible inside the flickering shadows, though the smell was strong enough to make her nostrils pinch.

"They've set fire to the pasture, milady."

"Don't worry. They'll not burn the house. We've done naught to them. And they'd be worse off without us. I'll go down and talk to them. Reason with them."

"There'll be no reasoning with a mob, milady. We should flee while we still have our lives."

"No, Agnes, we'll hold our ground. There will be someone among them whose mother, or child, or wife we've helped. You have probably fed most of them from your stewpot. They'll not harm two women alone."

Agnes only shook her head, muttering, "Even ye cannot talk sense with this rabble lot."

"Go back to the nursery. In case Magda forgets and returns there."

Kathryn pushed Agnes toward the door and reached for the handle, but it opened of its own volition.

"Simpson!"

Well, here was more trouble than a woman should have in a year of bad days! An unruly peasant rebellion and a traitorous devil all on the same day.

Her former steward stepped across her threshold. In his right hand he carried a torch. In his left a bucket.

Agnes stood her ground, between Kathryn and the steward. "I meant to warn ye, milady," she said. "This rotten apple came with the rebels. Using them for cover most like to worm his way back. Send him packin'. You don't need the likes of him."

For the briefest moment Kathryn entertained the notion of trying to draw him to her side. Bargain for his help against the rebels. But she could see the hard edge of hatred in his mocking smile. She would gain no champion here.

He set the bucket down, and grabbing Agnes by the arm, drew her dangerously close to the torch.

"I'm afraid you'll be needing a new cook before long, milady. This one is about to meet with an accident just inside your door. Killed by her own kind. Peasant rabble." He gave a mock bow. "But I'm still at your service."

He waved the flaming torch perilously close to Agnes's head, singeing some errant hairs that had escaped her cap. Agnes cried out in terror and slapped at the cap. Simpson laughed, tightening his grip on her. The smell of the burnt hair hovered with the smell of the burning fields.

Kathryn felt the old woman's terror like a pain in her stomach. Felt her fear of the flames, knew she saw only her husband's burnt body and hers beside it. She read, too, the mad intent in the overseer's eyes. He was just crazy enough to carry out his threat.

"Let her go, Simpson."

"*Let her go, Simpson,*" he mimicked in a falsetto voice. "Or you'll do what?"

Kathryn struggled to keep her voice even. Not stern, but not afraid.

"Let her go and we'll talk about your returning to Blackingham."

He threw back his head and laughed. "Return to what? A blackened heap of charred rubble?" But he lessened his grip on the cook.

"We can bargain, you and I. You help me save Blackingham from the rebels, and perhaps we can come to some permanent arrangement regarding your place at Blackingham. As you can see, it is difficult for a woman alone."

His eyes narrowed to slits. She could almost read the cunning behind them. He released the cook, but did not step away from the door. He still held the torch in his hand.

"Leave us, Agnes," Kathryn said. "Simpson and I have some terms of agreement to settle. Go to Saint Faith Priory until the trouble passes. I'll send Master Colin for you when it's over."

Agnes looked at her as though she were daft.

"But, milady—"

"Do as you are told, Agnes." Her voice, harsh now, demanding.

"Aye, milady." A small voice, unsteady. She edged between Simpson and the door. Squeezed through.

"Saint Faith Priory," Kathryn called after her sternly. She listened for the cook's footsteps on the stairs, heavy, plodding at first, then running.

When she could hear no more, she turned to the steward.

"How dare you enter my chamber! You are a thief and a liar. Get out before I order you the whipping that you should have gotten last harvest."

He stepped inside and shut the door behind him. Kathryn backed up, trying to keep a space between them.

"Tsk tsk, such harsh words! What about the bargain we just made, milady?" He feigned surprise, then his stare turned icy. "You think me an absolute fool? I know the old woman has gone for help."

The more Kathryn backed up, the more he pushed, until she was backed up against the bed. He held the bucket in one hand and the torch in the other.

"But I'll have satisfaction long before she can raise a cry." He set the bucket at her feet. "You remember the tar that you wanted. I brought you some."

The smell of smoke was stronger now, the house deadly quiet.

"Tar?" What was he blithering about? "What have you done with the others?" This time, it wasn't working. She couldn't bluff him as she had before. He sneered at her, staring her down. She could almost hear the hammering of her heart in the silence.

He waved the torch in her face, forcing her to draw back. "Others? There was only the old cook. It seems, milady, that you are abandoned. Nobody wants to be in service to an ill-tempered bitch. There are some *others*, but they're busy cleaning out your coffers. And smearing the old lord's room with pitch." He leered at her, curling his lip around the next words. "The illuminator's room. All that turpentine gum and paint soaked into the floors and table. It'll spark like lightning in a haywain."

Please, Holy Virgin, let Magda have remembered.

Kathryn started toward the door. "Get out of my way!"

He pushed her back toward the bed. She fell heavily against it.

"The tide has turned, milady. I'm giving the orders now." He leaned over and placed the lit torch in a wall sconce beside the bed. It teetered precariously, half in, half out. "I should have killed that old sow of a cook, sent her to join her drunken old shepherd, but the rebels will do it for me. She won't get far."

"You would murder an old woman who never harmed a living soul?"

Agnes was the closest thing she'd ever had to a mother. Holy Mother of God, keep her safe. And Jasmine. Please, God, please, let Magda keep her wits about her.

Simpson glowered at her as he busied himself with a brush and the contents of the bucket. He was painting something onto the bed curtains and the bedposts. It smelled strong and was black like pitch.

"What are you doing?" She tried to keep the panic out of her voice. She had faced him down once before. She could do it again. "You know if you do harm to me or my household, you'll hang for murder. I have but to ring this bell and my sons will come."

He threw back his head and laughed. The sound of it made her skin prickle. He was possessed by the devil.

"Muuurder." He gave a mock shudder. "It's so easy. I've gotten away with it, let's see, at least twice before."

"Twice?" Kathryn's mind was spinning as fast as her heart was pounding. She put her hands in her lap, gripping them tightly against her belly, pretending to listen. She felt the hard ridge of Finn's dagger. Yes. It was there. Beneath her overskirt. Hanging beside her rosary.

"I killed the priest."

Suddenly, his words had her full attention.

"Why so shocked? Never would've thought Ole Simpson, with his 'Yes, milady, no milady' would've had the gumption, eh? The priest overheard me selling the sheep, figured out, since you were always poor-mouthing, where some of your profits might be going. Milord scarcely paid attention. But you. You had to account for every bloody farthing. The bishop's priest said I owed a tithe of what I was stealing, or he'd have to turn me in." He lowered his voice to a husky whisper. "I gave him his tithe upside his head."

Fury gripped her. Fury at herself for being blind. For being so prideful that she thought she could intervene, twist matters around to save her sons. She should have trusted them. She should have trusted Finn. Yet there was that in her nature that only trusted herself. She repented that now. But it was too late. She thought of Finn's haunted eyes, the hard lines that framed his mouth whenever he said her name.

And it had all been this whoreson's doing.

She bit her lip until she tasted blood. She wanted to leap at him, spitting and biting, gouge out his eyes and tear his hair out by the roots. Her wrist tightened against the dagger under her skirts, twitching with the restraint that reason counseled. She longed to cut off his manhood and stuff it down his throat. But she would never be able to get her skirts up and loose the dagger in time. *Not yet.* She read what was in his eyes, bartered for time. "You said, 'twice,'" she said.

"You mean you haven't guessed? The wool house was my doing. The old shepherd knew I stole the wool pack. Threatened to tell you. Two pigeons with one stone. Made a nice bonfire. And then young Colin getting blamed. Well, that was just a bit of luck, a little something extra, you might say."

He put down the brush and reached out to stroke her breast. She shrugged him off, jerking her shoulders. But he just laughed. "Smoke's getting thicker. But I've one more piece of unfinished business. I mean to claim that which you stole from me."

"I? Stole from you?" She spat the words at him.

"Remember the little kitchen maid? The way I figure it, you're a good enough trade. A lay for a lay. A lady slut for a scullery slut." He lunged at her, pinning her to the bed.

She turned her face away, lest he read the lie in her eyes. "My flux is on me. Do you want to remove my bloody linen. Or shall I?"

He grimaced and froze momentarily, but recovered quickly, fumbling at the opening of his braies. "Jesu! I'll have what you owe me. I'm waist-steeped in blood already. Spread your legs, *milady*."

He was panting and his skin mottled, his features distorted, suffused with lust. He tore at her bodice with one hand, reached to push up her skirts with the other. One hand fastened on his, pushing it away. "I'll remove my own soiled linen. Do me that courtesy and spare yourself. Turn your head away." Her other hand groped beneath her skirt for the dagger. She jerked hard, pulling it from its sheath.

She lay still, the hand holding the dagger hidden at her side. She knew she would get but one chance. The smoke, the heavy weight of his disgusting body grinding on hers threatened to undo her spirit. She prayed she'd have the strength to strike. She had to live. *Holy Saviour, let my granddaughter be with Magda.*

Sweating and grunting, he gyrated on top of her. She willed herself not to fight him. *One more moment, Kathryn. One more moment.* And then she felt him push into her. She raised her arm high. She would only get one stab. She closed her eyes and prayed once more. *Holy Mother, guide my hand.* She fingered the heft of Finn's dagger for an instant, almost lovingly, as though she were seeking strength from it. And then, throwing her arm back until the joint hurt, she drove the dagger deep between Simpson's shoulder blades.

His body stiffened, his member wilted inside her. But he was still alive, his eyes rolling in his head, his lips forming a guttural curse. *Once more, Kathryn. It's no more than gutting an animal. You've seen Agnes do it enough.* But the knife would not withdraw. It was buried too far in, and he still held one arm pinned behind her. She worked the blade hard, up, then down until the blood spurted from his mouth. It dribbled hot against her skin, running in a stream between her breasts Then his body went limp on top of her, heavy, the lust on his face frozen into a death mask.

She stopped and closed her eyes, her hands dropping back against the bed. Her breath was labored. Her heart pounded a brutal rhythm that throbbed in her temples. Beneath his inert body, she was afraid she was going to drown in her own vomit. She pushed with what little strength she had left. His body rolled off her, his head thudding sickeningly against the bedpost, jarring it against the wall. The torch dislodged from its sconce and toppled onto the floor beside the bed.

Flames shot skyward, catching the edge of the counterpane, traveling up to Simpson's arm, which dangled beside the bed, little tongues of flame licking at his sleeve. Kathryn lurched forward, but her skirt was caught beneath Simpson's body. Tugging frantically at the fabric, she reached back to push him off her skirt, just as the curtains of the great four-poster bed burst into flame, igniting the feather ticking. The smell of burning hair and tar and feathers singed the air around her, choking her, burning her eyes. She struggled to pull herself free. Heat seared her lungs.

One last lunge and she felt the fabric of her skirt tear away.

The smoke was so dense she could see nothing but the silver crucifix hanging at the foot of her bed. It glowed in the heat and seemed to swell in size. The face of the suffering Christ, bathed with the light from the fire, looked almost as though it were made not of metal but flesh, warm melting flesh.

Kathryn struggled to breathe. Tiny flames attached to the burning feathers and floated through the air like some great fiery Pentecostal blaze.

She tried to run, but her legs did not respond. Skewered by a shred of fabric that still pinned her to the corpse of the man she'd just killed? Or transfixed by the face of the watching Christ? It was the same face that had watched over the widow's bed she'd shared with Finn. The same face that had watched over her when she birthed her sons, when they came squalling into the world, and the midwife had laid them on her stomach. The face that had watched during the long hours of her fevered ravings. The face she'd seen so often that it had become just another furnishing. And He had been there all the time.

Watching over her.

Dame Julian's Mother Christ.

Her clothing caught first, and then that great mass of silvery-white, unbound hair.

She didn't hear Finn climbing the steps. Didn't hear him frantically calling her name. She didn't hear her own voice calling to Colin and Alfred. But in the flames that danced around her, she saw their faces, glowing with radiance and bathed in a golden light.

Kathryn held out her arms to them and stood, transfixed by that illumination, until the fire offered up her body like a giant candle before a fiery molten altar.

THIRTY-TWO

Littera scripta manet.
THE WRITTEN WORD ABIDES.

aster Finn. We did all that we could do."

The prioress at Saint Faith's looked at him with sympathetic eyes. They sat in the small solar where the prioress received visitors. She sat beside him on a plain wooden bench across from a small altar. Finn didn't trust himself to speak. He kept his gaze averted.

"Lady Kathryn did not suffer more than she could bear." The prioress placed her hand on Finn's shoulder in a gesture meant to comfort. "Thanks to you, she was not burned as badly as we had feared. It was the smoke. Her breath was very labored."

She paused as if studying her words carefully, as if the saying of them pained her. "She lived through the night."

When he still said nothing, she added, "You must not blame yourself. You did right to bring her here. It was the will of our Lord." She opened her mouth as if to say more but did not.

Finally, he was able to look up, his voice gruff with misery. "I want to see her."

The prioress shook her head. Her wimple settled against her face so that he couldn't see her eyes. "She is being prepared . . . for her journey. It is best that you remember her as . . . as you knew her. Before . . . before the fire. You can do nothing for her now. She belongs to God."

He tried to conjure such a memory: Kathryn bent over her needlework in the garden, her face half-hidden in the shade of a hawthorne bush; Kathryn rising from his bed, trailing the bed linen behind her like a regal train; Kathryn holding his grandchild, her face glowing with love. He had tried to cling to these pictures, painted them painstakingly on his closed eyelids all through the night as he tossed, wide-eyed and horror-filled, on the straw mat in the priory guest house. He'd rifled the rooms of memory for her image: her face, her smile, the way her eyes softened when she spoke of her sons, the way her hair flowed round her slender neck when he kissed her, the taste of her mouth, the smell of her skin. But demons got inside his head and painted over the tender colors, the beloved forms, swiping furiously with the colors of smoke and fire, replacing all with that last hellish image no mortal's brush stroke could blot out.

She'd seemed so light when he carried her from the burning house that he feared her bones had turned to charcoal. Her hair was gone, even her eyebrows, and her face was dark and sooty. He dared not touch it, lest her skin fall away beneath his fingers. Her eyes were open, the pupils bright and dark like glittering onyx. Her mouth moved and he leaned forward to hear her. "Finn. You've come," she said as though she'd expected him all along. Then she whispered, "Take me to Saint Faith Priory."

There had been no one to help him with her. Everything was burning: house, stables, brewery. In the end, he'd ridden with her to the priory, cradling her in his arms like a child. She'd lain so still, he feared she was already dead. He begged her not to die, tried to ask her about the child. But she seemed not to hear. Once, she opened her eyes and spoke.

"I've seen him," she said. But the words were so soft, he wasn't sure he'd heard aright. And they made no sense.

Now, the prioress tried to spare his feelings, spoke tactfully of "her journey," but he knew what she meant. The sisters were sewing Kathryn into her shroud. And the prioress was right; it was an image he should forgo. His heart could not bear the weight of one more picture.

"You need not worry," the prioress assured him. "We will see that she sleeps in a holy place. It was her request that she rest here."

"Mother, I have no purse to pay for masses. But I will—"

She waved her hand in a gesture of dismissal. "None is necessary. Last night, before—before she went to sleep, she signed her deeds to us. She paid a corrody. She signed Blackingham over to us in return for sanctuary. And though the buildings are gone, the land is ample to see to her needs and fulfill the terms."

"The terms?"

"She asked that revenues from the land be used for translating the Holy Scripture into English." She averted her gaze, fingered nervously the beads of her rosary. "And I admit to secretly having some sympathy with this cause. I have read some of Master Wycliffe's writings on the subject. We will do it discreetly, of course. There will be enough left from the rents to care for her body and her soul."

"You've had no troubles from the rebels?"

She sighed. "We are a poor house, Master Finn. We've nothing to plunder. There's some security in poverty. And news came while you were gone back to Blackingham that Bishop Despenser has already hanged some of the rebels who attacked Saint Mary's College in Cambridge. They'll be afraid to bother us this close to Norwich."

The mention of the bishop's name penetrated the fog of grief that surrounded him. Should he go back? Turn himself in and offer to fight, gain some revenge by helping put down the rebels? But he'd no fight with them. He'd seen Simpson's body. A fool could figure out that he'd been the one responsible for the destruction at Blackingham. Other torches might have lit the fire, but his was the flint that set the spark. The whole world had gone mad. Where did a sane man's allegiance lie in such a time?

The prioress was talking again. He tried to concentrate on her words. She was his last connection to Kathryn.

"When you went back, did you find anyone else alive?" she asked.

"Nothing could be alive inside that hell. The roof had already collapsed. The house was a smoldering ember."

The prioress crossed herself. "You did not find your granddaughter, then. I'm sorry. But all may not be lost. Lady Kathryn said before . . . last night, she said to tell you to seek the child among Blackingham's crofters."

A tiny sliver of hope pricked his heart.

"She said she thought the child was alive. She gave her to a scullery maid to hide. Lady Kathryn said to tell you that Jasmine would be waiting for her grandfather to come for her."

"Is that all? Did she say anything else?"

"I'm afraid not. She was very weak."

Which maid? He was trying hard to remember the kitchen girl. Was she the quiet one who came to the prison with Kathryn and the babe?

"There was one other thing, now that I remember. When she signed for her corrody, I asked if she had any heirs."

"She does. She has two sons. Though I saw neither of them. Blackingham was apparently defenseless when it was attacked."

"She says her sons are dead. I asked her how she could be sure and she said a mother knows. We will say masses for their souls."

"There was another, a faithful servant who may have died in the fire. She was a good woman. I think Kathryn would want a mass said for her soul as well."

"We will abide by Lady Kathryn's wishes," the prioress said, getting up. "You may stay in the guest house as long as you like, Master Finn," she said. "I will pray for you that you will find your granddaughter. And that you will find our Lord's peace."

It was kindly put, but it was a dismissal. Finn stood up too. He thanked her for her concern and started to leave, then turned back. He reached inside his shirt and removed a pendant on a leather string from around his neck. "Mother, would you place this in her hand, bury it with her? It was given me once by a holy woman. As a kind of promise, a token of faith. I have no other remembrance to leave with her."

"I can think of no greater talisman to leave with a loved one than one worn close to the heart. It is better than gold."

The heavy oak door to the priory scraped closed behind him with all the finality of stone rolling across the opening of a tomb. The sun was struggling to break through the morning mist, the air already laden with June heat. In the distance, the booming call of a bittern nesting among the reeds sounded like a muffled foghorn.

❧

Finn searched for hours. He called on every crofter, peered into every weaver's hut between Blackingham and Aylsham. No mother had seen a child other than her own, each assured him with frightened eyes, hugging her little ones to her skirts when she heard his tale. If any had, would she have given his granddaughter up? Or would she hide the child from him out of fear of retribution? He could read anxiety in their eyes. Some of them must have guessed their menfolk had gone too far this time. Hungry for news, one or two made inquiry. Had he heard the bishop's soldiers were cutting down rebels? Had he heard the king had granted amnesty?

Finn answered them all curtly. He was too numb to care. His horse was almost as weary as he was, but he could not bring himself to go back to the priory guest house. Kathryn was too near there, sleeping in her linen shroud. He could ride toward Yarmouth Harbor, take ship to Flanders. Even a penniless artist could make ends meet there. Or he could return to his cell, to his paint pots, and throw himself on the bishop's mercy.

Maybe he would be lucky and Despenser would never even know he'd left. The prioress had said the bishop was in Cambridge putting down the rebellion. Unprecedented, in his memory, for a man of the Church to strap on a sword. But somehow it did not surprise him. He shuddered at the thought of the endless games of chess. the future commissions for paintings for which he had no heart. He would grow old and feeble in his cell like a hermit. His eyes would dim with the years, and when he became useless to the bishop, then what? Would they turn him out to beg in the streets or execute him for a crime long forgotten? Either way, he didn't much care.

In the end, he turned his horse back toward Norwich, to the only home he'd known these last two years.

It was almost dusk. There was an alehouse that he remembered just outside the town walls. He had a powerful thirst and not a penny to his name, but what alewife would not trade a pint for a flattering sketch? He hardly noticed the small party coming toward him—a woman and two small children. One of the children pointed at him excitedly. Or at his horse? He remembered he was riding the dead constable's mare Better to give them a wide berth. He dug his heels into the mare's side and averted his gaze.

And then he heard his name.

"Master Finn, please, Master Finn."

Finn reined in his horse and looked down. He had mistaken the dwarf for a child. It was his old friend and a young woman. And one child.

"Thank God it's you, Master Finn. I could hardly believe it. I feared you were dead. I was that scared when they said the rebels had attacked the prison, killed the constable. On our way to the fens, we were, Magda and me. And the babe. We lost hope of finding you. Thank God you stopped, Master Finn, thank God."

But Finn wasn't listening. He was looking at the blond child squirming in the girl's arms. It was Jasmine. It was his granddaughter. His arms twitched with wanting to grab her, yet he could not make the motion. He could do nothing but stare at her from the back of his horse. And she stared back at him out of cornflower-blue eyes, Colin's eyes. Her mouth was pretty, wide and bow-shaped. Kathryn's mouth. Her soft baby's skin was more cream than pink. Like Rose. Like Rebekka. It hurt to look and yet he could not turn away.

"My Magda saved the child from the fire. She hid her in the bee tree."

"Your Magda?"

"Aye. Mine. She says she'll marry with me." Then the swagger died from Tom's voice, as though he knew it was not right that he should display his happiness in so near sight of Finn's grief. "Now that milady is . . . now that milady doesn't need her."

"And the child?"

"We thought that you should know." The dwarf blushed crimson.

Finn did not respond.

"I mean to say, there's some talk that you . . . well, that you might want, that because of . . ."

"You've heard correctly, Tom. She is my grandchild. And you could have done me no greater service than to bring her to me." He turned to Magda. "And you, Mistress Magda, to keep her safe."

The girl curtsied shyly but said nothing. She cut her gaze at Half-Tom.

Finn continued, "I am a poor prisoner. I have nothing but the clothes on my back, but if there is anything I can do to repay—"

" 'Tis but an old debt discharged. And happy I am to have it off my shoulders."

The dwarf nodded in the direction of the stone cottage not far from where they were standing. For the first time, Finn recognized where they were. The first time he'd seen Half-Tom, the wounded child, the dead pig had been just a few yards beyond where they now stood. How sure of himself he'd been then, knowing what to do, shouting directions, riding fiercely into town on his borrowed horse with the bleeding child in his arms like some chivalrous knight out of an overwrought tale. But the child had died. And Rose. And Kathryn. That had been another man. That was an eternity ago. He looked down now at another blond child.

She reached out her arms to him. He could not take her. He had searched frantically to find her. But he had not thought beyond finding her.

Half-Tom looked at Magda. Magda looked at Half-Tom and nodded.

"Master Finn, we will take the child and care for her. We only thought . . ."

The child leaned toward the horse's head, reaching for the bright bits of metal on the bridle, and Finn saw that, next to the little silver cross, she too wore a hazelnut on a string. He could almost hear Dame Julian's voice explaining to him gently as she handed him a hazelnut—the hazelnut he'd left with Kathryn—from the wooden bowl on her writing table. *It lasts, and ever shall last; for God loveth it.* She had been so sure of that Divine Love. So sure that the Creator loved the created world which He held in the palm of His hand. And Finn had wanted to believe in that love too. But the anchoress was shut away, out of the world, away from the hurt and the pain and the calumny and the suffering of the innocent, with only her own pure heart for company. She did not see the world he lived in. And he could not feel the love she talked about.

He could not feel it now. But he had seen it. He'd seen it in Kathryn's sacrifice for her sons. He'd seen it in Rebekka's love for Rose. And he remembered. He remembered how he'd felt that same love for his daughter. But could the memory of that love cut through the numbness he felt? How could he, penniless, on the run, care for a child?

"Master Finn?" Half-Tom asked with his eyes. "It will be dark soon."

Finn held out his arms to the child. She went to him willingly, climbed up beside him, patted the horse's head. "Horsie," she said.

The tired horse pawed at the ground as if rejuvenated by the child's touch.

"I have nothing for her. I have nothing to buy food for her. I cannot even buy clean linen to wrap her in."

Magda smiled. "Sir, she is bright. She will tell you when she has to go. She will tug on your sleeve."

Tug on his sleeve. Finn felt as though he had been ambushed. Ambushed by Dame Julian's Mother Christ. How could he hand her back, surrender the gentle weight of her to another, this child of Rose, this child of his beloved Rebekka? Kathryn's grandchild. His grandchild. His child.

Magda reached into her pocket and withdrew a small parcel wrapped in linen. "I brought her some clothes from my mother's house. They are not fine, but they are clean." And she handed him the bundle. He watched as tears formed in the well of her eyes. She knew it too, this mother love. Even though she had never borne a child.

"Here, take this." Half-Tom, his voice raspy with emotion, pressed a small bag of coins into Finn's hand. " 'Tis not a lot, but it'll stand for a meal or two."

But Finn's mind was already working with strategy. "You keep it, Tom. You'll need it for your new bride. I'm too much in your debt already. I can sell the horse in Yarmouth. It should fetch fifteen pounds. More than enough for passage to Flanders and papers and pens and food for the two of us."

"Horsie," Jasmine said. She looked up at Finn, then at Magda, as though she was about to cry, held out her hands to be taken back. Magda patted her, whispered something in her ear. Finn couldn't hear what she said, but the child nodded, bravely fighting back her tears. She gave a subdued little sniffle. "Here. Look what I made for you," Magda said, loudly enough for him to hear. And she thrust a crudely stitched rag doll into Jasmine's arms. The child played with the doll for a minute before settling her head against Finn's chest.

"Ye'll not make Yarmouth tonight, Master Finn. Best to stop at Saint Faith's."

He could feel the weight of the child against him, oddly comforting. *I shall make all things well. I shall make all well that is not well and thou shall see it.*

Did he see it? All he saw was the sleeping child with her head resting against his breast. All he felt was the burden of his grief. He was too weak to choose, but the child had chosen for him.

Finn turned his horse toward Yarmouth.

Behind him, he thought he heard Magda give a stifled little whimper, but when he turned she was waving courageously and smiling at him. Half-Tom stood beside her with his arm around her.

With the dying light behind, he looked like a much taller man.

EPILOGUE

athryn woke slowly, pulled from her dream of Finn carrying her in his arms, his face close to hers, his eyes no longer cold and unforgiving. In her dream, he carried her lightly, as though her body were made of air.

In her dream she felt no pain.

But now Finn was gone. He *was* gone, *wasn't* he? Fled to safety with the child? Finn was gone, unless she'd dreamed that, too. And the pain was back. But not more than she could bear.

Her scalp felt tight, and her left hand ached with a drawing sensation. A burning pain crept up her neck and into her face, tingling, pricking. Her fingers touched a bandage beneath her cheekbone where the burning took root. She winced, and a soft groan escaped her lips.

Immediately, Agnes was there, bending over her, scolding.

"No. Don't touch your face." She held a cup to Kathryn's lips. "Here. Drink this. 'Tis wine laced with milk from the seedpod of a poppy. It will take away the hurt."

Kathryn pushed it away.

"It will take away my sense, too." The words felt clumsy on her lips. "The pain is tolerable. If I am to live, then I must live in this world. Not in a fog of dreams."

Agnes placed the cup on a chest beside her bed, no bigger than a cot, but soft with a down mattress. Kathryn lay on her back, propped up slightly on feather pillows. Apparently, her back was not burned. She shifted her weight tentatively, and the only pain that answered was along her left side.

The light from an east-facing window sliced into the cell-like room, hurting her eyes.

"Where are we?" she asked.

"Saint Faith Priory. I came here two weeks ago, like you told me." Agnes hesitated briefly. "The illuminator brought you." Her tone carried some accusation that she did not voice.

So Finn did carry her here, Kathryn thought. That part, at least, had not been a dream. And the forgiveness in Finn's eyes?

"Did he find Jasmine?"

"Ye don't remember? Aye, he found the little one. Magda kept her safe from the fire. She and the dwarf brought the babe to Finn. But I thought ye knew. Ye took naught for the pain until we heard."

She frowned as she said the next, her tone registering her disapproval. "Ye told the prioress to send Finn away. Ye deliberately deceived him."

Kathryn sighed with relief for the child and closed her eyes. The left eye closed slowly, sending a stab of pain shooting from its stretched lid. But she could feel the warmth from the candle flame on her right cheek. Its warmth was strangely comforting, reminding her of the vision of Julian's Mother Christ, glowing with life above her flaming bed, reminding her, too, of the faces of her sons bathed in holy light.

Colin and Alfred.

In trying to keep them, she had lost them forever. She felt a stab of grief, raw and bright as new blood. She pushed it aside.

"And Blackingham is gone?" she asked.

"Aye, milady. Blackingham is lost to us." Agnes's voice choked on the last word.

It was her home, too, Kathryn thought. Her home, as much as mine. Kathryn wanted to offer words of comfort, words of gratitude, but she lacked the strength.

Agnes removed the bandage from beneath Kathryn's eye. As the air hit it, Kathryn sucked in her breath with the pain. Agnes dressed the burn, gently, with a soothing ointment of comfrey leaves and flowers of Saint John's wort; then she laid on a cooling compress and reapplied the loose linen bandage. The ointment, or Agnes's touch, was soothing. Kathryn felt the muscles in her face relax.

"Ye know, milady, ye should never have sent the illuminator away. I never saw a man so besotted with a woman." Agnes wiped her hands of the ointment, and reaching into her voluminous skirt, withdrew an object. "He left this. He wanted you to take something of him to your grave. He told the prioress it was all he had."

Agnes laid the hazelnut, set in its little pewter backing like some great saint's relic, in the palm of Kathryn's right hand. She recognized it. Finn had said it was a gift from the anchoress. She wrapped her fingers around it, clutching it until the pewter bit into her flesh. The whole world in the palm of God's hand—or something like that. She couldn't remember what Finn said it meant, exactly. But it was enough that he had left it for her. Enough that it had once rested against his skin.

She lay against the soft pillows. The room receded until all she could see was Agnes's stern face in the glow of the candle.

"If the prioress—if I—had not sent Finn away, he would be dead by now," she said. "Or worse. He would live out his life as Henry Despenser's slave." It was hard to form the words. Then, murmuring low, more to satisfy herself than Agnes: "Finn has Jasmine. She will keep his spirit whole."

"And you, milady, what do you have?"

I have the memory of the forgiveness in his eyes. I have the memory of him.

"I have you, Agnes. And you have me," she said. "And that will have to be enough for now."

Her left hand had started to twitch with a tic, each tic a stab. "Now, I think, I'll have the tiniest sip of your special medicine to help me sleep. You need sleep, too, Agnes." She pointed to the pallet beside her bed where Agnes had kept her faithful vigil. "Don't sleep here tonight. The chapel bell tolls matins. There is a lot of the night left. Find yourself a bed of your own in the guest house. Tomorrow is soon enough for us to contemplate our future."

"If you are certain, milady. These old bones would like a soft bed, sure enough."

Agnes blew out the candle, but left the rushlight on in its sconce. It had burned low as well, casting long shadows in the room. Kathryn felt the sleeping draught begin its work, softening the edge of her pain. She clutched the hazelnut in her hand. Such a tiny thing.

A current of air stirred the room. She heard a sound, almost a whisper.

All will be well.

"Agnes, did you say something?"

But Agnes was gone. There was only silence in the room and the flickering shadows.

It must be the medicine, she thought. Or mayhap some inner voice, reminding her of Julian's words. She closed her eyes, searching for the dream, or memory, whichever it had been, that brought her comfort.

Again the whispered words filled her head.

This time each word was distinct and clear.

All will be well.

And Kathryn almost believed it.

AUTHOR'S NOTE

his is a work of fiction, but the characters of Bishop Henry
Despenser, John Wycliffe, Julian of Norwich, and John Ball are historical
figures whose histories I have braided with the lives of my fictional characters. Henry Despenser is best remembered as the "warring bishop" for the
bloody and violent manner in which he put down the Peasants' Revolt of
1381 and for his subsequent unsuccessful military campaign against Pope
Clement VII during the Great Schism of the West that divided the Roman
Catholic Church. He is also remembered for having made a gift of a five-
paneled altarpiece, known as the Despenser retable, or Despenser reredos, to
Norwich Cathedral in celebration of his bloody triumph over the Peasants'
Revolt. He had the reredos framed with the coats of arms of the families who
assisted him in this massacre. This altarpiece may be seen today in Saint
Luke's Chapel, Norwich Cathedral. During the Reformation it was turned
upside down and used as a table to hide it from the reformers and then forgotten for more than four hundred years. As the story goes, during the middle of the last century, someone dropped a pencil beneath the altar cloth and,

bending to retrieve it, found the wonderful paintings of the five panels depicting the Passion of Christ. The painter's name has been lost in history.

John Wycliffe is remembered as the "morning star of the reformation" because of his efforts at reform within the Church and because he was the first to translate the Bible into the English language, thereby reshaping not only Church history but cultural history. He was charged with heresy, dismissed from Oxford, and his writings were banned. But he was never brought to trial and continued to write and preach until his death by stroke in 1384 at his home in Lutterworth. His entire translation was completed by his followers in 1388, seven years after my story ends. In 1428, Pope Martin V ordered John Wycliffe's bones to be dug up, burned, and his ashes discarded in the river Swift. The Lollard movement he founded continued to thrive underground and eventually merged with the new Protestant forces of the Reformation.

John Ball was excommunicated around 1366 for inflammatory sermons advocating a classless society. According to historical sources, he urged the killing of lords and prelates. He was incarcerated in Maidstone Prison when the Peasants' Revolt of 1381 broke out but was released by Kentish rebels and accompanied them to London. After the rebellion collapsed, Ball was tried and hanged at Saint Albans.

About Julian of Norwich we know very little outside of her writings. She was the first woman to write in the English language. Her *Divine Revelations* have lately enjoyed a resurgence of interest, largely fostered by feminists who were intrigued by Julian's concept of a mother God. A close reading of her work certainly shows her to be an independent thinker for her times and a woman of deep and abiding faith. Historical documents indicate that she was still living as a recluse in Norwich as late as 1413, seven years after the demise of Bishop Despenser.

ACKNOWLEDGMENTS

I wish to acknowledge the readers who have given me valuable feedback during the writing of this book: Dick Davies, Mary Strandlund, and Ginger Moran, who critiqued my work when it was in its formative stage, and Leslie Lytle and Mac Clayton, who worked with me in the completion of it. Thanks also to Pat Wiser and to Noelle Spears (my youngest reader of seventeen), who read and commented on my final draft. A special thank-you is due to my writing partner of many years, Meg Waite Clayton, author of *The Language of Light*, who suffered with me through many drafts.

I wish also to acknowledge a debt to the writers from whom I have learned. Thanks to Manette Ansay for her valuable tips on the integration of internal and external landscape in fiction. Thanks to Valerie Miner for her excellent teaching on evoking a sense of place—one of the Half-Tom scenes developed from a writing exercise in her wonderful workshop in Key West—and thanks to Max Byrd for his excellent lecture on rhetorical devices delivered at the Squaw Valley Community of Writers workshop and for his timely and personal words of encouragement.

To my agent, Harvey Klinger, for rescuing me from the slough of the slush pile, and my editor, Hope Dellon, for her editorial skill and literary instincts, I offer heartfelt gratitude. I feel truly blessed to have two such consummate professionals on my side.

In the life of a writer, the importance of the role of encourager cannot be overstated. I wish to thank those who, with their words and actions, have helped me nurture my fragile dream of publication: Helen Wirth, who edited my first published short story; Dr. Jim Clark, for his professional advice and words of encouragement; the family members and friends who expressed interest and belief in my abilities, and finally, my love and appreciation to my husband, Don, whose unwavering support sustains me. Last, and most important, I thank the One from whom all blessings flow.

THE ILLUMINATOR

by Brenda Rickman Vantrease

For more reading group suggestions visit
www.readinggroupgold.com

St. Martin's Griffin

A Reading Group Gold Selection

Reading
Group
Gold

A NOTE FROM THE AUTHOR

I grew up in a series of small southern towns. My favorites were always the ones with the biggest libraries. Learning to read was the singular most liberating moment of my life. I still remember the day I brought home my third-grade reader, a book of real stories—not those skinny little See Spot Run books. This one had some heft and a yellow cover, and I read it all the way through in three days. I particularly liked a fairytale about a knight trying to win a fair maiden by the impossible feat of riding his horse up a glass mountain. I can still see the illustration of that plumed and helmeted knight spurring his white steed up that shimmering blue glass mountain.

My father was a Baptist minister, and some of his congregations were farther away from the library than my bicycle or roller skates could take me. When I ran out of books, I would dig out my father's old college text, a massive tome entitled *Masterworks of World Literature.* Boredom drove me to the epic poetry of John Milton and *The Nibelungenlied* and *El Cid,* the English poets, a little Sophocles, even Oscar Wilde, when I would have preferred to be reading Nancy Drew or a teenage romance novel—a beneficial deprivation.

I also made up stories in my head. My first published effort was a poem submitted by my ninth-grade English teacher to a student anthology. (I haven't written any poetry since—maybe because when I was called up to the stage in assembly to receive my award I stumbled on the steps. Overcoming shyness is not something one can learn in the pages of a book.) While still in high school, I received my first form rejection slip from *Ladies' Home Journal.* I'm still embarassed just thinking how awful that story was—and I still remember how much that first rejection hurt. At sixteen, my writer's heart was very naïve and very tender.

Libraries have always been important to me. I graduated with a B.A. in English from Belmont University, working my way through school in the college library, I met my husband Don on the steps of that same library, and late in my career in education went back to school for a library degree, finishing up my teaching career in the metropolitan Nashville school system as a librarian. During my twenty-five-year tenure, I earned a master's degree and a doctorate from Middle Tennessee State University, traveled, worked summer jobs, read books on writing—and even wrote a little fiction. But it was only after I retired from teaching in 1991 that I really had time and energy to pursue my dream. Don and I used our vacations to travel to writers' conferences and workshops from Maine to California. During that time I piled up a lot of rejection slips, but a few of my essays and short stories found homes in periodicals and anthologies, among them *VeriTales* (Fall Creek Press), *Thema,* and *Coast to Coast.*

Seeing my first novel in print has been the culmination of a lifetime of dreams. And the best part—*The Illuminator* is in my local library, and a lot of other libraries besides. Right there, on the shelf. With the call number Fic/Van. ❧

Photo Credit:
Nancy Crampton

AN INTERVIEW WITH BRENDA

Q: What inspired you to write *The Illuminator*?

A: The story of *The Illuminator* began with two documents. The first was *Revelations of Divine Love* by Julian of Norwich, the first woman to write in the English language. I was fascinated by the life of this anchoress and mystic: What would cause a woman to go voluntarily into a kind of tomb and give up all human contact, never to see the sky or smell the flowers again? Originally, I thought the book would be all about her, but as it turned out, the other characters just kind of bubbled up and took over.

The other document was the first original illuminated manuscript I had ever seen: *The Book of Kells,* at Trinity College in Dublin. To think that those brilliant colors and exquisite detail had survived since the ninth century gave me chills. I could almost hear the scratching of the pens on the vellum as the monks labored in their ancient scriptorium to complete the gospel in time for the dedication of their new monastery at Kells. It has 680 pages and we are told that only two have no color. It is thought by many to be the finest example of the illuminator's art in Western Europe.

Q: What is it like mixing fact with fiction? Julian of Norwich, John Wycliffe, Bishop Henry Despenser, and John Ball are all historical figures. How did you go about inventing your other characters?

A: It's a wonderful challenge—like taking two textures, silk and linen, and trying to weave them into a whole that has integrity and beauty. Sometimes I feel a little bit frightened, thinking that I'm taking too much liberty with a historical character, but I hope not; I try to stay attuned to the reputation and the character that person established in history. With the fictional characters, I try to conjure the people who might have interacted with these historical figures, mere silhouettes at first, then gradually they emerge for me like ghosts in a darkroom. That's the way Finn and Kathryn came. Occasionally, almost magically, a character just pops onto my computer screen fully formed, shoving and pushing her way in, and will not leave. The character of Magda, for example, was not planned; I never intended for this little urchin to develop her own subplot. I opened a door seeking a piece of furniture for my kitchen hearth and wise little Magda was there, seeing visions and colors and soul-lights; she was a gift. Half-Tom was the same. He was never intended to have any other use than to introduce Finn to the reader.

Q: Were any of the characters based on you?

A: None of the characters is based on me. The only connection I have with Kathryn is the miserable migraine headaches that plague her—and perhaps a little bit of the controlling personality that brings her such pain. It is much more fun to write about imaginary characters: I don't have to worry about misrepresenting a person who actually lived and breathed and exerted influence on others, though the research into their lives is very stimulating to my imagination. And therein lies the danger, I suppose.

Q: How did you go about researching *The Illuminator,* and what did you find particularly interesting or surprising?

A: I have always been a castle prowler. I love poking around cathedrals and old medieval ruins of castles and abbeys, and I love reading about them. A friend and I once got lost in the Doges' Palace and wound up in the dungeons, and another time I talked my way into Cardiff Castle after it had closed, just me and the pecocks and a few ghosts.

Since first seeing *The Book of Kells,* I've seen a lot of original manuscripts in museums—some books no bigger than a human hand. I think the most interesting thing to me is how varied the illuminations are, how much they reflect the personality of the artist, some pious and conventional in the pictures painted in the marginalia and some quite playful. And also how very expensive they must have been.

Q: What do you think about the role that organized religion plays in society, both at the time of this book and in the present day?

A: In many ways, organized religion has given us the gift of civilization. Great art, music, architecture, even universities, which were sponsored by the Church, came out of the very period when the Church appeared to be so corrupt. So organized religion has done much in our civilization—in Western civilization surely, and I think also in Eastern civilization—to further all good things.

At the same time, some people point to the fact that a lot of evil has come out of organized religion. In this book I am dealing with one of the most corrupt periods in the Catholic Church, and I think that's a warning to all of us: when any institution, whether political, religious, or corporate, becomes too powerful, it can act like a magnet for human frailty and become an instrument of evil rather than good—or, as John Wycliffe might say, a tool of the devil. History records such abuse of power. We witness it today in government and corporate scandals and atrocities committed in the name of religion.

Q: Why do you think there has been a renewal of interest in Julian of Norwich in recent years?

A: I believe her emphasis on Jesus as the "Mother God" has appealed to the feminist movement. It's not that Julian ever said that Jesus was a woman—far from it: she was just talking about how the love of Christ was most like a mother's love in nature. But I think the idea of a Mother God appeals to women who sometimes feel shut out by the strictures placed by the traditional church.

Q: Who are your favorite heroes or heroines in fiction? In real life?

A: I don't know that I have a favorite hero in fiction or real life. Maybe that's why I created Finn: my idea of the hero. But the most memorable characters are the ones who are tragically flawed in some way like the character of Heathcliff in *Wuthering Heights*. I love survivors, like Defoe's *Moll Flanders*. In real life the persons I admire most are those who can transcend self-interest in a way that most of us ordinary humans can never do—like the medics in Doctors Without Borders or Mother Teresa. We usually never even know their names.

Q: If you could meet any writer, alive or dead, who would it be, and what would you like to talk about?

A: William Shakespeare. He wrote about historical figures, lifting many of his characters from *Holinshed's Chronicles,* a history book published in 1578. He also wrote to please the crown—constantly sucking up. I'd like to talk to him about the artistic tension between representing history accurately and distorting it to please his patron, especially in the historical plays. The character of Macbeth, for example—Shakespeare really does a number on a man some historians believe was a good king. And I would especially like to ask him about the character of Sir John Oldcastle, the prototype for Falstaff, who figures hugely in my next novel. I know Shakespeare felt the pressure keenly. As it turned out, Sir John's descendent was the minister of entertainment at court and complained bitterly that the Bard had turned his illustrious ancestor, who died a Christian martyr, into a cowardly buffoon. Oops! Feeling the heat and not wanting to give up this wonderful character, Shakespeare hastily wrote a disclaimer and changed the name to Falstaff in his next play.

Q: Before becoming a novelist, you worked as a teacher and librarian. How has that influenced your writing?

A: Obviously, books and history have been a common theme in all of my endeavors, but beyond the subject matter, I believe that teaching has given me a sense of compassion for the human cond-ition. I have seen children—young children, older children, adolescents—lead very difficult, tortured lives, and I've come to understand that we all have a struggle, whatever our age. I like to think that watching these children as they develop and face their partic-ular challenges has helped me to understand human nature.

Q: Is imagined narrative as powerful as narrative based on factual experiences? Less powerful? Less true?

A: It is my opinion that the best fiction offers more truth than the best nonfiction because true fiction opens a window into the soul of the writer, revealing truths we as writers may not even know about ourselves. The pot simmers. The writer's subconscious bubbles up and a character emerges of whom the writer had no conscious awareness. Don't blame it or the muse. That character/event/emotion—glorious or monstrous as he or she or it may be—came from the heart and mind, the truth, of the writer. An intimacy exists between reader and writer in the best fiction because the writer exposes his soul or at least what lives in his imagination. And if the writer doesn't expose his soul, his fiction will be lacking. Like poetry, narrative provides a language that explains those metaphysical aspects of life that we cannot explain with facts. The quickest way to the heart is through the imagintion.

Q: How do we find and shape the story inside us? What are its elements?

A: We find the story much in the same way Michelangelo found his subject in marble. We free it. But before we can free it from the stone of our conscious mind, we must first discover it by finding a way in. It can begin with an image. C. S. Lewis says that his famous classic, *The Lion, the Witch and the Wardrobe*, began with a picture in his head of a faun carrying an umbrella and parcels in a snowy wood. It can begin with a scene, a question, a character—something hardly more than a spark, but if William Blake is to be believed that's a divine spark. Then we chisel away. Sometimes it takes years, sometimes it takes a life-time; think of Michelangelo's prisoners only half sculpted, half freed from their marble blocks. We find it by playing with the elements of narrative. ✍

Reading
Group
Gold

BEFORE GUTENBERG
Book Production in the Middle Ages

The image of a solitary monk toiling away at a slant-top desk comes readily to mind when we think of books produced before Johannes Gutenberg invented the printing press in the mid-1400s. And indeed many books were created just this way. But not all.

A book was a highly desirable commodity, a status symbol proclaiming that its owner—whether an illiterate knight who might not be able to read or a philosophy student in the burgeoning university system—was wealthy, educated, and religious, in an age when all of these things mattered greatly. An entire industry grew up to feed this need. From the largest guild of bookmakers in Paris to the monk-scribe toiling in his abbey scriptorium, book production provided employment in an economy that was shifting from the feudal model of farmers tied to their masters' land to artisans working in thriving towns and boroughs.

First, the parchment maker prepared the calfskin—a medium-sized prayer book required the skin of twenty animals—by curing, stretching, and scraping the hides. (Paper was also produced, but considered to be inferior because it was not lasting.) A stationer sold parchment, along with the nibs and quills, pens and brushes, paints and leather inkpots—these he might make in his shop or purchase wholesale from a cottage industry—and sometimes even the finished books. An apprentice prepared the parchment by drawing guidelines on it and mixed the fine pigments, taking great care not to waste such costly ingredients as saffron and lapis lazuli and cinnabar; then a scribe painstakingly copied the words using inks made from carbon black and oak galls.

It was the illuminator's task to illustrate the margins with miniature pictures, adding gold and silver to make them even more desirable. Indeed, in this context the word "illuminated" is not a synonym for illustrated, but a reference to the use of precious pigments and gold and silver. The illuminator's art would also be expressed in the carpet page, a full-page illustration at the very beginning of a gospel. This was brilliantly colored and meticulous in execution, with perfect symmetry that might require exacting compass work. (Think of some of the Turkish carpets you've seen, which is probably where carpet pages got their name.) The best ones are an intricate blend of Celtic knotwork and designs interwoven around a central motif—usually a cross, which would be blended over and over again in inventive ways, even into the border. Such a page would be a challenge to the imagination and the skill of a master illuminator, since it was the single biggest illustration in a manuscript, and the first thing his patron saw of his work. Finally the book binder would sew the pages, or "quires," together, attach the sewn manuscript to planed boards, and enclose the book in leather. If the book was destined for a wealthy churchman or nobleman, a goldsmith or silversmith enclosed the whole in a finely wrought cover studded with jewels. If it was intended for some humbler use, he would merely add a base metal clasp to keep the codex closed and protect its parchment pages from dust and curling. The whole process could take months, or even years, per book.

The text was often religious, a book of hours or psalms or hagiography, pilgrim guides, but sometimes secular, too, including husbandry tips, medical treatises, and secular verse. Books often contained errors from weary copyists. But whatever the wisdom or folly of the words inscribed, all were produced in the same laborious fashion. All were precious. ⌁

LONDON'S OTHER TOWER
Wycliffe and the Lollards

Many visitors to the infamous Tower of London are unaware that London holds another tower with an equally gruesome history. It's called the Lollards' Tower. And from the heavy iron rings imbedded in its stone to the aura of misery that still clings to its walls, it offers up a full measure of historical shivers.

It would seem an unlikely place for persecution and torture. Picturesque Lambeth Palace, situated on the south bank of the Thames, was for centuries the official residence of the Archbishop of Canterbury, where England's most venerable clergy met to discuss theology and make ecclesiastical policy. In medieval times, that mandated the confinement and torture of hundreds of heretical dissenters. Early in the fifteenth century a special tower was constructed to house these heretics, who were sometimes tethered to iron rings for days on end. Those who did not recant met their fate at the stake, while others—the luckier ones—had their hands bound behind them as a hot irons branded their skin with the letter H. H for heretic or L for Lollard.

The name Lollard refers to an anticlerical, antipapal movement that began in England during the last part of the fourteenth century, and was spread throughout the countryside by "poor priests" and lay preachers. Most scholars think the name came from a Flemish word *lollaert,* meaning to mumble or murmur softly. Some believe that this anti-Catholic movement, which in later decades expanded to Bohemia, Germany, Wales, and Scotland, would eventually influence North American belief systems through the Puritan fathers.

The movement began with the writings of the Oxford theologian John Wycliffe, who was deemed "the most significant Englishman of his time" in Barbara Tuchman's hstory, *A Distant Mirror: The Calamitous 14th Century*. Wycliffe gained powerful patronage at court because his early writings advocatec the supremacy of crown over Church in all matters of civil authority. Later, however, he went on to challenge Roman Church authority in spiritual matters as well, condemning the rich and powerful friars as thieves and liars and calling the Pope an Antichrist. Wycliffe and his "mumblers" advocated a personal faith and railed against relics, pilgrimages, and the sale of indulgences. But most impcrtantly, John Wycliffe proclaimed Scripture to be the only infallible authority in all spiritual matters and began the translation of the Scriptures into English.

Because of his powerful friends at court, Wycliffe never felt the full brunt of persecution. Although he was chased out of Oxford, he was allowed to retire to his parish in Lutterworth, where he died of natural causes. His followers would take up his fight and his effort to translate and disseminate the Scripture. Many of them would become all too familiar with the amenities offered in the Lollards' Tower. ❧

Reading Group Gold

RECOMMENDED READING

For general reading in the history of the period

Bainton, Ronald H. *The Horizon History of Christianity*. New York: American Heritage Publishing, 1964.

Calkins, Robert G. *Monuments of Medieval Art*. New York: E. P. Dutton, 1979.

Halliday, F. E. *An Illustrated Cultural History of England*. New York: Crescent Books, 1967.

Innes, Miranda. *Medieval Flowers*. London: Kylie Cathie Limited, 1997.

Jusserand, J. J. *English Wayfaring Life in the Middle Ages: XIV Century*. Williamstown, Massachusetts: Corner House Publishers, 1974.

Leyser, Henrietta. *Medieval Women: A Social History of Women in England 450–1500*. New York: St Martin's Press, 1995.

Nuth, Joan. *God's Lovers in an Age of Anxiety: The Medieval Mystics*. Maryknoll, New York: Orbis Books, 2001.

Shaw, Henry. *Dress and Decoration of the Middle Ages*. Cobb, California: First Glance Books, 1998.

Tuchman, Barbara W. *A Distant Mirror*. New York: Ballantine, 1978.

Wieck, Roger S. *Painted Prayers: The Book of Hours in Medieval and Renaissance Art*. New York: George Braziller, Inc., 1996.

The following are some of the author's favorite historical novels. They are all still widely available in various editions.

Ecco, Umberto. *The Name of the Rose*.

Seton, Anya. *Katherine*.

Stone, Irving. *The Agony and the Ecstacy*.

Tey, Josephine. *Daughter of Time*.

READING GROUP QUESTIONS

Reading Group Gold

1. Do you regard *The Illuminator* as primarily Kathryn's story or Finn's?

2. What do you think about Kathryn? Is she a good mother? In what ways do she and her sons, Colin and Alfred, help and hurt each other?

3. The author has said that she created Finn as a kind of ideal hero who doesn't exist in real life. How close does he come to your own ideal?

4. Agnes and her husband are caught in the shift between feudalism, when farmers were inextricably bound to the land where they were born, and the life of an itinerant worker. How do you regard Agnes's decision to stay with Kathryn, both before and after her husband's death?

5. The strict feudal class system exerts great pressure on the lives of other characters as well. For example, how does it affect Alfred's opportunities, and what choices does Half-Tom have open to him about his future? To what extent does class consciousness continue to influence our lives today?

6. Some have called the *Revelations of Divine Love* by Julian of Norwich feminist in her concept of Jesus as "Mother God." How do you view this interpretation? In light of the troubled times in which she lived, what do you think Julian means when she says "all will be well"?

7. Faith is obviously central to Julian's existence. What role does it play in other characters' lives? For example, how does Kathryn's faith change in the course of the novel? How important are Colin's religious beliefs to him?

8. What do you think about Magda? In what ways does her mysticism seem similar to, and different from, Julian's? What role does mysticism play in spirituality, and is that role greater during tumultuous periods in history?

9. What is the symbolism of the two necklaces described in the novel?

10. *The Illuminator* is set at a time of great corruption in the Catholic Church. What do you think accounts for corruption not only in religion, but also in other established institutions such as government, capitalist corporations, large philanthropic organizations, etc? Is that corruption inevitable?

11. Discuss how the social and political climate of the period brought Finn and Kathryn together while simultaneously pulling them apart. How could the actions of their children have led to a different outcome for their relationship?

12. The novel ends where it begins: Half-Tom meets Finn on the road outside Norwich and hands off another vulnerable child to him. How satisfying is the ending?

For more reading group suggestions visit
www.stmartins.com/smp/rgg.html
K St. Martin's Griffin

St. Martin's Griffin